D1636092

Praise for the novels
of Sandra Heath

"A rare talent." —Romance Fiction Forum

"A charming tale . . . full of adventure and romance, with a dash of mystery to spice the mix. The story and prose are vintage Sandra Heath, with vividly drawn characters, sparkling dialogue, and marvelous descriptions of people, places, and events that immerse the reader in the characters' lives and bring the Regency era to life . . . [an] entertaining, wonderfully written tale."
—Romance Reviews Today

"Sandra Heath has taken fantasy to heart and once again woven it through her Regency world. Drawing on Celtic lore and magic, Heath writes a tale reminiscent of the mischievousness and fey beauty of *A Midsummer Night's Dream*." —The Historical Novels Review

"Sandra Heath takes her considerable talent and leads a merry dance into the myths and legends of an ancient culture, while never missing a beat of the Regency waltz that is her setting. Delightful!" —*Romantic Times*

SIGNET

REGENCY ROMANCE
COMING IN JANUARY 2005

The Sandalwood Princess and *Knave's Wager*
by Loretta Chase
Two stories in one volume from Loretta Chase, hailed by Mary Jo Putney as "one of the finest and most delightful writers in romance."

0-451-21379-3

A Grand Deception
by Elizabeth Mansfield
Anthony Maitland, perplexed by Miss Georgy Verney's decision to run rather than be courted, embarks on a bold scheme to win her trust—and her heart.

0-451-21283-1

Miss Whitlow's Turn
by Jenna Mindel
Miss Harriet Whitlow's father wishes to see her married to a wealthy nobleman—but her heart belongs to George Clasby, a rake who wishes to reform. Now she must throw caution to the wind and find the courage to fulfill her heart's desire.

0-451-21035-2

Available wherever books are sold or at
www.penguin.com

My Lady Domino

and

A Commercial Enterprise

Sandra Heath

A SIGNET BOOK

SIGNET
Published by New American Library, a division of
Penguin Group (USA) Inc., 375 Hudson Street,
New York, New York 10014, USA
Penguin Group (Canada), 10 Alcorn Avenue, Toronto,
Ontario M4V 3B2, Canada (a division of Pearson Penguin Canada Inc.)
Penguin Books Ltd., 80 Strand, London WC2R 0RL, England
Penguin Ireland, 25 St. Stephen's Green, Dublin 2,
Ireland (a division of Penguin Books Ltd.)
Penguin Group (Australia), 250 Camberwell Road, Camberwell, Victoria 3124,
Australia (a division of Pearson Australia Group Pty. Ltd.)
Penguin Books India Pvt. Ltd., 11 Community Centre, Panchsheel Park,
New Delhi - 110 017, India
Penguin Group (NZ), Cnr Airborne and Rosedale Roads, Albany,
Auckland 1310, New Zealand (a division of Pearson New Zealand Ltd.)
Penguin Books (South Africa) (Pty.) Ltd., 24 Sturdee Avenue,
Rosebank, Johannesburg 2196, South Africa

Penguin Books Ltd., Registered Offices:
80 Strand, London WC2R 0RL, England

Published by Signet, an imprint of New American Library, a division of Penguin
Group (USA) Inc. *My Lady Domino* and *A Commercial Enterprise* were pre-
viously published in separate Signet editions.

First Signet Printing (Double Edition), December 2004
10 9 8 7 6 5 4 3 2 1

My Lady Domino copyright © Sandra Heath, 1983
A Commercial Enterprise copyright © Sandra Heath, 1984
All rights reserved

 REGISTERED TRADEMARK—MARCA REGISTRADA

Printed in the United States of America

Without limiting the rights under copyright reserved above, no part of this publication may be reproduced, stored in or introduced into a retrieval system, or
transmitted, in any form, or by any means (electronic, mechanical, photocopying,
recording, or otherwise), without the prior written permission of both the copyright owner and the above publisher of this book.

PUBLISHER'S NOTE
These are works of fiction. Names, characters, places, and incidents either are
the product of the author's imagination or are used fictitiously, and any resem-
blance to actual persons, living or dead, business establishments, events, or locales
is entirely coincidental.

If you purchased this book without a cover you should be aware that this book
is stolen property. It was reported as "unsold and destroyed" to the publisher
and neither the author nor the publisher has received any payment for this
"stripped book."

The scanning, uploading, and distribution of this book via the Internet or via any
other means without the permission of the publisher is illegal and punishable by
law. Please purchase only authorized electronic editions, and do not participate
in or encourage electronic piracy of copyrighted materials. Your support of the
author's rights is appreciated.

My Lady
Domino

Chapter 1

The sound of the alley door closing was only faint, but it was sufficient to carry through the open casement and into the bedroom at the rear of the small house in Bath's most fashionable shopping street. Adele stirred, drowsily opening her eyes and looking up, not at the half-expected elegance of a stuccoed ceiling adorned with birds and garlands of flowers, but at a low expanse of plain whitewash, unrelieved by any pretty decoration. She was not at Beech Park, she was in the haberdashery in Milsom Street.

As always when sleep left her, the reality of her severely reduced circumstances came as a dreadful shock. Each morning it was the same; sleep receded and with it so did the happy past, leaving only the awful truth of the present. She was no longer the heiress daughter of Bath's richest banker; she was dependent upon the kindness and love of Miss Cat Rogers, once her nurse at Beech Park but now the lessee of the haberdashery where Adele served behind the counter.

For a moment she lay there, and then, remembering the sound of the alley door, she threw back the patchwork counterpane and slipped from the bed. Please let that sound mean that the carrier had at last brought the fancy ribbons ordered so long ago from the London manufactory! Pouring some water from the chipped china jug into the bowl on the dressing table, she began to wash.

A little later she was attired in a neat dimity gown that smelled of cloves from the orange pomander she kept in the wardrobe. The gown's dusty lilac color became her very well, for it emphasized the largeness of her blue eyes and the cornfield hue of her hair. She wore the neat apron of a shop assistant, but there was something about her that betrayed the truth—that she had not been born to the life she now led, that she had been born into a world of lace and silks, of wealth and plenty, of elegant rooms with glittering chandeliers and fine furniture, of magnificent carriages and gracious parks. But for Miss Adele Russell this was all in the past, a vanished world that only returned when she was asleep.

Pushing the final curl beneath her day bonnet, she went to the window to look past the rooftops toward the stark ruins on the hillside overlooking the busy spa town. The scent of summer flowers rose from the garden below, but she hardly noticed it as she looked at Beech Park, her former home, the scene of so many happy years, but now just a shell after being destroyed by a mysterious fire one snowy January night five years ago.

After looking at the ruins for a moment, she turned and left the bedroom, hurrying down to the kitchen where Joanie, the maid, was busy sweeping the flagstoned floor.

"Good morning, Joanie."

"Good morning, Miss Russell."

"Did you hear the alley door a little while ago?"

"No." The maid stopped working, her eyes brightening. "Do you think it could have been the London ribbons?"

"Oh, I hope so, we seem to have been waiting for simply ages, and with the Duchess of Bellingham's masquerade almost upon us now . . . Well, the ladies of Bath will go to the shop which provides them with the latest thing, and if we don't, then they'll go elsewhere." Adele went to the back door and then paused, smiling a little wickedly at the maid. "Joanie Smith, I do believe you've missed a speck of dust in that corner over there, that won't do anymore, you know."

Joanie's plump, freckled face fell. "Miss Rogers isn't coming back from Bristol!"

"Yes, I'm afraid she is."

"Oh, no—"

"Let me give you a word of advice, Joanie," said Adele gently. "Only the Lord knows you should have learned it for yourself by now. Cat Rogers' bark is far worse than her bite; she doesn't mean half she says."

"That isn't how it seems to me."

"I should know, she was my nurse for long enough."

"I know she was your nurse, but she can't have scolded *you* like she scolds me! I mean, you were a fine lady in that great big house—"

"I was only a little girl then, a spoiled, willful one at that, but I soon learned how to conduct myself once Cat Rogers took charge of me." Hardly knowing that she did so, she glanced out through the window in the direction of Beech Park, but the surrounding buildings hid it from view. "Well," she said more briskly, "I'll go and see if those dratted ribbons have arrived."

The walled garden behind the haberdashery was a tiny piece of the English countryside transferred to the center of the busy spa. It was bright with July flowers, roses that nodded against the mellow stone and sweet-smelling herbs that bordered the ash path. Adele's skirts brushed against them as she passed, and their perfume was released into the warm air. It was a perfect morning, the sky was a flawless blue, and she felt lighthearted as she hurried toward the wash-house; she even hummed a little tune.

The wash-house was built against the alley wall, next to the door which every Thursday night was left unbolted to admit the London carrier, should he be expected. Inside, it was always cool, the same temperature whether it was winter or summer, and it always smelled of boiled linen and potato starch. Its red-raddled floor was spotless and it had the air of a place that was frequently used and that was always looked after with great care. One of Cat's best blankets had been washed the previous day and was hanging up to dry, and a basket of laundry awaiting ironing stood on the floor next to the door where Adele entered. In a far corner was the dolly tub, and leaning against it the scrubbing board, an indication that the carrier had indeed called. Her face breaking into a smile, she knelt by the tub to take the brown paper package which had been hidden in the agreed place. But as she stood again the wash-house went suddenly dark as a shadow blotted out the sunlight streaming in through the doorway.

With a frightened gasp, she whirled about to see the silhouette of a gentleman, a silver-handled cane swinging lightly in his hand. There was something very menacing about his silent appearance, and she backed slowly away, pressing against the wall, the package of ribbons clasped tightly to her breast. She knew who he was. "You!" she breathed, the loathing she felt only too evident in that single word.

Sir Frederick Repton sketched a graceful bow. "Miss Russell."

"Why have you come here?"

"That is hardly a gracious greeting, nor, given your circumstances, is it a sensible one."

"Why should I stoop to being polite to you?"

"Come now, you aren't the fine lady anymore, Miss Russell, and I am certainly not your father's clerk now."

"I don't need to be reminded of your spectacular advancement since my father was murdered, sir," she replied, hating him so much that she found it hard to even look at him.

"You make that sound dreadfully like an accusation, Miss Russell."

"It *is* an accusation!" she flashed, her eyes very bright. "You murdered my father, you and your fine patron, the Duke of Bellingham!"

"Do go on, you are really most entertaining."

"After promises of patronage and advancement from the duke, whose financial straits the world and his wife knew about, you embezzled huge sums from my father's bank." She paused, expecting him to silence her, but he merely smiled and so she went on. "My father found out and so you started that fire which killed him, and after that you laid the blame for the missing funds on him."

"Dear me, what a catalog of odious crime. I must credit you with exceptional powers of imagination."

"I haven't imagined anything; everything I've just said is the truth."

"But can you prove it? No, you cannot." The cool smile continued to play around his colorless lips. He had a sallow complexion, pale-lashed eyes, and those toneless, gaunt looks which do not seem to register the passing of the years. He was somewhere between fifty-five and sixty, but his figure was that of a man in his early thirties. He looked every inch a gentleman, which was the very thing he was not. Oh, he wore costly apparel, which had been tailored in London by the same craftsmen who clothed Mr. Brummel, his cravats were always wonders of starched intricacy and his waistcoats a byword in elegance, but no amount of peacock finery could turn Frederick Repton into anything remotely resembling a true gentleman.

The cologne he wore wafted over her as he came a little closer, pushing the blanket aside with the tip of his cane and coming to a halt at last within inches of her. "How very lovely you always manage to be, Miss Russell. In spite of all that has befallen you, you are still one of the most beautiful women I have ever seen. I recall how once you wore Paris muslin and Brussels lace, how the services of an excellent maid produced a coiffure which showed off your magnificent hair to such advantage that your appearance in a room eclipsed all other ladies present, no matter how grand they were. Oh yes, you were quite a lady, exquisite in appearance, vivacious in character and so very delightful in your charm. Denzil Russell's daughter, a famous beauty, fêted, courted, sought after by numerous young blades eager for such a dazzling bride . . . Dear me, how you must miss all that, but all things must pass," he said softly. "Even what remains of Beech Park will soon be gone forever and totally forgotten."

She looked away from him, but the silver handle of his cane pressed warningly against her cheek, forcing her to meet his gaze once more.

"I am tired of those grim ruins on that hillside, Miss Russell. They overlook Bath too much and can be seen from too many windows. They are a reminder of what once was, and I do not like that. So I have acquired your old home, and soon work will begin upon *my* new mansion. Repton Hall will rise from the ashes like a phoenix, and every last trace of Beech Park, every stone and every fragment of mortar, will be gone forever."

She stared at him. "No!"

"But yes, Beech Park is mine."

"Not legally!"

"Don't be childish, Miss Russell; it is hardly necessary to always work within the letter of the King's law! You should know that by now, or do you never learn your lessons?"

"One lesson I have learned, and that is to know that you are a rogue and a thief, a murderer and an arsonist!" she cried.

The cane pressed harshly against her cheek, the silver very cold. "How very tiresome you Russells are, always so innocent and above all else, *honest!* Your father was a brilliant banker, an extremely clever accountant and a bookkeeper par excellence. With skills such as his he should have had half a dozen estates like Beech Park. But he was an honest man, and he was a very dull fellow. How fortunate for me that I learned my skills from such a master, for I knew so much better how to go on in this world. I was prepared to manipulate books, transfer this to that, juggle a little here, assess something else there. I just had to wait until a suitable patron came along."

"The Duke of Bellingham."

"But of course, the noble Duke of Bellingham. He and I

understood each other from the outset, Miss Russell. *I* knew that he was in desperate financial straits, and *he* knew that I was ambitious. We worked very well together, very well indeed, an excellent partnership. Had the duke not come along, it could have been that I would still be your father's wretched clerk, still not fully appreciated and still chafing at the unfairness of my lot in life. But fate chose to advance me. I am where I am now, Miss Russell, but you, I am afraid, are where you are.''

"You have not set foot near me for five years, Sir Frederick, but then suddenly you came creeping along before Bath is fully awake, you use the side alley so that no one will see you, and then all you have to say seems to be that you've been exceeding clever over the years and that you've now acquired Beech Park to add to your list of stolen prizes. Somehow, I don't think that you've told me the real reason why you've come here this morning.''

"How very perceptive you are. Very well, Miss Russell, I will tell you that my true purpose this morning is to issue due warning that from this moment on I shall be watching your movements very closely indeed, and that should I suspect you of unwise actions, then it will be the worse for you—and for Miss Cat Rogers. What befell Beech Park and Denzil Russell can as swiftly and anonymously befall the haberdashery and its plump lessee.''

Her eyes widened. "But why?'' she whispered. "Why threaten me like this? I have not been able to harm you in five years, although God knows I would if I could, so why do you come here like this now?''

He looked a little taken aback and then a flat chuckle escaped him. "You haven't heard, have you? News has not reached your little establishment yet.''

"News of what?''

The humorless smile faded. "David Latimer, Earl of Blaisdon, is about to return to Bath. He has taken a house on Royal Crescent. Ah, I see that the gentleman's name is not lost upon you.''

"I recall him,'' she replied shortly.

"I'll warrant you do; you almost married him!''

"Why should I be interested in his return to Bath?''

"Come now, don't let's be silly. Of *course* you're interested in what he does.'' The cane tapped her cheek a little playfully. "His reason for returning is outwardly to accompany his mother, the countess, whose health requires her to take the cure, but apparently there is an ulterior motive—he is soon expected to announce his betrothal to the Duke of Bellingham's daughter, Lady Euphemia."

"But she is already married, to the Marquis of Heydon!"

"The *late* marquis; he passed away some ten months ago. The lady is very much free to marry again, I promise you. Which, alas, brings me to the crux of this whole matter—well, one of the cruxes anyway. Five and a half years ago, or thereabouts, the Earl of Blaisdon was again on the point of proposing to Lady Euphemia, after many years of patient work behind the scenes by the duke and duchess and by the Countess of Blaisdon. Then you came along, Miss Russell, and the earl abruptly terminated his association with Lady Euphemia and pursued you instead. You greatly interfered with matters, inflicting humiliation upon a great house. That is not to happen again."

"Earls do not pay court to haberdashers' assistants," she pointed out dryly.

"Maybe they don't, but haberdashers' assistants can make a dreadful amount of trouble by approaching earls and by seeing to it that the teacups of Bath rattle to the Russell tune again."

"Those teacups will rattle to a certain extent anyway the moment David Latimer sets foot in this town again. But you may rest easy, for I am fully aware that no purpose would be served by attempting to stir things up again. As you point out, sir, I cannot prove anything against you or the duke. Making noise now would be tantamount to beating my head against the proverbial wall, and whatever else I am, I am not a fool. As to approaching the Earl of Blaisdon, well I promise you that nothing on this earth would make me willingly do that, for I despise him almost as much as I despise you."

"What a waspish tongue you have, to be sure. But in this instance, I think you are protesting a little too much where the earl is concerned. Possibly you do regard him with some acrimony, for it must have been galling indeed to receive his curt note, ending the betrothal and expressing a wish never to communicate with you again. But then, that was after the fire and you were no longer rich. As you say, earls do not pay court to haberdashers' assistants." He smiled.

"There was no need for you to come here today. I am

totally uninterested in the earl's arrival here or in his betrothal to the Marchioness of Heydon.''

"Indeed? Then you will be the only unconcerned soul in Bath. You must understand, Miss Russell, that with so many important things about to happen where the House of Bellingham is concerned, too much care cannot be taken to see that all runs smoothly. The Waterloo masquerade promises to be *the* social event of the year, and it is taking place not in London but in out-of-season Bath. It is quite a coup for the duchess as a hostess. The last thing she wishes is for there to be any undue whispering to spoil it all. You do understand, don't you?''

She felt the cane touch her cheek once more. "Yes, I understand.''

"Excellent. Oh, there is just one more small item and this time it concerns my good self. I am an ambitious man, Miss Russell, but then you already know that, don't you?'' He smiled again. "I thrive on wealth and on power, and so I have turned my eyes toward the world of politics, where lies the greatest power of all for such as I. The duke has in his disposal a parliamentary seat which he has kindly promised to me. He is also, God bless him, a kinsman of our first minister, and I am soon to be a houseguest at Lord Liverpool's country estate. My sights are set very high indeed, as you can imagine, and so my reputation must be as pure as the driven snow. It would not please me at all to learn that you have been stirring undue chitter-chatter about your imagined wrongs—no, it would not please me at all. But if you behave yourself, I think the interest will all die down again nicely. Don't you think so?''

She said nothing.

"Just remember my warning, and think on the welfare of your Miss Rogers. You wouldn't like to have her on your conscience, would you? So, just be a good girl, serve dutifully behind the haberdashery counter, and go about your daily business without attracting any undue attention. All will be well for you if you do that, and in due course you will probably marry some cloddish wagoner or market porter and your life will pursue its allotted course.'' He lowered the cane. "There, that was not so bad, I think we both know where we stand now, hmm? Good day, Miss Russell, it was so pleasant talking with you again.''

Touching his top hat and inclining his head once, he turned

and was gone. She heard the alley door close behind him. Holding the package of ribbons tightly, she remained motionless. The brightness of the morning seemed duller now, and the lightheartedness with which she had come to look for the ribbons had vanished as if it had never been. The past, the unhappy past, had returned to envelop her, slipping over from her nightmares to her waking hours as it had not done for a long time now. Its bitter tendrils twined remorselessly around her.

Chapter 2

A short while later the time came to open the doors of the haberdashery for the day, and as she picked up the French and English tulles which were daily draped around the entrance, she strove to put Sir Frederick Repton's visit to the back of her mind.

The noise of Milsom Street was tremendous after the quiet of the house where only Joanie's tuneless humming disturbed the silence. For a moment Adele stood on the pavement looking at the broad, Palladian street with its impressive edging of shops and lodging houses, and the colorful streamers and bunting put up just over a week before to celebrate the victory of Waterloo. There were shops of all descriptions, from haberdasheries and confectionaries to repositories of music and circulating libraries, and many of them already had a carriage or two drawn up at the curb outside. A continuous stream of wagons, drays, carriages and horses passed to and fro, and mingled with them were the inevitable sedan chairs conveying invalids to the Pump Room for their first daily glass of the waters. A boy selling posies of flowers from a large basket tried to attract Adele's attention, but she shooed him away and then stretched up to begin draping the tulles.

A dandy, dressed very modishly indeed in a wide-brimmed, glossy hat, spotless white cravat, and exquisitely cut black coat, sauntered slowly along the pavement. His cravat was so high and tight that he could scarcely look down and certainly could not contemplate turning his head, and his skintight "inexpressibles" were gathered so closely into his waspish waist that he resembled a chicken, all puffed out at the top in front and similarly puffed out at the bottom at the back. His rose-colored waistcoat, like his coat, was worn open to display his embroidered cambric shirt and an array of fobs, jewels, and chains. He was very much the swell in his own opinion and no doubt in the opinion of other dandies, but the

14

truth was that he looked rather ridiculous, and Adele was careful to avoid catching his eye. Perceiving her ankles, so becomingly displayed as she stretched up, he paused dramatically, raising his quizzing glass to carefully inspect her from head to toe. He knew full well who she was and had for some time entertained the notion of pursuing her.

" 'Pon my soul," he declared at last, lowering the glass, "Who demmed well needs the cure when there are other, more uplifting remedies for the spirits?"

Flushing, she carried on with her work, her gaze fixed firmly on the tulles. She suffered frequently from the unwelcome attentions of such gentlemen, and without exception she kept them well and truly at arm's length. She may have had an interesting and intriguing background, but that did not make her in any way available to the likes of him.

He pondered pestering her a little but then remembered how very early it was in the day. How tiresome; one simply did not pursue the fair sex at this ungodly hour, one strolled in order to be seen. The fair Russell wench would have to wait for another, more suitable time. He sauntered on, but not before he had smartly slapped her posterior, remarking that she was a "demmed fine filly, in spite of her bloodline."

She still refused to be drawn, having long since discovered that a stony silence was the best deterrent. He had vanished among the crowds on the pavement when at last she stepped back to admire her finished work. She always took care about the doorway of the shop, for that was what enticed those who were new to Bath; those who came frequently were already aware of the excellence of Miss Rogers' haberdashery. Above her head the Waterloo bunting fluttered in the light breeze, and she glanced up at the red, white, and blue streamers she and Cat had hung from the upstairs windows. What a day that had been; the London coaches had arrived bedecked with laurels and flags and the people had taken joyfully to the streets, fêting the Duke of Wellington. There had been music, and fireworks in Sydney Gardens, and afterward she and Cat had toasted the duke's health with some of Cat's fine, homemade birch wine; birch wine—once it would have been the best champagne, chilled in the cool cellars at Beech Park.

Still, the victory at Waterloo had had one unexpectedly beneficial side effect for the haberdashery; it had produced the famous Waterloo masquerade and all the business this inevitably entailed for the shopkeepers of Bath. Normally the Bellinghams, like every other great family, would have been in London at this time of the year, enjoying the delights of the Season, but throughout the previous winter the duke had obstinately ignored his doctors' advice, choosing to follow the hounds every day instead of coming to Bath for the cure. The result had been that his gout was now very bad indeeed, he was confined to a Merlin chair a great deal of the time, and he and his family were forced to remain in out-of-season Bath, a fact which reportedly had made the duchess furious. Thus her decision to hold a masquerade to celebrate the great victory had meant the somewhat unfashionable surroundings of the assembly rooms rather than a glittering ballroom in Mayfair. It was said that some very grand names indeed were on the guest list, and although the masquerade was a week or so away still, it was already almost impossible to obtain lodgings in the town. More than once Adele had wondered if the assembly rooms, commodious as they were, would be able to accommodate such a vast number of people. Still, it was said that the greater the crush, the more successful the occasion! If that was true, then the duchess's masquerade promised to be the most successful event not only of this year but of many years past!

Adele was about to go into the shop again when something caught her attention a little way down the street. A fine landau drawn by matched bays was approaching, and the coachman and attendants were dressed in the mulberry and gold Bellingham livery. Her heart sank, for as the carriage's hoods were lowered she could see that its occupant was Euphemia, Marchioness of Heydon, who had been with her parents in Bath for most of the summer so far. Instinctively Adele knew that Euphemia was bound for the haberdashery, and it was at times like this that she cursed the duke's pigheadedness, wishing him hale and hearty, free of gout and miles away in London with his odious offspring!

A confrontation with the Marchioness of Heydon was always something to be dreaded, for Euphemia was the bane of Adele's life and had been ever since Adele had won the Earl of Blaisdon all those years before. Adele could have understood her jealousy and natural dislike of a successful rival, but she could not understand the vindictiveness, the unending spite, and cruel taunting Euphemia employed at all times. After Sir Frederick's visit, the thought of having to face the duke's daughter was more daunting than ever.

16

The lowered hoods of the landau displayed Euphemia's graceful beauty to the full. Unfortunately, it also displayed the glaring absence of any form of mourning. Ten months, Sir Frederick had said, but never once had Euphemia so much as appeared in a black rosette or weeper; small wonder Adele had not even known she was a widow! However, had the roles of the marchioness and her late husband been reversed, from all accounts he would have practically danced a jig upon his wife's grave. Unfortunately for him, and for Adele Russell, he had been the one to go first.

With a heavy sigh, Adele went into the shop, positioning herself behind the oak counter and pretending to sort through the new ribbons, rolling each one carefully, pinning it and placing it neatly in a waiting tray. The smells of the haberdashery closed over her, a strange blend of leather and cloth, of perfumed artificial flowers and ostrich plumes. The walls were lined with shelves and tiny drawers, and the handles of many parasols protruded high above. Normally Adele liked the atmosphere of the little shop, but when visited by Euphemia, Marchioness of Heydon, everything about the place served to be a painful reminder of the great gulf that now separated Denzil Russell's daughter from the daughter of the Duke of Bellingham.

The landau halted outside and a footman jumped down to assist Euphemia to alight. In a flurry of muslin, she stepped down to the pavement. She had the sort of dark beauty which was the envy of every lady of fashion. Her face was framed by a dark fringe of brown curls and her skin was pale and without blemish. She wore a delicate apricot walking gown and a brown spencer and carried a crimson parasol that was pinned with countless ribbons, a mode which had been the rage in Bath these past two years. The ribbons on her bonnet and on the parasol streamed prettily as she approached the shop door, and something in her demeanour warned Adele that this, like Sir Frederick's before it, was no ordinary visit. The bell tinkled.

In a rustle of expensive material, Euphemia crossed to the counter. "Well," she murmured, her dark eyes glittering. "The foolish Miss Rogers has seen fit to trust a Russell with the business. How very remiss, given past Russell activities."

Anger burned in Adele's heart, but she remained polite. "Good morning, Lady Euphemia, may I be of assistance to you?"

"Oh yes, certainly you can."

At that moment, to Adele's intense relief, the bell rang once more as the door opened to admit the two Misses Mortimer, newcomers to Bath for the masquerade and two of the silliest of creatures A flicker of annoyance passed over Euphemia's face, and Adele saw how tightly her hand clenched over the handle of the crimson parasol.

"Why, Lady Euphemia!" cried the Misses Mortimer together—they frequently spoke in unison. "How pleased we are we noticed your landau!"

"And how glad we are to see you once more," went on the younger one alone, her plump figure positively quivering in its unbecoming pink lawn.

"Yes," agreed her sister, "For we are in quite a tizzy about the masquerade."

"A tizzy?" said Euphemia coldly, making little secret of the fact that she found their appearance on the scene most unwelcome.

"Why yes, for we are quite undecided how to go," replied the younger.

"Indeed so." Her sister nodded. "For I am determined to go as Britannia, but my sister says that there will be *numerous* such costumes as it is quite unoriginal for a victory celebration!"

Euphemia took a long, slow breath, her glance positively withering, although the Misses Mortimer were too silly to notice anything amiss in her manner. "My dear ladies," she said coldly, "there will be no Britannias at all, unless you take account of the one sung of by Madame Giardi during the course of the evening. The masquerade is not in fancy dress; I thought that that had been made perfectly clear even to the dullest of wits."

They were crestfallen, but not because of her sarcasm; they were simply disappointed that it was not to be a fancy-dress occasion. "Oh," said the elder, "just masks and dominos?"

"Yes."

The younger recovered swiftly from the setback, seizing upon what Euphemia had said. "Oh, is Madame Giardi to sing for us? Oh, I do declare that this will be the finest evening of my life! I shall dance in celebration of the greatest victory of all time, and I shall hear the glorious singing of the sweetest of nightingales."

Euphemia's lip all but curled. "Personally I find Giardi quite abominable; she cackles like a hen, but my mother holds her to be the best and so she is to batter our poor ears with her noise.''

The Misses Mortimer glanced at each other, uncertain of what to say next. All they knew was that they must say something, for one simply did not allow conversation with such a personage to flag at all.

Then the younger one had an inspiration. ''Tell me, Lady Euphemia, is it true that your dear brother, Lord Talbourne, hopes to be back in England in time for the masquerade?''

Euphemia looked at her, dumbfounded. Dear God, the dreadful little creature still carried a torch for Rex, in spite of the unkind rebuff he had delivered on the last occasion they had met. Surely no one could be that thick-skinned! ''Rex? I really have no idea, Miss Mortimer. He has languished in India these past six years or more, finding it most agreeable, and he certainly has not communicated any change of plan to me.''

''Oh.'' Miss Mortimer lowered her doleful eyes.

Her sister, not smitten to the same degree by the absent Lord Talbourne, was determined not to let the conversation die away. ''Lady Euphemia,'' she said brightly, ''a little bird has whispered to me that soon congratulations will be in order—''

''Congratulations?''

''Concerning yourself and the dear Earl of Blaisdon.''

Adele kept her eyes on the tray of ribbons, but she felt the glance of pure malice Euphemia directed at her as she replied. ''Miss Mortimer,'' she purred, ''it is surely not done to anticipate events.''

''But you do not deny it!''

''I deny nothing.''

The sisters looked excitedly at each other, triumphant at being the first to have direct confirmation of the rumor. They were quite innocent of any desire to taunt Adele, for they knew nothing of what had happened five years before, but their innocence must have pleased Euphemia, whose sudden air of triumph was almost tangible.

''Oh, Lady Euphemia,'' cried the elder Miss Mortimer, ''how very exciting! To be sure the earl is quite the most handsome gentleman in the world!''

''If one discounts your dear brother, Lord Talbourne,'' added the younger hastily, the telltale blush returning to her plump face.

"Indeed, I must be the most fortunate of women," remarked Euphemia, "to be the sister of the most handsome man in the world, and about to be the wife of the second most handsome."

They giggled and then trilled in unison. "Oh, Lady Euphemia, now who is anticipating events?"

Euphemia all but gritted her teeth, turning suddenly toward Adele and extracting a particularly fine green velvet ribbon at random from the tray. She held it up so that the delicate golden threads with which it was embroidered gleamed in the shop's dim light. "I will take this," she said, holding Adele's gaze. "See that you deliver it to the house in the Circus this afternoon. In person." You will not escape me, said that malevolent gaze, you will not escape me. . . .

Slowly Adele took the ribbon and set it aside. "Certainly, Lady Euphemia." Forcing her to deliver small purchases by hand when those purchases could easily be tucked away in a reticule was one of Euphemia's greatest delights, for it demonstrated more than anything else how subservient Adele's position now was. Today, however, there was more behind the ploy, and Adele knew that it had something to do with the information Sir Frederick had imparted earlier.

Euphemia left, and a moment later the landau pulled away. Gathering herself together, Adele put Euphemia from her mind to concentrate upon the business in hand. With a bright smile, she turned to the patiently waiting Misses Mortimer. "Good morning, ladies, may I help you?"

They beamed. "We wish to purchase a parasol," they replied, still in perfect unison.

"Certainly."

"A fashionably pale one," they added, "Parisienne and simply *covered* with ribbons."

Adele nodded and brought the little steps so that she could reach the array of parasol handles high above. But as she went about her work she found it hard to concentrate after all, for one thought persisted, disturbing her more than she would have thought possible after all this time: David Latimer was returning to Bath.

Chapter 3

Just as Adele was closing the shop at midday, after a very
hectic morning's trading, Joanie came through from the kitchen
to announce that Cat had returned from visiting her sick sister
in Bristol. The maid looked anything but overjoyed, but
Adele was delighted, hurrying through to the back of the
house.

Joanie had obviously worked like a Trojan on the kitchen,
for its floor had been swept until it almost shone and the
reflection of the fire flickered pleasingly over the flagstones
and over the immense table that stood in the center. It was a
sunny room, and colorful with its chintz curtains and the pots
of pink geraniums on the windowsills. Brass and copper pans
and utensils gleamed brightly on the stone shelf to the side of
the fire, and everything suggested that Joanie was determined
not to fall foul of Cat's sharp tongue the moment that critical
lady stepped over the threshold. The kettle was singing on its
hook above the fire and a beefsteak pie, hot and smelling
delicious, stood before the brick oven.

Cat was by the fireplace, her back to the room as she gazed
up at the landscape picture worked in silks by Adele when
she had been only thirteen. She was a stout, homely woman
in her fifties, clad in a sensible gown of heavy brown cloth
that was gathered tightly beneath her ample bosom. Her
graying hair was pushed beneath a fresh white mobcap, and
she was tying on a clean apron as she heard Adele enter.

She turned with a warm smile. "Why, Adele, my dear,
how good it is to see you again!"

Adele hugged her tightly. "Welcome home, Cat. How is
your sister?"

"Oh, fair to middling. She'll go on all right now, providing she takes that there physic like the doctor told her. Oh,
it's good to be back, though. Tell me now, do I still have a

21

thriving business, or have you sent my fine customers packing with fleas in their ears?''

Adele laughed. "You still have a business, *and* you have those fancy new ribbons in good time for the masquerade.''

"That London manufactory certainly took its time. Still, they do say that it's better to be late than never to arrive at all. So, we shall be prospering handsomely out of the Duke of Bellingham's gout!'' A wicked smile spread across Cat's face. "Let's hope it's giving him agonies!''

"Amen to that.''

Cat nodded. "Well, reckon you've good cause to wish him suffering. Come on now, let's have that smile again. Tell you what, reckon we should celebrate my return, we'll get Joanie to go and buy us some of Nell Norfolk's pastries on her way back from the market this afternoon.''

Adele smiled. "Why aren't you honest enough to say that you just have an overwhelming desire to eat Nell's disgracefully sticky wares?'' she teased, and then her smile faded again. "I can buy them for you, and go to the market too.''

"You? Your place is in the shop, it's Joanie's task to—''

"But I have to go out this afternoon, Cat, to deliver some ribbon to the Circus.''

Cat's lips pressed crossly together as she realized immediately what had happened. "That darned Lady Euphemia is it?''

"Yes.''

"She's never let up, has she? Not from the very beginning. If ever there was an evil-hearted creature, it's that one!''

"Amen to that too.''

"I suppose she's remained in Bath because of the masquerade.''

"Partly.'' Adele looked away.

"Why only partly?'' asked Cat curiously, watching the thoughtful expression on Adele's face.

"She is soon to be betrothed to the Earl of Blaisdon. He's taking a house on Royal Crescent, or so I'm told.''

Cat stared at her. "She's what? Well, I never! She's only been widowed these past ten months!''

Adele laughed ruefully. "I wasn't even aware of that.''

"You don't read the newspaper enough, that's why.''

Adele pursed her lips. "It's my experience that newspapers do not always tell the truth,'' she replied, thinking of the reports of the inquiry after her father's death.

"Aye, well maybe that's so, but when it comes to reporting society chitchat the newspapers are seldom wrong. How did you hear about it?"

Reluctantly Adele told her of Sir Frederick's visit and Cat listened sadly, nodding when Adele finished with an account of Euphemia's conduct in the shop and the probability that she too was about to warn Denzil Russell's daughter off where the Earl of Blaisdon was concerned. "Happen you're right, Adele, happen you're right."

"They both seem to imagine that I'm still interested in David Latimer."

"And aren't you?" asked Cat softly.

"No!"

"You can't fool old Cat, my pet."

"I'm not trying to. I think he and Euphemia richly deserve each other and should make each other supremely unhappy—with a little luck!"

Cat took a long breath and then went to bring the pie to the table, as Joanie lifted the pan of potatoes and began to strain them. "Well," said Cat, glancing again at Adele, "reckon you'd best get it over with as soon as we've eaten, and not only because it's always an ordeal facing Lady Euphemia."

"Why else?"

"Because I reckon there's a thunderstorm on its way."

"Your big toe is aching, is it?"

"You may scoff, young Adele, you may scoff, but my big toe's infallible! Country folk learn to take notice of such things for they turn out in the end to be *proven* common sense."

"Like the powdered tansy on the back doorstep?"

"Yes, just like that; there's never been an ant cross that threshold, has there? Nor are there any flies in here since I put herbs up in that basket hanging from the rafter." Cat was brisk. "*And* we'll be in no danger from that thunderstorm on account of the Palm Sunday hawthorn I've got up in the attic."

"But—"

"Have we ever been struck by lightning? Well, have we?"

"No, but—"

"No, we haven't, and that's because good country wisdom knows a thing or two about how to protect against it, that's why." Cat almost gave a triumphant snort as she pierced the crisp pastry of the pie with the blade of her knife.

23

Adele smiled and said no more. What point was there in saying that nearly every house in Bath escaped lightning and managed to do so without the dubious benefit of Palm Sunday hawthorn, or that the last time there had been a thunderstorm Cat had walked all the way to her cousin in Swainswick and back again without even mentioning her famous big toe!

As they ate their meal Cat's thoughts returned once more to the news about Lady Euphemia and David Latimer. The one thing Adele had found it harder to cope with than anything else at the time of the scandal five years before had been her callous betrayal by the handsome, dashing Earl of Blaisdon. In Cat's considered opinion, the fact that he had remained away from Bath ever since had been the best thing; but now he was coming back. With luck his resumed courtship of Lady Euphemia would keep him away from Adele, and Cat prayed that this would indeed prove to be the case, for he had done damage enough in the past without bringing more pain now. But as she glanced at Adele's withdrawn face she knew that the pain was already there.

A little later, wearing her light gray cape and plain straw bonnet, in case Cat's predictions about thunder were correct, Adele set off to deliver Euphemia's purchase to the Bellingham residence in the fashionable and exclusive circle of houses known as the Circus. She looked up frequently at the darkening skies, wondering if she would have been wiser to take her pattens too, for she doubted very much if she would have completed her errands before the storm broke.

That strange calm that sometimes precedes a storm had settled over the town, making the still air feel clammy and unpleasant. The Waterloo bunting hung motionless and the noise of constant traffic was made inordinately loud by the stone terraces and raised pavements. A Bristol stagecoach passed, having just left the nearby York House Hotel, and the outside passengers were equipped with umbrellas and overcoats. Their faces were very glum as they prepared for what was bound to be a wet and uncomfortable experience, for they had no hope at all of completing their journey before the storm.

The Colosseum in Rome had been the inspiration behind the Circus, which as its name suggested was a circle of houses, but where the Colosseum was viewed at its best from the outside, the Circus could only be viewed properly from the paved area in the center. The terraced curve of houses, so warm and pleasing in honey-colored stone, was richly decorated and adorned with columns, and the overall effect was one of grace and beauty. The rim of the circle was broken in three places by adjoining streets, one of which led to Royal Crescent where David Latimer was soon expected to take up residence, but these breaks in the continuity of the design seemed to enhance the glory of the Circus rather than detract from it. All in all it was one of Adele's favorite parts of Bath, in spite of the fact that one of its houses was occupied by people she loathed.

As she approached the Duke of Bellingham's residence the first gust of wind rose dustily, ruffling the ribbons of her bonnet and billowing some of the celebratory flags draped from upper-story windows. Something made her glance up at one of those windows, and to her dismay she saw a lace curtain twitching—her arrival had not gone unnoticed. Her vague hope of being able to leave the ribbon and hurry away without Euphemia knowing was dashed in that brief moment, and her steps became noticeably slower.

A footman opened the door and without a word ushered her into the cool, closed atmosphere of the vestibule, gesturing for her to wait. She watched him walk proudly away to the staircase, his livery very splendid in the dull light which rested across the many portraits lining the wall.

There was beautiful green silk on the walls of the hall and gilded plasterwork surrounding the doors. A bowl of sweet-smelling flowers stood upon a polished satinwood table and beside it was an impressively full dish of calling cards. She wondered wryly how long it would be before David Latimer's card joined them. Perhaps it was already there. . . .

The footman returned, a disdainful expression on his face as he beckoned to her from the stairs. As she followed him up to the next floor, however, she had the immense satisfaction of noticing that his perfection was considerably marred by the fact that one of the calf pads that were intended to give his leg the necessary shape, had slipped, giving him a decidedly lopsided look. Serve him right for being so high and mighty!

The sound of piano music drifted through the house. Someone was playing a waltz, and as she was shown into a chamber adjoining the drawing room she realized that Euphemia was receiving instruction from a dancing master. A cane rapped loudly upon the floor and a petulant male voice interrupted the music. "No, no *no!* My lady, the waltz is an

25

intimate dance, an excuse to embrace in public. It is *not* enhanced by treading upon your partner's toes!''

Euphemia was cross. "But how can I dance that close? It simply is not possible to move *without* treading on toes!''

"My lady,'' he said with that tone of patience one adopted with a difficult child. "In London *everyone* is managing to waltz without causing permanent lameness. We will try again.'' The cane rapped and the pianist launched once again into the music.

Adele glanced around. Tasseled damask hangings graced the windows and the walls were covered with costly Chinese silk in soft pink and white. A large portrait of the duke and duchess with their two children dominated one side of the room. It had been executed some years ago, for Euphemia was an angelic little baby, and her brother, the absent Lord Talbourne, was a mere boy. Adele wrinkled her nose at the portrait and then looked elsewhere. There was a particularly handsome buhl cabinet and several embroidered sofas scattered with soft cushions. Apart from these pieces of furniture, the rest of the things in the room had been carefully placed by Euphemia. Great thought had been given to their artfully haphazard arrangement so that whoever entered the room would see evidence of the fashionable and ladylike pursuits that occupied Euphemia's day. Embroidery was stretched on a rosewood tambour frame, the colored silks lying in a tangle on the floor. Miss Austen's latest book, *Mansfield Park,* lay on the cabinet, the book marker acquainting one with the fact that its reader had almost finished the final volume. Nearby was a folder of pressed flowers, left casually open at a page of rare wild orchids—proof that Euphemia was most diligent in her search for specimens. There was even a paint-stained cloth tossed on the windowsill, silent witness to the fact that she was also an artist, although she had not gone so far as to have the easel placed in the room. It was an artificial room, filled with vanity, and was just what Adele would have expected of Euphemia, Marchioness of Heydon.

A small sound from behind made her turn sharply, and to her surprise she saw a tiny monkey chained to a perch. It was dressed like a miniature Indian rajah, its bead-bright eyes shining with mischief as it ate sultanas from a dish. Adele guessed that it was a gift from Lord Talbourne, who had lived these past six years in India.

She did not notice that the music had ended in the adjoining room; she was so intent upon the monkey, that she gave a start when the folding doors were opened suddenly. Euphemia entered, her muslin skirts swishing as she turned to draw the doors to again. Then she leaned back against them, surveying Adele in silence. Her dark eyes shone; she looked bewitchingly lovely and yet at the same time malevolent—like a poisonous flower.

"So," she said after a moment, "You've brought the ribbon, have you?"

"Yes, my lady."

"How obliging of you."

Adele placed the tiny package on the cabinet. "If there's nothing else—"

"Oh, but there is. You know, it truly is very gratifying to have you of all creatures at my beck and call." Euphemia came closer, the many golden chains at her throat flashing in the sunlight streaming through the window. "You've lost everything, absolutely everything, and you'll never know how glad I am about it. You stole him from me five years ago, but you've paid the price now, haven't you? He's mine once again and this time he will not even glance at you."

Not trusting her tongue, Adele turned to leave, but Euphemia caught her wrist. "Stay away from him, do you hear me? I swear that I'll make you rue the day you were born if you so much as—"

"You need have no concern, my lady, for I have no desire even to glance in his direction! He is beneath my contempt and you are very welcome to him!"

She had gone too far, for Euphemia's furious hand stung across her cheek, leaving a fiery mark. "Don't be insolent, for you are no longer in any position to adopt such an attitude. Remember your benefactress now, Miss Russell, for she is very vulnerable should you offend!"

Adele stared at her. To be warned and threatened like this twice in one day was almost unbelievable. "I swear," she repeated quietly, "that I have no intention of doing anything untoward."

"See that you adhere to that, for if you do not, then you will find out exactly how virulent my loathing for you really is."

At that moment the folding doors were flung back and a tall young gentleman with blond hair appeared. At first Adele took him for the dancing master, for there was something about his almost feminine good looks and the very particular attention he had obviously paid to his exceedingly fashionable clothes, but almost immediately she realized her mistake, for he addressed Euphemia by her first name, something no dancing master would dare to do. "I say, 'Phemia," he drawled, "me toes are about capable of putting up with another battering—" He broke off as he saw Adele. His warm, appreciative glance swept over her and he smiled. "Now *there's* beauty for you," he murmured.

Euphemia was irritated. "I will not keep you a moment, Tarquin."

"Who is she?" he asked, not taking his eyes off Adele.

"No one you need concern yourself with."

He saw the package containing the ribbon and realized that Adele had brought it. Before Euphemia knew what he was about, he had broken open the package and taken out the length of ribbon. He looked again at Adele then, a hint of lazy amusement gleaming in his gray eyes. "Ribbon," he said softly. "Delivered from a haberdashery, no doubt. Would it be too much to wonder if that haberdashery is situated in Milsom Street and that you are the notorious Miss—?"

Euphemia snatched the ribbon away furiously. "Your conduct is hardly that of a guest, Tarquin."

"Temper, temper."

"Be so good as to go back into the other room," she said, trying to compose herself, "And I will join you in a moment."

A thoughtful smile played around his fine lips and he sketched a bow, sauntering back and closing the doors quietly behind him. Euphemia threw Adele a venomous look. "You may leave!"

Adele was only to glad to obey and almost flew down the stairs in her eagerness to comply. The footman was just opening the front door to admit another caller, and she halted in surprise as she saw Dr. Septimus Enleigh, rector of Benwick parish and owner of the premises where Cat ran her haberdashery.

Dr. Enleigh was a huge man, broad-shouldered and of immense girth, and would have been imposing even without his clerical dress. On his head was a large frizzed wig that had been liberally powdered and on his face an habitually benign and saintly expression that somehow did not seem quite believable—it was too angelic. He announced that the Marchioness of Heydon had requested him to call, a state-

28

ment which surprised Adele, for Euphemia was hardly a lady of high religious principles.

Stepping into the hallway, the clergyman handed his hat to the footman and then saw Adele. "Good day to you, Miss Russell," he said, his eyes resting an unconscionably long time on her ankles. Yes, there was something far too worldly about the rector of Benwick!

"Good day, sir." She curtsied and then hurried past him to where the footman was pointedly holding the door open. With a sigh of relief, she emerged from the Bellingham residence.

The wind was noticeably stronger now, blowing the coats of a chairman who hurried past with a heavily laden sedan. Some swallows dipped low over the paved center of the Circus as Adele began to walk in the general direction of the market. As she went back down into the town she didn't know that this momentous day had still not finished with her, for she was about to see the very gentleman whose return to Bath was causing so much concern among her enemies.

The hurly-burly of the market was still unnerving to her, even after five years, but then perhaps that was because some of the most salutary lessons she had had to learn had been taught in this very place. Her life at Beech Park had not prepared her in any way to argue over the price of cabbages or the condition of onions. Frequently in the beginning, she had returned to Cat with purchases which that lady had considered definitely inferior. Knowing that Adele would have to learn the hard way, Cat had sent her back to the market, and after being despatched in this ignominious fashion several times, she had indeed soon learned to stand her ground. Now she was as demanding as any of the red-cloaked country wives thronging the walks between the stalls, although she still found such haggling very alien indeed.

The imminence of the storm meant that the market was particularly busy. Everyone hurried to finish their purchases in good time, and Adele was glad to place the last item on Cat's list in her basket and begin to push her way through the crowds to return to Milsom Street. The thoroughfare edging the market was cluttered with farm carts and wagons, and consequently there was a great crush of vehicles trying to pass. The jam was not aided in any way by the "Age" stagecoach, setting out for London with a young gentleman of fashion at the ribbons, he having coaxed the coachman into letting him have this honor. Tempers began to fray as he managed to lock the wheels completely and the irate coachman had to clamber down to try to maneuver the confused team out of the predicament. There was so much shouting and gesticulating that Adele stopped to watch, and had it not been for this small incident, she would have been long gone when the blue town carriage drawn by four matched grays passed the very spot where she stood.

The "Age" was at last sorted out and the traffic began to move, but as Adele turned to go on her way she found herself facing the blue carriage. Her eyes were drawn inexorably to the coat-of-arms emblazoned on the gleaming panel, a crimson eagle rising regally from a golden coronet, the escutcheon of the Latimer family. The noise of the market seemed suddenly deadened as she slowly raised her eyes to the windows.

The old Countess of Blaisdon sat erectly in one seat, her lace-gloved hands clasped on the handle of her ivory cane. Her graying hair was hidden beneath a black calash, but Adele could just see her face, as proud as ever, although marked now by the paleness of ill health.

Opposite sat David Latimer himself. He lounged back against the velvet upholstery, with no idea that he was so close to the woman he had once nearly made his wife. He wore a dark ruby coat and an oyster waistcoat, both of which were unbuttoned to reveal the crisp frills of his shirt. He still wore his cravat in the same knot and still looked in the very height of fashion, without being in any way dandified or foppish. And he was still as devastatingly handsome as she remembered. His dark hair curled just a little and his lips were twisted in that faint, cynical smile which had once affected her so much. His eyes were steely blue and his profile strong, and his complexion was tanned from many hours spent in the fresh air—he had never been one to languish in smoky drawing rooms or sit at the green baize tables until well into the night. His ringed hand rested idly against the glass window and his face bore a pensive expression; he did not glance out or sense her presence in any way, but continued to gaze at nothing in particular, as if deep in thought.

The first raindrops began to fall as she stood there, transfixed by the shock of seeing him again after all this time. He had been on her mind since Sir Frederick's visit that morning, and yet it still came as a considerable jolt to find herself looking at him. Mixed emotions tumbled through her, a bewildering blend of hatred and memories of a love that had meant so much to her. He had hurt her badly and had done so without apparently caring at all, but in spite of that she could recall the ecstasy of being held in his arms.

The carriage moved on, carrying him from her sight, and her eyes were bright with tears as she stared after it, oblivious to the now heavy rain. A jagged flash of lightning illuminated the sky and she was roused at last by the loud clap of thunder that followed. Blinking back the tears, she hurried on her way, deaf to the clinking metallic sound of pattens and blind to the bobbing stream of umbrellas. She moved in a daze, forgetting to pull up her hood and reaching the beginning of Milsom Street without feeling the cold rain seeping through her light cape.

She passed the entrance of Nell Norfolk's confectionary shop but no thought crossed her mind of the pastries she was expected to purchase there for Cat. She was unaware of anything but the haunting memory of David Latimer's warm lips over hers; oh, so very long ago now. . . .

Chapter 4

Cat said nothing to Adele on her return, either about her bedraggled appearance or about the forgotten pastries, rightly putting both things down to the upset of the day's revelations. Instead the hapless Joanie was sent out in the rain a little later to procure the pastries Cat was determined to have that evening. None of the maid's protests about being frightened of thunder had the least effect; the pastries would be sampled that evening and that was the end of it.

The storm continued unabated and Cat soon decided on an early closing, for there were fewer and fewer souls prepared to brave the weather or the increasingly dirty pavements.

With something akin to relief, she bolted the door of the haberdashery. A short day was just the thing as far as she was concerned, for she was no longer as young and spry as she had once been and she had found the coach journey from Bristol tiring. It would be good to enjoy a strong cup of orange pekoe with Nell Norfolk's pastries, and then there would be the pleasing prospect of an hour or so reading the newspaper and doing a little knitting before retiring to the comfort of her bed—yes, that was just what Doctor Rogers ordered for herself!

It was so dark in the kitchen that they enjoyed the tea and pastries by the uncertain light of the only oil lamp. The lamp had been giving trouble for some time, but as it was summer and the evenings very long, Cat had just not bothered about having it repaired. Besides, there were always the candles, or the old lamp up in the attic if there should be an emergency. As Joanie cleared away the tea board, Cat took herself to her favorite chair where the newspaper and knitting lay waiting. With a contented sigh she settled herself.

Adele sat by the window, the novel she had been reading lying unopened on her lap. She gazed at the rain sluicing down the pane and could hear the wind howling around the house as it forced the scudding clouds across the low skies. Her reflection looked back at her by the light of the oil lamp on the table, but her face was indistinct, distorted by the uneven glass.

Joanie carefully washed the blue and white crockery and replaced it on the shelf, gasping a little as another rumble of thunder growled over the heavens. But then the thunder died away again and there was just the noise of the rain on the window and the rustle of Cat's newspaper, and the maid relaxed a little, taking an out-of-date copy of *La Belle Assemblée* from under her apron and seating herself by the table where the lamplight was good. Carefully she opened the first page and settled down to pore over the fashion illustrations.

Cat glanced up at her, tutting a little crossly. "You shouldn't be filling your head up with such things, my girl; you've neither the time nor the money to contemplate anything out of *that* fancy publication!"

"Oh, but the clothes are so beautiful," sighed the maid. "There's a bonnet here all made of peach satin and trimmed with huge bunches of cherries; it's the prettiest thing you ever saw."

Cat snorted. "Fruit? On your head? That's for porters at Covent Garden! Joanie, my girl, you've got some foolish notions and that's a fact. Before I went to Bristol you got yourself a new blue cloak—a new one when there was nothing amiss with the old. Then there was the matter of those Spanish leather shoes. Shoes like that are for gadabout wenches, not for good girls. *Sensible* footwear is what you should be looking for."

Joanie scowled a little, although she hid the fact from Cat's eagle eyes. "Sensible things don't make me feel good," she muttered.

"And what has feeling good got to do with what we're talking about?"

"An awful lot, especially when you've been—" Joanie had been about to say "nagging at me," but wisely thought better of it.

Cat sniffed. "Feeling good from spending sprees is for ladies of quality and wealth, not for kitchen maids!"

Adele abstained from the conversation; indeed she did not hear a great deal of it. She watched the storm. How grimly this day was ending, especially when you thought how fine it had been at the beginning. How grim a day it had been in many ways. . . .

Cat glanced at the silent figure by the window, but said nothing. Best leave her for the time being, she'd had a hard day of it. The old nurse turned another page of the newspaper, adjusted her spectacles on the end of her nose, and began to read the society announcements. One item caught her eye. "Well now, it says here that there's been twice as many people invited to the masquerade as the assembly rooms can reasonably hold! They'll be packed in there like large peas in a small pod, that's for sure! Lord above, I'm glad my name got missed off the list somehow!"

Adele smiled at her. "What a dreadful omission, what can the dear duchess have been thinking of?"

"Can't imagine," replied Cat drily, glad to have drawn a smile. "Perhaps it was to make room for her son, Lord Talbourne; he's daily expected to return to England."

"That will please the younger Miss Mortimer."

"Eh?"

"The younger Miss Mortimer. She is very smitten with Lord Talbourne."

Cat was scornful. "That silly creature will never find a husband of any worth, certainly not the future Duke of Bellingham!"

"Especially if Euphemia has anything to do with it."

"No doubt."

At that very moment there was a loud rumble of thunder, and the oil lamp chose to expire. The kitchen went immediately dark and Joanie gave a squeak of fright. "Ooh, Miss Rogers!"

"Don't fret, you dafty, it's only that dratted lamp. Adele? Can you light a candle, I swear I can't see my hand in front of my face."

Adele got up, feeling her way to the mantelpiece where the bottle of lucifers was kept. A moment later one flared into life and she held it to a candle. The frail light flickered and swayed, revealing Joanie's terrified face. Adele smiled reassuringly. "Don't be afraid, Joanie, the storm won't harm us. We've Cat's word for that."

Cat threw her a sideways look. "Do I detect a note of sarcasm, young Adele? Still, now that you come to mention what's in the loft, it calls to mind that there's another lamp up

34

there somewhere too. It's a bit old, but it still works. Joanie, can you go up there and—?''

"*Me?*" gasped the horrified maid. "Go up there with all those spiders? Oh, please don't ask me, Miss Rogers!" She shook from head to toe, more afraid of creepy crawlies than she was of thunder.

"For heaven's sake!" began Cat, becoming irritated with such an apparent nincompoop, but Adele spoke up hurriedly.

"It's all right, Cat, I'll go up and look for it.''

"It's Joanie's place to—''

"Ah, but I think I know where the lamp is," fibbed Adele quickly.

"Oh. Very well, you go on up there. Light us another candle before you go, though.''

Adele held the candle to another and set it on the table next to Joanie. Then, shielding the delicate flame with her hand, she left the kitchen and made her way up the dark stairs. She could hear the storm raging as she reached the first-floor landing, and holding the curtain aside, she looked out over the deserted street where the lamplighter was struggling to do his work, his boy holding the ladder steady.

She went on up to the next floor, her steps silent on the carpeted stairs, but as she began the final flight to the attic, there was no longer any carpet and each step sounded unnaturally loud and eery. The wind howled around the eaves, sucking beneath the roof and making the tiny cobwebs which seemed to be everywhere tremble in the chilly draught. The candle flickered, making shadows leap and fade alarmingly, and she looked around nervously, conscious of the odd noises— the scratching and squeaking of unseen mice, and the creaking of a board, for all the world as if someone was hiding nearby.

Holding the candle higher, she looked around at the paraphernalia which always seemed to collect in attics. There were old boxes and crates, disused chairs, battered pots and pans, and even an ancient portmanteau. In fact there was everything that Cat thought "might come in useful someday," but which seldom did. Turning a little, Adele saw the withered, almost unrecognizable bunch of hawthorn in its place among the rafters, and she could not help hoping that it would prove as efficacious as Cat insisted, for up here she felt rather too close to the storm for comfort.

At last her glance fell upon the oil lamp, lying on the floor next to a dusty old trunk, and holding up the hem of her gown, she picked her way toward it. As she bent to pick it up, however, the candle's light fell across some embossed initials upon the trunk's lid. D.V.L.R. Denzil Vivian Lionel Russell. This trunk was one of the few things to have been rescued from Beech Park on the night of the fire.

Slowly she put down the candle and lamp and knelt before the trunk, turning the rusty key in the lock. The old hinges groaned as she lifted the lid, and her breath caught as she looked down upon something that winked and shimmered in the candlelight. With a trembling hand, she took out the dainty domino her mother had once worn. Sequins and spangles flashed in her hand as she looked at the flimsy, foolish thing with its little mask and the delicate veil to conceal the lower part of the face. She remembered her mother wearing it, and the beautiful ballgown—which lay folded at the bottom of the trunk where a grieving Denzil had so lovingly placed it after his wife's untimely death from the smallpox. Putting the domino aside, Adele took out the gown and stood up to hold it against herself. It was of white muslin, sheer and soft and sprigged with nasturtium embroidery. Its high-waisted bodice was gathered by a red-gold string and the skirt swung as Adele twirled a little, the draught making the candle flicker wildly and almost go out. She gazed at the gown. How strange it was that although it was more than eight years old now, it was only made old-fashioned by its train and the fact that its hemline lacked any particular embellishment. Fashion had indeed not progressed a great deal in the past few years.

Slowly she folded it again and replaced it in the trunk, resting the domino on top again and closing the trunk. The past, both happy and unhappy, seemed determined to intrude today, and in so many ways. Picking up the candle and the lamp, she retraced her steps to the stairs and descended with some relief.

Adele closed the door of her own room a little later and carefully placed the candlestick on the white-draped dressing table, which looked far too grand for such a room. Indeed, it had once occupied a much grander room in a large house, but which room and where would never be known as it had been purchased secondhand.

Lightning pierced the gloom outside and she went to the

window to look out over the crowding rooftops and smoking chimneys toward the hillside where another flash of lightning momentarily revealed the stark ruins of Beech Park. The image remained imprinted on her vision long after the lightning had faded, and she closed the curtains swiftly, turning back into the room.

It was a small room, but not by any means cramped. The walls were a pale blue and the floorboards were dark-stained, scattered with three or four little rugs that gave it a cozy look. The bed was narrow and plain and an ornate dressing table dominated the room. It was bare except for her brush and comb and a little bowl of pins and a bowl and jug of cold water.

Undressing, she slipped into her voluminous nightgown and then she unpinned her golden hair and began to brush it, halting only when she had reached a count of one hundred. Tying on her night bonnet, she extinguished the candle and climbed into the bed. Sleep soon overtook her—but with sleep, the unhappy past came into its own. . . .

The flames consuming Beech Park roared and spiraled into the ice-cold night, melting the snowflakes as they wandered down. The inferno could be seen for miles; a thick pall of smoke spread across the hillside above Bath and light illuminated the great park that swept down from the house between the two woods to the narrow lake and the elegant Palladian bridge that spanned the dark water.

Adele stood barefoot in the snow, numbed into immobility by the horror of what was happening. The flames were reflected in her eyes and tears were wet on her cheeks. The night breeze stirred the rich ribbons at the throat of her silk night robe and she was unaware of anything around her except the dreadful knowledge that her father was still in the blazing house, and all hope of rescuing him had been abandoned.

The insurance company's engines had labored up the steep hill, but all their efforts could not stem such a blaze, and one by one they gave up, the firemen standing wearily by as they stared at the collapse one of the proudest and most beautiful of houses. The servants huddled together, frightened and bewildered, and soon only the fire itself could be heard, devouring the elegant furnishings and destroying the house room by magnificent room.

A carriage came slowly up the drive, the sound of its

approach drowned by the roar of the fire. It came to a halt and two men alighted, the one well built and almost gaudily dressed, the other plainly clothed, tall and thin. They glanced at each other, not saying a word, but their satisfaction would have been evident to anyone who happened to glance at them.

Adele turned, sensing their presence. They were the cause of this! The vain, popinjay Duke of Bellingham and his toadying creature, her father's clerk, Frederick Repton! They alone had reason to want this tragedy to befall Denzil Russell. Now their crimes would never be exposed; they had seen to that!

"Murderers!" she screamed, the single word echoing over the stunned gathering.

All eyes turned toward the carriage and the two climbed hastily back inside. The coachman whipped his weary horses into action and the equipage moved away down the drive.

Adele's terrible accusation followed it. "Murderers! Murderers! murderers . . ."

With a start she awoke, sitting up in the narrow bed. The roar of the flames and the acrid smell of the smoke still seemed to cling to her, but gradually the threads of the nightmare slipped away into the night and it was July again, not a bitter January night in 1810.

She heard Cat's anxious voice at the door. "Adele? Adele, are you all right?"

"Cat?" Adele's voice broke a little, and in a moment Cat had opened the door and hurried inside. She carried a candle, which she hastily put down on the dressing table and then came to sit on the bedside, putting her arms comfortingly around Adele, just as she had done many years before when as a little girl she had woken up from a bad dream.

"It's all right, my pet, don't cry now. Cat's here."

Adele clung to her for a moment and gradually recovered enough to draw away, smiling ruefully. "I'm sorry, did I call out very much this time?"

"Enough to have Joanie shaking like a leaf."

"I'm sorry—"

"You can't help it, my dear. It's been a long time since you dreamed like this, but then after today, I suppose I'm not surprised."

Adele looked fondly at the plump face with its framing nightcap and wisps of gray hair. A long plait hung down over

Cat's shoulder, trailing almost to the remnants of her waistline, and she looked so very reassuring that the effects of the nightmare disappeared completely.

Cat took Adele's hand gently. "Don't start thinking you can right all those wrongs," she said anxiously. "For there's no way at all that you can bring down the likes of the Duke of Bellingham and Sir Frederick Repton. They are the victors, my dear, and you and your poor dear father are the losers."

"I know."

"It's hard for you, I know, but there truly isn't anything you can do. Your father had evidence, we both know that, but we also know that it was destroyed in the fire. Without proof there is nothing that can be done."

"Unless proof is manufactured," said Adele bitterly. "As it was manufactured against my father."

"Aye, well that's another matter entirely." Cat squeezed Adele's hands warmly. "Do you know, I've been thinking about what that foolish Joanie said earlier, about buying fancy clothes to make yourself feel good. Maybe she's right. You haven't bought yourself anything frivolous in a long time, why don't you indulge yourself a little, hmm? Go out and be extravagant over some silly new bonnet or shawl? I reckon Joanie's not far out when she says it makes you feel good."

"Maybe—"

"You think about it. Shall I make you a cup of chocolate?"

"No, I'll be all right now."

"I'll leave your door open and I'll come the moment you call for me."

"Oh, Cat, I do love you so," whispered Adele, putting her arms around the older woman's neck and kissing her cheek. "You'll never know how much I love you."

"And to think that after that fire your first thought was to take yourself off to London or some such devilish spot," said Cat, blinking back pleased tears. "The very idea, as if I'd let my pet go off like that when I had a good home to offer her."

Adele smiled. "I'll warrant there were times in the beginning, when I was cutting the wrong lengths, dropping things, and sending out the wrong number of this and that, that you began to wish you'd let me go!"

"Never!" said Cat firmly, "Never, in a million years! With Beech Park gone like that, your place was with me.

There'll always be a place with me for you, my dear, for you are the daughter I never had. I raised you and I look upon you as my own flesh and blood. Now then, I'll leave you to try to go back to sleep.''

"Good night, Cat."

"Good night, my sweeting."

Chapter 5

The presence in Bath of the three main protagonists of one of the causes célèbre of 1810 did indeed produce the whispers Sir Frederick was concerned to keep at bay. The whispers were discreet, however, for no one wished to antagonize either the Bellingham family or the Latimers. No mention was therefore made in front of them, which Sir Frederick was pleased to note, but when they were not present the drawing rooms were filled with it. Bath society was titillated by the thought of the Earl of Blaisdon perhaps coming face-to-face with his former fiancée and by the hope that if such a confrontation should take place, the Marchioness of Heydon would be present as well. A great many ladies would have given their eye-teeth to be present at such a momentous meeting, and as a result the haberdashery, already doing remarkably well because of the masquerade, began to do quite handsomely.

Adele endured the renewed interest as stoically as possible, being ever-mindful of the warnings she had been given, but Euphemia was finding the situation unexpectedly trying. She had always taken great delight in taunting Adele about what had happened, but now it was the marchioness herself who was the butt of much chitter-chatter and spiteful innuendo. She knew only too well that the moment she left a room, she became the topic of conversation. The incident with Tarquin had warned her what to expect, but nevertheless she did not find it easy to maintain her usual composure. Of the trio, only the Earl of Blaisdon seemed totally unaware of what was going on, but then where that gentleman was concerned people were more discreet than ever, for he was not someone to cross.

But the longed-for confrontation showed no signs of taking place and the haberdashery did not become the scene of a great dénouement. Adele did not even see the earl from a distance after the one glimpse in his carriage at the market. She *heard* a great deal, however, from the number of times he had escorted his mother to the Pump Room to the duration of his visits to the Bellingham residence.

Each day she served in the haberdashery, closing her eyes and ears to the undercurrents as she had learned to do over the past five years. The sheer volume of customers made it easier for her, if anything, for she had little time to think. The Misses Mortimer were a prime example of the spate of interest, for they came far more frequently than they would normally have done, and they came simply in the hope of being there when something of consequence occurred. The haberdashery did well out of their curiosity, for it sold them a whole card of fine white lace, another parasol, a pair of embroidered gloves, and some fancy handkerchiefs, which lightened their purses quite considerably. Adele groaned inwardly whenever they arrived, for they stared so at her and then exchanged meaningful glances, their dumpy faces even more pink than usual. They were, she thought savagely, quite the most stupid of creatures, empty-headed and lacking all sense of tact, and she was very thankful if Cat served them. When that was not to be, however, Adele was outwardly all charm and attentiveness, smiling as she brought item after item for their perusal, and being at all times the very model of politeness. They must have found it all most frustrating, for they were simply *dying* for something to happen, and it never did!

This was the pattern of her life then when some three days after being ordered on Euphemia's business, Adele found herself on an errand for the Duchess of Bellingham herself. It happened one morning when a very haughty running footman in the distinctive mulberry and gold livery of the Bellinghams entered the haberdashery. Both Adele and Cat were busy serving and he made little secret of his impatience that a personage of his importance should be kept waiting. At last his turn came and he rapped purposefully upon the oak counter.

"The Duchess of Bellingham requires the immediate delivery to the assembly rooms of three hundred ostrich plumes. One hundred to be red, one hundred white, and the remainder blue." His expression was lofty and disdainful and both Cat and Adele disliked him immediately.

Cat was short with him. "Do you honestly imagine I am able to stock such vast numbers in this small shop?"

"It is nothing to do with me what you've got here, I am merely charged to tell you the duchess's urgent desire."

Cat's lips pressed angrily together, and she took a deep breath. "I will be able to carry out the duchess's wish in an hour or so."

His expression changed. "But the duchess said *immediate* delivery!"

"I'll warrant she did, and that she said it at least two hours ago, you insolent young puppy! I can smell the ale on your breath from here. How many taverns did you *run* through on your way here, eh? If the duchess's wrath is to come down upon anyone, it will be upon you, so don't you go coming the high-and-mighty swell with me! I will attend to the duchess's requirements as swiftly as I can and you may tell her so. But if you so much as say one word to try to lay the blame for the delay upon me, then I promise you that your mistress will hear the truth—and double quick at that!"

He clenched his fists but said nothing more, turning on his heel to march out, his ears red with humiliation. Once outside, however, he was once again the picture of majesty, adjusting his tricorn hat on his powdered wig and drawing himself up to strut importantly along the pavement, breaking into a run only when within sight of the assembly rooms where the duchess was striving to see that all was to her liking for the masquerade.

A moment or so later, Adele was dispatched with Joanie to scour the shops for the necessary number of plumes. Joanie grumbled all the time, for she was wearing her Spanish leather shoes and was afraid of ruining them with so much walking. At last, however, they had all they required and carried the huge, bouncing armfuls of patriotic plumes up through the town to the assembly rooms.

These rooms, sometimes simply known as the upper rooms, to distinguish them from the lower rooms, which were of little consequence, lay up the hill from Milsom Street, and Joanie's complaining grew louder with each step they took. The rooms were very elegant, and at the height of Bath's glory had been considered very fashionable indeed. They were still a focal point of the town's social life, even though the days of Beau Nash were long since gone, and as the two young women approached the porticoed main entrance Adele recalled the occasions during her father's lifetime when she had accompanied him here in the carriage.

The western front of the building was marred now by the thoughtless addition of Mr. Bartley's billiard rooms to one side of the main entrance and by the reading room on the other. Neither of these accretions matched and so the symmetry of the whole building was destroyed. The aesthetic qualities of the architecture did not concern Adele and Joanie, however, as they toiled the final yards, their feet and arms aching.

The Bellingham landau was drawn up outside the rooms, the coachman lounging on his seat in a way that suggested that he had been waiting there some considerable time, which indeed he had, for inside the duchess was finding life quite a trial. Her wishes were being challenged by the primping, but nevertheless important, figure of the master of ceremonies, whose word could still be law in the assembly rooms.

Adele and Joanie passed through the heavy doors and into the glittering hallway. Laurel wreaths, oak leaves and ribbons had been placed on the walls, although it could not help but be noticed that the ribbons were Bellingham mulberry and gold, not the expected red, white, and blue. One must not be allowed to forget that this was first and foremost a *Bellingham* celebration—Waterloo and the Duke of Wellington took second and third place respectively to such a consideration. Everywhere there was immense activity and not a little chaos as groups of workmen erected displays of suitably victorious scenes from the classics or draped the walls with swathes of linen. The chandelier in the center of the ceiling vibrated with all the noise, its candle flames swaying sufficiently to make the crystals flash from time to time. No one paid any attention to the two women as they picked their way over planks of wood, bolts of cloth, and half-painted Greek heroes fashioned out of wood toward the octagon room, which provided access to all the other principal chambers—the ballroom, tea room, and card room.

Joanie's grumbling had ceased the moment they entered the building. She had never been to the assembly rooms before—her knowledge of dances ran more to the occasional evening at the White Hart—and her eyes were huge with wonder as she gazed around at the dazzling luxury. Even in its present state of uproar, the building looked grand, and she could only guess how it would look on the night of the masquerade. Clutching the ostrich plumes close, the maid looked at everything, taking in the minutest detail and committing it to memory, just as she had committed to memory every illustration in *La Belle Assemblée*.

In the octagon room they paused for a moment, Adele looking around for the footman who had come to the haberdashery, but there was no sign of him, indeed there was no sign of a footman at all and certainly no one of sufficient importance to entrust with the duchess's plumes.

Joanie appeared to have forgotten the purpose of their visit; she was still gazing at the portraits lining the upper walls and at the four perfectly placed fireplaces that provided much-needed warmth on cold winter evenings. There were no fires burning now; the fireplaces were decorated with large vases of artificial flowers—red, white, and blue—which in turn were decorated with more Bellingham mulberry and gold. The blend of colors was dreadful, but evidently met with the duchess's approval.

Hearing the duchess's raised voice emanating from the noisy ballroom, Adele caught Joanie's arm and drew her toward the entrance, where they peeped inside. The great chamber with its five large chandeliers, pale blue walls, and high windows flanked by Corinthian columns was very beautiful indeed, although one might be forgiven for failing to appreciate that fact at the moment, for just as the entrance hall was a scene of mayhem, so was the ballroom. Scores of workmen swarmed everywhere, some up ladders to drape linen on the walls, others putting laurel wreaths, and still others balancing precariously to put transparencies in the windows. The noise of hammering and sawing came from the far end where a new stand was being erected to accommodate the orchestra, which at that unhappy moment was attempting the impossible—to rehearse for the grand night. Behind the orchestra and half-completed stand was the doorway into the billiard room. The lights were on inside and Adele could well imagine the tenor of the language of the gentlemen trying to enjoy a quiet game with all the uproar going on in the ballroom.

Even as she thought this the door opened and a young gentleman emerged, his face aglow with impatience and irritation. The moment she saw him, she held the plumes closer to conceal her face, for it was Tarquin. He was obviously intent upon leaving, but the duchess perceived him immediately and beckoned to him. With a sigh, he complied.

The Duchess of Bellingham was a tall woman who had

been, and still was, a great beauty. There was a coldness about her, however, which now deterred gentlemen, but at one time her string of illustrious lovers had been very impressive. After observing the unwritten rule that a wife must provide her husband with a son and heir before playing the rest of the field, she had played with a vengeance. Lord Talbourne, it was universally acknowledged, was indeed the duke's offspring, but Euphemia was whispered to be the daughter of a certain Lord Wenworth—whose dark good looks she certainly appeared to share.

Tarquin bowed low before the duchess, whose face was thunderous, not because of his attempted exit from the billiard room but because she was beset by the pesterings of the little master of ceremonies who was continually at her heels like a furious little dog. The curling feathers in her beaver hat quivered and her expression was one that would have reduced even the duke to instant silence. She spoke to Tarquin, but her voice was drowned by all the noise. Her face still and admirably controlled, she addressed the master of ceremonies.

Drawing himself up to his full height, which brought him to the duchess's shoulder, he turned and flicked his fingers importantly at a small boy sitting against one wall. The boy put a trumpet to his lips and blew a discordant blast upon it. Immediately there was silence.

The duchess took a long breath. "That, sir, is a vast improvement," she said coldly to the master of ceremonies. "Lord Tarquin, I would like your opinion about the positioning of the orchestra stand. Should it be there, or should it be somewhere against that wall over there?"

Tarquin flacked a lace-edged handkerchief over his wine-red sleeve. "Truly, Your Grace, I believe it is quite satisfactory where it is at present." At which reply the workmen laboring upon the stand looked justifiably relieved.

"You think so? Really, it is too bad of the duke not to have arrived yet, I simply cannot manage everything by myself."

Tarquin smiled. "But you do it so well, Your Grace," he said gallantly.

She looked pleased. "Why, how kind of you to say so; I do believe your new bride has a positive treasure in you. By the way, how *is* Amelia? Will she be attending the masquerade?"

"I trust so, Your Grace." But he did not look at all certain, or so Adele thought. In fact, she had the distinct impression that all was not well between Lord Tarquin and his wife Amelia.

The duchess did not seem to notice anything amiss. "She is with your mother, is she not?"

"Er, yes. At least, she was."

"Are you not certain?"

"No."

"Really?" The duchess at last looked a little nonplussed. "Oh. Oh, well don't let me detain you now, my lord. I realize that you have other things to do." She inclined her head graciously.

He bent a very elegant leg and then turned to approach the door where Adele and Joanie were standing, waiting in vain for the appearance of a footman to relieve them of the plumes. Adele kept her face hidden, not wishing to attract his attention, but he did not even glance at them as he passed.

Immediately after he had gone, the duchess found herself facing the master of ceremonies again. He was very splendid in his blue coat with its oyster silk lining, his black tights and silk stockings and pumps. An eyeglass was suspended on a wide ribbon around his neck and he had a gold watch and huge bunch of seals at his fob. He carried an ivory-handled cane and was dressed for a grand occasion, but then he always had to dress like that, for masters of ceremonies must always be prepared to be ceremonious. In Bath he was an important figure, presiding over many social functions, and he was determined to preside over the duchess's Waterloo masquerade as well. In the duchess, however, he had met his match. She had most definitely had enough of him. She drew herself up, the plumes in her hat quivering a little more than before. "Yes?"

"Your Grace, it is customary for *me* to lead the first dance."

"I will dance the first dance with the duke, his gout permitting."

"But, Your Grace, it simply is not done!"

"I *beg* your pardon?" she said icily. "Are you questioning my right to say what will and will not be done at my own masquerade?"

"But—"

"No, sir!" she said shortly, "Most definitely no!"

He looked outraged, but wisdom prevailed for the moment and he left the subject of the first dance to broach another issue of equal moment. "Your Grace, about your insistence that the billiard room be closed on the night of the masquerade . . ."

"What of it?"

"I do not know that it will be possible."

"Of course it is possible! I will *not* have gentlemen slipping away and denying the ladies their company for the dancing. No, sir, I will not hear of it."

He toyed with his cane, sure proof of his upset. "Th-then there is the matter of the refreshments, Your Grace," he said, determined to persevere.

"Go on."

"At the assembly rooms we always serve tea and lemonade, certainly nothing of an alcoholic nature."

"On this occasion there is to be iced champagne."

"But, Your Grace," he protested, "in all my years as master—"

"My dear sir, do you seek to *cheapen* the victory at Waterloo?"

He blinked. "Cheapen it? But I assure you, the tea is the very finest—"

"It is still tea, sir. Only champagne is suitable for such an occasion as my masquerade. We have defeated the French, sir, or had that fact slipped your mind? We will toast a British victory with *French* champagne. I will not hear any more of your tiresome objections. The élite of the land will be converging upon this town, do you honestly imagine they will be pleased to know that because of your interference they have been reduced to drinking tea and lemonade? I would not give much for your dandy little hide, sir, no, I would indeed not give much for it!"

The duchess's pond became once again serene and calm as the master of ceremonies finally sank without trace, leaving not a ripple behind him. The duchess swept on her way, demanding that a laurel wreath be moved a fraction of an inch, without a glance back at the little man, who looked totally defeated. Adele would have felt sorry for him had she not known him to be an officious insect, always puffed up with his own importance and always too ready to say what would and would not be done. His comeuppance was long overdue.

Joanie grinned at Adele. "That told him, eh?"

"Yes. Small wonder the Duke of Bellingham is said to be a *five*-bottle-a-day man," replied Adele, aware suddenly that she had forgotten all about the plumes. Now she looked around again for a footman but froze with shock, for coming across the octagon toward the very door where she and Joanie were standing was David Latimer, with Euphemia leaning adoringly on his arm.

Adele turned sharply back, her mind racing. Once again she hid her face with the plumes, catching Joanie's arm and pushing the startled maid urgently into the ballroom and pressing back against the wall. Puzzled, Joanie complied, just as the Earl of Blaisdon and the Marchioness of Heydon entered the ballroom.

Euphemia looked very graceful and fresh in pale blue lawn, a ribboned parasol twirling over her shoulder, but Adele hardly noticed her; she could only look at David Latimer. He was taller than she remembered, his shoulders a little broader, but his hips were as slender as she recalled. He looked superb in a plain dark gray coat and breeches, carrying his top hat under his arm, and he smiled as Euphemia spoke. That smile cut into Adele's heart, and the pain he had caused her was suddenly as fresh as if he had written that cruel note only the day before. Cruel. That was the word to describe him. Cruel and heartless. How easily he bent towards Euphemia once more, just as easily as he had before he turned his fickle attention to Denzil Russell's foolish, trusting daughter. He was all that was false, all that was despicable.

Joanie glanced uncertainly at her, sensing the sharpness of her thoughts. "Miss Russell, is that not the Earl of—"

"Yes. It is."

"He's so handsome," breathed the maid, staring in open admiration.

"You cannot tell a book by its cover, Joanie; inside he is very ugly indeed." Adele turned back into the octagon room, where to her intense relief she almost immediately saw the very footman who had come to the haberdashery. Thrusting the plumes into his startled arms, she and Joanie left the assembly rooms.

Outside, the Bellingham landau was still waiting, its coachman dozing now, but there was another vehicle drawn up nearby, a smart green curricle drawn by two matched grays. A tiny groom held the reins, and Adele quickly averted her head, for she recognized him. That same groom had been perched behind a similar curricle five years before when the Earl of Blaisdon had called upon her at Beech Park.

Before the assembly rooms passed finally from sight behind them, Joanie turned to look back. "Oh, I wish I was going to that masquerade; I'd love to dress up in fashionable finery and dance with a handsome gentleman—a Guards officer maybe."

Adele said nothing as she looked at the elegant building. Yes, it would be good to attend such a gathering again, to be once more a part of that world she missed so very much still. It was a hard, glittering world, unkind and unfeeling, but it was her world for all that. She was an outcast now, but no matter how hard she tried to accept that fact, she could not.

Forcing such thoughts away, she smiled briskly. "Come on, we've left a certain lady alone to cope in a certain haberdashery for long enough already; she'll be rushed off her feet."

"Oh, don't talk to me about feet," groaned the maid. "I'm going to have hundreds of blisters tomorrow, simply hundreds!"

Chapter 6

The next morning Adele came downstairs to be greeted by the sound of Cat's raised voice. The unfortunate Joanie was in trouble on two counts; first because she had forgotten to buy bread the day before, and second because her vain insistence upon wearing shoes of flimsy Spanish leather had indeed resulted in painful blisters, which overnight had reduced her to little more than a hobble. Cat was extremely vexed, not only because the maid had proved unreliable again but also because there was one thing in the world she enjoyed above all others, and that was what she called a "civilized" breakfast—a good pot of strong tea, a boiled egg or possibly two, and fine white bread.

Seeing Joanie's eyes brimming with tears, Adele hastened to intervene on her behalf. Soothingly she said that she could go to the baker straight away and be back with the necessary bread before the kettle had even begun to boil. Maybe that was something of an exaggeration, for such an errand would take a little longer than that, but it had the desired effect of placating Cat and rescuing the maid.

Adele put a clean cloth in the basket, tied on her cape and bonnet, and a moment or so later was hurrying down Milsom Street toward the bakery. Across the road from the bakery, she paused on the curb as a lumbering ox wagon passed by. She could hear the wavering but belligerent notes of the notorious Chippenham "Arrow" stage leaving the White Hart further down in the town opposite the Pump Room and she smiled a little at the sound, wondering if anyone would ever claim the prize that was said to be there for the first person who could find the "Arrow" traveling the King's highway *legally!* The Chippenham stage was famed for its reckless, uncouth coachmen and for its many infringements of the law. It was nearly always overloaded with baggage and frequently carried too many outsiders, the coachmen pocketing the extra fares themselves.

The ox wagon moved on its way and she crossed the road to the bakery, emerging after a minute or so with a warm loaf. Her only thought was to return to the haberdashery as quickly as possible, and with this single purpose in mind she stepped heedlessly into the road, straight into the path of the oncoming "Arrow."

The coachman cursed roundly as he tried to rein the startled team in, and Adele screamed as the leaders reared only inches away from her. The basket was struck from her hands, the bread tumbling out into the gutter. Shouting a string of obscenities, the coachman waved his clenched fist at her, and in a blur she saw the nervous faces of the outsiders peering down at her.

At last she found her tongue. "Don't you speak to me like that!" she cried, the nature of his language at last making an impression upon her scattered senses. "And don't *you* accuse *me* of being a danger to other folk! There's no coach more dangerous than yours and no coach more illegally loaded!"

"Illegally loaded?" he bellowed, his round, red face going almost purple above the capes of his box coat, "There ent nothin' illegal about this drag!"

"No? I see three outsiders too many and hampers fixed so badly that they are unsafe! Hadn't you better be on your way before some vigilant informer seeks to earn himself a fine reward for sneaking on you?"

Muttering beneath his breath, he gathered the reins again. Informers were not to be forgotten, and he was drawing attention to himself by shouting at a bit of muslin with less sense than a pig's trotter! Breaking the law could incur heavy fines for the likes of him and he'd too much to lose by remaining to jaw at stupid, damned . . . He did not finish the thought but urged the team on again.

Adele stepped hastily out of the way and then bent down to retrieve the basket and the bread, which had remained miraculously safe in the protective cloth. But as she reached out to pick the bread up, she saw something lying next to it which made her breath catch in her throat. It was a small white card embossed with gold lettering, an invitation to the Duchess of Bellingham's grand Waterloo masquerade!

Slowly she picked it up and read. *The Duke and Duchess of Bellingham desire the honor of your company on the occasion of their grand masquerade at the Upper Assembly Rooms in commemoration of the glorious victory at Waterloo, commencing at ten o'clock in the evening.* She turned it over, seeking the owner's name, but there was nothing. It was completely anonymous. She glanced up and down the street, but apart from several street vendors there was no one, certainly no one dressed fashionably enough to have been the owner of such an invitation. Her mind was racing. She was holding a card which would admit her to *the* social event of the year, an "open sesame" to a chance of enjoying once again the life she had known at Beech Park. The moment such a thought entered her head, she pushed it away, for down such a path lay certain disaster, not only for herself but also for Cat, whose business would suffer greatly if her assistant were to be discovered in such an act. But she did not throw the little card away. Picking up the loaf and the basket, she hid the card and hurried on across the street, taking care to look both ways this time.

As she reached the side alley and the door into the garden, however, the invitation card and the possibilities it offered filled her head. She said nothing at all to Cat, but as she untied her cape and removed her bonnet, she remembered the trunk in the attic—and the ballgown and domino which lay inside it.

The candle flickered in the cool air of the loft and for a moment she thought she heard someone behind her on the stairs, but as she listened there was only silence; both Joanie and Cat were well asleep by now. Carefully she tiptoed across the dusty floor to the trunk, setting the candle gently down and opening the trunk as she had before. Her breath held, she took out the little domino and then the ballgown. The soft white muslin felt so fine against her hands, and the nasturtium embroidery looked so very dainty. It would not be difficult to alter such a gown and bring it bang up to the mark. She bit her lip, crushing the garment against her breast in a gesture of guilt. It was wrong; she shouldn't be even *thinking* such thoughts! She had no right to risk harming Cat. But then it *was* a masquerade; everyone would be hidden behind masks and no one could possibly know who she was. And it was for just one night, one brilliant, glittering night. Was it so much to want to go? Was it so wicked to want to return just for a while to the world from which she had been cast? How could it really be wicked when there was practically no risk at all of discovery?

Slowly she folded the gown and looked at it again, indecision clouding her face. She knew what she *should* do, but she also knew what she desperately *wanted* to do. Suddenly she picked up the gown and the domino and closed the trunk; her mind was made up, she was persuaded that she could not be found out, not if she really took pains to conceal her identity. Taking the candle, she made her way back to the stairs and then down into the house.

In her room, with the curtains tightly drawn and the door locked, she tried on the gown that her mother had worn all those years before. Her mother had been a slender woman, and the gown fitted her daughter to perfection. Adele stared at herself in the looking glass. She was transformed. She was no longer a dull little shop assistant, she was a lady of quality again. Slowly she put on the domino, draping the shimmering veil over the lower part of her face. Only her hair offered any clue to her identity now, for its vivid golden color was so very distinctive, but it would be easy to conceal it beneath a little hood, something as light and brightly spangled as the veil.

She twisted first one way and then the other. The gown's train would have to be removed and then the hemline embellished with fringes and ribbons or something equally as fashionable. Maybe the little sleeves could be adorned with matching trimmings; yes, that would be the thing. Her plain fan could be given new life by the careful application of sequins and the addition of a particularly handsome golden tassel she knew was in the haberdashery. She would have to purchase a new shawl, for she simply did not have anything remotely suitable, but that should not be too difficult, and then there was the matter of a reticule. She paused to think for a moment and then smiled, for she could make one from the discarded train of the gown! The haberdashery stocked the necessary white silk stockings and after that her outfit would be complete, except, of course, for the new, lightly boned corset which was de rigueur now. Such a corset would be very expensive, and although she had funds enough to purchase her other accessories, she could not have afforded that as well. No doubt she would be considered forward and lacking in modesty, but then as no one would know who she was, what did it matter?

A surge of excitement swept through her and her eyes shone in the light of the candle. She hugged herself tightly, whirling about so that the soft muslin swung richly, outlining her figure very clearly indeed. She was going to the Duchess of Bellingham's masquerade!

Cat nodded approvingly when Adele took out the new shawl she had purchased. "There, I was right then, eh? Treating yourself to something a little extravagant has done you the world of good; your eyes look all of a sparkle. My, but that's a handsome shawl." Cat took the shawl and held it up, admiring the softness of the Kashmir and the unusual design of orange flowers on the white background.

Momentarily Adele felt a twinge of conscience, but almost immediately it was gone. She wasn't doing any harm, she *wasn't*. . . .

The gown lay spread out carefully on the bedroom floor, the candle beside it. The haberdashery's best scissors gleamed in the light as Adele picked them up, her hand trembling. If she should make a mistake, then the whole dream would be ended in a moment. She had measured and measured, over and over again, and the neat line of pins marked the very spot where she must cut. But what if she had misjudged? It was so difficult to do without anyone to help, so hard to know if the new hemline would show just the right amount of ankle or far too much. Taking a deep breath, she made the first incision. There it was begun now, she must go on. The scissors snip-snipped in the quiet room and several minutes later she pulled away the unwanted hem and the train.

Satisfied that her measurements had been correct after all, she retired to the comfort of the bed, carefully turning up the new hem and beginning to stitch. The candle burned low. Outside, Bath was silent, but for the occasional calling of the watch. A piece of delicate gauze lay folded at her side, waiting to be made into a little hood, and the tiny golden spangles and sequins she had chosen shone richly in their dish. She had purchased many yards of fine nasturtium ribbon from another haberdashery, not daring to use Cat's stock as that lady would certainly have noticed such a thing, and the golden tassel for the fan lay on the floor where it had fallen. The needle flashed in and out and Adele's eyes grew tired, so tired that at last she had to concede that she must sleep if she were to remain alert in the shop the next morning. Carefully she put everything away in the drawer, hiding it beneath her old clothes in case Joanie should happen to open the drawer to put something away.

Yawning, she lazily stretched her arms above her head. She felt deliciously tired, for she had been working on something that meant a very great deal to her. As she curled up in bed, however, a fleeting anxiety touched her. What if she *was* discovered? But sleep overtook her a moment later and the anxiety was gone.

Three long nights later everything was complete. She had altered the gown, made the reticule, and refurbished the fan. The little hood was all that remained and that would not take her long. Everything lay on the floor for her close inspection. The white silk stockings had cost the dreadful sum of twelve shillings, but she had to admit that they were very fine indeed and were worth such a price—not, perhaps, for just one evening though! With all the other accessories, there were also two lemons and a little bottle of Yardley's lavender water. One lemon was for her hair, the other to blanch her hands, and the lavender water was an absolute must to dab behind her ears and on her wrists. There, she could not possibly have forgotten anything!

She picked up the little invitation card and gazed at it. Such a little card, a mere piece of paper found in a gutter, but to her it was priceless beyond belief, a ticket to her lost paradise.

The masquerade was in two days' time, but in the meantime something happened to almost change her mind about the wisdom of using that ticket.

Chapter 7

A family with five daughters, all unmarried and all invited to the masquerade, was lodging at the White Hart opposite the Pump Room, and between them they had ordered a variety of items from the haberdashery. With the shop relatively quiet for once, Cat decided that it was an opportune moment for Adele to take the various parcels to the White Hart, and on the way back she could call in at Nell Norfolk's and buy some more pastries. Cat did not pretend this time; she openly admitted that she simply liked the pastries, even if they were expensive and decidedly bad for the figure.

Adele found the yard of the White Hart even more bustling than usual. An important coaching inn, it was always filled to capacity with stages and mails, but now it was positively bursting with private drags too, for with lodgings so scarce at the moment, many of the duchess's guests had had to resort to hotels and inns for accommodation. Catching a glimpse of the unpleasant coachman of the Chippenham "Arrow," Adele thankfully left the parcels with the landlord and scuttled out again, wanting to avoid a confrontation with such an ill-tempered fellow at all costs.

Nell Norfolk's confectionery shop was a popular establishment, a place where society frequently met, and consequently it was elegantly appointed, furnished more like a drawing room than a shop. True, behind the highly polished counter there were shelves weighed down with pots of currant and raspberry jam, quince marmalade, and bottled fruit, but the rest of the shop was quite different. There were sofas and candelabra, and mirrors on the walls, and the tables were covered with snowy white tablecloths on which were set out the array of delicacies prepared to the rear of the premises. There were biscuits and cakes and sugar plums, all to be sampled on the spot, to say nothing of the famous pastries. In the windows everything was displayed beneath gleaming glass domes, and the curtains were a rich, eye-catching crimson trimmed with heavy golden fringes.

Nell herself was a plump woman, giving the impression that she enjoyed her own cooking, and she always dressed in cherry-red muslin. Her hennaed hair was always twisted up beneath the white day cap, but never neatly enough to prevent long, fiery strands from hanging down past her rouged cheeks. This preoccupation with red was not accidental; it came from Nell's firm conviction that red was a color that enticed people to eat, and there was no reason to suppose that she was wrong, for there was indeed something very inviting about the shop with its warm hues and equally warm, appetizing smells.

Adele was glad to find the shop empty and Nell herself behind the counter. Nell smiled when she saw who her customer was, for Adele would always have a special place in her heart. Had it not been for Adele, the shop would never have caught society's eye. The sight of the Russell barouche drawn up outside had meant that soon other carriages had drawn up there too, and now the mouth-watering pastries and preserves were served in every fashionable drawing room. Nell had much to thank Denzil Russell's daughter for, and the scandal and Adele's fall from grace had not made the slightest difference to the proprietress of Bath's most exclusive confectioner.

"Why, Adele, my dear, does this visit mean that Mistress Rogers is once again consigning her waistline to perdition?"

"It does indeed."

Nell patted her own vanished middle. "It comes to us all, I fear, especially if there is a sweet tooth to contend with as well. Still, I doubt if you will ever have to worry about such things, for I remember that your poor dear mama was as slender as a girl to the end."

"Yes, she was." A brief vision of the ballgown passed before Adele's eyes.

"What is it to be today? Some pastries?"

"Naturally—the stickier and more wicked the better."

"I have the very thing. How many do you want?"

"Half a dozen."

Nell went to select them from beneath one of the glass domes in the window, but then her sharp gasp of dismay made Adele look up swiftly. Nell was looking out the window at the green curricle that had drawn up outside, and Adele's horrified gaze followed the gentleman on the pavement as he went to help down his lady companion. David Latimer and Euphemia!

"Oh, my lordy, lordy!" muttered Nell swiftly, replacing the glass dome and scurrying back toward the counter. She beckoned swiftly to Adele to follow her to the back where another of the crimson curtains soon hid the girl from view.

Smoothing her skirts and straightening her cap, Nell returned to her place behind the counter just as the bell sounded. Holding the curtains aside a little, Adele managed to peep out. Euphemia was wearing a mauve pelisse and a military hat with bouncing tassels. "My dear earl," she was saying, "I cannot help but admire the wondrous shine on your boots. Could it be that you have taken a leaf out of Mr. Brummel's inestimable book and polished them with the froth of champagne?"

"Mr. Brummel's inescapable book, did you say?"

"Fie on you, you know that I did not."

He leaned against the counter, tipping his top hat back slightly on his unruly dark hair with the tip of his cane. "An understandable error on my part," he murmured. "For I swear the wretched fellow *is* inescapable. His effect upon male fashion can only be described as beyond reproach, but the rest of him is ludicrous in the extreme. As to the froth of champagne, alas no, my valet uses nothing but elbow grease."

"How very excellent a valet he must be," she said softly, her gaze moving appreciatively over him. He wore the dark ruby coat Adele had seen in the carriage, and his long legs were encased in close-fitting breeches. A jeweled pin shone in the folds of his cravat and the cane tapped softly against the side of his boot as he looked at her. His face was quite inscrutable, as was the slightly cynical smile that Adele remembered so very, very well.

"My lady, have you not come here to make a purchase?" he asked after a moment.

Euphemia flushed a little and turned to the patient woman behind the counter. "Some of your Madeira citron, if you please."

Nell took down a jar from one of the shelves, but as she placed it before Euphemia that lady turned suddenly to go to one of the tables. "I do believe I have a notion to sample some sugarplums." It was an obvious ploy to delay, which the amused twist on the earl's lips showed had not gone undetected.

"My lady, I swear that such confections are ruinous to the figure," he said.

"Not *my* figure," she retorted, smiling coquettishly.

"Possibly."

She pouted. "Is there some fault in my appearance, sir?"

"No, your appearance is quite magnificent."

"Why, thank you, sir."

"I speak only the truth, my lady, although such disgraceful compliment seeking on your part deserved less." He spoke lightly, almost teasingly, but Adele felt somehow that he meant every word.

Euphemia did not notice anything. "How unkind you are, my lord earl. I warn you that I will exact revenge on the night of the masquerade."

"If that be the ominous threat, then maybe I will stay safely at home with Mama."

"But you have to come!" she protested.

"Certainly I have to. I cannot possibly miss hearing la Giardi sing."

She flushed again, but this time much more deeply. "I wonder you are interested in her *voice*, sir, when the world knows the closeness of your liaison with her *person*!"

He smiled. "How nosy the world is."

"It is Madame Giardi who is 'nosy,' " she retorted, alluding to that lady's singular appearance. He said nothing in reply, and as the moments passed Euphemia began to feel uncomfortable. She cleared her throat. "So, you *are* coming?"

"I am."

"Promise me that you will dance the waltz with me."

"The waltz? It shocks me to learn that a young lady knows anything about such a shameless measure."

"Oh, I have been dancing the waltz for simply ages now," she replied airily. Adele smothered a smile at such a fib. How sweet it would be if her dancing master should enter the shop at that moment and ask her if she had perfected the dance yet!

"I am surprised that the duchess should permit such a licentious dance at her masquerade."

"She does not know."

"That I'll warrant," he said with a short laugh.

"Promise me that you will dance with me?"

"I cannot promise any such thing."

"Why ever not?"

"Because we are not supposed to be able to recognize each other, are we? That is the whole point of a masquerade."

"That is *not* the whole point of a masquerade. I shall know everyone immediately."

Behind the curtain, Adele's heart sank.

"Everyone? That is a boast which cannot possibly be true; there are hundreds attending! I'll warrant there'll be many uninvited intruders and you will not notice any of them."

"I know everyone who was invited, sir, and my eye is very keen."

"Then I bow to your conviction." He inclined his head.

Adele swallowed, for quite suddenly her plans seemed full of danger, far too much danger to be sensible.

Euphemia was smiling. "I shall certainly know you, my lord earl," she said softly, returning to the counter. "And if you will not promise me that waltz, then I shall come and demand it."

"You seem determined to be embraced in full view of the world, my lady."

"I am."

He straightened. "Do you not have something to purchase in the circulating library?" he asked, deliberately changing the subject.

Euphemia knew that she had been a little too forward. "Yes, I do," she said, looking slightly flustered. "And I have to take out a book for your Mother; she was most careful to ask me before we left."

"A book? What book?"

"Miss Austen's *Northanger Abbey*."

He seemed nonplussed. "I did not know that my mother read such books."

"She informed me that she has recently begun to read all Miss Austen's books. I believe she said she was fortunate enough to have met the author."

He gave a short laugh. "You are better informed than I am, my lady."

"Ladies usually are," she retorted, her composure returning a little. "Now then, you promised me a drive in your curricle."

"You twisted an invitation out of me," he corrected.

She picked up the Madeira citron and pushed it in his hand. "Maybe this will help to sweeten you a little, sir," she said, sweeping to the door and out into the street.

Smiling a little, he pulled his top hat forward again and then followed her. The bell tinkled and there was silence.

Nell came to pull the curtain aside. "Are you all right, Adele?"

"Yes."

"That was close. Well, to think that the confrontation the whole of Bath waits gleefully for nearly took place right here in my confectionary, and with only me to witness it."

Adele smiled. "No one would have believed you."

"Probably." Nell's answering smile faded then. "You know, the ways of grand folk always make me feel uneasy."

"Ways? What ways."

"Their attitude to marriage. Everyone says the earl and the marchioness are soon to announce their betrothal, but they did not seem close enough to be contemplating such a course. I know that arranged marriages are still very much the thing, but it still does not seem right."

"Oh, I think the marchioness loves him," said Adele, remembering Euphemia's fiery warning.

"Maybe she does, but I doubt very much if *he* loves her."

"The Earl of Blaisdon is incapable of loving anyone but himself," replied Adele.

"So sour, Adele?"

"I have every reason to be."

"Aye, I suppose you do. Three names above all others you must despise—Bellingham, Repton, and Latimer."

Adele smiled at that. "You make them sound like a firm of dishonest lawyers!"

Nell chuckled, going to get the six pastries. She placed them in Adele's basket. "There, now Mistress Rogers can munch away to her heart's content."

Adele was thoughtful. "Nell, do you think it possible that Lady Euphemia will know everyone at the masquerade?"

"She seems to think so."

"But do you?"

"Well, I think that she won't have time to wonder about everyone, she'll be too busy chasing after the Earl of Blaisdon. She'll certainly know a great many, though, that's for sure."

"Yes. Well, good-bye for now, Nell."

"Good-bye, Adele, and tell Mistress Rogers not to eat all those pastries at once."

Adele walked slowly back to the haberdashery. All the doubts that had lurked on the edge of her consciousness now came flooding to the fore. It *was* a foolish and dangerous escapade; she was moonstruck to be even thinking about it!

For the remainder of that day common sense prevailed and she was decided against the whole enterprise. But after a long night's sleep, the gloom and despondency had departed, the doubts had retreated, and the determination had returned. She opened her eyes on the day of the masquerade, quite set upon going after all.

Chapter 8

Dame Fortune smiled upon Adele that evening, for Cat decided to accompany Joanie, who was visiting a sick relative. Adele pleaded a headache and said she would be retiring early, and after promising Cat that she would take a soothing posset before retiring, she watched them go down the garden and out into the side alley.

The sun's rays were blood red as the evening sank into dusk, and Adele's pulse was racing almost unbearably as she went up to her room to begin to get ready. She refused to let any doubts creep in and determinedly began to brush and pin her hair, which glinted with paler lights after being washed earlier with lemon. Her face was a little drawn and tense, and although it would be hidden by the domino, she still felt the need to put a touch of rouge on her cheeks. The scent of lavender water hung in the still room as she stepped at last into the white muslin gown, shivering just a little as the cool, light material touched her skin. The nasturtium sprigging was intensified by the brightness of the sunset beyond the window and the heavily trimmed hemline swung as she turned at last to pick up the domino. She held her breath as she arranged the little veil before putting on the dainty little hood that would completely conceal her hair. There, she was anonymous, completely incognito—just another guest who could dance the night away without fear of discovery! As she drew on her long white gloves she had a moment's uncertainty about the lack of a corset, for the muslin was so very fine and soft that any gentleman would know immediately . . . Taking a deep breath, she put her reticule and fan over her wrist and then arranged her shawl around her shoulders. She couldn't turn back at this eleventh hour, she *couldn't*! There might never again be an opportunity of returning, albeit fleetingly, to that life she had loved so much.

She paused at the door of the bedroom, looking back at the

bolster she had put carefully in her bed. Yes, it did look as if she were sleeping there should Cat peep in later. . . .

Several carriages drove up Milsom Street conveying guests to the rooms, and Adele waited until a chair had passed the entrance of the side alley before she emerged. She could see the watch further down the street, and she now hurried toward the little group of men with their lanterns and staves. A woman walking alone could hardly feel safe, but she would be very safe indeed if she enlisted the aid of the watch!

They turned as they heard her call them and their faces changed as they saw the elegant figure in sequined hood and domino and rich evening gown.

"Pray, sirs!" she cried, "I beg of you to help me. My wretched rakehell of a cousin was to have escorted me to the rooms tonight, but he has been too forward by far and I cannot possibly contemplate placing myself in his care now! Gentlemen, will you please escort me to some place where I may hire a chair?" Her eyes were wide and pleading and she hoped she appeared disconcerted enough to make her story convincing.

They didn't bother to conceal their amusement, but they obviously thought her genuine enough, for they immediately agreed to walk with her to the yard of the White Hart where there would be chairs in plenty. She felt a little conspicuous as she walked between them, but at least she was perfectly safe, and she felt rather pleased with herself for successfully carrying out the ruse.

At the White Hart an old ostler with a lantern was calling out the arrival of the "Comet" stagecoach and his voice was completely drowned by the guard of a departing coach, which had choosen that very moment to give a long blast of "Off she goes." Adele looked up at the coach as it passed her, its team straining and the wheels rattling on the cobblestones. The outside passengers braced themselves for the first sharp corner and then the horn sounded again as the coach gathered speed and vanished into the darkening night.

The watch escorted her right to the waiting sedans, advising her before they left that she would be best advised to tell her papa about her untrustworthy cousin. She promised that she would inform "Sir Algernon" at the very first opportunity and then thanked them for their kindness. They waited long enough to be assured of a glimpse of her silk-clad ankles as she climbed into the nearest chair and then went on their way.

The chair was preceded from the yard by a link boy, and the flame of his torch smoked as the chair conveyed her up through Bath toward the rooms. The streets were filled with carriages and sedans now as everyone in the town seemed to be converging upon that one destination. As she neared the rooms, however, the first real qualms of the evening beset her. There was still time to call off this foolhardiness, time to go back to the haberdashery. . . . But then the sedan halted outside Mr. Bartley's billiard room and she felt the cool evening air on her face as the chairman opened the door for her.

Shaking out her skirts and pulling her shawl around her arms, she stood for a moment watching the entrance to the rooms. The duchess had acquired the services of red-uniformed soldiers to escort the guests those last few steps, a fittingly military touch for such a celebration. Colorful lanterns hung beneath the portico and garlands of greenery, mainly laurel, had been draped around the columns. The sound of music drifted out from the high windows of the ballroom as one of the soldiers bowed before her, and taking a deep breath, she followed him toward the entrance. Fate smiled upon her, however, for at that moment she saw Dr. Enleigh, the rector of Benwick, and his nervous, mousy little wife also approaching. There was no mistaking the identity of those two; he was so very large and she so very small, and Adele found it a simple matter to place herself immediately behind them, for all the world as if she accompanied them.

Holding the precious invitation in her hand, she moved nearer and nearer to the liveried footman guarding the portal. He cast a seemingly cursory look over each card as it was presented to him, but was that glance so cursory, she wondered? Perhaps he was looking for something that was missing from her card, which to her mind seemed suddenly very naked indeed without a name or any other identifying mark. Second thoughts began to press urgently upon her as Dr. Enleigh and his wife presented their cards, but then it was too late and it was her turn. Her hand was shaking; she tried to appear casual and unconcerned but was really so very nervous that she feared to give herself away, but he hardly glanced at her card before he was looking beyond her to the next guests. The warm, close air of the entrance hall seemed to sweep welcomingly over her. She was inside.

But the surge of triumph faded almost immediately, for

ahead she saw a far greater hazard, and it was one she should have foreseen. All the guests were being presented to the duke and duchess, and also to Euphemia, and as if that was not bad enough, Euphemia appeared to be accompanied by Sir Frederick Repton. The foursome stood in a line, and feeling suddenly quite numb, Adele moved slowly nearer. Behind the mask and domino, which no longer seemed to afford her enough anonymity, Adele's face drained of color, and Euphemia's words, overheard so clearly in the confectionary, seemed to echo in her head. *I know everyone who was invited, sir, and my eye is very keen. . . .*

The duke, author of Denzil Russell's destruction, was very splendid in the uniform of colonel-in-chief of the Prince of Wales' Royal Somerset Militia, although truth to tell he could not boast of any military service worth mentioning, certainly nothing worth mentioning on a night that celebrated heroic Waterloo. He was no longer as slender as he had once been; his waist had been thickened and his complexion mottled by taking far too much port wine. His commendable thatch of chestnut hair looked suspiciously artificial, and all this, together with the fact that he was endeavoring to look elegant and impressive in spite of considerable pain from his bandaged, gouty foot, made him look far less grand than he would have wished. Behind his brief satin mask, his eyes were small and set close together over his pointed nose, and there was something in his whole manner that suggested the true nature of the man: dishonest, sly, corrupt, and capable of stooping to any depth to achieve what he wanted. He smiled as Adele sank to a curtsy before him, and his tongue passed briefly over his lips as he gazed long and hard at the low neckline of her gown.

"Good evening, m'dear, I trust you'll enjoy this evening."

"Good evening, Your Grace."

"Do I know you?"

Her heart began to beat even more swiftly. "But, Your Grace," she said, "you must not ask such questions."

He laughed and received a freezing glance from the duchess. Clearing his throat, he looked away from Adele and gave his attention to the somewhat safer lady of ample proportions who stood behind her.

Adele moved on to curtsy before the duchess, whose freezing glance was now resting upon the object of her husband's interest. Euphemia's mother was daunting in pure white, for such virginal purity did not rest easily upon a lady of such an interesting past. Her lengthy list of lovers, thought Adele sourly, would seem to warrant fiery scarlet rather than the color of driven snow. A very tall ostrich feather, held in place by a glittering diamond pin, curled up from the duchess's hair and swept richly through the air at the slightest movement. She wore the briefest of masks, but then there seemed little point in trying to hide her identity if she was then to immediately make herself known by greeting each guest!

The frosty gaze did not waver from Adele's masked eyes. "Good evening."

"Good evening, Your Grace."

Adele obviously did not warrant any further greeting, having committed an undoubted faux pas in the duchess's eyes by gaining too much attention from the duke, and so she moved on to what was the greatest hazard of all—Euphemia.

The rector of Benwick and his wife were at that moment being presented, and in spite of her own agitation, Adele could not help noticing how cool was Euphemia's nod. Not a word of greeting passed her lips and the hand she held out was limp. The snub obviously disconcerted Mrs. Enleigh, but the rector, if Adele was not mistaken, had been half expecting such a reception. Why would that be? What could have passed between Dr. Enleigh and Euphemia to make such a decided chill?

Euphemia turned pointedly toward Adele, standing behind the clergyman and his lady, and they passed on, nodding briefly at Sir Frederick. Adele sank into a curtsy, keeping her eyes lowered respectfully as she rose again. Euphemia looked quite dazzling in a gown of pale rose japan muslin upon which countless emerald spangles had been stitched. The fancy ribbon she had purchased from the haberdashery had been looped through the hem, catching it up to one side to reveal a dainty underskirt of the frailest gauze imaginable—too frail for modesty, for the outline of her legs was quite plain to see. There were emeralds at her throat and in her dark hair, and her fan wafted slowly to and fro as she inspected Adele's appearance, her practiced, knowing glance taking in every last detail of trimming, style, and material. Her lips twitched a little and Adele knew that her long hours of labor in the secrecy of her bedroom had not been in vain— Euphemia reluctantly approved.

Euphemia smiled graciously, inclining her head, and Adele passed thankfully on, nodding briefly at Sir Frederick.

He appeared to be trying to out-Brummel Mr. Brummel, for he wore so severe and subdued a style that he looked like a thin, black crow presiding over a flock of birds of paradise. There was no relief from the somber black of his excellent coat and pantaloons, except the pristine white of a remarkably restrained shirt which did not boast a single frill. There was no pin in his cravat, and his waistcoat, unlike those of the other gentlemen present, was as black as his coat. Of all those gathered in the rooms that night, he alone had chosen to go without a mask. His pale, cold eyes moved constantly over the sea of faces around him. It was the gaze of a bookkeeper and clerk; it calculated, assessed, and judged; it added and subtracted and concluded, and it seemed capable of seeing right into the heart. But it did not perceive the identity of the lady in the domino as she passed, although it paused to sweep approvingly over her dainty figure and neat ankles.

Adele passed on into the building, mingling with the elegant crowd and enjoying the simple pleasure of just smiling graciously when a gentleman bowed admiringly. She took a glass of champagne from the silver tray a footman held out to her, and as she sipped it she glanced up at the glittering chandeliers and the exquisite plasterwork. The noise of the evening was all around her, recalling times gone by when she had left Beech Park in her father's beautiful landau to be wined and dined in the most important houses in Bath. Just to be here tonight was all she had craved, just to be part of it again.

A masked gentleman bowed before her. "A dance, fair incognita?" he asked, offering her his arm.

She hardly hesitated, putting down her glass and resting her hand lightly on his sleeve. They walked through into the ballroom where the chalked floor was ranged on either side now by tiers of crimson sofas where many of the guests sat simply watching the dancing. The orchestra began to play a minuet, and Adele and her partner stepped out onto the floor to take their places. The dance was delayed from starting by the fussing of the master of ceremonies as he strove to find partners for several single ladies, but at last he declared that all was satisfactory and the orchestra struck up again.

The golden spangles and sequins of Adele's hood and domino flashed as she moved to the stately measure, her heavy hem swinging as she twisted and turned. Her heart was almost bursting with happiness as she danced, and she was aware of several gentlemen glancing at her in appreciation. She looked good and she knew it, and what finer thing can there be for a woman than that? As the dance came to an end, for Adele it was as if the haberdashery had ceased to exist. She was a lady again, not a shop assistant.

The garlands and festoons with which the ballroom was decorated seemed to pass her by in a blur over the next hour as she danced every single dance. Not for her the ignominy of having to find somewhere to sit, for she had a succession of partners, from a portly military gentleman to a dandy in pink satin. During one cotillion she even found herself partnered by Sir Frederick, and she had the infinite satisfaction of deliberately dropping her handkerchief favor, thus forcing him to bend to retrieve it.

She saw David Latimer the moment he entered the ballroom, with Euphemia draped clingingly on his arm. They took up their positions for another cotillion, and Adele's heart began to beat more swiftly as she realized that the dance's sequence would bring her opposite him at the end! The music began and she took the first few steps, but she was aware of an almost unbearable rushing in her ears when at last she faced him. Their hands touched momentarily and it was as if a shaft of lightning had struck her, so intense was the wave of sensation that passed through her. She was glad of the domino, not only because it hid her identity, but because it also concealed the utter confusion that had beset her in that moment. They came together again and he bent forward to kiss her cheek, as the measure demanded, and then the dance parted them again and she was opposite her original partner. The orchestra played the final note and she sank into a curtsy. When she glanced up she saw him walking away with Euphemia.

The incident was disturbing to her and she refused the next dance, choosing instead to leave the ballroom and go into the relative quiet of the card room, where many ladies and gentlemen sat earnestly around the green baize tables. She stood watching for a while, composing herself and chiding herself for being so silly. Turning, she removed her hood momentarily to adjust a pin in her hair, and then she returned to the ballroom, her face and head as much concealed as before.

A country dance was already in progress and so she went to sit down on the end of a line of sofas. For the first time she

70

noticed Lord Tarquin lounging on another sofa nearby, his mask tossed aside. He looked, she decided, absolutely furious, for he fidgeted with the frills at his cuff and his cheeks were flushed a dull red. Beside him sat a young woman in orange gauze, and she too looked in a towering rage, her face as fiery as her auburn hair and her back stiff and straight as she perched on the edge of the crimson seat. Her feather-trimmed fan moved to and fro at such a rate that it was virtually invisible and everything about her bristled. She wore a wedding ring, and somehow Adele knew that she was Amelia, Lord Tarquin's wife. Things were obviously still far from well in that quarter.

Adele looked away from them then, surveying the crowded floor instead. The colorful company moved beneath the glow of the hundreds of candles in the chandeliers, and the atmosphere was hot and beginning to feel uncomfortable. She could see Euphemia dancing, although not with David Latimer, who for the moment seemed to have disappeared. The country dance came to an end, and Adele watched Euphemia curtsy to her partner and then hurry toward the orchestra, beckoning to the leader. He nodded and then Euphemia turned back to the ballroom, her whole manner one of triumph as she began to make her way purposefully in Adele's direction. The orchestra played the first few notes of a waltz, and immediately a ripple of surprise went around the room. The master of ceremonies looked positively furious, and the duke and duchess did not quite seem to know what attitude to strike over their daughter's daring.

A voice suddenly addressed Adele and she turned with a startled gasp, looking up into David Latimer's masked face. She knew it was he; she recognized his voice even before her eyes met his. He bowed. "Would you care to dance?" he inquired, holding out his hand.

She was frozen with shock, and then slowly she stood. His fingers closed over hers as he drew her hand through his arm, and they walked on to the deserted floor where no one had yet dared to take a place for the immodest, wicked waltz.

Chapter 9

She moved in a daze to the center of the floor. She had known that she would see him tonight, but she had not for a moment anticipated being asked to dance with him like this. She did not dare to speak, for she knew that he might recognize her voice, and she was aware of all eyes upon them as he turned toward her and put his hand to her waist. They began to dance.

Someone gave a cheer, and within moments they had been joined by others, glad of a lead to follow—and what better lead than the Earl of Blaisdon? She caught a glimpse of Euphemia's furious face but then concentrated instead upon the steps, once learned so painstakingly from illustrations in a journal. They whirled to the music, so close together and yet so far away still, and she could feel the warmth of his gloved hand against her uncorseted waist.

He smiled at her. "I wonder," he asked softly, "who my fair partner could be, who not only dares to dance the barbarous waltz but also considers whalebone to be totally unnecessary?"

Her hidden face felt hot and her mouth was dry. She did not reply, and he smiled again, saying nothing more. The dance seemed endless, the seductive music exerting its magic over them and holding them spellbound until the very last note. She sank thankfully into a deep curtsy, her head bowed, and when she stood she was horrified to see everyone turn toward them, applauding them for having had the nerve to be the first couple to walk onto the deserted floor. The earl still held her hand and drew it to his lips, which produced a cheer. Unnerved, she withdrew her hand, turning on her heel to walk away, and she heard the gasps this action caused. It was too late then; she had seemed to snub him very deliberately, but she had done so out of panic rather than with any deliberate intention. But as she mingled with the crowd again she was glad that she had done it, glad that she had caused him a little discomfort even though it was nothing when set beside his monstrous sins!

"These rooms are the holy place of high fashion tonight, are they not?"

She turned at the sound of the voice and found herself looking at a tall young man whose face was almost entirely concealed by a black satin mask. He had tawny hair that curled a little and his eyes behind the mask were a soft brown. He was dressed exquisitely in black velvet and there was a large sapphire pin shining in his cravat. His tight pantaloons revealed his legs to perfection and the ring on his finger flashed as he took out his fob watch and flicked it open, smiling a little then as he glanced at her.

"I am sure you are not about to leave, for the evening is young and you could not be so cruel as to deprive me of your presence just yet." He reached out and took her hand, raising it to his lips. "Bath is surely favored, for to be true you can only be here to increase and embellish the number of beauties."

She laughed. "And how can you possibly say that with any conviction, sir? You can see nothing of my face at all, I could be as ugly as a warthog for all you know."

"Ah, that could not be, not with that low, melodious voice and that figure which Venus herself would envy. No, your face is as beautiful as the morning sun, of that I can be quite certain."

"Are you a poet, sir, for to be sure you use a poet's words?"

"A poet?" He laughed. "No, I assure you that I am not one of that breed—although I admit to being a romantic. A romantic, my lady, who is intrigued to learn more of you."

"Why?"

"Now that is not gracious. Here I am, being all agreeable and flatteringly full of eagerness, and you put me down with a *dis*agreeable query about my motives. My motives are most improper. There, will that do for an answer?"

She smiled, liking him. "You wish to know more about me, sir, but that cannot be permitted, for we are at a masquerade, and *not* knowing about each other is the whole thing of it."

He bowed. "Very well, I grant you victory on that score, but I must at least have a name if we are to spend the rest of the evening in each other's company."

"You presume, sir."

"Come now, admit that you find me appealing and lovable."

"I find you impudent."

"Then tell me your name and I promise to be all goodness and etiquette."

"No names, sir."

"Why? Have you removed a telltale ring from your pretty finger?"

"My husband is a six-foot giant who felled Tom Belcher in five minutes when last they met."

"Indeed? Your husband must also be a veritable monster for following the pleasures of the fancy rather than the pleasures of Venus," he said softly. "From which remark you will have gathered that I am not to be put off with fiblings about nonexistent pugilists lurking in the background. You will not tell me who you are, so I must give you a name. I will call you my Lady Domino, and you may call me Sir Mask. There, that is all the politeness done with and we may converse quite happily for the rest of the evening."

"You are very forceful, Sir Mask."

"I am—when I am as drawn as I am now."

She looked away "Forceful—and forward."

"And honest."

She smiled in spite of herself.

Encouraged, he pressed her. "Have I won you over? I perceive that I have and that it would be in order now for me to lay claim to every single dance from now on."

She nodded; Her decision was made on the spur of the moment. "Very well, Sir Mask."

Again he drew her hand to his lips. "And I swear that one way or another I will find out who you are."

"No, sir, you will not."

"There cannot be many ladies who would deliver Blaisdon such a monumental snub."

"And is that why you have engaged me in conversation?"

"Partly, I admit."

"Are you his enemy?"

"Yes." The single word was said softly but in such a way that she felt the urge to shiver. He smiled again then. "So you see, anyone who finds him as abhorrent as you obviously do is automatically a bosom friend of mine. We are allies, Lady Domino, and therefore destined to share this evening."

She said nothing, wondering what it was that lay between this man and David Latimer.

He took her hand once again to lead her onto the floor as a cotillion was announced. "And I promise you," he said lightly, "that I shall persuade you to meet me again and that then I shall truly see your loveliness and learn your name."

"You will need a silver tongue, Sir Mask."

"Silver I have in plenty," he murmured as the music began.

For the rest of that part of the masquerade she danced only with him, knowing that she was not a little flattered by his obvious admiration—that it had been caused initially by her conduct toward the Earl of Blaisdon did not really enter into it, for he did not mention Blaisdon again and it was obvious in his whole manner that he found her desirable and interesting.

The time approached at last when the great singer Madame Giardi was to sing. The orchestra took a short rest and everyone flocked to the tea room where more iced champagne was served. The master of ceremonies stood in the door of the tea room looking blackly at the champagne and obviously bemoaning the absence of tea, but it had to be admitted that the evening's success was partly due to the absence of that staid beverage! Everyone was enjoying the occasion to the full, and the Bellinghams could already be satisfied that their masquerade was a triumph—not that the duke would remember much about it, for he had fallen asleep in an armchair in the octagon as a result of the numerous stolen cognacs he had consumed before even setting off for the rooms. He slept on, his mouth open in a most unbecoming way, and Adele paused to look at him in disgust; this was the fine fellow whose financial straits had brought her father to ruin and death! How ignoble and contemptible he looked now, how totally lacking in all claim to respect!

Sir Mask glanced curiously at her. "Our exalted host would appear to be bored by the proceedings," he said lightly.

"Yes."

They thought no more of the Duke of Bellingham as they approached the entrance of the tea room. There were a great number waiting to be served, so Sir Mask escorted her back to the ballroom and left her sitting on one of the sofas while he went alone to procure some champagne.

He was still away when the crowd began to drift back to

hear Madame Giardi sing. The orchestra was tuning up and everyone pressed close to be able to see the great singer who was the talk of England. Adele looked anxiously toward the doorway, but there was still no sign of Sir Mask, so she got up to join the crowd by the orchestra, pushing her way down the side next to the lacquered screen now standing before the door of the billiard room.

Madame Giardi appeared, draped in the robes of Britannia herself, complete with shield, helmet, and trident, and a great roar of approval went up. Bowing impressively, she placed herself before the orchestra and the first notes of "Rule Britannia" began. The choice was so popular that the shouts of approbation continued until almost half the song was completed. Madame Giardi's voice was as impressive as her physical appearance, and Adele could not take her eyes off the statuesque figure in the flowing drapery, wondering if the singer had indeed been anything to the Earl of Blaisdon.

What happened next was so sudden and was over so swiftly that she had no time to call out for help and no one even noticed she had been plucked from their midst. A gloved hand closed over her mouth and she was thrust roughly behind the screen; her attacker opened the door of the billiard room and dragged her inside, then closed the door again behind them both. She was alone in the darkness with an unknown assailant! Desperately afraid that she had been found out, she remained silent.

The hand remained over her mouth until she ceased to struggle, and only then did he release her, knowing somehow that she was too afraid to cry out. Terror coursed through her veins as she backed away, trying to make out his face but unable to do so for the lack of light. The brilliance of the ballroom and the magnificence of Madame Giardi's singing were a world away now; there was only the velvet darkness and the terrifying thunder of her heart. She gasped aloud as her questing fingertips dislodged a rack of cues, which fell to the floor with a clatter. She was vaguely aware of someone walking past her toward the barely discernible table and then a lucifer blazed, illuminating the green cloth table and the white ivory balls. Her assailant reached up to light the revolving lamp suspended above the table, but still she could not see his face. In the brief second before he turned at last toward her, she was aware of the stark, raised glass ceiling high above, of the wooden marking boards on the walls, and the settles where the players sat to wait their turn, and then her eyes were drawn sharply to the silhouetted figure by the table. It was David Latimer. There was a cynical smile on his lips as he folded his arms and leaned back against the table. She felt the cool sweep of his eyes and then he spoke.

"I make no apologies for treating you roughly, madam, for your recent conduct toward me would not seem to merit any politeness on my part." He waited but she did not reply. "Are you still that most unusual of creatures—the silent woman?"

Weakening relief spread through her—he didn't know who she was!

He gave a low laugh at her continued silence. "Well, your silence leads me to the inevitable conclusion that you are afraid I will recognize your voice. Perhaps it is best, therefore, that we keep your identity the secret it now is, for I swear that if I knew who you were, madam, I would not be able to keep the dislike from my eyes the next time we met in polite company. Whoever you are, you are an ill-mannered, willful jade with little notion of how to behave in society."

Behind the domino her face was hot and her anger rose sharply at the deliberate, cool way he set about insulting her. How she loathed him! How she *loathed* him!

"I grow tired of this one-sided conversation, madam," he continued. "So I will come directly to the point. My sole purpose in thrusting you in here is to warn you against the blackguard you have seen fit to spend the last hour with."

She stared at him. That he, *he* should have the face to condemn another as a blackguard! It passed belief!

He straightened then. "I will not say his name, since names are obviously de trop; suffice it that he is not fit company for a gentlewoman, and I now consider myself to have done what is required of a gentleman."

For a long, quivering moment their eyes met—his disdainful, hers bright with dislike—and then she turned, gathering her skirts as she went to the door. The noise and glitter of the ballroom seemed to leap at her as she left the billiard room, not glancing back.

Fury blazed through her as she glanced around for a glimpse of Sir Mask. The Earl of Blaisdon condemned him as a blackguard; well such a condemnation from such a fellow could only mean that Sir Mask was the very opposite of a blackguard! Determined at all costs to ignore the earl's warning, and determined as well to be *seen* ignoring it, she pushed her way through the crowd toward the sofa where she could see a very perplexed Sir Mask sitting with two glasses of iced champagne.

He seemed to sense her approach, for he turned suddenly and smiled as he got to his feet. "I feared you had left—"

"I was detained a moment." She accepted the glass he held out.

He raised his glass. "To us, my Lady Domino."

"To us, Sir Mask." She felt reckless now, and above all defiant. How dare David Latimer, of *all* low creatures, presume to cast doubt upon the honor of another! How *dare* he!

Sir Mask allowed his gaze to move appreciatively over her. She was truly the most exquisite creature present, her skin so flawless and perfect, her figure so rounded where it should be rounded and so slender where it should be slender. He could see by the way her gown clung that her legs were long, and he instinctively knew that her hair would be fair—probably the color of corn, or of gold. . . . He glanced away momentarily, knowing that he was allowing his imagination to run away with him, but there was something about her, something so very fresh and different, something that drew him like a pin to a magnet. He wondered anew who she was. And he knew that possessing her was something he had to achieve. He had to make her his own. . . .

Madame Giardi gave another rendering of "Rule Britannia," but thereafter resisted all further attempts to persuade her to sing more. Obviously enjoying the adulation, she accepted several bouquets of flowers and then made an exit, which was, if anything, even more impressive than her entry. The crowds drifted away from the orchestra dais, and Adele glanced around to see the lacquer screen being removed from the door of the billiard room.

The orchestra played the first bars of a cotillion, and Sir Mask smiled at her. "Would you like to dance?" She nodded, returning the warm smile, and a moment later they had taken their place on the floor. As they began to dance she saw David Latimer standing to one side, his lips a firm line of disapproval. She all but tossed her head in the air as the dance took her right past him, and she twitched her skirts aside, making her decision to ignore his warning as plain as it was possible to make. She would dance every dance with Sir Mask, she would remain at his side for the rest of the evening, and she would show the noble Earl of Blaisdon what she thought of his *gentlemanly* advice!

And for the remainder of that dazzling evening she did just that. She danced until her feet were sore and enjoyed Sir Mask's company more than it was wise to enjoy it, for she knew she was only making heartache for herself when the night ended and she had to put him from her mind forever. For the moment, however, it was good to bask in his ardent attention, good to flirt a little and know that the warmth in his voice was proof of his desire.

The Duchess of Bellingham's insistence upon champagne produced the sort of happy horseplay that signified the success of an evening. The guests laughed and joked together, and Adele saw Euphemia being pursued by several young men intent upon stealing the trailing ribbon from her hem. She squealed aloud as one of them snatched it at last, pulling it from the soft rose muslin and then waving it triumphantly aloft. Euphemia, obviously exulting in all the attention, made a great noise about trying to retrieve it, and the wretched ribbon, once so very beautiful and elegant, became twisted and trampled upon in the general scuffle that followed. Many of the more sedate guests departed at this juncture, fearing that the whole evening would degenerate into something resembling a bear garden.

Adele saw little more of David Latimer, for he adjourned to the card room and remained there. To be truthful, he did not cross her mind a great deal, for she was too happy in Sir Mask's pleasing company, but it wasn't until the orchestra played another waltz that she became aware of exactly how much she was enjoying being with him. They moved to the intoxicating music and she knew that he was holding her closer than he should, but she wanted to be in his arms and the dance was weaving an elusive spell around her which made her want to cast caution to the four winds. When at last the music came to an end, they stood motionless on the floor, oblivious to the crowds around them and aware only of each other. He still held her hand and still had his arm around her waist. His eyes were dark and fathomless behind his mask, and the moment was so charged with feeling that she knew she would not have resisted had he pulled her close there and then and kissed her. Slowly she at last drew away, glad of having the domino to hide her confusion.

He still held her hand. "Who are you?" he asked softly, his voice almost a caress.

She shook her head. "I cannot tell you."

"At least promise me that you will meet me again."

"No."

"You cannot enter my life, steal my heart, and then run away from me again. Please meet me again, let me see your face and—"

Tears filled her eyes. Oh, to be able to make an assignation with him, to be able to enter into a liaison! "I-I must leave now—"

"Stay, I beg of you."

"No, I dare not stay any longer."

"I will be in Sydney Gardens tomorrow at noon. I will wait by the eastern bridge. I know that you will come."

Blinking back the tears, she turned to walk from the floor. He caught her up and seized her hand, drawing it gently through his arm and still holding it firmly as they walked down the entrance hall. Sir Mask hailed a chair for her himself, and as she was about to climb in he turned her toward him, raising the veil just sufficiently to kiss her on the lips.

"Until tomorrow," he whispered. "Until tomorrow, my Lady Domino."

She pulled away and climbed into the chair, averting her face as the chairman conveyed her away from him. The tears were wet on her cheeks. Tonight had been the stuff of dreams, but to continue that dream into the morrow would be to turn it into a nightmare. . . .

The chairmen had reached the bottom of Milsom Street when she told them to stop. As she paid them, she looked up the deserted street, and then she gathered her skirts and hurried along the pavement, her slippers making only a slight sound. She could feel the curious chairmen watching her flight, but by the time she had reached the entrance of the side alley they had shrugged at the antics of the rich and had gone on their way.

No one saw her enter the side alley. The house was in darkness, Cat and Joanie having long since retired to their beds, and as she went up the path she had her fingers crossed that in her usual forgetfulness Cat would have left the back door unlocked. To her relief, it responded to her touch and in a moment she was inside.

She listened for a moment, but there was not a sound. Glancing at the clock on the mantelpiece, she saw that it was past three o'clock; she would have to be up again in an hour or so! She needed a little sleep at least, but she still felt overexcited and knew that sleep was a long way away. Poking the embers of the fire a little, she put a pan of milk on and heated it through.

As she sat with the cup of milk she remembered times gone by when she would have been served warm wine and water after such an evening. She smiled a little. Tonight she had reentered that lost, yearned-for world again, tonight she had lived a dream that would remain with her for the rest of her life. She would always remember Sir Mask, always. . . .

Chapter 10

It seemed that she had hardly fallen asleep before Cat was calling impatiently at her door. "Wake up in there, sleepyhead, I've called you twice already! Hurry up now, I've already opened the shop!"

With a gasp, Adele hurried out of bed, glancing out at the gray skies and at the rivulets of rain running down the pane. Rain! How could it *rain* after such a magical night? Memories of Sir Mask returned and she glanced at herself in the looking glass. Last night she had looked like a princess; this morning she would look like a shop assistant again! She would never be able to meet Sir Mask and tell him the truth about herself; he would never understand. . . . With a sigh, she began to wash.

The haberdashery was quiet that morning. The bustle that preceded the masquerade was over now, and those customers who might normally have come stayed away because of the weather. Cat was concerned by Adele's obvious tiredness and declared that she must be sickening for something. Nothing Adele could say would deter her from producing some physic which she insisted Adele must take. Adele did as she was commanded, grimacing as the vile liquid slid down her throat, but at least Cat was satisfied now that any lurking ailment would think twice before making its presence known!

One of the few customers that morning was Euphemia's maid, Euphemia herself was no doubt still lying in her warm bed, sleeping away the aftereffects of the long night, something Adele herself would dearly have liked to do. But all thoughts of sleep were dispersed and replaced with a burning anger the moment the maid revealed the reason for her visit. Producing the length of green ribbon Euphemia had purchased in the shop, she announced that her mistress was very displeased with the quality. Cat looked in surprise at the crushed ribbon, damaged beyond redemption by the horse-play at the masquerade.

"How did that happen?" she asked.

"My mistress merely removed it from the hem of her gown."

"But—"

"She says that unless you replace it immediately she will take her custom elsewhere."

Adele seethed with rage. Nothing could have withstood that horseplay at the masquerade, *nothing*! How dare Euphemia demand new ribbon! But Adele could say nothing at all; she had to bite back the retort and stand meekly by as Cat matched the ribbon and wrapped the replacement carefully, assuring the maid that she deeply regretted having sold an item that failed to please. The maid took the new ribbon and left.

As the door closed, Cat picked up the offending ribbon again. "Well, I don't know what's been done to it, but *something* has."

"It looks as if someone's danced on it," remarked Adele dryly.

"And likely that's just it. Look at this powder. I reckon that's chalk dust, except that it's almost *ground* into the velvet! Still, I can't afford for the likes of Lady Euphemia to go elsewhere."

Adele looked away, a shaft of conscience passing through her. If her actions the night before should become common knowledge, then not only Euphemia would go elsewhere— every lady in Bath would shun the haberdashery!

"Adele?" Cat's voice interrupted her thoughts.

"Yes?"

"Whatever is the matter with you this morning? First you slept on and on and now I've asked you something three times and you've not even heard me!"

"Oh, I'm sorry, Cat. What did you ask me?"

"If you were feeling better."

"There's nothing wrong with me."

"Well, I'm going to have to trust that's so, for you must go on an errand for me. I clean forgot about Mrs. Harriman's lace. She left an order here first thing—while *you* were still in your bed—and asked that it be sent around to Great Pulteney Street as soon as possible. Get your cape and bonnet, there's a good lass, you can take my umbrella."

The sound of the rain filled the air as Adele walked down

Milsom Street a little later, her pattens clinking. The clock outside the circulating library stood at a quarter to twelve as she made her way toward Pulteney Bridge where the River Avon rushed over the weir.

The rain pattered on the umbrella as she crossed Laura Place and entered Great Pulteney Street. Ahead, closing the magnificence of Bath's longest and widest avenue, was the Sydney Hotel—and behind it the trees of Sydney Gardens Vauxhall. It was almost time; in a matter of minutes Sir Mask would be at the bridge waiting for his Lady Domino. . . .

Mrs. Harriman's footman opened the door, almost snatched the package of lace and then slammed the door again. Adele turned away and began to retrace her steps, but then she halted. The street was deserted but for a solitary chaise drawing up on the opposite side of the road, and the rain was falling more heavily than ever. The skies were low and gray and the clouds scudded endlessly past. She was so near and yet so far. There would be few people in the gardens, and her face would be concealed by the hood of her cape. She could go there, she could steal a look at Sir Mask, see if he was indeed as handsome as she believed he was, and then she could be gone again—as anonymously as at the masquerade itself! Even as she thought it the warnings crowded into her head—it was madness, *madness*! But she turned around and began to walk toward the Vauxhall, her heart was ruling her head. She *had* to see him; she had to at least know that he had kept the tryst.

She did not even glance at the nondescript chaise on the other side of the street, its tired horse holding its head low and its driver looking wet and bedraggled. Had she looked, she might have caught a glimpse of its occupant, Euphemia, Marchioness of Heydon, glancing anxiously and irritably at her fob watch, her gloved fingers drumming. A tall, shabbily dressed man moved silently along the pavement to the chaise and immediately Euphemia lowered the glass, her expression questioning. He shook his head and her annoyance was immediately apparent. "Nothing at all?" she inquired stonily.

"No, my lady."

"There *must* be."

"I've tried everything—"

"You haven't tried enough," she replied coldly. "See that you unearth something between now and our next meeting, sir!'' She raised the glass again, rapping on the roof of the chaise with the handle of her parasol. The chaise drew away and the shabbily dressed man scowled after it. He spat once into the gutter and then walked away again.

Adele witnessed nothing of this strange meeting. If she had, she would have wondered at the nondescript chaise that conveyed the rich, elegant Marchioness of Heydon, and she would have wondered even more at the possible reason why that lady would keep an appointment with such a strange fellow. As it was, as she paused briefly on the curb across the road from the Sydney Hotel, Adele was concerned only with the prospect of maybe seeing Sir Mask again.

The Sydney Hotel was a handsome building with a pedimented portico and Corinthian columns, an exclusive place where society gathered during the winter. A single woman would not normally have been permitted to enter the hotel, let alone the gardens, for fear that she might be a prostitute, but a maid seeking her mistress would not be given a second glance, and it was this disguise that Adele intended to use if challenged. She found that she was holding her breath as she entered the hotel lobby. As she had suspected, the doormen paid no attention to her as she approached the doorway of the large coffee room, which in the height of the Bath season would be filled to capacity with fashionable people intent upon being seen there and upon enjoying the matchless view along the three hundred yards of Great Pulteney Street. The weather had kept everyone away; not a table was occupied. A waiter looked inquiringly at her.

"I, er, I'm looking for my mistress," she said quickly. "She must be in the gardens."

"There's not many out there."

"She likes the rain."

"Aye, well she's got someone to clean her togs up for her afterwards, hasn't she?" he said with a sniff, his expression showing his envy of the privileges enjoyed by the rich.

Glancing at the doormen again, she turned away from the coffee room and went on down the lobby toward the handsome double doors under the arched recess that gave on to the rear loggia. Above the loggia was the conservatory where the orchestra played, and as there was to be a concert that night she could hear them tuning up; it was somehow a very dismal sound on such a wet day. There were so few people about that the attendant did not seem to think it necessary to remain at his post, and so she entered the gardens themselves without paying an entrance fee.

She emerged from the hotel into the semicircular area edged by private alcoves which could be hired for parties. A gust of damp wind carried the sound of the orchestra and of laughter from the Sydney Garden Tavern in the basement of the hotel. Even out of season the tavern was busy attending to the needs of chairmen and coachmen eager for their midday tankards of strong beer.

There were puddles on the gravel walk as she passed the bowling green and began the climb up the tree-lined way through the heart of the octagonal gardens. The terraces of Sydney Place overlooked the Vauxhall, but apart from that the gardens were on the edge of open country, the soft green hills stretching away into the misty horizon, and everywhere was the noise of the rain and the wind soughing through the trees.

Horsemen were making good use of the wide grass rides provided for them, and the hoofbeats made an agreeable noise on the wet earth, but Adele paid them scant attention. Her heart was beating wildly now, for she would soon see the bridges spanning the Kennet and Avon canal, which passed right through the gardens. She saw nothing of the artificial waterfalls, the grottoes, the thatched pavilions or even the famous labyrinth; her eyes sought only one thing—that first glimpse of the eastern bridge. As she neared it she pressed back against a laurel, parting the leaves a little to look.

She saw the horse first, a large chestnut beast with a startling blaze, but it was positioned in such a way that she could not see the man holding its reins. She could see his boots and spurs, and she could see his top hat, its brim upturned at the sides, but she could not see his face. Was it Sir Mask? Who else could it be on this particular bridge at this precise time? She waited, her breath held, and then at last the horse shifted, arching its magnificent neck and snorting a little as it danced impatiently around. Now she could see him, and it *was* Sir Mask; she recognized his curling tawny hair!

He defied the rain, his cloak flung dashingly back over his shoulders to reveal his blue coat and cord breeches. He wore a black-and-gray-striped marcella waistcoat, and the collar of his shirt was turned up so that it brushed his chin. A starched black muslin cravat was tied nonchalantly at his throat, and even in the gloom of the rain she could see the large diamond pin sparkling there. As she watched he took out his fob watch, flicked it open, and then glanced around. She gasped and pressed further into the laurel. For the first time she saw his face fully; he was indeed as handsome as she had imagined, from the soft hazel of his long-lashed eyes to the slight curve of his fine lips. She stared at him from the safety of the laurel. There was something vaguely familiar about him, and yet she was sure she did not know him. Surely she could not have met him once at Beech Park? No, she was sure she would have remembered him. Last night she had been in his arms and he had kissed her, but she would never know who he was.

Knowing that she had already tempted Providence too far, she turned away to go back down the walk toward the hotel, Cat's umbrella over her shoulder so that he could not possibly see anything of her. But some sixth sense seemed to guide him, for he called after her.

"Lady Domino?"

She walked a little more swiftly, but he called her again.

"Lady Domino? I know that it is you."

She halted then, turning slowly to look at him. Dismay spread unerringly through her as he walked toward her. He would see by her clothing that she was not what she had led him to believe. But no, she wore a cape that totally concealed; he could know nothing of what she wore beneath!

He halted before her, smiling a little. "Would you truly have walked away without speaking?"

"That would have been best."

"Best?" His eyes swept over her and then came to rest warmly on her face. "How could that be?" he asked softly.

"Because this is foolish."

"Why? Because your bruiser of a husband will come after my hide?"

She smiled. "Maybe."

"But still you kept our tryst." He took her hand and raised it to his lips, at the last moment turning the palm toward him.

A flush spread through her and he smiled. "How very beautiful you are, as exquisite a rose as ever bloomed in an English garden."

"I see you wear your poet's hat again today."

"Are only poets expected to speak the truth? You *are* exquisite and you *do* put the rose to shame. Who are you?"

"I am Lady Domino."

His eyes were quizzical. "You still hide your identity?"

"Yes."

"Even from me?"

Her eyes were huge as she looked at him. "Yes," she whispered.

"I have kissed those lips and yet must not know who those lips belong to?"

"Please—"

"Please don't remind you of how very *fast* things were? But I must remind you; I must make you recall every sweet moment—"

"I do not need reminding of anything," she interrupted softly. "For I will never forget. I should not have done what I did last night, and even less should I have come here to meet you today."

He studied her anxious face. Sweet Jesu, how lovely she was. She had not been out of his thoughts, and the desire that had leaped into being the night before now rose sharply within him again. The air of mystery that surrounded her served only to heighten that desire, making the need to possess her completely all the more urgent. But who was she? He had made inquiries at the Pump Room that morning, but no one seemed to know the name of the lady who had so magnificently snubbed the Earl of Blaisdon. Was she indeed married? Was that why she refused to say who she was? No, on reflection he did not think that that was so, for there was something so very untouched, so unawakened about her. Oh, to be the first man to rouse her from that innocence. . . .

"You say that you should not have come here today," he said. "But still you came, and you came because your heart overruled dull common sense."

"Yes."

"Then you admit that your heart is not immune to me."

"You know that it is not," she breathed, every nerve alive to his closeness, every fiber yearning to be in his arms. The truth about her real self remained starkly on the edge of her thoughts, refusing to go away, refusing to be even pushed aside for these few precious moments. Tears filled her eyes and she looked away from him.

He put his hand to her cheek, making her look at him. "Don't cry," he whispered, "please don't cry, for I could not bear it. Stay with me for just a while, Lady Domino. I do not know your reason for refusing to tell me who you are, but

I will respect your wish. Just stay with me, as anonymously as last night, and we will walk a while. Will you stay?"

His thumb gently caressed her cheek and she slowly nodded. "Just for a while."

He smiled. "What would you like to do? Go into the labyrinth? I am told that altogether it is half a mile long—"

"I think I would just like to walk."

He tethered the horse and then drew her arm through his. They said little as they walked, and in spite of the rain she wanted those minutes to last forever. But she knew that she must go, and when a church bell struck the half hour she drew her hand away and halted. "I must leave now."

"Meet me again tomorrow."

"No."

"I will be here at the same time."

She looked unhappily into his eyes and he could not resist drawing her into his arms. Although she knew that it was wrong, that she was allowing a great liberty, she came willingly into his embrace, raising her lips toward his, unable to help herself. For a breathless moment they kissed, and then she pulled finally away, turning to hurry back to the hotel.

He watched her go. Dear God, how he wanted her! And by fair means or foul, he would possess her, there could be no doubt about that. Whoever she was, she had aroused him as few other women had done, and his eyes were very dark as he watched until she passed from sight. She would meet him the next day, he was certain of that, for he recognized the answering desire in her kiss.

But she guessed nothing of his thoughts as she hurried down Great Pulteney Street, and indeed she was determined that the very last thing she would do would be to meet him again the following day. She had already erred to the point of lunacy; there must be no more Lady Domino, no more assignations, and no more foolish dreaming. She was Adele Russell, she owed too much to Cat, and she could not—*dared* not—risk any more, not even for the sake of something that was perilously close to love itself. Not even for that.

Chapter 11

There seemed no end to the rain; it continued through the rest of the day and into the night. There was something very depressing about it, from the low, unfriendly skies to the deep puddles which formed everywhere. By day there was the clink-clink of pattens and by night just the rushing of the raindrops. But when the next day dawned and it was still raining, Adele inevitably thought of the possibility of meeting Sir Mask again. She could not help herself; she knew it was wrong and that it was courting disaster, but the desire to see him again was simply too strong. Knowing that she was contemplating such a course made her jittery, and Cat watched her with growing concern; there was surely something wrong with the girl. . . .

Adele dwelt upon the quandary she was in, a quandary that was entirely of her own creation. Memories of the masquerade and of the meeting in Sydney Gardens kept returning to her, and she could not concentrate on her work. When the younger Miss Mortimer asked to see lilac silk, Adele placed pink before her, and then she proceeded through the morning to drop a drawer of gloves, miscalculate two yards of braiding, count the incorrect number of buttons, and bring the wrong size handkerchief. The moment the shop was empty, Cat took her aside.

"Is something wrong? You don't seem at all yourself this morning."

"I-I'm quite all right, truly I am."

"Well you don't seem it, and that's a fact."

Adele knew that she must say something, something to put Cat's mind at ease. "I-I have a headache."

Cat smiled then. "My poor pet. We aren't very busy again on account of this dratted weather, so I will make you a good draught of camomile tea, then I want you to wrap up well and go out for a good long walk. There's nothing better for banishing a headache.''

Adele was inwardly dismayed, for this suggestion would make it so very easy for her to add to her already considerable catalog of sins. She glanced at the clock and saw that it was half-past eleven. "I-I'll be all right as I am," she began. "I expect that once I've had some luncheon—"

"No, I insist upon the camomile tea and the walk in the fresh air. Come on now, there's no time like the present."

It was as if all the fates were determined to thrust her deeper into that enticing, beckoning entanglement, at the same time so bitter and yet so sweet.

She sipped the camomile tea while Joanie brought her cape and pattens and Cat's umbrella. Cat fussed around her and then ushered her to the back door. "There, you take a good long walk now, and when you come back we'll have some of that there beefsteak pie young Joanie's made. That'll either kill or cure you!"

Joanie scowled, still unable to tell when Cat was teasing and when she meant what she said. Adele put up the umbrella and walked down the garden path. Emerging from the side alley, she turned down Milsom Street and set off in the direction of Great Pulteney Street and Sydney Gardens, she just could not help herself. The rain was indeed keeping people off the streets and it seemed that there were only the less fortunate footmen and maidservants out and about on errands, their top halves concealed by the enormous umbrellas they carried.

Adele reached the Sydney Hotel just as the clock struck twelve. She followed the same procedure as she had the day before and was soon hurrying up the tree-lined walk toward the bridge, but as she did so the rain suddenly stopped. She glanced up and saw a large patch of blue sky directly above and in a moment the gardens were sparkling in the sunlight, the raindrops glittering like so many diamonds. The blue sky stretched further and further as the clouds rolled away to the east and Adele came to a halt. Now she did not dare meet Sir Mask, for there was too much risk of being seen and recognized; she would not have the protection of the umbrella or of her hood. She could see the bridge and saw that he was there, without his horse this time. Her heart ached, but she knew that today a meeting was impossible.

For a moment she stood there looking at him. How very elegant he was in a sage-green coat and pale gray corduroy trousers. A green silk scarf was tied at his throat and a beaver hat was pushed to the back of his head, revealing his rather unruly hair. He looked quite perfect, and everything that was manly and handsome. For the briefest of moments she was tempted to the final insanity of walking up to him, but then common sense returned as she saw several couples strolling up from the hotel. She recognized Mrs. Harriman and in a moment she was almost running back down the slope toward the hotel. Tears filled her eyes and she blinked them back. He would think that she had meant what she had said the day before, and maybe he would never come to the gardens again at twelve. . . . She felt as if her heart was breaking. A bewildering confusion of emotions beset her as she went through the hotel and out into the safety of Great Pulteney Street: she wanted to see him again and yet she didn't, she wanted him to know that she had come again and yet knew that it was for the best that he thought the opposite. Ending the whole sorry affair was the sensible, safe solution—continuing with it was the exciting, dangerous alternative.

She had reached Pulteney Bridge when she saw the green curricle drawn by two high-stepping grays, their tails and manes unfashionably long and feathery. David Latimer tooled the nervous team over the bridge, smiling as he glanced at Euphemia, who sat beside him.

Euphemia looked very lovely and very dainty in a rose-and-white-checkered walking gown. She carried a marquise parasol she had purchased from the haberdashery tilted back so that her face was revealed. The sunlight streamed from behind her, softening her face and enhancing its loveliness.

But it was at David Latimer that Adele looked as the curricle passed. His harsh words echoed in her head, and she loathed him anew as she watched him bring the team up to a smart pace. How good it had been to deliberately ignore his advice, and how good it had been to know that she had caused him some embarrassment at the masquerade! But as the curricle passed from sight she knew a sense of regret too. How different it might have been had there been no scandal and no fire at Beech Park. If none of that had happened, she would have been Countess of Blaisdon now and *she* would have been sitting beside him in that curricle. . . .

Cat was helping Joanie lay the table when she returned to the haberdashery. "How is your headache, Adele?"

"It's gone."

"That's better. You'll be in fine fettle once you've eaten."

They had been sitting at their meal for a short while when Adele glanced at Cat. "Cat, do you happen to know the name of a young gentleman I've seen. He is very good-looking and has tawny hair, and he rides a very large chestnut horse with a blaze."

"Well now, there's many a gentleman rides a chestnut horse."

"He's new in Bath, I'm sure of that."

"My dear Adele, with the duchess's masquerade and all that there are many gentlemen new in town."

"I suppose so."

"Caught your eye, did he?"

Adele smiled. "Yes."

"I wish I could help, but I can't." Cat laughed then. "The only gentleman I'm sure of being new in town is Lord Talbourne."

"The Duke of Bellingham's son?"

"The very same. He turned up the day after the masquerade, so I'm told, but as to what he looks like—"

"It can't be him," said Adele quickly. "Not if he arrived after the masquerade."

"So this paragon, this Corinthian has replaced the Earl of Blaisdon in your thoughts, has he?"

"The earl hasn't been in my thoughts."

"No?"

"No."

"He's most certainly in Lady Euphemia's, but she's *un*certain enough of him to make sure he did not enter the haberdashery earlier."

Adele stared at her. "What do you mean?"

"While you were out walking, the earl accompanied Lady Euphemia to the shop. They were in his curricle, and when she alighted and he began to escort her in, she most pointedly made some excuse to make him remain outside. She didn't want him to come in and see you, Adele, that is the only explanation."

"She may have been about to purchase something a gentleman should know nothing of."

"A pair of scissors? Hardly unmentionable. No, she was afraid that he would see you. She fears you still, Adele, especially where the Earl of Blaisdon is concerned."

"Rubbish."

"And that is why," went on Cat, ignoring the interjection, "she's always so mean and spiteful toward you. She's jealous."

"She has no need."

"I think she does."

"Why?"

"Oh, Lord above, I don't know. Perhaps he still loves you."

"He never loved me, that was perfectly clear."

"Oh, I give up with you. I know what I saw and I know what I think it meant."

"Miss Rogers is right," said Joanie quite suddenly, speaking for the first time. "I was in the shop when Lady Euphemia came in and she was positively *relieved* when she saw you weren't there, Miss Russell."

"I expect she was," remarked Adele drily, "She doesn't want any hint of the past to be remembered now, not when she's about to get to the altar after all."

Cat pursed her lips. "But what if I'm right?"

"You aren't."

Cat glanced around at the clock on the mantelpiece. "Good Lord above, is that the time? Come on, Adele, we'd best get ourselves back behind the counter!" She smoothed her apron as she stood, then she cast a baleful look at Joanie. "That pie was very good, young Joanie."

"It was?" Joanie was perplexed by the frown, which did not match the compliment.

"It was. I can't understand why you can make such a fine beefsteak pie and yet make an apple tart with pastry you could break your teeth on!" With that Cat swept out of the kitchen.

Adele smiled at the maid. "I liked your apple tart, Joanie."

"Thank you, Miss Russell. Miss Russell?"

"Yes?"

"You're wrong about Lady Euphemia, you know. I'm sure

she didn't want the earl to come in because she's afraid he still feels something for you."

Adele stared at the maid, surprised. "And *I'm* sure *you're* wrong, Joanie."

"No, I'm not. I recognized that look on her face, for I've worn it myself—when I was afraid Tom Wainwright would see Sally Roberts at the fair. I was right to be afraid an' all; she's Mrs. Wainwright now, and I'm still plain Joanie Smith."

Chapter 12

By the next morning it was raining again, and once more the streets were virtually deserted. There were no pretty summer parasols and light slippers, only black umbrellas and pattens, and on the roads only the hardy stages, mails, and carriers ventured forth. Everyone complained bitterly about the weather, for the streets were so dirty, with deep puddles, and like all the other traders in Milsom Street, Cat was forever having to have the floor of the shop mopped up.

For Adele there was something inevitable about the reappearance of the rain. It was as if fate was still determined to throw temptation in her path. She half expected Cat to ask her to deliver something to an address close to Sydney Gardens, but it still came as a jolt when that is exactly what happened. At about a quarter past eleven, with the rain still pouring relentlessly down, she was dispatched to deliver a package in Laura Place. Her hood up and Cat's umbrella shielding her, she made her way down through the town, crossing Pulteney Bridge and completing her errand swiftly. Determined not to give in to the overwhelming desire to see Sir Mask once more, she turned back toward the bridge, putting Great Pulteney Street and the Sydney Hotel firmly behind her, but she could not ignore the urgency of her heart. Her thoughts were thrown into turmoil as slowly she turned to look back along the vista of Great Pulteney Street and at the green of the trees in the Vauxhall behind the hotel. He would be there, he would be there right now. . . . Biting her lip, ashamed of her own weakness, she began to walk toward the hotel. Conscience fled, leaving only the desperate need to see the man she could not put out of her every waking moment. Let him be there today, please let him be there.

The Countess of Blaisdon's cane tapped audibly on the floor of the card room in the Sydney Hotel as she and the earl came to a standstill in the doorway. She frowned disapprovingly at the group of gentlemen already well into the delights of whist. She did not mind gentlemen indulging their seemingly endless craving for gambling, but she disliked such activities taking place so early in the day. Gaming, in her opinion, was for the evening and night, certainly not for the morning. But this particular morning she was in an irritable mood anyway, for the weather depressed her and she had been looking forward to a dish or two or the Sydney Hotel's fine Turkish coffee. After going to some length to persuade her son to accompany her, she had now discovered that her table—*her* table—was already occupied. Those dreadful Mortimer creatures had chosen *her* table. Really, it was too bad, *everything* about Bath was too bad! She loathed the place, loathed the cure, loathed the weather, and loathed the conversation, which turned so frequently upon the discussion of ailments.

The matter of the coffee rankled as she glowered at the whist players. "I find Bath in the winter barely tolerable," she grumbled. "But in the summer it is odious in the extreme. The waters taste like molten iron and must be sampled in that Pump Room where nothing can be said above the squawling of that odious band!"

"Hardly odious, they play very well indeed."

"But not at the crack of dawn! And then there is the necessity of attending daily service in the abbey. I *never* go to church every day and to my mind such apparent devotion smacks of hypocrisy."

"Then don't go."

"How can I not? What *would* be said of me?"

"It could be that they will thank you for setting a precedent."

"That I doubt very much indeed. Oh, if only I could sip a glass or two of wine, I am sure my constitution would recover, but instead all I am permitted is barley water or some other such wishy-washy stuff! It really is too much."

"Your doctors prescribed the cure."

"They do not have to endure it."

He smiled. "That is true enough, although if old Aitcheson continues with the port at his present rate he will be toddling down here soon enough."

The countess's foot tapped crossly. "And now my table in

97

the coffee room here is taken—by those, those Mortimers! It is really too vexing, David."

"Mother, there are any number of tables free; it is surely not necessary to demand that particular one," he said wearily.

"I *always* have that table; it offers the finest view down Great Pulteney Street."

"The windows are so misted over because of the rain that there is no view at all today. Indeed the abduction and rape of the Sabine women could take place within feet of you and you'd know nothing of it!"

"David!"

"It's true," he said, smiling.

"You are very tiresome at times. Which brings me to another matter—"

"Oh, no, not that again."

"Yes, that again."

"I hardly think the doorway of the Sydney Hotel card room is the wisest place for such a discussion."

"You are a captive audience here, my laddo. *When* do you intend to name the day with the Marchioness of Heydon? I confess to finding the whole affair a little embarrassing, for *everyone* expects an announcement and yet there is nothing. You drive her here, there, and everywhere, you call upon her, you appear to be making it positively certain, and yet nothing has definitely come of it. Why?"

"Perhaps I need to be sure."

"About what?"

"That she is the wife for me."

"But of *course* she is! She is well connected, rich, and beautiful, and what's more she dotes on you—although sometimes for the life of me I can't think why. She is the perfect match."

"I once believed that of someone else."

The countess took a deep breath. "That disastrous interval is well and truly over, which is just as well, given Denzil Russell's subsequent ruin."

"You never did approve, did you?"

"Hardly. Arranged matches are the best matches of all, and that is why I firmly believe that your future lies with the Marchioness."

"You may be right, Mother, but I will move in my own good time, I will *not* be bludgeoned into anything."

"Bludgeoned? No one's *bludgeoning* you!"

"No?"

"No!"

"I promise you that you will be the first to learn of any development."

"And I'm to be content with that?"

"It's all I'm prepared to say on the matter."

"Well, I'm *not* content, far from it. Maybe at one time it would not have been so urgent, for there would have been your brother Jamie to carry on the Latimer line . . ." Her voice trailed away and she stared at her son, seeing something pass through his eyes. "You know the truth, don't you?" she breathed, "You've always known—"

"That Jamie was strictly speaking my half brother, with no Latimer blood in his veins? Yes."

"How? Did Hester tell you?"

"Your sister? No, she is innocent of the charge."

"I didn't think anyone knew."

"There is only me."

"You've never said a word."

"Naturally not—that would hardly have been the thing now, would it?" He smiled, touching her cheek briefly. "Now then, shall we adjourn to that coffee room?"

She composed herself, for the discovery that her well-kept secret was known to him had come as something of a shock. "Only if those Mortimer creatures have vacated my table," she said after a moment.

"If we go into that coffee room," he said with commendable patience, "we will sit down at a table, *any* table! I am not about to lend myself further to tabby-cat yowlings about personal places. You inveigled me into coming here and I've gone along with your wishes so far, but I'm fast tiring of the whole thing."

"Are you about to be disagreeable?"

"Me? As if I would. I am an angel, Mother, a positive angel."

"Except when you're tiresome."

He smiled. "Except then, of course." He offered her his arm once more and after a moment she took it.

Adele passed through the hotel without knowing how close she came to encountering the Earl and Countess of Blaisdon. She emerged at the rear of the building and hurried up the tree-lined avenue where the noise of the rain was magnified by the countless leaves. With each step she took, her heart seemed to pound a little more, and then she came within sight of the bridge. She hardly dared to look, for fear that he would think that after yesterday she had ended the liaison once and for all. But he *was* there. She saw him immediately, leaning on the iron balustrade, looking down at a barge conveying Bath stone to London. It glided silently beneath the bridge, the bows cutting through the dark, rain-mottled waters.

He once again wore the sage green coat, and his cloak was tossed carelessly back over his shoulders as if he scorned the downpour. The rain dampened his hair, making it curl tightly, and his face bore a withdrawn, pensive expression. She knew that although he waited there, he did not expect to see her.

A smile sprang to his lips as he saw her approach, and he caught her hand, swiftly drawing her close. An unbelievable ecstasy flooded through her and she was oblivious to everything but the joy of being in his arms. She did not think of the impropriety of the situation; it did not pass through her head that his conduct was not really that of a gentleman when he embraced and kissed her as he did when he knew that she was virtually helpless to deny him. In that long moment as he held her close, there was no thought of danger either; she did not feel the risk of discovery or consequence, there was just happiness.

He cupped her face in his gloved hands. "Why didn't you come yesterday?"

"I couldn't."

"Why? Will you not tell me?" He smiled at her silence. "Oh, what mystery lies behind all this? And what madness is it which makes me your willing slave? Is it possible to love a dream, a spirit without a name?" His lips brushed hers again and he felt her tremble.

How tantalizing she was, so innocent and yet so very sensuous—and always with that devastating hint of the unknown. She enticed him as no other woman had enticed him before, and the thoughts passing through his mind in that moment were far from honorable.

A gust of wind billowed her cloak and disturbed a stray lock of her golden hair. Gently he pushed the damp curl back beneath her hood. "I sometimes think," he said softly, "That I have willed you into existence, that I alone can see and touch you."

"I am real."

He decided that this was the moment to carry the liaison on to its next logical step. "Yes," he whispered. "You are real. We are both real, so let us dispense with further formality. I desire you, I want you so much that I ask you to come to me. Leave whatever life you now have and let me set you up, let me be your protector."

She drew away slowly, staring at him in sudden dismay, horrified and shaken that he should make such a very improper suggestion. It was as if he had struck her. "Y-you mean you wish to keep me?" she asked faintly, the dull red of shame staining her hot cheeks.

"We should be lovers in fact, not just in wish—"

"No!" she cried, "I will never be any man's mistress, sir!" Her eyes flashed with anger as she at last recovered from the initial shock.

"Do not misunderstand me," he said quickly, beginning to realize his mistake.

"I don't, sir, I don't misunderstand you at all."

It was too late; he had completely misjudged her and had blundered almost irretrievably. Hastily he tried to make good his error. "Forgive me," he murmured, "Forgive me, I beg of you."

"I am not a demimondaine, sir, even though I have foolishly allowed you certain liberties."

"Not foolishly," he whispered, "never foolishly. Please forgive me, for I cannot bear to be closed out of your heart." He put his warm hand to her cheek, once again caressing her with his fingertips.

The spell began to fold around her again, and in spite of her anger she did not move away. There was something in his touch and in his soft voice that trapped her and rendered her almost defenseless.

"Forgive me," he whispered again, drawing her into his arms.

But as his arms tightened around her, the spell was shattered when another gust of wind blew her hood back from her face and at the same time twisted the umbrella out of her hand. She drew away with a sharp gasp as the umbrella bowled away down the hill, and as she turned to try to try to catch it she found herself looking at the two Misses Mortimer.

Dragging her hood back over her distinctive hair, she began to run away, ignoring Sir Mask's calls and holding her hood to prevent it slipping back again. Tears filled her eyes, for the Mortimer sisters must have recognized her. Soon the extent of her stupid, inexcusable sins would be known to one and all. Now too Sir Mask would learn the truth, that his Lady Domino was the infamous Miss Russell, the almost-countess who was now a mere haberdasher's assistant. How he would loathe her for her deception. . . .

Blinded by her tears, she did not see David Latimer in the hotel doorway, but he had seen everything and, having glimpsed her hair when she had repinned it at the masquerade, knew she was the woman who had snubbed him. He caught her arm as she made to pass him, and her breath caught with a jerk as he forced her to halt.

His voice was low and angry. "Do you *never* listen to advice, madam?" he demanded coldly. "Or are you hell-bent upon ruining yourself with that coxcomb?" He turned her roughly toward him, and for the first time realized exactly who she was. His face grew white in that brief moment, as if he were looking into the eyes of a ghost. "You!" he whispered incredulously. "All the time it was you!"

With a choked sob, she pulled herself free, pushing blindly on into the hotel and out again through the main doors without a glance back over her shoulder. She ran all the way along the blessed anonymity of Great Pulteney Street, conscious all the time that that anonymity would not be hers for much longer; soon the drawing rooms of the town would ring of nothing else but the misdeeds of Denzil Russell's daughter. She had played with fire and had been badly burned. Worse, she had brought certain ruin upon Cat, Cat who had done nothing to warrant such a cruel fate.

Joanie was alone in the kitchen when Adele returned, and the maid took one horrified look at Adele's distraught face and went hurrying through to the shop to call Cat. Leaving the maid in charge, Cat came through to the kitchen where Adele was sitting motionless in a chair by the table. Her head was bent and her shoulders shook with silent tears.

Gently Cat put her hands on those trembling shoulders. "Adele, whatever's happened?"

"Oh, Cat, don't be kind to me for that is the very last thing I deserve. I've let you down terribly, I've done things I shouldn't—"

"Tell me."

Slowly Adele poured everything out, leaving no detail

untold, and all the time the ashamed tears stained her pale cheeks. Cat's lips parted in dismay as the sorry tale unfolded, but she said nothing until Adele had finished.

Then she straightened. "I *knew* something was wrong, you simply weren't yourself, but I thought you were ill."

Adele dissolved into helpless weeping at that, overcome with guilt and remorse. "I shouldn't have done it, I should have known better! I should have thought of someone other than myself. Oh, Cat, can you ever forgive me?"

"Of course I can forgive you," soothed Cat anxiously, stroking the tangled golden hair.

"I'll go away," said Adele, "I'll go away just as I should have done five years ago! Then you'll have nothing more to worry over."

"Nothing more? I'd have three times as much to worry about if you did that!" cried Cat, horrified. "I'd be wondering all the time what'd become of you. No, Adele, you are not to go away, we'll weather this one out together!"

"But—"

"No buts, my lass! Let's consider the whole affair in its proper light. I think we may discount the Misses Mortimer, for their eyesight is very poor and they are too vain to wear spectacles. Why, I doubt if they have any idea at all what they witnessed in the gardens. As to the Earl of Blaisdon, well I believe he will keep silent on the matter as well; after all he has as much reason as the duke and Sir Frederick to wish to keep your name out of the public eye at the moment, hasn't he? Well, hasn't he?"

"I suppose so," agreed Adele in a small voice.

"Right, so if I'm right then nothing will come of it. You are not to be thinking of leaving, I just will not hear of it."

"I'm so sorry for what I've done," whispered Adele, trying to wipe away the tears. "I just could not think of anything else but being part of it all again, just for a while."

"I know, my pet, I know how you miss all that you had at Beech Park."

"But that should not make me behave like a spoiled brat."

"You didn't; you just didn't think, that's all. Now then, we must look on the bright side and trust that my judgment of the affair is the right one, hmm?"

Adele tried to glean hope from Cat's forced cheerfulness, but somehow she couldn't. Only if David Latimer's affections were engaged as far as Euphemia was concerned was there any real possibility of his wishing to suppress anything, but as Adele herself knew from the conversation she had overheard in the confectionary, it was highly unlikely that he felt anything at all for his prospective bride. He seemed incapable of any real depth of feeling and she could expect no mercy from him; she knew that from past experience.

Cat was determined to be as optimistic as possible. She patted Adele's shoulders and went to fill the kettle. "A good pot of tea wouldn't go amiss, and after that we'll just have to wait." She smiled a little sadly as she hung the kettle above the fire. "We can do nothing else, we're in the hands of Providence now."

Adele glanced at the rain-washed window. Yes, they could only wait—and each second would seem like a minute, each minute an hour. Her eyes filled with fresh tears and she hid her face in her hands.

The afternoon passed oh, so slowly, and there seemed no change in the attitude of the customers who braved the atrocious weather. Nothing had happened by the time the shop was closed for the night and Cat felt a little encouraged by this, telling Adele that had the Misses Mortimer recognized her, not even such weather would have kept them indoors. They would have felt compelled to go out to spread the scandalous tidbit as far and wide as possible. Their silence could only mean their ignorance of what they had come upon in Sydney Gardens.

Adele tried to cling to this, but the doubt and fear would not go away. Hers was the responsibility and so she was the one who must put it right. Maybe Cat was right about the Misses Mortimer; indeed that seemed to be the definite case, but there was still David Latimer to contend with. As Adele went to her bed that night she knew that she must go to see him, to beg him face-to-face to keep her secret. She would go first thing the next morning, before the shop opened.

Chapter 13

She wore her best gown, a lawn checkered in blue and white; it was not anywhere near as grand a garment as she had worn the last time she had called upon the Earl of Blaisdon, but it was the finest in her small wardrobe. With her hair pinned up and hidden beneath a straw gypsy bonnet and her blue spencer neatly buttoned, she went quietly down the stairs. Joanie was humming as she poked the fire. She stopped, her eyes widening as she saw Adele, who put a warning finger to her lips and the words died on the maid's lips. Adele slipped out into the sunlit garden, and Joanie watched her go, guessing her destination. Slowly the maid closed the door and returned to her work, but she no longer hummed.

Once again the weather had changed dramatically; the clouds had gone and the sky was a clear blue, the color of forget-me-nots. Adele hurried up Gay Street and had reached the spacious Circus before something made her halt. Ever afterward she was not to know what hidden sense had warned her, but something did, making her draw into a doorway as a highly sprung yellow phaeton drawn by four bays dashed up the street behind her and turned into the Circus, its huge five-foot wheels sending small stones flying. The dangerous drag was the sort considered to be of the first stare by gentlemen-about-town and was very eye-catching as the handsome team came to a standstill outside the Bellingham residence. The tiger in his striped waistcoat and beaver hat jumped down immediately from his perch at the back and hurried around to take the reins as the gentleman who had been driving slowly prepared to climb down from the precarious seat so high above the ground. Adele stared at him. It was Sir Mask.

He jumped lightly down, removing his top hat and running his fingers swiftly through his tawny hair. He slapped the rump of the nearest horse and grinned at the tiger. "They were uncommon active this morning, eh, Thomas?"

"They were indeed, my lord."

"Well, they set me back enough, the least they could do in return is cut the dash of dashes."

At that moment the door of the house opened and Euphemia emerged in a walking dress of heavy cream muslin. The scarlet ribbons of her bonnet fluttered prettily as she hurried toward the phaeton. "Rex!" she cried, "Wherever have you been? I believe I've been waiting hours! Which demimondaine occupied you so completely that you forgot your early-morning appointment with your only sister?"

"Hush!" he replied, "Would you have the whole of Bath hear you?"

They lowered their voices then and Adele heard no more, but she stared at them in the utmost dismay. Sir Mask was none other than Rex, Lord Talbourne, brother of the Marchioness of Heydon and only son of the hated Duke of Bellingham! She had been guilty of an association with a member of the family that had ruined her own family! Closing her eyes, she turned away.

In the Circus, Rex folded his arms, looking at his sister. "Now then, what's all this about waiting hours? I have not kept you one minute past the appointed time."

"That's a fib, and you know it." She spoke a little petulantly.

"You're still miffed with me, aren't you?"

"Why should I be?"

"Because I was at that masquerade and you didn't know it."

"It was a mean trick after being away for six long years."

"It was a necessary trick. I had to see how things stood between you and Blaisdon."

"And now that you know?"

"I am not exactly pleased."

"Must I remind you again that I am a widow, free to do as I please with whom I please?"

"Meaning free to conduct a liaison with Blaisdon?"

"Hardly a liaison. I mean to get him to the altar this time."

"The fish ain't landed yet, sis," he warned.

"And aren't you pleased," she said drily. "Tell me, what is it exactly between you and him?"

106

"That isn't any of your business."

"Oh, yes it is, when it intrudes upon my plans."

"He and I simply do not like each other."

"There's much more to it than that."

"Maybe there is, but you aren't about to find out what it is."

"I intend to have him, Rex, unless you can give me a very good reason why I should accede to your wishes. Well? Can you give me such a reason?"

He said nothing, and brother and sister eyed each other, their strong wills well matched. She smiled then. "Don't interfere with my life, Rex, and I shall not interfere in yours. Content yourself with finding your mysterious Lady Domino."

Glad to leave the subject of his dealings with the Earl of Blaisdon, he seized upon her mention of Lady Domino. "Would that I *could* find her; but no one in this damnable place seems to know anything about her."

"Well, from the description you've given me, I wouldn't think it would be all that difficult to find her. She's a veritable paragon, of matchless beauty, with large blue eyes and golden hair the color of the sun itself. My, my, you have waxed poetic on the lady." She gave a short laugh. "Actually, there *is* someone who fits the description. . . ."

"Who?" he demanded swiftly.

"She is hardly likely to be your temptress, for she is hardly a lady—in fact she is in trade."

He pressed his lips angrily together, irritated by his sister's apparent amusement. "Don't play games with me, Euphemia," he said coldly. "For it means a great deal to me that I find her, and it is hardly likely that the woman I speak of is in *trade*!

"No? I thought you wished to make a kept woman of her, and is that not one of the oldest of trades? Perhaps not *the* oldest, but bordering on it."

"How full of sisterly love you are," he said. "The joy of being with you threatens to overwhelm me."

"Then you know exactly how I feel where you are concerned," she replied. "Now then, shall we sheathe our claws again and take that drive, or shall we continue to scratch and spit?"

"We'll sheathe them for the time being." He took her hand and helped her up into the phaeton. A moment later the high-flyer sprang away from the curb, the team setting off at a grand pace, but as it passed down Gay Street there was no sign of Adele.

She was making her way up Crescent Fields toward the magnificent curve of Royal Crescent spreading majestically across the hillside above. The whole edifice was arrayed with over one hundred magnificent columns along the second and third stories, and in the morning sunlight the stone was a mellow, warm gold that contributed more than a little to the glory of the scene. Perched on its exposed site, it caught even the slightest breeze and could be a devastating place for ladies' coiffures, but it was the jewel in Bath's crown, commanding a fine view down over the Fields, worthy indeed of being the most-sought-after address in the town.

But Adele did not look up as she climbed toward it; she was still filled with immeasurable dismay at discovering the real identity of Sir Mask. Her foolishness now became even greater, for Sir Mask was not just any young nobleman, he was a scion of the very house that had placed itself implacably against the Russells. He had a name so vile that the memory of his kiss filled her with loathing now, and the urgency with which she must seek David Latimer's aid became all the greater. He *must* keep her secret, he must!

She reached the wide pavement before Royal Crescent and paused at last to look at the grand vista. The pavement invited promenading and the carriageway was wide, seemingly capable of accommodating a great number of carriages at once. To have one's equipage drawn up outside one's house in this desirable place must be the finest of achievements, but she must not think about such unimportant things at a time like this, for behind one of those elegant doors was the man who once again held her future in the palm of his hand.

She walked along the pavement and then crossed the bridgelike approach to the door, glancing briefly down at the small yard before the kitchens. She could hear a maid singing as she worked and the sound reminded her of Joanie. Her hand trembled as she stretched up to knock. The sound seemed to reverberate through the silent house and the maid stopped singing.

Suddenly the door opened and she was looking at a young footman clad in the dark blue livery of the Latimers. He looked inquiringly at her.

"Yes?"

"I—I am Miss Russell. W-would it be possible for me to

see the Earl of Blaisdon?'' Her voice sounded very unsure, lame even, and she half expected the door to close in her face.

But it did not. "The earl is expecting you," he said, standing aside for her to enter.

Expecting her? Her heart sank even more as she went inside and the door closed softly behind her.

The earl received her in the library, a rather dark chamber at the back of the house. He stood by the window and did not turn as she was shown in. He wore a green and beige ankle-length dressing gown, tied loosely at the waist, and when he turned at last to face her she saw that beneath it he wore breeches and top boots and that his frilled shirt was partially undone. He looked the very model of male stylishness, as always he did, but there was no warmth in his greeting when at last he turned to face her.

"Good morning, Miss Russell."

"Good morning."

"How strange that we should meet again."

"Y-you were expecting me to call?"

"I was, once I discovered your present circumstances. I confess that it came as something of a surprise to me to find out yesterday that you now reside at a haberdashery where you also serve behind the counter, but the discovery did make it quite clear that the lady in the domino would wish at all costs to keep her identity and her activities a secret from society."

"I do not come on my own account."

"No?"

She flushed. "I come because of Cat, I mean, Miss Rogers."

"Ah yes, the lessee of the haberdashery. Forgive me if I am little skeptical about your sudden attack of conscience. You deliberately attended the masquerade and then you flouted the rules by meeting Talbourne afterwards. That does not smack of anxiety for Miss Rogers, Miss Russell; it smacks of a willful lack of consideration for the unfortunate lady."

Her flush deepened, for his words, spoken with such contempt, came miserably close to the truth. She *was* guilty, so very guilty. "I make no excuses, sir."

"No, because you cannot. There *is* no excuse for what you have done."

"Was the crime so very great?" she cried. "So very heinous?"

"The crime must indeed be great for you to be here now, Miss Russell; your own action this morning is proof of that."

Oh, how she hated him. There he stood, so safe and secure, so superior and arrogant. What did he know of being thrust into poverty, of being denied all that had meant anything? "Very well," she said quietly. "Very well; I stand convicted. I merely ask you to pass a light sentence."

"Did you honestly imagine that I would go around with a bell, madam? I do not concern myself with the spreading of tittle-tattle."

She was stung then. "No, I'll warrant that in this instance you don't!"

"And what does that mean?"

"It means that you probably have as little desire as I to have my activities broadcast, as it will stir up all the mud which has so providentially settled after the passage of five years. The imminence of your betrothal to the Marchioness of Heydon requires the discreet omission of any mention of former betrothals!"

His eyes darkened angrily. "Tread softly, madam, tread very softly indeed! What happened in the past between you and me is most certainly not ever to be mentioned between us again, is that quite clear? I heartily wish I had never set eyes on you, Miss Russell, either then or again now, and I have a variety of excellent reasons for feeling that way, as you well know. As far as I am concerned you simply do not exist; you are still as dead to me as you have been these past five years."

She stared disbelievingly at him, a shaft of pain sweeping bitterly through her at the force of his unkindness. This man was not even the palest shadow of that wonderful ideal she had once believed him to be! Her voice shook a little when she replied; she could not conceal that, but she held his gaze steadily, her coldness matching his.

"Do not concern yourself, my lord earl, for I will never approach you again or cause you even the slightest embarrassment. I will indeed be as if dead."

He looked away. "Forgive me for speaking so harshly; there was no cause."

"No, there wasn't."

He smiled a little wryly. "I was right at the assembly rooms when I suspected that your silence was because I would know your voice. I know it so very well still, just as you know mine. Did it please you greatly to insult me in front of everyone?"

She said nothing.

"Your silence is, as before, very eloquent. Once I thought I knew you so very well, but I have never really known you at all, and I have certainly never understood you."

"I could say the same of you."

He nodded. "Perhaps. However, it no longer matters. But one thing does matter, and that is that you begin to heed my warnings about Talbourne."

"There is no need to warn me anymore, sir."

"After yesterday it would seem to me that there is."

"I did not know who he was then."

He raised a cynical eyebrow. "Oh, come now, you knew exactly who he was!"

"No, sir, I did not."

"You expect me to believe that you were unaware that you were with the heir to a fine, fat dukedom?"

"I don't expect you to believe anything, sir, for to do that would be foolish in the extreme. I say again that I didn't know who he was and that if I had, then I would have dealt him a snub which more than equaled the one I dealt you."

There was an unwilling glint of humor in his eyes. "Indeed? My, my, how busy that would have made you, Miss Russell. Busy, but not without resource, for to be sure snubs appear to be your speciality." The humor faded. "Why would Talbourne warrant such a rebuff? What is he to you?"

"I suggest, sir, that if you wish to know why I loathe the family into which you are about to marry, then you have recourse to the premises of the *Bath Chronicle* and the *Bath Herald* where you may read past editions of both—five years past, to be precise." She opened the door. "Good day to you, my lord earl. You must forgive me if I do not wish you every happiness with your future bride."

He inclined his head coolly. "Good day to you, Miss Russell." He pointedly returned his attention to the prospect from the window as she left.

She emerged from the house and hurried along the wide pavement toward the Circus, halting in horror almost immediately as she saw the two Misses Mortimer sauntering toward her, arm in arm. Parasols twirling, they walked with their heads together, giggling from time to time. Now she would know, for their reaction on seeing her would tell her if they had indeed recognized her the day before.

They glanced at her but did not acknowledge her, for ladies did not acknowledge shop assistants. They continued with their whispering and giggling and she knew that she was safe; they had no idea at all that she had been the woman in Sydney Gardens the day before. A flood of relief washed over her. They didn't know! Her secret, and therefore Cat's well-being, was safe. She glanced back once at the house. Her indiscretions would not be made known and her life would be able to continue as it had before she had found that invitation card. But there were tears shining in her eyes; David Latimer's words seemed to echo in her head as she looked at the house. *As far as I am concerned you simply do not exist, you are still as dead to me as you have been these past five years.*

David remained where he was long after she had gone, and his expression was thoughtful when at last he turned to ring for the butler, who appeared a moment later.

"Yes, my lord?"

"I will not be in to luncheon today, Frederick, and when my mother arises you may inform her that if she requires me at all I will be at the premises of one or other of the local newspapers."

"Very well, sir." The butler hesitated.

"What is it?"

"I was wondering, my lord, if it had slipped your mind that you are expected by the Marchioness of Heydon later this morning?"

He had forgotten Euphemia and her invitation to some sort of morning reception where he would be forced to endure idle society chitchat and where he would most probably find himself face-to-face with Rex, Lord Talbourne. "Send a footman around and inform the marchioness that I am unavoidably detained. Oh, and proffer my sincere apologies and so on."

"Very well, my lord."

112

Chapter 14

Cat was aghast to learn who Sir Mask really was, but the shock faded into relief when she learned the outcome of Adele's meeting with the earl. "The Lord be praised," she whispered, "The Lord be praised indeed! I confess I was very anxious when Joanie here said she believed you'd gone to the Royal Crescent to see him, and not only because of what happened in the past between you and him. I was also worried on account of the warning Sir Frederick Repton gave you about having anything to do with the earl."

Adele stared at her—she had forgotten all about Sir Frederick's warning! She gave a quick, nervous laugh. "To be honest, Sir Frederick had somehow slipped my mind. Still, he will probably never know. I think we may forget about my misdoings; the earl will say nothing, and the Misses Mortimer, as you said, do not seem to know what they witnessed." She took Cat's hands. "I'm truly sorry for what I did, Cat, truly sorry."

Cat squeezed her fingers. "It's all over now, my love, over and finished with once and for all."

"I hope so."

"The only risk would appear to be Lord Talbourne recognizing you. You'll have to be extra careful when you are out, and if he should accompany Lady Euphemia to the shop, well then you can step back here until they have gone. With luck he'll soon take himself back to India for another six years."

Adele smiled. "With luck. Oh, Cat, if you only knew the horror I felt when I realized who my handsome Sir Mask was!"

"I can imagine." Cat smiled, getting to her feet. "Now then, there's no point in us sitting around congratulating ourselves on getting out of a scrape if we then proceed to lose our customers anyway through not opening the shop doors in good time! Come on now, there's work to be done."

"Not least of which is the Dowager Countess of Bainie's annual visit."

Cat heaved a heavy sigh. "Don't remind me, just don't remind me!"

Adele smiled as she followed Cat through to the shop. The Dowager Countess of Bainie was an extremely old and extremely particular lady who would have no other but Cat herself to serve her on her once-a-year sallying forth to the premises in Milsom Street from her eyrie in the Mendips near the little village of Cheddar. On that one day in the year she demanded Cat's full attention for almost an entire day, spending a great deal of time over a seemingly endless list of requirements, from a mere handful of pearl buttons to an amazing variety of different ribbons, each one described in the minutest detail in the little book she brought with her. As the Dowager Countess did not leave her estate except on this one occasion, it was difficult to know what on earth she needed all that ribbon for, unless it was to clothe a veritable army of maypoles! Still, she spent a great deal of money and was therefore to be welcomed, even if her fussiness and constant mind changing virtually drove Cat to the nearest lamp post with a suitable length of rope!

But this year, the dowager countess's annual visit was to have a very unfortunate consequence for Adele, for it meant that Cat was fully occupied at a time when there was an urgent summons to the Duchess of Bellingham. With Joanie away at the market, there was only Adele to complete this unwelcome errand. Following so soon on the almost inexpressible relief of believing herself safe from exposure, the errand to the duchess at the Circus was one of the most difficult and daunting tasks Adele had ever performed. Donning her little cape and her bonnet, she left the haberdashery and made her way to the Bellingham residence. Please, please let Lord Talbourne be absent, let him be far away when his Lady Domino appeared in her true light. . . .

The Bellingham footman seemed taken aback when she told him why she was there. "The duchess? But the duchess is not at home today; indeed she is away for the next two days."

Lord Tarquin suddenly appeared at the top of the stairs. "That's all right, John," he said, "I will deal with this."

The footman turned in surprise. "You, my lord?"

"Yes. You may go." Tarquin descended the stairs. He

was exquisitely attired in a russet coat and camel breeches and a quizzing glass swung idly in his pale hand as he dismissed the dumbfounded footman.

Adele felt suddenly on her guard. Something was not quite what it should be here. Tarquin swept her an extravagant bow, smiling all the while. "Tarquin, Earl of Bainie—your servant, sweet lady."

Earl of *Bainie*? He was the dowager countess's grandson? "Sir?" she asked, not returning his smile.

"You are still as beautiful as that brief glimpse promised."

"If the duchess is not here, I will go—"

"Tush now, no protestings, my sweet. Here you are, and here, for the moment, you shall remain."

"I came to see the duchess."

"I know." The smile continued to play around his fine lips. "I know because I sent the message to the haberdashery."

"*You* sent it?" A little fear was creeping into her now and she began to move toward the door, but he caught her arm.

"Don't deprive me of your delightful company, Miss Russell."

"Please let me go."

"I promise that I will; once you have succeeded in ruffling a few proud, scheming feathers."

He drew her toward the stairs.

"Please!" she cried.

"It will not avail you to raise your voice. The servants will not hear you and the gay company thronging the drawing room is too preoccupied to bother. I promise you again that this will not take long, and I swear too that—on this occasion at least—I do not have designs upon your honor." He paused at the foot of the stairs, his warm glance sweeping over her. "Just on this occasion, I must emphasize."

"Please let me go," she begged, feeling very frightened now.

He moved a little closer, smiling down into her pale face, his lips barely inches from hers. "Oh, how very tempting your loveliness is; your looks would put to shame the most sought-after courtesan in the realm. I could almost give in to your pleas—at a price, of course—but that would be to spoil the game, a game which I have waited some number of days to play."

"What game?"

"Punishing those who displease me. I had to wait, because

my dear grandmother does not come up to Bath until today. I know that she takes up your employer's entire day, leaving, as I hoped, your sweet self to come here at the 'duchess's' bidding.''

''If you are a gentleman, sir, you will let me go. I have done nothing to you and indeed am nothing to you—''

''Unfortunately I must agree with that last remark, would that the opposite were true. Perhaps a little later I will be able to—persuade you. However, for the moment I shall begin to be a little irritated with you if you do not toddle along nicely with Uncle Tarquin and behave yourself like a good little thing.'' With this, his grip tightened on her arm and she was virtually propelled up the stairs.

She could hear the sound of laughter and merriment as he pushed her into the little antechamber where before she had faced Euphemia. The little monkey was still on its perch; the evidence of Euphemia's leisure pursuits still scattered around in contrived profusion.

Desperately Adele tried to persuade the young earl not to go on. ''Please, my lord earl, *please,* I beg of you!''

''I will not be denied my revenge.''

''Please,'' she whispered brokenly, ''please let me go.''

''Why?'' he asked, turning her toward him, his eyes suddenly shrewd. ''Why don't you want to go into that drawing room? It's not just because you fear my plans, is it? There's something more; what is it?''

She stared helplessly at him. She couldn't tell him the truth, that she feared coming face-to-face with Lord Talbourne. She couldn't tell him that.

Still smiling, he drew her toward the folding doors which he flung open. The noise leaped into the antechamber and she found herself looking at a gathering of young ladies and gentlemen. At first she could not see Lord Talbourne anywhere.

A particularly pretty woman in fawn-and-white-striped lawn was in the middle of a complaint. ''If one must be out of Town at this time of year,'' she said, ''then one must be at Brighton or some other such seaside place. Not Bath! Bath is a place for old fogies, ailing clergymen, and retired army officers! I hanker after London, but must do with Bath!'' She noticed Adele and the Earl of Bainie for the first time and turned in surprise, her fan moving busily as her glance took Adele in. ''Why, what have we here, dear Tarquin? Where did you find her—in the kitchens?''

A small ripple of laughter greeted this, but to Adele's immense relief there was so much noise in the rest of the room that only a small number of guests noticed what was going on. She had never in her life before been so glad that human beings can make so much noise when they are enjoying themselves, for in this particular instance that noise saved her from being discovered by Lord Talbourne. He was seated at a faro table in an alcove, his back to her, and he was so engrossed in the cards that he was not aware of anything going on around him. She watched him write out an IOU and place it confidently on the ace on the painted board before him. A small smile spread across one opponent's face.

Euphemia was moving among her guests, the picture of charm and attentiveness, but then suddenly she saw Adele—and Lord Tarquin's grinning face. Her face became rigid with anger, at first pale and then red, and she crossed swiftly to the new arrivals.

In dread, Adele watched Rex, but he did not glance around; his whole attention was upon the turn of the cards.

Euphemia halted in front of Adele but looked furiously at the Earl of Bainie. "I suppose you think this highly amusing, Tarquin."

"Who? Me?" He was all innocence.

"Yes, you," she hissed furiously, glancing self-consciously at the interested onlookers and then lowering her voice. "It is just the sort of puerile prank I would expect from someone whose mentality has not progressed beyond his first year at Eton!"

"How unkind you are, to be sure," he murmured, his eyes hardening. "And how forgetful—I went to Harrow. As to this prank being puerile, well you should know, for I stole the trick from you, Euphemia, my dear. I recall that you considered it to be the very grandest of japes to invite my damned mistress to that masquerade when you knew my wife would be present."

Her mouth clamped shut, her whole body shaking with fury.

He smiled then, glancing again at Adele. "Yes," he said softly, "under the circumstances, I thought it particularly apt to have Miss Russell here when Blaisdon arrives—such a laugh, don't you think, 'Phemia?"

"I'm sorry to disappoint you!" she snapped. "But the Earl

has sent word that he is unavoidably detained. Now get out of here, Tarquin, and take her with you.''

''With pleasure, but remember not to play games with me again, for I promise you that I am a match for you.'' He sketched a brief bow, taking Adele's arm and steering her back into the antechamber. As the folding doors were closed she caught a glimpse of Rex rising from the faro table, his run of luck having deserted him at last. He had seen nothing, knew nothing of what had just happened.

Adele wrenched her arm away from the earl at last. ''You are unspeakable,'' she breathed. ''Unspeakable!''

''How kind of you to say so,'' he replied, smiling. ''And if compliments are to be the order of the day, let me say again that I find you a quite exquisite creature.''

''I cannot say the same of you.''

''No? What a pity. But perhaps I can make up for my failings with my attributes in—shall we say—other directions? I promise you that the ladies in my life have never had cause to complain, as you could find out for yourself had you a mind.''

''You flatter yourself, sirrah.''

His smile faded a little, but she gave him no opportunity to say any more for she hurried from the room and down the stairs, ignoring him as he called her back. A moment later she was out on the pavement and running to the safety of Gay Street.

On the corner, she paused to look back, just to make sure that he was not giving pursuit, but there was no sign of anyone except a burly man in an unseasonally heavy box coat. It was the box coat that made her notice him, for not only was it heavy but it was far too big for him, giving him a very strange appearance. But she thought nothing more of the man as she turned to go on her way again. She had escaped, but only just. . . .

At the haberdashery the dowager countess had reached the middle of her lengthy list and was now inspecting an array of purl-edged satin ribbons. Cat glanced anxiously at Adele and looked relieved when Adele smiled. For the remainder of the day, life in the shop went on in its usual fashion, but at last the time came for Adele to take down the tulles from around the doorway and prepare to close for the night. And so it was that she again noticed the man in the box coat. He was leaning against a railing across the street, apparently engrossed in a newspaper. She looked at him curiously, thinking how strange it was that she should see him again. Folding the tulles, she went back into the shop and locked the door.

In the kitchen, Cat had seated herself in her favorite chair, glad indeed that the day was over. "That's the end of a particularly trying day," she said. "And as tomorrow's the Sabbath, I intend to have a good rest. Is that braised beef ready yet, Joanie?"

"Almost, Miss Rogers," said the maid, bending to remove the lid from the pan steaming on the fire.

Cat smiled as Adele entered the kitchen. "I take it that you escaped Lord Talbourne."

"By the narrowest of squeaks." Adele explained what had really happened.

Cat was taken aback. "It was the Earl of Bainie's trickery? I'll warrant his grandmother would skin him alive if she knew!"

"Well, nothing came of it anyway."

"No thanks to him."

"No, no thanks to him."

"I should have suspected there was something odd about the duchess's summons."

"You weren't to know. How was anyone to know?" Adele saw Joanie struggling with the braised beef and went to help her.

Cat opened the newspaper and settled back for a short browse. After a moment or two she sniffed disparagingly. "I see that Sir Federick's tarnished star is about to rise as promised."

"What do you mean?" asked Adele, slicing the beef as thinly as she could.

"It says here that he's received a definite invitation to the prime minister's private estate, which means he's set off on his political career. Oh, if anything should make all good men vote Whig from now on, this news should!"

Adele smiled, but the smile was halfhearted. She had defied Sir Frederick when she had gone to see David Latimer—she was remembering this only too clearly now. She hoped and prayed that her apparent defiance would go undiscovered, but Sir Frederick Repton was like a large spider, lurking at the center of the web that was Bath.

Cat looked up from the newspaper and saw the thoughtful look. She misinterpreted it. "Adele, to my mind you still look peaky and out of sorts, which isn't surprising after all that's gone on of late. It's Sunday tomorrow, why don't you take the opportunity to go for a good long walk—up on the hill maybe.''

"To Beech Park?''

"Yes.''

"I don't think so, I'll just have a quiet laze here instead.''

"But I believe you should go up there, my dear.''

Adele looked at her, detecting an odd note in her voice. "Why?''

"Because of something the Dowager Countess of Bainie happened to mention today. She said that Sir Frederick has begun the work up there; some laborers began the task at the beginning of the week. There won't be a Beech Park soon, my dear, so I think you should go there while you can.''

Chapter 15

The air on the hillside was warm as Adele walked along the flower-edged lane. Bath spread along the valleys and slopes below, a glorious gold against the vivid green of the English summer landscape. The recent heavy rain had left deep ruts in the track and the undergrowth seemed more dense and luxuriant than usual, a riot of creamy-lace ground elder, shining yellow buttercups, scarlet poppies, and pale lilac scabious the shade of her eyes. There was color everywhere, enhanced by the heady scent of wild honeysuckle high in the straggling hedge, which in the time of Denzil Russell would have been kept under strict control. She could hear the wind whispering in the great elms and ash trees that towered over the lane, casting their delicate, leafy shadows on the ground where she walked. She preferred the lane as it was now, for when left to her own devices, nature had created a pageant mere man could not hope to emulate.

There was a small cottage at the bend in the lane, and beyond it she could see the great iron gates of Beech Park for the first time. She hardly glanced at the stout cottage wife in her gray stuff gown and checkered apron standing in her porched doorway, but the silent woman watched every step she took, recognizing her instantly but not daring to greet her.

Adele halted at the rusting gates by the lodge with its boarded windows and overgrown garden, once so neat but now untidy and wild. The roses that had once bloomed so prettily around the door now climbed freely to the weatherbeaten roof where the gales of several hard winters had dislodged several tiles. The little weathercock she had loved so much as a child still stood on the chimney, its proud blue and gold paint faded almost beyond recognition now. It creaked dolefully as the light breeze played around it.

She was about to walk through into the park when something made her glance behind. The lane was deserted, the cottage wife had gone from her doorway, and there were only the gently moving shadows of the trees dappling the ground. For a moment she continued to look back, for she would have sworn that someone had been there, then she pushed through the ill-fitting gates.

The grounds of Beech Park had been laid out by the great "Capability" Brown himself, but the panorama the landscape gardener had envisaged was now little more than a tract of open countryside. An army of gardeners with scythes had once tended the expanse of land between the cedar trees, but now dog daisies swayed among the tall grass, which moved like the sea in the stream of warm air that swept up the hillside from the valley below. There were no red deer wandering between the trees now and no green-coated gamekeepers at work in the woods that edged the park, which had formed a natural frame to a scene that drew the eye inevitably to the magnificent house overlooking everything. Just as the park itself was no longer glorious, so too had the house faded and died, its smoke-blackened shell a sad reminder of how it had once been.

She walked slowly along the overgrown drive, which had once been raked over daily but was now giving way to the encroaching grass. There were tracks, however, proof that several vehicles had passed over it recently, heavy wagons that had left deep marks in the mossy gravel.

As originally intended, the lake seemed to appear quite suddenly from nowhere, a stretch of glittering silver that narrowed to a neck and tumbled beneath the span of the elegant Palladian bridge. She could hear the steady, remembered rush of the water as she neared the bridge, and then her steps were echoing between the classical stone columns and pedimented porticoes.

The drive stretched on up the hillside between the dark green woods from which drifted the unmistakable perfume of the balsam trees, and the Arcadian scene ended with the sweep of great stone steps of a terrace. As always, a lump came to Adele's throat as she looked at what was left of her beloved home, and she could almost smell again the acrid smoke, hear the roar of the devouring flames, and sense the fear of the servants as they stood together at the foot of those steps. . . . She walked on, the past folding softly over her with its poignant memories of happy days filled with the love of her parents and the comfort of knowing that it would go on for ever. And ever.

There were weeds growing in every crack of the steps now as well as in the stone urns that topped the newel posts. The closer she came to the house, the more she could see evidence of Sir Frederick Repton's activities, for several walls had already been demolished and the stone and bricks piled high ready to be taken away. There were several sheds erected on the elegant terrace, their doors heavily padlocked against thieves, and the remains of a large bonfire where those few timbers that had survived the earlier conflagration had been finally burned. Elderberry bushes had begun to grow among the ruins now, their roots thrust deep into the cracks, and the flagstones of the terrace had become uneven as more weeds forced their way between them, but as Adele sat down on the top step, looking back down into the valley far below, it was possible to forget the decay all around her and remember it all as it had been.

At this distance Bath had become a glare of white in the sun, and the only sound was of the skylarks tumbling high in the sky above, their rippling song carrying far over the beautiful countryside. When she had been small she had loved to sit here, just looking and now as she stared down at the view she suddenly remembered one particular occasion. Carrying her precious collection of beads in its little silver casket, she had escaped from her harassed governess to sit here. She had worn a tightly waisted muslin frock with a wide pink sash, and her hair had been pushed up beneath a large cap that sported a bow of the same pink. She had heard her governess quite clearly, but had ignored her, being too intent upon the new bead she had found to add to her collection. The open casket stood on the step beside her, its bright contents glittering in the sunlight, but it was only the new bead that had held her breathless, fascinated attention. It had shone with dazzling glory, a many-faceted jewel shot with rich ruby, which she was sure was precious beyond belief, but which in fact was mere glass. The tears had brimmed instantly in her eyes when the bead slipped from her plump little fingers to roll between two flagstones and vanish from sight. With a sob she tried to retrieve it from that dark, enclosed space, but then the sobs died as she stared down to where a thin shaft of sunlight had caught the bead, flashing it with crimson rays of fire that made it ten times more beautiful than before. She left it there,

123

her secret treasure, known only to her and there for her to look at whenever she chose. Her sorely tried governess found her a moment or so later and dragged her before her father. Denzil laughed to see his scowling daughter, still clutching her casket, but he scolded her for being disobedient and she had to forgo the privilege of taking dinner with her parents for the rest of that week. Her father spoke gently to his Little Miss Magpie, as he always called her, but he was always firm when she misbehaved, and thus she learned that she must do as her governess said.

Adele smiled to herself as she remembered, for she had not thought of her nickname in many years, and had certainly forgotten all about that particular bead—why, it was probably still there. . . . On impulse, she bent over to look down between the flagstones, and there, sure enough, was the gleam of a crimson fire, as beautiful and mysterious as it had always been.

A horse snorted nearby and she sat up nervously. Someone was here! She looked up and heard the sound again. Slowly she got up, moving silently across the terrace and peeping very stealthily over to the long grass below.

A gray riding horse was tethered to a bush and had obviously been there for some time. David Latimer lounged on the ground nearby, his long legs sheathed in expensive, close-fitting breeches and stretched out nonchalantly before him. His dark blue coat was undone and his loosened silk cravat moved a little in the breeze. His dark hair looked disheveled and yet perfect as ever and the rings on his fingers flashed momentarily in the sunlight as he raised a glass of champagne to his lips. The half-finished bottle was propped up on the grass beside him and he appeared very pensive as he gazed down toward the valley, his view of the lake and the drive quite clear. He must have watched her every step!

She was about to draw back when he spoke, without bothering to glance up at her. "Good day to you, Miss Russell, I trust you are not too exhausted by your exertions."

She didn't reply and he turned then, smiling a little. "Surely you are not the silent woman again?"

"Good morning, sir."

"That's better." He gestured toward the park with his glass. "A fine view, is it not? Too fine for the likes of Fred Repton, don't you agree?"

"Yes."

His eyes were lazy as he sat up. "I presume you often make this pilgrimage?"

"Not often."

Putting the glass down next to the bottle, he got up, coming to the terrace steps and slowly mounting them. "Your reluctance to converse implies that I am intruding upon your solitude, Miss Russell."

"I certainly did not expect to see you here."

"How welcome you make me feel."

"I no longer have the right to any opinion where Beech Park is concerned."

"No. However, perhaps it is just as well that chance has placed us both here at the same time."

"Why?"

He did not reply immediately, studying her face for a moment. "Will you share a glass of champagne with me, Miss Russell?" he asked suddenly. "I cannot offer you the convenience of a glass to yourself, but at least you will know that I do not offer you a poisoned draught."

She stared at him.

"I realize that after our encounter yesterday the invitation may seem a little unexpected," he went on. "But I do believe that it would be better if we talked."

"About what, sir? Haberdashers' assistants have little in common with earls."

"Possibly, but Denzil Russell's daughter surely has something in common with someone who liked and respected her father a great deal and who is forced now to believe that events were not what they seemed five years ago. Ah, I see that I have your attention now. Will you accept my offer of champagne?"

"I will speak with you."

She took the arm he presented and together they descended the steps to the grass where she sat down, removing her bonnet and tossing her hair free. He sat down beside her, watching her for a moment before handing her the glass. "You are still a very beautiful woman; that is one thing about you I had not forgotten."

"You wished to talk about my father."

He smiled wryly. "Yes, indeed I did. You suggested yesterday that I read past editions of the local newspapers. I took your advice. The exercise proved most interesting."

She wondered what was passing through his mind, for if he

had indeed read the reports of the inquiry, then he was now fully aware of her open accusations against his future father-in-law and Sir Frederick Repton. "Interesting?" she asked.

"Yes, for until yesterday I knew only that you—that your father had died in the fire and that he had been found to have embezzled a rather large sum from his bank—which was always something I found a little unbelievable."

"And now?"

"Now I agree with your accusations. Someone deliberately started the fire, knowing your father was confined to his bed, the intention being to kill him and also to destroy any evidence he may have kept here."

Her glance was mocking. "*Someone*, my lord?"

"I don't shrink from naming the Duke of Bellingham. Or Repton."

"Don't you?"

"No. The fact that the duke is Euphemia's father makes no difference whatsoever."

"How flattering for her."

"Now is hardly the time for sarcasm, Miss Russell."

"Well, to be perfectly honest, sir, I cannot imagine that you are about to join me in accusing your future bride's father of murder and embezzlement, to say nothing of a little arson too!"

"I would hardly do that, Miss Russell, for there is no evidence."

"How very fortunate for you."

His lips pressed angrily together. "I begin to think, madam, that the ending of our engagement was more of a blessing than I had hitherto realized!"

She thrust the champagne glass back into his hand and got up, her face flushed with anger. "Again I say," she breathed, "how very fortunate for you!"

He caught her hand before she could walk away. "Did your father have any evidence against Repton and the duke?"

"He did, but if that evidence were still in existence do you honestly imagine I would have held my tongue about it? More than anything else in the world I want to clear my father's name and see his murderers pay the penalty for their odious crimes, but there isn't any evidence now and so my hands are tied! If their intention was to destroy the evidence as well as my father, then they certainly succeeded. Look at all that is left of this house, my lord earl, look at it! Blackened walls and the sky for a roof, and rat-infested cellars which have long since been ransacked of anything even remotely usable!''

She wrenched her hand away. ''Sir Frederick and the duke did their work very well indeed; they left nothing to chance and so have been able to wax fine and fat these past five years. You have come very late on the scene, sir, for things have been going along very nicely for those two evil men, and will continue to go along in the same comfortable way.''

He got up, seeing that she was trembling with emotion, and he took her hand again, but more gently this time. ''Forgive me, I did not mean to upset you so.''

''And you will have to forgive me, sir, if I find your sudden interest a little hard to stomach!''

He released her. ''I am obviously guilty of a great deal in your eyes, madam, but whatever I may have done, my crimes surely do not rank alongside those of Repton and Bellingham! Well, do they?''

''No.''

''Thank you for that small crumb of comfort,'' he replied coldly.

She turned to walk away.

''So, you are going to turn your back on the past, are you?'' he called after her.

''How dare you say that!'' she cried, halting.

''Why? It's true, isn't it? I have told you that I agree with your evidence at the inquiry, but rather than speak further of it you choose to leave. I realize that we are strangers to each other now, Miss Russell, but I had not realized that we spoke alien tongues too.

''We might as well for all the good it does to try to converse; the past intrudes far too much, sir.''

''Then let us attempt to converse as two people who revere Denzil Russell and who wish to rewrite his epitaph.''

Slowly she looked at him. ''What is the point?'' she whispered, her voice barely audible.

But he heard her. ''The mighty have been known to tumble, Miss Russell.

Her mouth twisted wryly. ''Oh, I know, sir, I know only too well.''

''Yes, I suppose you do. Well? Are you still going to walk away?''

''What will it achieve if I stay?''

''Maybe nothing at all, but at least we will have tried.''

We? Why was he suddenly bothering about it? It could only be a belated guilty conscience, the sure knowledge that he had played his own despicable part in destroying her. . . .

He could see the antipathy in her eyes, but chose to ignore it. "Tell me about the evidence your father had."

"To do that would be to accuse again the family you are about to join, my lord."

"I already know you accuse them, so telling me the details will hardly make all that much difference, madam."

"Very well." She went up to the terrace again, for from there she could see the house more clearly, and one room in particular. "It was something which happened in the library some two days before the fire. It was very late, I remember, and Mrs. Kean, the housekeeper, came to tell me that my father was still in the library and she didn't like to disturb him to ask him if he wished to have supper. It wasn't like my father to remain so long in the library in the evenings, especially in the winter; he preferred to bring whatever he was reading into the drawing room to sit with me. He couldn't bear being alone after my mother died. . . ."

"Go on."

"So I went to see him. He was sitting in darkness, the curtains undrawn so that I could clearly see the snow falling outside. At first I thought he wasn't there, but then I saw him, sitting in his favorite chair by the fire. Do you remember that chair, my lord? It was very large and had a high back and was upholstered in fine French tapestry."

"Yes, I remember it."

Their eyes met for a moment and then she looked away toward the little that remained of the library again. "I was alarmed because he hadn't even lit a candle, and I asked him if something was wrong. He didn't reply, so I took a spill to the lamp on his desk. There were a number of bank ledgers there and a little book containing page after page of figures, all in my father's neat hand. He must have been laboring for hours and had gone through those ledgers with a fine-tooth comb. He spoke then, he said: *'I don't know how long it's been going on, Adele, but I do know how much has been embezzled. I know how it was done, by whom and why, and I believe that I will be able to prove it.'* I asked him who had done it, but at first he wouldn't say, then he admitted that Frederick Repton had done it in order to aid the Duke of Bellingham, who had promised him fat rewards in return."

"So that book was the evidence?"

"Yes."

"What happened then."

"Well, the next morning my father was taken ill with an ague. I believe it was caused by a combination of sitting for so long in a cold room and by the shock of what he had found out. He was very ill indeed, and so I sent for the doctor. I was with the doctor in the library, discussing my father, when Frederick Repton came to the house. He said that he needed the ledgers my father had taken home, but I could tell that he was afraid his activities had been discovered. I was wary enough to play the innocent, I gave him the ledgers without betraying what I knew. The notebook was gone, I don't know where it went."

"Your father had already hidden it?"

"He must have done, but I have no idea where. Two days later, when my father was still too ill to move from his bed, the fire began and the flames were terrible outside his room almost immediately. It was impossible to save him." Her voice broke a little and she turned her face away, trying to compose herself before going on. "The house was burned to the ground and within days the scandal began. Sir Frederick and your future father-in-law are safe, my lord earl. You do not need to concern yourself about the wisdom of allying yourself to the House of Bellingham, which, unlike the House of Russell, is not about to fall."

"And what, pray, would you know about my thoughts or intentions, Miss Russell?" he asked frostily.

"Nothing, sir, and nor—to be honest—do I wish to. You have been out of my life for five years and I have long since learned that you care very little about anything in particular, except perhaps yourself. Maybe your conscience prodded you into issuing a timely warning to me about Lord Talbourne, but that was all it was, wasn't it? Perhaps, now that you have learned the truth about what happened when this house burned to the ground, you will understand why learning the identity of Lord Talbourne made all the difference in the world to me. I despise his family, sir, and would not willingly have anything to do with any member of that breed."

"You despise them—and you despise me," he said coolly. "Once again I am aware of intruding. Perhaps you were right after all; it was a mistake to think anything constructive could come out of a conversation between us. I believe we have exhausted the politenesses, don't you? He bowed. "Good day, Miss Russell."

"Good day."

Forgetting her bonnet, she hurried away, descending the sweep of steps to the drive and almost running down the hillside toward the bridge and the lake.

He stood on the terrace watching her. The bells of Bath Abbey suddenly pealed out joyfully in the valley below, just as they would have had he made Miss Adele Russell his wife. Those bells seemed to be mocking him now. His face expressionless, he turned away to go back where his horse was tethered. Lying on the grass once more, he picked up the glass of champagne and refilled it before raising it to the empty air. "Your health, Miss Russell," he murmured, "your health."

Chapter 16

It was not until she reached the deserted lodge again that Adele stopped her headlong flight. The bells still echoed over the surrounding countryside, a sound which was meant to uplift the spirits, but which did nothing at all to lighten her heart. Meeting David Latimer again, in Beech Park of all places, had affected her a great deal, for although she knew she despised him, she was still inordinately disturbed by him. Everything he said and did made her very aware of him, each expression that passed over his face, each inflection of his voice had the power to reach through her defenses and remind her of how very much she had once yearned for him. His smile, even when ironic could wreak havoc with her senses, making the past with its sweet memories all important and the present almost meaningless. . . . And all this in spite of the fact that she could now only despise and distrust him. To compose herself, she walked slowly back down the leafy lane, trying to put him from her thoughts, but not succeeding very well at all.

The unpleasant sensation that she was being followed came over her quite slowly, creeping like a shiver. Her first thought was that it must be the earl riding down from Beech Park, but when she turned, the lane was deserted. Everything was very still, except for the noise of the church bells resounding from the valley. She stood there for a while, looking around, then walked on, but the feeling remained, growing in intensity. It was unnerving to suspect that someone was there, behind her somewhere, watching everything she did but remaining out of sight all the time.

She had reached a row of small new villas on the outskirts of the town when at last the sensation became reality. The stretch of road was open, offering no shelter, and without warning she turned sharply to look back. The man had no time to step out of sight and was forced to stand there by the entrance of one of the villas, trying to look as if he was waiting for someone. She recognized him as the man she had seen in the Circus, the same man she had also noticed in Milsom Street. Her heart began to beat more swiftly and her thoughts raced. Surely it could not be coincidence that this was the third time she had seen him—but what else could it be? Why would he follow her? She had nothing worth stealing, so robbery was not his purpose, and nor was assault, for he had had opportunity enough in the emptiness of Beech Park. But he was following her, she was not mistaken about that.

Fear seized her then and she hurried on to the center of the town, her steps becoming more and more swift as the minutes passed. She glanced frequently behind and saw that the man was keeping pace with her, making no attempt now to conceal himself, as if he knew he had been detected. She ran as if she had wings, her frightened steps sounding inordinately loud in a narrow lane and then broadening to a distant patter as she reached a wide thoroughfare where several carriages were moving slowly away from the curb outside a church. But even the safety of the small crowd of worshipers did not halt her flight; she did not stop until she had reached the entrance of the side alley by the haberdashery. There, at last, she came to a standstill, looking back across Milsom Street to where her follower had also come to a standstill. He was breathing heavily, leaning one hand against a railing as he watched her, his face a white blur, featureless and alarming to her in her taut state.

She fled down the alley then, thrusting open the garden door and pushing the bolt across.

Cat and Joanie looked up in surprise as she burst breathlessly into the kitchen. "Lord above!" cried Cat, standing up immediately. "Whatever is the matter?"

"Someone's following me."

Cat stared. "*Following* you?"

"Come through to the shop and I'll show you." Adele caught the older woman's hand and led her from the kitchen. Removing the vase of ostrich plumes from its place right by the window, Adele put a finger to her lips and then carefully pointed out the man who was still leaning breathlessly by the railing. "Do you see him?"

"I do, but what makes you think—"

"I don't just think, Cat, I *know*. He followed me all the way down from Beech Park. When I went faster he went

132

faster, and so I ran nearly all the way. Look at him, he's out of breath from having to run to keep up with me!''

Cat nodded. "But why would he follow you?''

"I don't know.''

Joanie leaned forward then. "I know him,'' she said. "His name's Jake Cottler; he's Sir Frederick Repton's creature.''

Adele's eyes widened with dismay and Cat stepped slowly back from the window, her voice heavy. "Oh, my lordy, lordy. Still, he may not have seen anything, he may not know you went to see the earl at Royal Crescent.''

"No, he may not, but he will certainly have seen me with him today.''

"Today?''

"The Earl of Blaisdon was at Beech Park, Cat. I spent some time talking to him. Mr. Jake Cottler cannot have failed to see.'' A great coldness wrapped itself around Adele as she continued to stare out at the man. "Oh, Cat,'' she whispered fearfully, "what if he knows about the masquerade? What if he knows about my meetings with Lord Talbourne in Sydney Gardens?''

Cat seized her hands swiftly. "He cannot know about all that, Adele, for if he did, then Sir Frederick would have been here before now.''

"He's going now; no doubt Sir Frederick is about to learn all about my latest tryst with the Earl of Blaisdon.'' Adele watched the man walk quickly down Milsom Street.

"Well, there's nothing we can do about it, is there?'' Cat smiled, for it was a statement rather than a question.

"Except try to think of something convincing to say.''

"Convincing enough to persuade Sir Frederick that you haven't gone against him? I doubt if there's anything *that* convincing, Adele.''

"It will have to be, Cat, it will have to be.''

Later that Sunday darkness had fallen and the oil lamp cast its soft light over the kitchen when the three women distinctly heard someone knocking at the shop door. Cat slowly lowered her newspaper and Joanie looked up fearfully from the engrossing pages of *La Belle Assemblée*. There was something about the peremptory knocking that told them all that their visitor was Sir Frederick Repton.

Adele got up. All day she had been waiting for this moment and now it was upon her. She did not know if she would be able to bluff her way through the next few minutes, but she would have to try for all her worth. Pulling her shawl nervously around her shoulders, she went through to the shop where the noise of the silver cane upon the door was very loud. She unbolted the door and stood aside for him to enter. His top hat was pulled down over his forehead and he had turned up the collar of his overcoat. He pushed the door open the final few inches with his cane, removing his hat only when he had stepped into the shelter of the shop.

She closed the door and turned to face him. His pale gaze swept over her like the touch of ice. "I believe you know why I am here," he said softly, the very softness of his voice filling those simple words with menace.

"If you will come through to the back, sir . . ."

"I will not step beyond this point, Miss Russell. I say again, I believe you know why I am here. I issued you a very specific warning and you have chosen to ignore it."

She took a deep breath, holding his chill gaze as squarely as she could and hoping that her fear did not stare out of her eyes. "I didn't ignore what you said to me, Sir Frederick."

"Come now, my man tells me you were with Blaisdon at Beech Park this very morning."

"I did not know he was there. Our meeting was quite accidental, Sir Frederick, I swear that it was." She could say this with all honesty, for it was the truth.

He detected the ring of truth. "Very well, and if I accept that to be so, will you also say that you happened by accident to walk from here to his town house, knock upon the door, and gain admittance? Will you say that you happened to remain there, still accidentally, for some fifteen minutes before leaving?"

Her gaze did not waver. "Of course I will not pretend that to have been an accident, Sir Frederick. The earl sent for me."

His eyebrow flickered. "Indeed? And why would he do that?"

"For the same reasons you came to see me."

"Is that so?"

"Like you, he has no wish to have past events raked over now and he sent for me to tell me so."

He pursed his thin, colorless lips, his shrewd, penetrating eyes not moving from hers. She waited in an agony of anxiety. Was that enough? Had she convinced him? Or would

134

he now move on to other things—the masquerade, perhaps, or the meetings in the Vauxhall. . . .

At last he nodded a little, obviously crediting David Latimer with the same aims he himself had. "Very well, I accept that you had no choice in the matter."

"I would not be foolish enough to flagrantly disobey your warning, Sir Frederick," she replied, trying to conceal the rush of relief that washed through her.

"Oh, you would, Miss Russell, you would, for old habits die hard, and I think you forget that I am no longer merely your father's clerk."

"No, Sir Frederick, I never forget who you are."

The cold silver of the cane handle was raised to her cheek, pressing softly. "Be warned again, and remember that this will be the last time, for I can accept one transgression, but two transgressions stretch my credulity. Three would convince me that you are a danger to me. I told you before to be content with your lengths of ribbon and your safety, but if I hear again that you have had dealings—no matter how seemingly innocent!—with the Earl of Blaisdon, then you may kiss farewell to those pretty ribbons and that blessed safety. My fear of scandal does not give you the ultimate protection, Miss Russell, for my determination to safeguard all I now have and all that I will have in the near future will not let me hesitate to dispose of you—and those who are near to you. The momentary flurry of excitement caused by your extinction would swiftly be forgotten; you would be no more and my existence would go on as before. Do I make myself supremely clear this time?"

"Yes." Her voice was almost silent.

"I did not hear you, Miss Russell."

"Yes, you are supremely clear to me, Sir Frederick."

"Good. I will not dally here in further idle chitchat, even in your delightful company. What a pleasure it is to speak with you, such a change from the dull conversation of ladies of quality. Good night, Miss Russell."

"Good night."

He put on his top hat again and then stepped out into the darkness, his steps dying away into the night. Slowly, and with shaking hands, she closed the door again, turning with a gasp as someone touched her shoulder—but it was only Cat.

"Are you all right, Adele?"

"I think so."

"I heard everything he said. He meant each word."

"I know."

"Please, my dear, pay good heed to him. Don't have anything more to do with the Earl of Blaisdon. Oh, I know that today was not your fault, but—"

"What can I do if I happen to see him as I did up at Beech Park? I will do all I can to stay on the right side of Sir Frederick, but I cannot promise the moon as well."

Cat nodded sadly. "I know, my love, I know. Come on back into the kitchen now, we'll all have something good and strong in a warm drink. Joanie too, for she looks fit to faint clean away."

Adele smiled and nodded. But as she followed Cat her smile faded a little and there was a hint of apprehension in her eyes. When would all this end? When would she be left alone to settle back into the life she had so struggled to accept? She felt so very vulnerable, threatened not only by Sir Frederick Repton and the Duke of Bellingham, but also by the duke's son and daughter. And there was always David Latimer. . . . When would they leave her alone, leave her to get on with her life?

Chapter 17

Several days passed before events inexorably closed in upon Adele, and when they did it was at a moment when she was feeling strangely safe again, simply because nothing had happened.

Not wanting to run any risk whatsoever, she had remained in the haberdashery since Sir Frederick's second visit, but as the days passed she began to feel confined. As so it was that one morning, a particularly fine and sunny morning, when the haberdashery was not doing much in the way of trade, she volunteered to go to buy some more tea. Promising to be on her guard, she emerged from the side alley in her dimity gown and shawl, a gypsy bonnet with mauve ribbons on her head. Across the street she immediately noticed Jake Cottler in his usual position, but he was more interested in the charms of a saucy milkmaid than he was in attending to his duty. He did not see Adele leave and set off down Milsom Street to purchase the orange pekoe.

She had finished her errand and was on her way home again when she noticed the small crowd gathered by the window of the print shop. When she joined them she saw that the attraction was Mr. Cruickshank's latest caricature of the Prince Regent. The drawing was very accurate and very unkind, but in spite of this she had to smile, for there was no mistaking the artist's genius—the unfortunate Prince was there for all to grin at, a ridiculous figure in tight fashions that revealed only too clearly his immense girth.

Milsom Street was as busy as ever as she stood there, looking at the other prints displayed in the window, and the general noise was such that at first she did not hear the voice hailing her from the carriageway.

"Lady Domino!"

At last the voice made an impression upon her and she froze, her heart almost stopping. Only one person would call her that—Lord Talbourne. Why, oh *why* had she paused by this cursed window? Slowly and reluctantly she turned in the direction of the voice. From the perch of the yellow phaeton drawn up at curb he smiled at her.

He jumped down lightly, handing the reins to the waiting tiger. "So, at last I have found you again, just when I thought I had exhausted all avenues." Removing his top hat, he bowed over her cold hand. His hazel eyes were as warm and lazily inviting as ever and he looked very handsome indeed in his sage-green coat and gray trousers, but there was no trace in her heart now of that former attraction, no trace at all. He was no longer her Sir Mask; he was Lord Talbourne, only son and heir of the hated Duke of Bellingham. She felt no pleasure at all at seeing him again, only a growing fear and a desperate desire to flee. But he held her hand still, his thumb moving softly against her palm as he continued to smile into her frightened eyes, not noticing her obvious reluctance and dismay.

"Fate is determined to be kind to me at last," he said, drawing her aside from the crowd by the print shop. "I thought when you ran away from me that I would never see you again. I know that I failed you, that I sinned very much indeed when I said what I did, but now I only want the chance to set matters right between us, to begin again. Say that you forgive me."

She stared at him in confusion. What was he talking about? "F-forgive you?"

"Come now, I know that I upset you greatly and that that is why you ran from me. I had no business at all asking you what I did; it was just that I let my desire for you take precedence over everything."

At last she understood; he was referring to asking her to be his mistress. "Oh. I forgive you, of course I do." She glanced miserably around, wondering if it would be possible to dart away from him into the crowds, but he still had not released her hand.

He smiled again, drawing her palm to his lips. "Say you will meet me again," he pleaded softly. "For I have never been more desolate in my life than I have been these past days without seeing you."

"Please, I cannot."

"Yes, you can. You wear no ring and I do not believe you are promised to anyone. There is no reason why you cannot allow me one small favor. All I ask is that you meet me again.''

''No!'' The word came out more sharply than she had intended.

At last her unease communicated itself fully to him and his smile began to fade. ''You tell me that I am forgiven, and yet you are cool with me. You are become an ice queen, madam, and I believe I have the right to know why, for you were certainly no snow maiden at the masquerade, nor again when you allowed certain liberties in Sydney Gardens!'' Anger stirred in his eyes and his grip tightened on her hand, making escape an impossibility. ''Well, madam? I believe I await your reply.''

Desperation made her hasty and she tried to twist away. Sensing now that there was far more to this than met the eye, he maintained his hold, his gaze very dark with anger now.

''So,'' he breathed, ''you have played the coquette with me, teasing and enticing, promising with your every gesture! I am not a man to be toyed with in that easy manner, madam, and I will not submit lightly to your damned caprices!''

Sir Frederick's warning was ever present as she glanced fearfully around, afraid that her predicament would attract the very attention she must at all costs avoid, but no one was paying any heed at all. To all intents and purposes she and Lord Talborne looked like lovers; he held her close, her hand clasped in both his, his face barely inches from hers. ''Please,'' she begged again, ''please let me go.''

For the first time, he noticed her clothes, his astounded glance taking in the neat but hardly expensive gypsy bonnet and the plain, serviceable dimity gown. These were not the clothes of a fine lady! His eyes hardened. ''Who are you?'' he asked softly. ''Who the devil *are* you?''

Feeling his grip relax just a little, she wrenched away from him, turning into the crowds on the pavement and fleeing for all she was worth.

Stunned, for a moment he remained where he was, but then he snatched the reins from the tiger and leaped up into the high seat, whipping the nervous team of bays into action. The tiger barely had time to jump to his place at the rear of the vehicle as it began to move swiftly away. From his vantage point above the heads of the crowd, Rex could see everything, including the bouncing mauve ribbons of Adele's bonnet as she ran up the street. In her haste she saw nothing of the phaeton. As she fled into the haberdashery Rex slowed down, drawing his vehicle to a standstill close to the shop.

He waited for some time for her to come out again, thinking that she had gone to make a purchase, but as the minutes passed and lady after lady emerged, he began to grow suspicious. He urged the team just a little further along the street, halting right by the doorway of the shop, and then he saw her. His Lady Domino was serving behind the counter. She was an assistant, a damned shop wench! She was the woman in trade his sister had mentioned!

A spark of bitter anger flared into his heart, and the veneer of charm faded from his face, leaving only his prideful, selfish, and unpleasant self. A nerve twitched at his temple and he clenched the reins so harshly that the leather of his fine gloves was stretched and taut. No wonder she had been so anxious and afraid all the time! No wonder she had refused to identify herself! How could he have been so besotted, so blind that he had not noticed her poor clothing? What a fool she had made of him. How the world would curl up with mirth when it learned that Lord Talbourne had been duped by a haberdasher's assistant! Humiliation and the fear of ridicule seized him in its relentless grasp. By God she would pay dearly for her sins; she would regret her pretense, her falseness, and her impudence! She would regret the day she had been born when at last he had finished taking his full revenge. And that revenge would begin with a taste of what her kisses had promised; he would take his counterfeit lady and enjoy those charms that had filled his thoughts since the first moment he had seen her!

The whip cracked loudly as he galvanized the team into action again, turning the vehicle in the middle of the busy street and almost causing an accident before he whipped the bays again, bringing them up to a foolhardy pace.

In the haberdashery Adele looked up from serving Mrs. Harriman, hearing the whip cracks and the shouts of the other road users, but she didn't give the moment more than passing consideration. She believed she had escaped from Rex and that she was safe again. She had no idea that it was already too late, that all attempts to conceal her actions had been in vain and the world was about to learn of her activities after all.

She had managed to put the incident by the print shop out of her mind when at last the time came to close the shop and take down the tulles. She had almost completed tidying up the doorway and was humming a little as she took down the last length of gauze, but the humming was abruptly extinguished a moment later when someone roughly caught her arms and propelled her into the shadows of the side alley. The tulles spilled from her hands and were trampled as she was overpowered and thrust back against the wall, a hand over her mouth to silence her.

Her eyes were huge and frightened as she stared up into Rex's cold, mocking face. "So," he murmured, "we meet yet again, my *lady*! Is it a new rage then, for ladies of quality to pretend to be shop assistants? Or is it perhaps the other way around—shop assistants like to pretend they are ladies! Oh, you must have thought yourself quite the tippy, dressed up in finery, dancing with gentlemen and even going so far as to dare to make an assignation with the son of a duke!"

Slowly he removed his hand from her mouth, but he still pressed her against the wall so that she could not escape. "Please," she whispered, "I didn't mean any harm and I didn't mean to insult you in any way."

"But you did insult me, my sweet, you insulted me very much indeed. And you made a fool of me, something I cannot and will not forgive."

"No. No—"

"You thought you would trifle with me, leading me on, promising me everything with your kisses and soft words—"

"No!"

"You played the coquette, my love, and now the time has come for you to pay the price."

Her eyes widened. "I didn't play the coquette; I didn't lead you on! Not in that way!"

"No? Does a *lady* behave the way you did? Does a lady permit kisses on her very first meeting, or keep assignations with a man she knows nothing of? I think not. You played the whore, sweetheart, and you have been found out. There is a forfeit." He put his hand softly to her pale cheek, caressing her a little.

"I would as soon take poison as have you for my lover," she breathed.

His eyes flickered a little. "The choice is yours, my love; either you come to me or your tawdry little secret will be announced to the world. Think carefully now."

At that moment she heard the watch calling further down

141

the street, and before Rex knew what had happened, she screamed for help. With a sharp intake of breath, he moved away from her, his lips white with rage.

"Very well," he breathed. "Very well; you have made your choice!" Then he was gone and she leaned her head weakly against the wall, trying to quell the sobs that rose sharply within her. He had gone and she could hear the watch shouting, for they had heard her scream but did not know from where the sound had come. Ever mindful of Sir Frederick Repton, she remained silent, her eyes closed as she struggled to overcome the violent trembling. Gradually the shouts of the watch faded into the distance and everything was quiet again.

Slowly she bent to pick up the trampled tulles. There was no escape anymore; her misdeeds had finally caught up with her and she could expect no mercy from Lord Talbourne. She would be punished—and Cat would be punished too. Tears sprang to her eyes; it was all her own fault; she had done it all without being forced; she had *chosen* to conduct herself in a way that would bring the wrath of society down upon her should she be found out, and now she had been found out, once and for all.

How Cat would wish that she had after all left Bath five years before. Even as the thought came into her head, Adele knew that that was still the only solution. If she left Bath now, then the haberdashery would stand a chance of coming through the storm Lord Talbourne intended should break. Yes, that was the only way, for none of this was Cat's fault; she and Joanie should not suffer because of Adele Russell's vanity and selfishness!

She folded the tulles. She would have to wait until later when Cat and Joanie had gone to bed before she would be able to slip around to the York House Hotel, the nearest coaching inn, to find out the times of the mails and stages that went to London. And for the rest of the evening she would have to behave as if all were well.

Chapter 18

Dinner at the Bellingham residence was a silent affair that evening. The duke was in a gloomy mood after being denied a bottle of port, and the duchess was in high dudgeon because he had dared to demand it. Euphemia had commenced the meal philosophically enough, but the surrounding atmosphere proved too much and her attempts at conversation had died away. Her parents' surliness toward each other was nothing new; she had lived with that all her life, but there was something odd about Rex. His face was withdrawn and—yes, it was angry—a quivering, barely controlled anger, which was really quite frightening.

He retired to his room directly after dinner, taking with him a decanter of cognac, and Euphemia did not delay to follow him. She found him lounging in a chair by the window that looked out over the cobbled inner area of the Circus.

She sat down on the edge of his bed. "Well?" she said. "Are you going to tell me what's wrong?"

"And why should something be wrong?"

"You are as cheerful as a requiem and you look set to finish that entire decanter."

"You're too sharp; you'll cut yourself one day."

"So Heydon used to frequently pray."

He drained the glass of cognac and refilled it. "Which haberdashery do you go to in this damned place?"

She stared at him and then gave a short laugh. "Which *haberdashery*? Rex, what is all this?"

"It was a perfectly reasonable question," he replied, the cognac swirling.

"All right. I go to Miss Rogers."

"At the top of Milsom Street?"

"Near the top. Why?" Her face became still. "Why, Rex?"

"The assistant there, a certain jade with golden hair—" He

143

gave a thin smile. "The woman in trade I believe you once mentioned to me."

"What of her?" Euphemia's voice was sharp.

"Who is she?"

"No one of any importance."

"I can find out simply by asking elsewhere, but I believe it would be better if I learned the truth from you. You say that she is of no importance, but she is very important indeed to me at the moment. And I believe by your reaction that she is important to you too, for some reason or other. Who is she?"

"Her name is Russell."

A light passed through his hazel eyes. "*The* Russell?"

She avoided his gaze. "I don't know what you mean."

"Oh, come on, Euphemia! Is she the same wench who once took Blaisdon from you?"

"She is Denzil Russell's daughter, yes."

He laughed then. "Dear God above, Latimer's first love! No *wonder* any mention of her brings out the poison in you, dear sister!"

"What is she to you?"

"I think you already know. I asked you if you knew any ladies who fitted a certain description—"

"Adele Russell is hardly a lady!" she snapped.

"Possibly not, but she certainly remembers how to conduct herself as one."

Euphemia's cheeks were flushed with anger. "Are you telling me that she is definitely your—your Lady Domino?"

"I am. She attended Mama's precious masquerade, danced a wicked waltz with the Earl of Blaisdon, snubbed him quite magnificently—I still doff my hat to her for that— and then she kept several assignations with me in Sydney Gardens."

Euphemia's cheeks paled as she got slowly to her feet. "How dare she," she breathed. "How *dare* she!"

He smiled. "My sentiments precisely."

"How did you find out the truth?"

"I saw her today, serving behind the counter. She duped me completely; she made the greatest of fools of me, which insult she will pay dearly for."

"You must have been very easy to fool," replied Euphemia, rounding on him. "How could you not notice that she was no lady of high fashion? Oh, I admit that at the masquerade she somehow produced clothes fit for such an occasion, but I doubt very much whether that appearance could have been maintained all the time."

"True, but then I was hardly aware of what she was wearing. She is a very tasty little morsel, sis, very tasty indeed. Besides, she wore a cape most of the time and I merely assumed that beneath the cape she wore togs as elegant as yours."

"But now you know better, and I'll warrant the realization is giving your digestion considerable torment."

"As what I've just told you is giving *you* similar torment. It must be supremely galling to realize that after five years Latimer picked her out at the masquerade. Even with her face and hair hidden, she could lure him."

"Stop it!"

"Face the truth, sis; your hold upon him is no greater now than it was then. However, it could be that all this will turn out to your advantage in the end."

"How?"

"I intend to expose her—as publicly as possible."

"I don't want her in the public eye," his sister replied swiftly.

"Possibly not, but you want to make certain of driving a wedge between the lady and Blaisdon once and for all, don't you?"

"What sort of wedge?"

"I hardly imagine he would respect in any way a woman who had eagerly entered into a torrid affair with a bitter enemy of his."

"Are you telling me that you and she—?"

"I did not go unrewarded, if that is what you are wondering," he replied, surveying the amber liquid in his glass. "I was her lover."

Euphemia flinched. "I don't wish to know—" Her eyes sharpened then and she looked at her brother. "*Why* are you such a bitter enemy of his?"

"Ah, that would be telling."

"I think I have a right to know."

"No, sis, you don't."

"I shall marry him if I can, Rex," she warned.

"And I shall obstruct such a wedding, if I can," he replied, draining the glass.

"You will not be able to."

"I shall do my damnedest, for if there is one man on this

145

earth I refuse to accept as a member of my family, it's Blaisdon!"

"He must have made a bigger fool of you than she has," she said lightly, her skirts rustling as she went to the window.

It was his turn to flush now. "You know nothing of it!" he snapped.

"No, so I shall make up a suitable story to fit what I know of him—and you, dear brother."

He put the glass down. "You don't know me at all, Euphemia, even though you pride yourself that you do. I have been away from you for six years, and that is a damned long time in the life of any man. Besides, it hardly matters at the moment what lies between myself and Blaisdon. I am more concerned at punishing Miss Adele Russell for her presumption!"

"Punishing her?" she asked guardedly. "In what way?"

"By exposing her, as I have already said."

"Yes, but in what way? By placing a notice in the newspaper?" She laughed. "That would reach the attention of all those who should know."

"Very droll. I was thinking more along the lines of facing her in the haberdashery—when there are a number of influential ladies present, if possible. I thought we could go there tomorrow."

"You can leave me out of this."

His eyes moved instantly to her. "You would prefer to let her get away with it?" he asked incredulously. "I can't believe that of you, my dear sister."

"I intend to deal with Miss Russell in my own way," she said mysteriously. "And that way certainly does not include dramatic confrontations in crowded haberdasheries. You do as you please, Rex, but I will not be associated with your actions in any way."

"What does your 'own way' mean?"

She smiled a little. "My dear Rex, I have no intention of telling you. You have your little secrets, and so do I."

"*Touché!*" He smiled at her. "Very well, we agree to differ. I don't even begin to guess what you are plotting, but I believe that my own way of dealing with the lady is the best one. I shall visit that haberdashery tomorrow, and by the end of the day the whole of Bath will be acquainted with her daunting list of sins against society."

Euphemia did not reply, but her face was thoughtful.

Adele was enduring one of the most difficult evenings of her life, employing every last shred of acting ability in order to appear as natural as possible in front of Cat. At all costs, Cat must believe that all was well, so Adele forced herself to eat as much as possible of the ham and salad Joanie served at the evening meal. Afterward she sat trying to appear very engrossed in Mrs. Radcliffe's much-praised novel, *The Mysteries of Udolpho*, but although she turned the pages, she did not see a single word. Her heart was breaking, but not by so much as a flicker did she betray this. Cat was a mother to her now, and leaving her was like turning her back on her own flesh and blood; but leaving Bath and thus giving the haberdashery a chance of salvaging something seemed the only solution.

Joanie retired early, but Cat seemed in no particular hurry, patiently reading every word of every column of the newspaper before at last folding it and getting up.

Stretching, the old nurse looked down at Adele, still apparently deep in the book. "Well, that's my day over and done with. Are you coming up now, Adele?"

"I-I think I'll just finish this bit—"

"Very well. Good night then, and don't stay up too long; we've a shop to open in the morning."

The tears sprang to Adele's eyes at those words, but she managed a smile. She waited until the house was silent and then went to pick up her reticule and shawl, tying on her bonnet and listening again on the landing before creeping stealthily down and out of the back door.

Luckily the York House Hotel was not far; since the watch could be heard nearby, she didn't feel in any danger as she hurried up Milsom Street and turned right into George Street. The coaching inn was fairly quiet, and the booking clerk sat in his small office, a weak lamp throwing a pale glow over his wrinkled face. There was little for him to do at this time of night, and he jumped when Adele rapped on his glass window.

Cautiously he opened it. "Yes?"

"What time is there a coach to London?"

"Mail or stage?"

"Either."

"You've missed the mail."

"A stage then," she said patiently.

147

"Not until morning."

Her heart sank. "Isn't there one at midnight?"

"Not anymore, not enough fares. You should've come earlier."

"What time in the morning is it leaving?"

"Nine."

She took a long, heavy breath. That was so late, after the shop had opened. It would be very difficult indeed for her to leave without Cat or Joanie seeing. But what choice did she have? She seized a straw. "Is there another coach tonight?"

"Where to?"

"Anywhere."

He sniffed. "You're desperate, aren't you? Well there's nothing going anywhere, not until that London stage goes anyway. It's not the season; there isn't much call for nighttime travel."

"All right, I wish to travel on the London stage. Is there an inside seat left?"

"No, only outside."

"Are you sure?"

"Listen, it's my job to know things like that," he said testily, a grubby, ink-stained finger tapping on the open ledger before him. "All insides are taken. So if you want to get to London on that stage, you'll have to take your chance on the top."

"Please make sure, someone might have canceled their—"

"Now you look here," he growled. "If I say there's no insides, then there's no insides—right? I know exactly what's what because if I overbook, then the proprietor must provide the extra passengers with some other form of transport, and that means a post chaise at ninepence a mile instead of about fourpence. If that happens, then it isn't the proprietor who puts his hand in his pocket, it's me! Now then, if we've got that straight, perhaps you'd like to book on a later coach if you're set upon an inside seat."

"No," she said resignedly. "No, I'll go outside on the nine o'clock."

"Right." He picked up his quill and dipped it in the huge inkwell. "Let's have your name and details."

"Details?"

"Luggage and so on."

"My name is Miss Smith."

"Oh yes?" he remarked drily, "And mine's Napoleon

148

Bonaparte. Still, it's your business. Will you be carrying luggage, Miss Smith?"

"A portmanteau."

"Over five pounds in value? If so then there's an extra premium to be paid."

"No, not over five pounds."

He finished scratching across the ledger with the quill. "That's half fare to be paid in advance, and you forfeit it if you don't turn up."

She pushed the coins through the opening and he picked them up, counting them laboriously into a wooden bowl. Then he sniffed. "You're booked on the nine o'clock then."

"Thank you."

"And you'd best start praying for fine weather, hadn't you?"

She said nothing, turning slowly away and leaving the quiet yard where there was a solitary stagecoach, its team sweating and its weary passengers climbing thankfully down at the end of their journey. For a moment she looked at them. Tomorrow she would be alighting from a stagecoach as they did now. Tomorrow she would be in London.

Chapter 19

The following morning dawned blustery and overcast, and Adele sat on the edge of her bed as Cat called a little crossly from the bottom of the stairs. "Adele, you lazybones! Hurry up now, it's half-past eight and I have to open the shop!"

Adele bowed her head and a solitary tear wended its slow way down her pale cheek before she got up to put on her gray cape and the gypsy bonnet. Looking in the mirror, she saw that her face was very drawn and that there were shadows beneath her tear-reddened eyes. A frame of golden curls peeped from beneath her bonnet, but the pretty mauve ribbons looked forlorn instead of gay, and there was a heaviness about her movements as she bent to pick up the portmanteau. Glancing around her little room for the last time, she went out, closing the door very softly before carefully descending the stairs, listening all the while for sound of Cat or Joanie.

The kitchen was silent and she hurried through to the back door, realizing that Cat had dragooned the maid into helping open the shop. The herbs lining the ash path smelled particularly fresh and the wind had blown some rose petals to the ground, but she hardly noticed anything in the garden; she was intent only upon reaching the side alley without either Cat or Joanie realizing what had happened. From there it would be easy enough to wait until they had finished working at the shop door and gone back inside, leaving her free to cross Milsom Street and make her way to the York House Hotel in good time for the nine o'clock stagecoach. But as she opened the alley door and stepped through, her plans fell into immediate disarray, for at the end of the alley she saw a yellow phaeton drawing to a standstill and a gentleman climbing down to hand the ribbons to the waiting tiger. It was Rex, and he was right by the alley, leaving her no chance at all of escaping without him seeing. Dismay filled her and she could have wept, having got so far only to be trapped virtually at the post. Pressing back among the shadows, she waited for a moment, but he remained there on the pavement, an elegant figure in his dull blue coat and slate-gray trousers, his silk cravat blowing a little in the wind. How very handsome he was; it was difficult even now to believe that beneath that charming, attractive exterior he was cold and despicable, the very opposite in every way to a gentleman. She waited, willing him to go away, but he remained where he was, glancing now and then at his fob watch as if he were waiting for something. She knew as she watched him that it was no coincidence that he was there at this early hour; he had come to carry out his threat.

Miserably she turned back into the garden. She did not dare to linger for the minutes were passing inexorably by and she must be at the York House Hotel before nine. Each second that passed was vital if she was to slip through his closing net. Her only chance now would be to leave through the shop, trusting that her bonnet and cape would give her a little protection and maybe conceal her identity from him. Once in the crowds on the pavement, she could perhaps reach the hotel. But first she must get past Cat!

The kitchen was still mercifully empty, but even as she went softly toward the door to the shop, it opened and she came face-to-face with Joanie. The maid's startled glance immediately took in the significance of the cape, bonnet, and portmanteau. Her mouth opened to call Cat, but Adele silenced her with a glare.

"Not one word will pass your lips, Joanie Smith! Not one word!"

"But—"

"Is there anyone in the shop with Cat?"

Dumbly the maid nodded. "Several. The Misses Mortimer and—"

"Is Cat busy then?"

"Yes."

"I want you to call her through to the kitchen."

"Me?" Joanie was horrified. "But why? What must I say? She'll kill me, Miss Russell, you know that she will!"

"If you value your position here, Joanie, you'll do this for me. If you do not, then you'll have no position to consider. Lord Talbourne knows everything, and he has threatened to make my actions known to one and all. I must leave and give

Cat and the haberdashery a chance. You do see that, don't you?''

The maid's eyes filled with tears and she nodded. ''Oh, Miss Russell—''

''Call her for me, Joanie.''

Impulsively the maid flung her arms around Adele's neck, hugging her tightly. ''God bless you and keep you safe, Miss Russell,'' she cried, and then she stepped back, smoothing her hands on her apron nervously. Taking a deep breath, she called Cat. ''Miss Rogers? Miss Rogers, will you come and see? Quickly!''

Adele stepped out of sight behind a heavy curtain next to the door, and a moment later she heard Cat bustling through crossly, muttering that she'd have Joanie's hide upon the wall if there was nothing! As soon as Cat had gone past into the kitchen, Adele hurried into the shop, but there, for the second time that morning, her steps halted and she stood looking miserably at the door as Rex came in, having judged that the shop was now sufficiently full for his purpose. She was too late; by a matter of seconds she was too late! Resignedly she stood there, and the customers in the shop looked curiously at her, gradually becoming aware that her strange behavior was caused by the arrival of Lord Talbourne. The younger Miss Mortimer turned to look at him and immediately became all of a dither, her plump little face becoming quite pink and her eyes round with adoration. But Rex did not even know that she was there.

He smiled coolly at Adele. ''Why good morning, Miss Russell. Don't tell me you are about to depart?''

''I-I was going out—''

''But now you will remain to speak to me.'' Slowly he removed his top hat and teased off his gloves finger by finger.

She heard Cat come back into the shop behind her. ''Adele? What is it?''

Rex glanced at her. ''It's nothing for you to concern yourself with—yet.''

''What can I do for you, my lord?'' asked Adele.

''Ah, well I believe that question comes a little late, does it not?'' His eyes moved lazily over her and then came to rest on her large, frightened eyes. ''I came to inquire if you enjoyed my mother's Waterloo masquerade, Miss Russell.''

Gasps greeted this remark and the Misses Mortimer stepped back from the counter as if they feared being burned. Adele

152

was conscious of the sudden hostility in the shop as the gulf between the customers and herself suddenly widened.

Rex smiled. "Does your silence mean that the get-together of the year did not meet with your approval—for to be sure it cannot mean that you don't know what I'm talking about. You were there, weren't you? You masqueraded at a masquerade, Miss Russell. No doubt you even stole the invitation card in order to do so, for the world knows what thieves the Russells are."

Adele's face was ghastly and Cat stepped hastily forward. "My lord, I don't think—"

"Keep out of this, Miss Rogers, if you know what is good for you. Unless, of course, you are as guilty as Miss Russell. Yes, on reflection, you probably are, for you no doubt aided and abetted her throughout."

Cat fell silent. He returned his attention to Adele. "Now then, where were we? Ah, yes, the masquerade. Do admit that you were there, pretending to be the fine lady, for it ill becomes you to try to dissociate yourself from your sins at this late stage."

"I admit that I was there."

She heard the sharp intakes of breath and the almost tangible closing of ranks as the customers looked at her, outrage written large upon their faces.

Rex's smile was triumphant. "Yes," he said softly. "You were there, setting yourself up as the equal of every guest, daring to dance with gentlemen who knew nothing of the truth, that you are the disgraced daughter of a disgraced father, that you serve behind the counter in this shop and are not fit to look them in the eye let alone dance a measure with them." He turned, catching the younger Miss Mortimer's eye. She is quite shameless," he remarked conversationally. "Quite, quite shameless. Do you know, she even neglected that essential item of feminine apparel, a corset? Shameless, immodest, and impudent— those are the words to describe Miss Russell, a brazen adventuress who sought to make good her losses of the past by attempting to ensnare a duke's son."

"She—she attempted to—?" Miss Mortimer couldn't bring herself to say any more, being rendered speechless both by the honor of being addressed by the object of her passion and by the terrible revelations about Adele.

He smiled coolly. "She embarked upon a liaison, or at

153

least she attempted to embark upon one; unfortunately for her she was found out."

At that moment the shop door suddenly opened, the bell ringing loudly in the silence that had fallen. The murmur of surprise that the newcomer caused made Adele look up sharply and Rex turn. David Latimer closed the door, his gaze moving thoughtfully over the little gathering before finally coming to rest on Adele.

"Ah," he said lightly, "I see you are ready."

"Ready?" she asked faintly. Why had he come? Was he too intent upon her destruction once and for all?

"Our appointment."

She stared blankly at him, unable to think clearly anymore and certainly unable to cope with puzzles.

He put his top hat on the counter next to Rex's. "My mother expects you, Miss Russell, and as you are ready to leave, perhaps we should waste no further time—"

The ladies in the shop gaped at him. He was about to become betrothed to the Marchioness of Heydon but was taking *Miss Russell* to an appointment with his mother? Whatever could it mean? Could it possibly be that the haberdasher's assistant was back in favor after all? Bemused glances were exchanged and the atmosphere underwent a faint but perceptible change. If Adele stood a chance of becoming Countess of Blaisdon after all, then not one lady present was about to be fool enough to offend her, not even to please Lord Talbourne!

Rex felt the change. "Look here, Blaisdon," he said. "I don't think you'll be so keen to take Miss Russell anywhere when you know the truth about her."

David turned slowly to look at him, his blue eyes full of withering contempt. "Oh, good morning, Talbourne, I had not noticed you there."

Rex flushed.

"What were you saying about Miss Russell?"

"That she is not fit to meet a lady like your mother."

"Indeed? And why would that be?" David's voice was deceptively light.

"Because she presumed to attend my mother's masquerade, without being invited, and because she then willingly and flagrantly entered into a liaison with me. She is a whore, Blaisdon, and I do not imagine that your mother would wish to be acquainted with such a person."

A pin could have been heard to drop as all eyes moved

154

from Rex to David. A nerve flickered briefly at his temple as he leaned back against the counter, his arms folded and his cold gaze not moving from Rex. "Well now, let us take those accusations one by one, hmm? Miss Russell did indeed attend the masquerade, but there I am afraid that *I* am at fault."

"You?" Rex became wary.

"Yes. You see, I invited her. Oh, it was a liberty, I agree, for I was a mere guest myself, but it seemed such a shame to leave my mother's invitation card unused."

The silence in the shop became deafening as everyone waited.

Rex gave a slight smile. "Very well, Blaisdon, I cannot of course gainsay your words, but I do not believe you can excuse my other accusation."

"Ah, yes, the second accusation." The softly spoken words were followed without warning by a lightning movement that had Rex caught tightly by the knot of his cravat, lifted bodily from the floor, and thrust ignominiously against the array of drawers and trays along the far wall of the shop. The ladies scattered with squeals of alarm and Rex slumped heavily to the floor, winded by the force of the attack. The contents of the drawers spilled over him, a demeaning cascade of ribbons, little feather flowers, and glittering sequins. His elegant, arrogant appearance was no more and he now looked a little ridiculous. Fury darkened his face, twisted his mouth into an ugly snarl as he made to get up again, but David pushed him back down with the toe of a shining boot.

"Not so swiftly, my little lordling. We have yet to discuss your second accusation."

"I'll not do so from here!"

"You'll do so from wherever I choose, my dear fellow."

Rex subsided, his face crimson with frustrated anger and with helpless humiliation. He did not dare defy David Latimer, and that fact was now only too clear to the interested ladies who had gathered together in the relative safety of the opposite corner.

David folded his arms. "Now then, Talbourne, what were you ill advised enough to say of Miss Russell?"

Discretion was belatedly the better part of valor and Rex said nothing.

"Silence, Talbourne?"

Stung, Rex retorted angrily. "You'll regret laying hands upon me, Blaisdon, so help me you will!"

"Really? I doubt that very much." David bent to pick up a

155

little flower fashioned out of dainty white feathers. He dropped it into Rex's lap. "The cowardly game cock sports a white feather again, as he always will, for he is a poor bird."

Adele stared at Rex, whose fury had been replaced by sudden trepidation. His face assumed a ghastly pallor as he looked down at the little flower.

David looked down at him contemptuously. "Now then, shall we set aside your abhorrent accusation? Yes, I think we shall, but first you must apologize to Miss Russell, whose good name you have so gravely sullied."

Defiance flared briefly into life again. "Are you so very sure I've lied about her, Blaisdon?"

"Oh, yes. You see, I know Miss Russell, but I also know you. Would you like me to tell these good ladies of your exploits? No, I can see from your face that that is the very last thing you wish me to do. So apologize nicely to the lady, Talbourne, or so help me you'll hear from my seconds."

The defiance was extinguished, leaving only pure hatred as Rex struggled at last to his feet. But fear of David Latimer held sway, for he turned slowly toward Adele. "I apologize."

David thrust his hat and gloves into his hands. "That was not well done, but it will do to save your pretty life. And now, I fancy your presence here is no longer required. Toddle along, there's a good chap. Oh, and Talbourne—?"

"Yes?"

"Stay away from Miss Russell from now on. She has my protection to call upon should she desire it, and I don't really think you wish to tangle with me again, do you?"

Rex said nothing more, flinging the door open and striding out into the street. A moment later they heard the loud whip crack and briefly saw the phaeton leap past the shop, the nervous, alarmed team tossing their heads wildly.

"Damned fellow never could master the art of driving," murmured David, turning to incline his head apologetically to Cat. "Forgive me for causing such a disturbance, Miss Rogers."

"Th-think nothing of it, my lord."

He glanced at the cluster of ladies. "You may come out now, for I promise you that the excitement is over and you are quite safe."

They stared at him, still totally bemused. What had it all really been about? Was the match with the Marchioness of Heydon on or off? Was it to be the Russell match after all?

156

Or was it nothing to do with any match but simply a bitter antagonism between two men whose paths had crossed before? Whatever the truth of it was, one thing was certain: the Earl of Blaisdon had defended Miss Russell and apologized to Miss Rogers, which meant that it would be socially unwise to avoid the haberdashery. Better to cross the Bellinghams than the Blaisdons.

David offered Adele his arm. "Shall we go now, Miss Russell?"

Cat nodded at her and Adele emerged slowly from behind the counter. He tapped his top hat on his dark curls, inclined his head politely at the silent ladies, and then left with Adele. The moment the door closed behind them the ladies scuttled eagerly forward to ply Cat with questions, questions she was very careful indeed to answer diplomatically, for the battle was not yet entirely won.

Adele hardly knew what was happening as the earl escorted her to his curricle, handed her into it, and then took his place beside her. The tiger gave the earl the ribbons and then took his own position at the rear of the vehicle as the handsome team moved easily away toward George Street, but instead of turning left toward Royal Crescent the curricle was brought around to the right, passing the Royal York Hotel, where Adele's coach had long since departed for London. Bringing the team up to a spanking trot, the earl drove on past the Paragon building and entered London Road with its raised pavements and terraces of pale golden houses. The curricle moved effortlessly along the wide carriageway. Ahead now lay the outskirts of the town and the open countryside.

Adele was dazed, bewildered by the swift sequence of events that had somehow totally changed her plans. By now she should be on her way to London, but instead she was driving with the Earl of Blaisdon. The long catalog of her misdeeds had been announced to the world, but each one had been disposed of by the man now at her side. She gazed ahead as the last houses slipped away behind. She owed everything to him, but why had he done it? Why?

Chapter 20

Adele said nothing as the curricle began the long climb up Swainswick Hill. David glanced at her from time to time. She seemed oblivious to everything, her eyes downcast and her hands clasped neatly in her lap. The mauve ribbons of her bonnet fluttered wildly in the breeze and the hem of her cape flapped as the curricle sped on. She looked so very lost and defenseless and so very appealing that it would be easy to forget the past and how much she disliked him. The road reclaimed his attention and he maneuvered the curricle around a ponderous stagecoach, which was toiling up the notorious hill, its passengers walking wearily beside it.

Ahead lay the tollgate, which had just swung open to allow a mail to pass through on its way to Bath. The shining maroon vehicle descended rapidly, its guard very splendid in his scarlet coat and gilt hatband, his horn blowing loudly to clear the road. A shower of small stones were scattered by the red wheels as it passed, but Adele did not even glance at it. She remained silent as the tollkeeper was paid and the curricle moved on once more, the team appearing to make light work of the long, long incline. Bath fell further and further behind and there was only the rattle of the wheels and the steady drumming of the horses' hooves.

He broke the silence at last. "Not a Sussex bit of road, you will agree."

"Sussex? I don't understand."

"The roads of that county are said to be the worst in the realm."

"Oh."

"Your conversation is dazzling this morning."

"You surely do not expect drawing-room sparkle after what has happened." She looked at him. "Why did you do it? Why did you rescue me from the results of my own folly?"

"I am insulted to think you need to ask why I did a gentlemanly act."

She looked away again, her lips moving wryly. Why should she expect gentlemanly behavior from him when in the past he had hardly come up to such a standard?

"Another eloquent silence, Miss Russell? I shall hasten to fill the gap you have allowed to appear in our chitter-chatter. I did what I did this morning because the moment I saw Talbourne's phaeton outside the shop, I knew he was up to no good. I may have lacked the shining armor and the white steed, but I certainly had the villainous dragon and the damsel in distress. I needed no further prompting to show my valor to the world."

"And for your pains you have got your name connected with mine again and you have crossed a future duke. Perhaps you would have been wiser to have driven on by, my lord."

"Perhaps I would," he replied a little wearily, "for then I would have spared myself the company of an ungrateful creature. As to enduring the tedium of having my name connected with yours, Miss Russell, I survived before and no doubt will survive again. I must also correct you about crossing the future duke, for I crossed swords with Talbourne long before you reentered my boring, uneventful little life, so you may rest easy on that score."

"I think it would be better if you returned me to Bath, sir," she said stiffly, aware that she deserved the rebuke and aware too that the strain of the morning's events was catching up on her, bringing her perilously close to tears.

"If I do that, the world will swiftly realize that I have fibbed little."

"We have had more than enough time for me to meet the countess, my lord."

"We haven't, you know," he said, moving the curricle slowly through a small flock of sheep which were being driven along by a shepherd and his dog. "For my mother is not conveniently at Royal Crescent today; she is visiting Dyrham Park, which happens to lie along this very road."

She stared at him horror-struck. "You aren't really taking me to meet her, are you?"

He smiled a little. "No, Miss Russell, I am not. I am merely still doing my unusually gallant act by keeping you away from that damned shop long enough to convince the inquisitive ladies of Bath that you are indeed doing what I so shamelessly told them you were. Which reminds me, Miss Russell, I have not heard one word of thanks for my efforts. You are very remiss, madam.''

The reprimand proved the final straw for her. Tears brimmed in her eyes and she turned her face away, but a single, stifled sob told him the truth. He reined the team in immediately, halting the curricle beneath the overhanging branches of an oak tree.

''Forgive me,'' he said apologetically. ''I should not have spoken like that. I should have realized how distressed you were.''

She tried to fight the tears, furious with herself for revealing her weakness to him but unable to do anything to stop herself. Slowly he reached over to take one of her hands, and when she did not snatch it away, he drew her gently to him, putting his arms around her. She could not resist, her misery and unhappiness were too great. Her arms slipped slowly around his neck and she hid her face against his shoulder, her whole body trembling as she wept.

He touched the foolish ribbons of her bonnet, and the past seemed to move nearer suddenly as he remembered holding her in his arms before. But things had been so different then. . . .

After a while, her sobs subsided and she drew slowly and deliberately away, sharply aware of the intimacy of their situation and aware too that she found it too pleasing to be in his embrace once more. She would not let her foolish heart betray her again, not with this man. He had saved her from a dreadful fate at Rex's hands a little earlier, but he had not been there to protect her five years before when her need had been so much greater. Where had he been then with his strength and comforting presence? The answer was simple—he had not had a conscience to move him then, nothing to shame him into doing the gentlemanly thing!

He drew back too, the moment of closeness and understanding dying as swiftly as it had flared into life.

The little flock of sheep moved slowly past, the shepherd making no secret of his curiosity as he stared at the curricle and its silent occupants.

Adele moved uncomfortably. ''I think perhaps it would be better if we returned to Bath now, my lord.''

''Why?''

She looked swiftly at him. ''There is little point in continuing as we now do. Besides—''

"Yes?"

"What of the Marchioness of Heydon? She will have heard all about it by now and she will not be at all pleased."

"No, I don't suppose she will be," he replied dryly, picking up the reins and slapping the team into action once more. But he seemed to have no intention of bowing to Adele's suggestion, for instead of turning the curricle back the way they had come, he drove on, threading his way through the sheep once more and this time doffing his hat to the startled shepherd.

The Three Tuns was a large wayside inn, a straggling thatched building that dominated the hillside ahead and provided weary travelers with a final stage before Bath. Like all such inns, its gardens provided the fare that was served at its tables. A large kitchen garden stretched up the hill behind it, a treasure trove of fine stick beans, peas, cabbages, carrots, and every other summer vegetable. There were flowers too, swaying spikes of blue larkspur and beds of bright golden marigolds. Beehives were dotted among the apple trees in the little orchard to one side of the inn, and there was a large brew house, which seemed to be much used and in excellent order.

Chickens scratched in the yard as the curricle arrived, and a packhorse looked up from the water trough. A peddler was showing some of the maids his range of trinkets and a covered wagon was being unloaded, the canvas flung back to make the task easier. It was a very peaceful scene and one which was disturbed a moment or so later by the arrival of a gaudy blue and yellow stagecoach. The chickens scattered in all directions as the heavy vehicle came to a noisy standstill at one of the inn doors, the coachman shouting loudly. "Please to alight, gentlemen!" Ostlers hurried out with ladders for the stiff outsiders to climb down.

David brought the curricle to a halt in a quiet corner next to the well and then turned to Adele. "I take it that you are prepared to eat with me, or will you choke upon any thought of accepting my hospitality?"

"The question seems to defy an answer, sir."

He smiled a little at that. "Perhaps it does. Miss Russell, I consider the enjoyment of a good meal at a fine inn to be a very civilized pastime and so think it would be an excellent notion if we declared a truce for a while. There are few finer tables than that provided by the Three Tuns. What do you say?"

"Are you sure you wish to take luncheon in my company, my lord?"

"I am asking you if you will."

"Then I am pleased to accept."

A brief light of amusement passed through his eyes. "You do not look pleased, but I will believe you if you say you are."

"Thousands wouldn't?"

"Something of the sort." He held his hand out to her and she alighted.

She didn't want to eat with him, she just wanted to escape, to be free of the confusion with which he filled her. He pierced her armor so very easily and did so with each glance, each word. . . .

He turned to the waiting tiger. "See to the horses, Thomas, and then sup what you will." He pushed some coins into the groom's hand.

"Thank you, my lord."

"And go easy on the strong ale this time. I have no wish to keep halting during the return journey simply to haul you up off the road."

The tiger grinned sheepishly. "That won't happen again, my lord."

"I know, for this time I am of a mind to leave you where you fall."

The innkeeper had seen the curricle arrive and was waiting in the doorway. It was immediately obvious that he knew David well. "Good day to you, my lord, and welcome to the Three Tuns."

"Good day to you, Dick, how goes the world with you?"

"Excellently, my lord. Were you wishing to partake of luncheon?"

"That was the general notion."

"I'm afraid the small parlor is taken up with a meeting of justices."

"God forbid."

"I can offer you one of the tables in the main parlor, if that will not be too inconvenient."

"Is the food as excellent there?"

"The food at the Three Tuns is always excellent, whichever room it is served in," retorted the innkeeper proudly, drawing himself up so that his starched white apron seemed to crackle.

162

"Then the main parlor will not be inconvenient," said David, smiling at him.

They were shown into the main parlor, which contained two white-clothed tables, one of which was occupied by the travelers from the newly arrived stagecoach. The red-brick floor was sanded and there was a fine rug before the cold, empty fireplace. A plain mirror hung on the handsome chimney piece and a clutter of hats and coats were draped over the pegs next to the door. There were a number of horse prints on one wall and some highly polished pots and pans gleaming on another. As the innkeeper led David and Adele to the empty table another door opened and a waiter and the innkeeper's rosy-cheeked daughter brought hot, covered dishes to the waiting customers at the other. The lids were removed to reveal a leg of mutton, a joint of boiled beef, boiled potatoes, and some stick beans from the garden.

David drew out a chair for Adele and then sat down himself, glancing across at the other table. "Dick," he said to the innkeeper, "I trust that you have something a little less gargantuan for us to eat."

"Yes, my lord, there is dressed fowl and salad."

"Fowl?" drawled David, hiding a smile. "Could that mean pheasant?"

"It could not!" protested the innkeeper, bridling at the implication that he accepted poached birds. "It means chicken!"

"What a pity. Still no doubt it will go down sweetly with one of your best wines; you know the one I prefer."

"Yes, my lord, I'll attend to it immediately."

Adele sat back when he had gone, and as she glanced around the chamber she noticed that the innkeeper's daughter looked a great many times in the direction of the Earl of Blaisdon. "You appear to be well known here, sir," she said.

"I am."

"So it seems."

He followed her gaze and then laughed. "You flatter me if you think I have conquered the luscious Betsy, for she is the most expert flirt in the land and has yet to oblige any hopeful young blood with the delights her warm glance would appear to promise."

"Do you speak from experience?"

"No, from hearsay."

"I suppose I must believe your protestations of innocence."

163

"Yes, you must. But would it matter to you if I bedded her in the hay each time I came here?"

She flushed a little. "No."

"Then the whole subject is rather pointless, isn't it?

She looked out of the window at the stagecoach. The grooms and ostlers were hurrying about their business and the coachman was overseeing their labors with a critical eye. Had things gone as she intended, she would probably have been at some other wayside inn now, picking at a meal and pondering the awfulness of what lay ahead.

"Do you always find stagecoaches so engrossing, Miss Russell?"

"I do today."

"Why?"

"Because when I got up this morning, I fully intended leaving Bath and going to London. Instead I am at the Three Tuns taking luncheon with you."

"Where were you going in London?"

"I don't really know."

"You don't *know*? Great God, woman, had you taken leave of your senses?"

"No, I had come to those senses, sir," she replied quietly. "I knew Lord Talbourne was coming to do as much mischief as he could and that Cat would be the one to suffer. I was the cause of it all, and so I knew that I should leave and give Cat a chance."

His gaze was piercing. "So you were just going to take yourself to London. Perhaps you should thank Talbourne then, for by arriving when he did and catching my eye when he did, he certainly saved you from a fate worse than death! You are young and beautiful, very beautiful. What on earth do you imagine would have happened to you? London is filled to capacity with gentlemen eager to trap innocents like you, Miss Russell."

Again she flushed. "I am not a fool, sir."

"No? I beg to differ. And I beg to find fault with Miss Rogers's part in all this. What can she have been thinking of, condoning such a foolish escapade?"

"She didn't know what I planned!" cried Adele, conscious immediately of the attention her raised tone was receiving from the adjoining table. She lowered her voice to continue. "She wouldn't have let me go had she known, which is why I didn't tell her."

164

"I'm relieved to hear it." He studied her flushed face for a moment. "I take it that you will now change your alarming plans and remain in the safety of Bath."

"I don't know." She avoided his eyes.

"And what is that supposed to mean?"

"It means that I don't know if I will be able to remain in Bath."

"Because of Talbourne? I don't think you need to fear him anymore, I have effectively spiked his guns for him, I promise you."

"It isn't only Lord Talbourne."

His penetrating gaze seemed to reach right into her soul. "You are threatened from some other direction? Bellingham? Or Repton?"

"Sir Frederick. Even as I sit here with you, I am flouting Sir Frederick's wishes. I am also going against the Marchioness of Heydon's express warning. All in all, my lord, I have been most definitely warned off you."

"I begin to feel like a damned bone." He smiled for a moment. "I have already disposed of Talbourne; I will see to it that the other threats are removed too."

She stared at him. "I do not think that the Marchioness will see such a move on your part in a very good light, sir."

"I am tired of others making it their business to interfere in my life."

She fell silent.

"You may rest easy, Miss Russell, and I trust that from now on you will desist from all foolish talk of fleeing to London."

"It seems to be my lot to be in your debt today, sir."

"Don't let that worry you unduly."

The innkeeper brought the dressed fowl, which was appetizingly served on a platter surrounded by a salad so fresh and crisp that it must have come barely a minute before from the garden. The cork of the wine bottle slid out with a dull pop and the pale liquid was poured into two sparkling glasses. Bowing and wishing them a hearty appetite, the innkeeper turned to leave but was hailed by an elderly gentleman on the other table.

"Some hot brandy and water, if you please."

"*Hot* brandy and water, sir? At this time of the year?"

"It's damned cold on the top of that accursed stage and I need something to keep body and soul together if I am not to be a corpse before reaching my destination."

"Very well, sir."

The elderly gentleman did not look hale and hearty enough to travel as an outsider, even in the middle of the summer, thought Adele. He looked thin and peaky, his rounded shoulders being well wrapped in a shawl that would have deterred an arctic gale.

The meal was as excellent as it looked, and Adele found herself feeling surprisingly hungry, so that she forgot about the elderly gentleman until the coachman appeared in the doorway to collect his passengers. "Time's up, gentlemen," he said, pinning a posy of flowers to his lapel and winking at the maid who had presented it to him.

The passengers grumbled a little, but got up from the table—with the exception of the elderly gentleman who had at that very moment been presented with his hot brandy and water. It was far too hot for him to drink swiftly and he protested to the coachman, who would not listen. There was a schedule to maintain, and old men with a penchant for hot brandy in the middle of the summer were not going to be allowed to interfere with that! Obviously very put out, the elderly gentleman put the brandy down and began to rise.

David had been watching the scene with growing disapproval, his fingers drumming a little on the table as he eyed the puffed-up importance of the coachman. Everyone had filed out, except the old man, when suddenly David got up and removed some of the cutlery from the deserted table, thrusting them into a vase of flowers and putting his finger to his lips as the startled old gentleman stared at him. Then David called to the waiter. "I think you had better check the knives and forks, for it would seem to me that some are missing."

The waiter looked hastily at the table, mentally counting the cutlery, and then with a shout he ran out after the passengers, calling them all back. The coachman was furious and the passengers a little cross, but they had to obey. The elderly gentleman had not wasted his time and was already back in his chair sipping the hot brandy and water, a beam of delight spreading across his wrinkled face.

Mayhem reigned for the next few minutes as a search was made, and the old gentleman enjoyed his hot drink at his leisure. David continued with his meal as if totally unaware of what was happening, and Adele had to look out of the window to conceal her mirth as the furious coachman stomped up and down demanding that his passengers be allowed to leave. The old gentleman put down his glass at last, and David slowly got to his feet.

"Why," he said casually, "I do believe I see something in the vase. Yes, it is a knife. And another. Well, who could have put them there?" His eyes exuded innocence and surprise. The passengers stared at the cutlery, the waiter looked relieved, and the coachman bristled, throwing a positively venomous glance at David. It was an old trick, one which he should have detected, but instead he'd made a fool of himself by falling for it.

The elderly gentleman got to his feet, bowing gladly at David. "I thank you, sir, you are a gentleman after my own heart."

"Mere timetables should not come between a man and his brandy, sir."

Within a minute the blue and yellow stagecoach was pulling away, the elderly passenger clinging grimly to the rail, his cheeks glowing and his eyes bright, and the chickens scattered once more. David sat down again.

"That was handsomely done, sir," said Adele.

"Praise?"

"There is supposed to be a truce."

"So there is. Does it extend to taking a stroll? I think a little exercise would not go amiss after such a meal."

A strip of woodland spread down from the road opposite the inn into a tree-choked valley where a stream rushed and chattered over rocks. The birdsong was deafening, echoing all around, and the wind swept constantly through the trees, rustling the leaves and bending the branches beneath the gray skies.

They stood on the mossy bank, watching the clear, cold water spilling between the rocks and babbling over the gravelly bed, and then suddenly Adele glanced up as a magpie darted from a nearby tree in a flash of black and white. She smiled.

"Why do you smile?" he asked.

"I was remembering."

"What?"

"That my father used to call me Little Miss Magpie because I collected beads."

"I trust that that was when you were very small."

"I certainly gave up bead hoarding some time before I met you, my lord," she responded swiftly.

"Thank goodness for that mercy; otherwise I might have found myself with a wife whose curiously acquisitive habits were arousing comment."

"Well, you were spared that dreadful possibility, weren't you?" she said coolly.

"That is one way of putting it."

"You know of another?"

His eyes darkened with anger then. "I know of many, Miss Russell, but I do not intend discussing them with you. You are free to see events of five years ago as you wish, that is your privilege, and it is a privilege you have obviously employed time and time again since those days."

"I see events as they were, sir, not as I wish."

"I think, madam," he said quietly, "that our truce is in danger of coming to a very ragged end and that we should make our way back to Bath before it becomes irretrievably trampled underfoot." Tapping his top hat on his head, he turned to walk away, back up through the woods to the inn.

They made the return journey in a rather uneasy silence, each wrapped in thoughts the other could only guess at. Adele was conscious of a sadness that the day was coming to an end, for in spite of everything she had enjoyed being with him, and the mere fact that she had to keep reminding herself of his past conduct and failings was proof enough to her innermost heart that he still meant far too much to her. Just as when she had met him so unexpectedly at Beech Park several days before, she was again very aware of everything about him. She behaved now as her pride permitted, for without pride what was she? She had lost everything and only had her pride to sustain her. To give in to the emotions he had once again aroused in her would be to destroy that precious pride, for his reentry into her life was a transient thing; it would be over soon and she would be left to carry on. These thoughts milled unhappily in her head as the curricle spun back toward Bath.

They halted once, on Swainswick Hill, where they were afforded a fine view across to Beech Park. She stared at the ruins.

"Are you sure that there is nowhere your father could have put that evidence?" he asked after a moment. "Sure that he put it somewhere which was destroyed by the fire?"

"I've looked everywhere, thought of everywhere."

"There is not much time now, for Repton is demolishing

absolutely all the remains of Beech Park, even the cellars. Nothing is to be left of Denzil Russell's house.''

She looked at the ruins again. "I don't believe the evidence exists anymore, my lord," she said quietly. "There is no way at all of proving my father's innocence.''

"And you think that eases my mind, don't you?''

"It must if you are to make the Marchioness of Heydon your bride.''

He touched the team again and the curricle continued on its way down the long hill. Their arrival outside the haberdashery attracted a good deal of interest, for everyone seemed to know about what had happened earlier in the day. David climbed out and then handed Adele to the pavement. His fingers felt very warm around hers and he held her hand a little longer than necessary, as if he would say something more. But then he released her and she knew that the words he spoke were not the ones that had first been on his lips.

"I trust you enjoyed meeting my mother, Miss Russell," he said.

"It was an—unexpected honor, sir.''

"An honor? I thought you regarded it as an imposition.''

"My manners were sadly lacking then, sir.''

"Once or twice I rather fancy mine were too.''

She smiled a little. "I am very grateful to you for helping me today, please believe that. If you had not come—''

"But I did," he said, putting his hand to her cheek for a moment. Then he was gone, climbing back into the curricle and driving away without a backward glance.

She watched him, her eyes very bright. She could still feel the touch of his hand. "You fool," she whispered to herself. "You utter fool, you love him still!'' She became aware of the flower boy looking curiously at her, and she turned away, hurrying down the side alley.

As she walked up the ash path, away from the curious gaze of Milsom Street, the sun came out, bathing the garden in its warm glow. But sunshine had no place in her unhappy heart.

Chapter 21

Adele found that her portmanteau had been unpacked and all her belongings put back in their usual place, and when she came down to the kitchen, Cat was waiting for her.

"Adele, you must promise me that you will never think of leaving like that again. You would have gone, wouldn't you? If Lord Talbourne had not come in at that very moment?"

"Yes." The word was barely audible.

"Promise me you won't ever do it again."

"I promise."

Cat nodded heavily. "Then I am satisfied."

"I was only doing it because—"

"I know why you were doing it." A smile touched the older woman's lips. "And bless you for it, but as things have turned out there's no need to be anxious, is there?"

"Trade was brisk again?"

"Oh, yes, almost as if another masquerade was in the offing. The tale of the confrontation between Lord Talbourne and the Earl of Blaisdon was around Bath like a flame along a gunpowder trail. Of course, that means that Sir Frederick will have heard—"

"The earl is going to see Sir Frederick."

Cat's eyes widened a little. "He is?"

"He isn't at all pleased; he says he dislikes feeling like a fought-over bone."

"I take it that you had a long conversation with the earl."

"We spoke."

"And?"

"And nothing."

"There is speculation that you will after all become the Countess of Blaisdon."

"The speculation is ill founded. He is intending to marry Lady Euphemia."

"Then I'm surprised."

"Because he is so openly at odds with her brother?"

"No, because of the way he came to your rescue today."

"Like a knight in shining armor?" said Adele, smiling a little as she remembered his words.

"Like a man who thinks more of you than you realize."

"I am his conscience, Cat, that is all there is to it."

"Are you sure?"

"Quite sure."

"Then there is nothing more to be said, except to ask you what your feelings are toward him?"

Adele turned away. "My feelings are not of any consequence."

"They are to me, my pet."

"I don't think you need to ask me how I feel about him, for my love for him has never died, in spite of anything I may have said to the contrary."

"He is a very hard man to put out of your heart."

"But I will. In the end."

Cat gave another nod. "Maybe. But in the meantime we must carry on—but we do it together, Adele. I shall hold you to your promise. We sink or we swim, but together."

Adele turned back to her, running into her arms and holding her very tight. "I love you so much, Cat."

Tears shone in the older woman's eyes as she returned the embrace.

In the early evening of the same day, Sir Frederick Repton was seated in his favorite chair in his club in Queen Square. Opposite him sat the Duke of Bellingham, but a large dinner and two bottles of forbidden wine had made that gentleman sleepy. His eyes closed and his head fell forward on his chest, crushing the starched excellence of his cravat. He looked very untidy as he sprawled in his chair, his heavily bandaged foot resting very gingerly on a stool. The game of chess they had been about to commence was left untouched.

Sir Frederick shifted a little, irritation gleaming momentarily in his pale eyes. He may only be a glorified clerk, but he had more refinement and style than His Grace the Duke of Bellingham would ever aspire to! An accident of birth, a unkind quirk of fate, had placed Frederick Repton low on the social ladder, and this avaricious lord far too high! Picking up a copy of *The Times*, Sir Frederick made himself more comfortable and then sat back to read.

Outside, the sound of a carriage was muffled by the tall

windows and by the heavy green drapes with their golden fringes and tassels. The smell of tobacco smoke clung to the room, and from beyond a partition came the dull drone of male conversation.

Footsteps echoed on the marble floor of the vestibule and Sir Frederick distinctly heard someone mention his name. He lowered the newspaper as the steps approached the polished oak doors. David Latimer entered.

Slowly Sir Frederick got to his feet. "Good evening, my lord."

"Repton."

"I had not realized that you were a member—"

"I'm not."

Something in the tone warned Sir Frederick that this was not merely a social call. "I take it that you wish to speak with me?"

"I do."

"How may I be of service to you?"

"By keeping out of my affairs."

Sir Frederick's colorless lips parted in surprise. "I beg your pardon? I'm afraid I don't understand—"

"You have been taking extraordinary liberties, Repton, for who are you to decide who does and does not have dealings with me?"

"I don't know what you mean." The pale eyes were wary.

"No? I think you do." David glanced at the slumbering duke. "You have dined with His Grace?"

"I have."

"Then you will be fully cognizant of what occurred in a certain haberdashery in Milsom Street this morning."

"I have heard a little, yes."

"I'll warrant you have. Well, let me point out that what I did to Talbourne I can do to you. *I* choose who I do and do not speak to; it has nothing whatsoever to do with you. I warned Talbourne that Miss Russell has my protection from now on, and that warning is now cordially extended to you, sir. I am not by nature a violent man, but I do have my moments, and when aroused I am told I have a very unpleasant and ugly temper. It so happens that the change of air has made me a little touchy, so you would be wise not to cross my path again. Keep well away from Miss Russell, for unless you do, you will need to glance frequently over your shoulder."

Sir Frederick's tongue passed nervously over his lips. "Come now, my lord, are you not being a little hasty? Surely Miss Russell is of little consequence. What is a shop wench compared to a marchioness? Your forthcoming match with the duke's daughter should come before a disagreement with the duke's friend.''

David's eyes glittered and his voice was icy. "And for you the thought of preserving your neat, well-tailored hide should come before all else, Repton. It would give me great pleasure to rub your vile nose in the mud from which you have somehow risen, and if you make one more remark like the one you have just allowed to slip from your unwise lips, then I will deem myself to have been given the very excuse I need.'' David smiled a little. "And just in case I have not made myself sufficiently clear to you, let me impress upon you the fact that you would be most unwise to fall foul of me, for I can harm you in a great many ways, not least where your political ambitions are concerned. I am told that you are soon to be the prime minister's guest.''

"I am.'' The pale eyes were very wary indeed now.

"The Duke of Bellingham may be Liverpool's kinsman, but really the link is rather tenuous—whereas my connection with him is a great deal closer, and therefore my influence with him that much greater. He is my first cousin, Repton, my mother being his favorite aunt. Offend me any more now and you may kiss farewell to any political aspirations while this government is in power.'' David smiled coldly. "I think we know where we stand now, don't we? Good night, Repton.''

Sir Frederick did not reply.

The sun was beginning to set as David entered the elegant drawing room of the house on Royal Crescent. The countess was seated on a chair that was drawn up very close to the fire. The room was almost unbearably hot, and he smiled a little as he bowed before her, for she deliberately ignored him.

She wore a black muslin gown sprigged with dainty flowers, and its long, voluminous sleeves were gathered in tightly at her thin wrists. A black day cap rested on her graying hair, and she had pulled a heavy rug around her knees, even though she must have been roasting from the heat of the fire. She looked very cross.

He removed himself to a cooler position by the window. Even had he not seen her wrathful expression he would still

173

have known that she was very displeased with him, for at such times she always played upon her infirmities, ordering fires that were not really required and then huddling over them as if her very life depended upon it. It was a ploy she frequently resorted to when all else failed, and the moment he had seen her, her face glowing with heat, he knew that she had been fully informed about the events at the haberdashery—probably by Mrs. Harriman, who had called the very instant the countess's landau had returned from Dyrham Park. Such information as would have been eagerly imparted would indeed result in a call for fires and the comfort of a rug. He waited, gazing up at the stucco ceiling with its beautiful design of swans, flowers, and garlands.

A maid entered with a silver tea tray, setting it carefully beside the countess. The porcelain tea pot chinked against the first cup as the maid retreated again.

The tea poured, the countess tweaked her Kashmir shawl around her shoulders and then sat back a little, her back stiff. "Is it true?"

"Is what true?"

"That you had a common dusting with Lord Talbourne today."

"Yes."

"In—in a *haberdashery?*" Her voice quivered.

"Yes."

"And that is only part of it, isn't it? I confess that I cannot believe it all—"

"What have you been told?"

"That you and Lord Talbourne had a set-to over a shop girl, not just *any* shop girl but one whose name appears to be Russell."

"That is correct."

She drew herself up a little. "And you then took this Russell creature out in your curricle, telling the world that she was expected to meet me?"

"Yes, I did."

"How dare you say such a thing, how dare you imply that it is my habit to receive tradespeople as my guests!"

"Come now, Mother, that is not why you are in such a pother about it. You are alarmed because the shop girl involved is identified as Miss Adele Russell, who once nearly became your daughter-in-law."

"Is it she?"

"Yes."

"But I thought she was—well, never mind what I thought, I was obviously wrong. How did you meet her again. Don't tell me you purchased a yard of ribbon in the haberdashery!"

"She attended the masquerade."

His mother bristled. "So I heard. I also heard the undoubted fib you gave out to spare her."

"She did not deserve to suffer at Talbourne's hands."

"That is a matter of opinion, David."

"You would agree with me were she anyone else but Adele Russell."

"That is not fair."

"It's very fair indeed, and you know it."

"I have a right to be miffed about all this, for where does your little bout with Talbourne leave your match with his sister?"

"It leaves it exactly where it was before," he said shortly.

"Don't be so infuriating; you remind me of your father!"

"Thank you."

"It was not a compliment."

"I realize that. Very well, Mother, what do you wish me to do?"

She looked nonplussed at this question. "Do?"

"You have gone on and on *ad yawnum* about the Heydon match, my hind leg has long since dropped off, and now I swear I loathe the very name Heydon. What do you really wish me to do?"

"I wish you to settle the matter."

"I will do so." He got up. "I will go there immediately."

She was startled. "So quickly?"

"I was under the impression that that was what you wished."

"Yes, but—"

"No buts." He bowed over her hand and left.

Euphemia got to her feet as her brother entered the drawing room. "So," she said in a voice shaking with barely suppressed fury, "you've decided to show your face here at last!"

"Have you been waiting for me?" His face was a little flushed and she knew that he had been drinking.

"You know that I have! I hope you're satisfied with the way things went this morning. The whole of Bath is laughing at *you*, not at her!"

He loosened his cravat before flinging himself on a sofa, lounging back to look at her. "And at you, my dear sister, for your efforts to snap Blaisdon up are beginning to look more and more sick."

"I have you to thank for that."

"Come now, you weren't exactly making progress before I returned."

"But now your great plan for her destruction has resulted in her being thrust into his arms!"

"I wasn't to know the damned fellow would arrive; things were going very well until then."

"How right I was to dissociate myself from you and your brilliance," she said coldly.

"You may pat yourself on the back," he replied, reaching over to pick up the decanter of cognac.

"Don't you think you've had enough of that already?"

"When I have I will let you know."

Her heavy skirts swished as she went to the window to look out. The sun's rays had sunk behind the Circus now, but there was still an amber hue to the evening air. The clouds had vanished and the wind had dropped, leaving the warm calm of a summer's day drawing to a close. The rays of the dying sun made the ruby at Euphemia's throat look blood red; her apple-green gown was blushed to crimson, and she looked particularly pretty but for the angry twist on her lips and the glint sharpening her brown eyes.

She glanced momentarily at her brother. "Something very interesting happened today while you were out."

"What?"

"Something which at last gives me ammunition to use against Adele Russell."

"Move against her now and you'll bitch up your last chance with Blaisdon. He's set himself up as her Lord Protector."

"There are more ways of skinning a cat than leaping at it with a knife."

"I presume we are referring to your more subtle plans."

"Yes."

"Do tell," he said drily, swirling the glass of cognac, his glance mocking.

"Your brashness this morning was as ill advised as I believed it would be. But I can move against her without

176

even vaguely arousing the Earl of Blaisdon's suspicions that I am involved.''

''How?''

''Does the name Enleigh mean anything to you? Dr. Enleigh, rector of Benwick parish?''

''Can't say it does; I'm not exactly a regular churchgoer.''

''No, I suppose you're not. However, in this case neither am I—at least not to Benwick church. Dr. Enleigh happens to own the premises in Milsom Street which contain that cursed haberdashery.''

''Ah, I have it! You've purchased the deeds!''

''Not quite, but they will soon be mine.''

''There is a delay?''

''Until today there was. Dr. Enleigh was rather tedious; he refused to sell to me.'' She sighed, her lips pursed a little. ''He is such a very solid, upright son of the church, trusted, respected, *et cetera, et cetera*. Indeed his reputation is so saintly that it positively glows with holy light. It did not seem possible to me that *anyone* could be that good.''

Rex smiled slowly. ''So you began to dig around the Enleigh muckheap.''

''Not personally. I employed the services of a fellow who is said to be the very best at such things. I confess that I did not always enjoy following all this through, for it was most demeaning to have to hire a dreadful old chaise and take to secretive assignations with a fellow whose very clothes damned him as an odious creature. However, in the end it has proved profitable.''

''The Enleigh halo has slipped a little?''

''Oh yes,'' she replied with a sleek smile. ''It appears that the saintly rector of Benwick has been amusing himself with a handsome Irish wench, by whom he now has three children. Mrs. Enleigh, a very mousy little thing, has not presented him with any children—nor with any joy in bed, by the look of her—and she knows nothing of this secret amour.''

''But she will, unless the good rector does as you wish.''

''Correct. Once such a tale got out, I wouldn't give much for the rector's career in the church.''

''And you found this out today?''

''Yes, while you were making an utter fool of yourself.''

He ignored the taunt. ''So you will turn Miss Russell and her beloved old nurse out into the streets.''

''Not exactly.''

"What then? I don't see the point of getting your hands on the deeds unless—"

"I want them out of those premises and out of Bath too. In fact I want them as far away from this town as possible." She smiled. "I want them out of this country."

"Sis, you could have rid yourself of this tiresome thorn in your side a very long time ago simply by using your considerable influence to put the place out of business. If you had done that, none of this would have arisen now, would it?"

"So, it's my fault that your pride has taken a battering, is it?"

"If I wanted a set-to right now, I would agree with you, but I am in no mood for arguments." He raised his glass to her, smiling.

"It so happens that I did consider trying to close the place, but that might not have worked. I could have come unstuck, as they say, and that would not have done at all."

"How could *you* have come unstuck?"

"Too many important ladies use the place, ladies like the Dowager Countess of Bainie and Mrs. Harriman. No, I could not risk defeat. I was on top of the problem anyway, until recently, when the Earl of Blaisdon returned to Bath. Things did not go well from then on, and that is when I decided to attempt to rid myself of the problem through the rector of Benwick. Tomorrow morning he will be informed about what I now know, and I am confident that the deeds will be mine before the day is out. I shall then seek a meeting with Miss Rogers; she will be told that she is to leave the premises, and I will give her a sum of money if she will leave the country, taking Miss Adele Russell with her."

"And if she refuses?"

"She won't; she will not be able to afford to."

"What if Miss Russell does not comply with your wishes?"

"She will, for her old nurse's sake."

"How quaint that you should credit her with qualities you sadly lack yourself," he said coolly, his eyes half closed as he watched the stain of anger flush across her face.

She turned, her eyes glittering. "As quaint as it is for you to pretend that your thirst for revenge is prompted simply by your sense of outrage at what she did. You aren't moved to such fury just because she attended the masquerade, or because she met you while still pretending to be a lady. You're furious because she denied you the one thing you've been bragging she gave to you. The haberdasher's assistant refused the advances of the duke's son, didn't she? She wouldn't bed with you!''

He sat up angrily. ''Have a care—''

''If you can't take it, brother-of-mine, don't attempt to give it either!''

He got up and went to the door.

''Where are you going?'' she called after him.

''Out.''

''Where?''

''To find more pleasant company. Celibacy has no place in my existence, Euphemia, so I shall seek the charms of a courtesan. With luck I shall not return before dawn.''

From the window she saw him climb into the yellow phaeton and drive away, the vehicle swaying alarmingly as it sped across the Circus and entered Gay Street. It had hardly passed from sight when another vehicle entered the cobbled area before the house, a green curricle that drew to a standstill in the very spot that had so recently been occupied by Rex's phaeton. The Earl of Blaisdon climbed down and handed the reins to the tiger before he approached the door.

Her heart began to beat with excitement, and she hurried to the antechamber, listening carefully as David announced himself to the footman. Gathering her skirts, Euphemia went back into the drawing room, sat on the sofa, and arranged her skirts very carefully. Her eyes were bright and her hands trembled with hope. The incident in the shop had not deterred him; he had still called upon her!

The footman announced him. ''The Earl of Blaisdon, my lady.''

She smiled, her eyes shining. ''Good evening, my lord.''

''Good evening, Euphemia.''

The footman retreated and the doors were drawn to once more.

She patted the sofa beside her. ''Will you sit down?''

He remained standing. ''I take it that this morning's episode has not made me persona non grata with you.''

''I do not profess to know what lies between you and my brother, my lord, but I do not have a quarrel with you.''

''I believe we have things to talk of, you and I.''

''Do we?''

He nodded. ''Yes, and I think that we may talk more
179

comfortably if we take a drive together. It is a very fine evening, quite perfect for such an expedition."

"Very well. If you will wait while I put on my pelisse and so on?"

"But of course."

She hurried out, pausing in the anteroom to compose herself. Her eyes were very bright indeed and her pulse was racing almost unbearably. His purpose could only be to ask for her hand; she had won him after all!

The haberdashery was closing and Cat stood watching as Adele took down the tulles from the doorway. The nurse glanced up as the breeze caught the Waterloo bunting that was draped from the bedroom window above. "That's looking a little unhappy now; all that rain didn't do it much good," she said.

"Shall I take it down?" asked Adele.

"If you would; you're more lithe than I am."

Adele went up the stairs and into Cat's bedroom, raising the window and leaning out to begin untying the bunting. She heard the curricle and looked up to see Euphemia seated beside David, smiling a great deal and looking the picture of happiness. David did not glance up at the window as the light vehicle sped past, and it seemed to Adele that Euphemia's tinkling laughter echoed in the street long after the curricle had passed from sight.

Slowly Adele continued untying the bunting and then dragged it all inside. Her heart was very heavy as she closed the window again. Down in the kitchen Cat glanced at her, and Adele knew that the old nurse had seen the curricle.

Adele put the bunting down. "She looked very happy, didn't she?"

"So it would seem."

"I think we may expect an announcement soon."

"Probably. It won't be a happy match, though, for he's made a bad choice. You mark my words."

Chapter 22

Adele sat in the moonlit window, clasping her knees tightly as she gazed out over the rooftops toward Beech Park. The moon made her nightgown very white and turned her hair to silver, and she looked almost ghostly as she sat there, so silent and still. Outside there wasn't a cloud to spoil the perfection of the starry night, and even the sounds of Bath seemed muted. There was no sign now of the dull weather and winds of earlier, everything was peaceful and warm, just as a perfect night should be.

She was lost in her thoughts and memories. How different life might have been for her, how happy she might have been had she become David Latimer's wife. If she had married him she would not be sitting alone in the moonlight now, she would be lying in his arms. . . . She lowered her eyes, a despairing sadness passing through her. She had tried to hate him, she had tried so very hard, but she could not, she loved him too much. Why had he had to come back into her life? Why couldn't cruel fate relent a little after all this time and leave her alone? Hadn't she endured enough?

Her eyes moved slowly toward the ruins again. How often had she sat here like this, just looking? Soon she would no longer be able to gaze at them for they would be gone forever and there would be no trace at all of Beech Park, that once-glorious house that had looked down so proudly over the town. Not even the cellars would remain; Sir Frederick Repton was seeing to that.

The watch called in a nearby street, and with a jolt she realized that it was past midnight. She got up, her bare feet making no sound on the cool floor as she drew the curtains across, blotting out the moonlight. She slipped into the narrow bed, curling up warmly and closing her eyes. She drifted on the rim of sleep, thinking of Beech Park still. Who could have known how life would turn out for Little Miss Magpie, that carefree little girl who had scampered so happily across the wide terrace, taking her casket of treasures back to its hiding place in . . . Her eyes flew open and the dreamy world halfway between wakefulness and sleep suddenly fled into the night. The hiding place in the cellar! She had kept her casket in the wall, behind a loose stone, and her father had known about that place! Slowly she sat up, her pulse beginning to race excitedly. The cellars were the only part of Beech Park to remain intact and she had gone through them many times since the fire, but she had not remembered the hiding place. Why? Oh, *why* hadn't she thought of it before? Why hadn't she even remembered being called Little Miss Magpie until a few days ago?

She could hear her heartbeats pounding with the rush of almost unbearable excitement. She must go there, she *must!* Flinging the bedclothes back, she got out of the bed, fumbling with the strings of her nightgown with fingers that seemed unable to perform their proper function. She could see the hiding place so clearly; she could even remember the noise the stone had made when it was pulled away. Had her father put the evidence there? *Had* he?

The night was warm, but she shivered as the nightgown slithered to the floor. Hope and apprehension vied for superiority as she put on her beige dimity gown and swiftly brushed her hair, tying it back with a white ribbon. Picking up her plain shawl, she went softly to the door, opening it and listening carefully for any sound from Cat or Joanie. The house was quiet.

She crept down the stairs and once in the kitchen lit the oil lamp. The little bottle of lucifers was on the mantelpiece, but as she reached up for them she dislodged a candlestick and it fell with an unearthly crash to the flagstones before the fireplace. The sound seemed to echo again and again through the silent house, and almost immediately she heard Cat's door opening.

"Who's there?" called a querulous voice from the floor above.

Adele knew that she would have to reassure her that all was well. "It's only me," she called back.

"Adele?"

Cat came down immediately, stopping in surprise when she saw that Adele was dressed and obviously about to go out. "What are you doing? It's past midnight. You're not leaving?"

"No, no, I'm not going back on my word, I promise you."

"But why are you dressed? What's happened?"

"I've thought of somewhere my father might have hidden the evidence against Sir Frederick and the Duke of Bellingham."

"But there isn't anywhere, we both know that there isn't—"

"There is. Do you remember Little Miss Magpie?"

"Of course I do, that is the name your father called you by when you were small. Why?"

"I used to hide my collection of beads behind a stone in the cellar and my father knew about that hiding place. It's just possible that—"

"You aren't considering going up there to Beech Park *now?*" cried Cat in dismay. "You can't possibly do that!"

"I must. I shall positively burst unless I go straight away."

"There will be those out and about now who are up to no good, Adele, you must not go alone. Let me come with you."

"You couldn't manage that long climb," Adele pointed out gently.

"Please, Adele."

"No, I will go now, there's no other way."

Before the old woman could say anything more, Adele picked up the lucifers and then took a candle from a drawer. Helplessly Cat put out a restraining hand, but Adele went to the door and slipped out into the moonlit garden. Cat heard her light steps on the ash path, the creak of the side door into the alley, and then there was silence.

The phaeton moved slowly along the road as it entered the outskirts of Bath. Rex was in no particular hurry to return to the Circus; he had spent an excellent evening at a certain house of ill repute some two miles outside the town, enjoying the charms of a courtesan whose flattering attentions had compensated a little for the humiliations of earlier. He pondered her bold eyes and ample figure, and no one could have been further from his thoughts in that moment than Miss Adele Russell, but then he saw the lithe figure hurry across the road some little way ahead and set off up the lane to Beech Park. He reined the phaeton in, watching, his eyes lingering in particular upon the pale hair, which was so silvery in the moonlight. Only one woman in Bath could have hair like that—and she was alone in the night, moving further and further away from the last

183

villas where help might possibly lie. His hazel eyes gleamed as he climbed swiftly down from the phaeton, calling to the tiger.

"Drive on back to the Circus without me."

"But, my lord—"

"Do as I tell you, damn you!"

"Yes, my lord." The little groom scrambled up to the high perch and slapped the team into action. Rex stood in the road for a moment when it had gone, and then he crossed over to the lane. Adele Russell had made a fool of him, but he would still take payment in full for those insults and slights; he would taste the delights of that beauty that had tormented him from the moment he had first seen her. Lady Domino would be his yet, and there would be no watch, no Earl of Blaisdon to save her this time. . . .

Cat waited anxiously in the haberdashery, glancing out time and time again through the bow window in the hope of seeing Adele return. Please God let her have second thoughts, let her retrace her steps and come back before something dreadful happened! She had been gone only fifteen minutes, but those minutes had dragged on leaden feet so that Cat felt she had been waiting for an hour or more.

She heard the phaeton before she saw it. Leaning forward, she looked out and saw the tiger driving past. She recognized the vehicle immediately, but where was Lord Talbourne? A dreadful thought crept into her head. The phaeton had come from the very direction Adele would have taken! Panic seized the old nurse then; the possibility was too horrible to contemplate, but it was still a possibility! Lord Talbourne had a score to settle and he was not a man to let such a score fade into mere memory.

Gathering her voluminous skirts, Cat hurried to the foot of the stairs. "Joanie? Joanie! Wake up and come down here immediately! And be quick about it!"

The maid almost scrambled down the stairs in her haste, tying the belt of her loose wrap and blinking the sleep from her eyes. "Miss Rogers?"

"Get on out to the shop door and keep a look out for a chair, or for the watch."

"But—"

"Don't argue with me, girl. I'm going to get dressed and I

won't be a minute and I need to reach Royal Crescent in safety.''

''R-royal Crescent?'' The maid gaped.

Cat hurried up the stairs and Joanie went through to the shop, sliding back the bolts. What was happening? Why on earth did Miss Rogers want to go to Royal Crescent at this hour? The maid went out cautiously to the pavement, glancing up and down the deserted street where the few lamps threw isolated pools of light. Everything was horribly quiet; there was no sign of the watch or of a chair.

Two minutes later Cat emerged from the shop door, still pushing her hair beneath her bonnet, and as she reached Joanie they both heard the rhythmic sound of boots upon cobbles, two pairs of boots—a chair! It came into Milsom Steet from the direction of the Circus, having obviously just returned a late reveler to his home.

The chairmen were far from pleased when Cat hailed them, and even less pleased when they learned that she wished to be conveyed all the way back up to Royal Crescent. They had just come from there and viewed the thought of Cat's weight with some dismay. However, she pleaded with them and they agreed to do as she wished. She squeezed into the narrow sedan and a moment later was being carried swiftly away from Joanie, who stood alone on the pavement, still completely unaware of what was going on.

Royal Crescent was as quiet as the rest of the town. There were hardly any lights in any of the windows, and the Earl of Blaisdon's house was in complete darkness. The chairmen set Cat down outside and then stood to watch as she hurried to the gleaming door and began to hammer loudly upon it. The noise thundered through the night like cannon fire, and the bemused chairmen could no more have left the scene than they could have flown, for it was far too interesting to see a plump matron apparently trying to rouse one of Bath's most illustrious visitors.

A pale light flickered inside as someone at last approached the door where Cat had not ceased her frantic knocking. A footman, his wig put on very hastily and his dressing gown flapping loose, looked out in obvious annoyance and amazement.

''I must speak with the earl!'' cried Cat immediately, her round face very anxious in the light of the candle he held.

''I am not going to call the master at this hour!'' he retorted. ''Be off with you!''

"It's very, very important."

"If you do not go away, I shall send for the watch—"

"Please, I beg of you, go to the earl and tell him that Miss Rogers of Milsom Street wishes to speak urgently with him!"

Another voice came from within the house behind him. "What in God's name is going on?" It was David, coming lightly and a little angrily down the stairs to see what the disturbance was.

With a cry of relief, Cat pushed past the startled footman. "My lord, I must speak with you!"

"Miss Rogers? What is it?"

"It's Adele, my lord, she's gone up to Beech Park."

He looked taken aback. "At this hour? Why?"

"Because she suddenly remembered a hiding place in the cellars there. She wouldn't wait until morning, my lord. I tried to stop her from going but she was adamant."

"Dear God above, she must have taken leave of her senses—"

"There's something more, my lord. It may be nothing but it may also be very important. I saw Lord Talbourne's phaeton; there was no sign of his lordship and the tiger was driving it. It came from the direction Adele would have taken, my lord, and I'm so very afraid for her!"

He seized her arms urgently. "How long ago was this?"

"She left half an hour ago." Tears brimmed from Cat's eyes. "I did the right thing, didn't I? I came to you because you said she was under your protection—"

"Of course you did the right thing," he said gently. "I will go to Beech Park immediately."

"P-please bring her back safely, my lord," begged Cat, so distraught that she was on the verge of collapse.

"I will do all I can." He glanced at the footman. "See that my horse is made ready as swiftly as possible."

"Yes, my lord."

"And then have someone inform my mother—"

"I already know," said the countess from the top of the stairs. "You did not imagine that even I could sleep through such a commotion!"

He took Cat's arm and led her up the staircase. "Mother, will you look after Miss Rogers, for me? I have to go out."

"Searching for the elusive Miss Russell?"

"Yes."

The countess nodded resignedly, looking then to Cat, who

186

really was in a dreadful state. "Come, Miss Rogers," said the countess gently. "Let us adjourn to the drawing room where we will take a fortifying glass of something."

Cat allowed herself to be led away, and David hurried to his room, where his valet, who had also overheard most of what had happened, had already laid out his riding clothes.

Barely five minutes later, the Earl of Blaisdon was riding swiftly along Royal Crescent, the clatter of hoofbeats rousing those few residents who had managed to slumber through the earlier interruption.

Chapter 23

The night breeze whispered through the trees overhanging the narrow lane as Adele neared the cottage where before she had seen the country wife. The scent of honeysuckle seemed to fill the air, as always it does after dark, and the moonlight lay across the land in a silver sheen that was ethereal and beautiful. A dog barked somewhere; it could have been fairly near or some distance away, but the silence of the night distorted her senses, and such was her mounting excitement as she at last saw the lodge and the gates that she hardly started at the sound. Her steps quickened a little. She felt no tiredness after the long climb from the valley, the strength of her eager hopefulness carried her onward as if she was weightless.

By the gates she heard the creak of the old weathercock on the lodge roof, and she paused, looking ahead across the waving, gray grass of the park. The breeze murmured over the open landscape, shivering the rippling surface as if it were all a vast extension of the lake which lay unseen ahead. Something made her glance back, just as she had the last time she had reached this point, but the lane was deserted. Thoughts of Jake Cottler crossed her mind but were immediately dismissed, for he would not be watching her at this hour.

She hurried on, her hair threatening to fall loose from its single restraining ribbon and the fringe of her shawl flapping wildly as she ran. On the bridge she halted again, feeling vaguely uneasy, but there was only the silent expanse of water and the gentle rushing of the clear, glittering stream. Again she looked behind. Was that a shadow she had seen so briefly against the skyline? Had something moved? Holding her breath, she continued to look, but the ghostly moonlight was uncertain and everything seemed too still now. Ahead lay the final climb to the terrace, and above the terrace the stark, grim silhouette of the ruins. The gentle perfume of the balsam trees in the woods spread over the hillside as she left the bridge and began that last portion of the climb.

Time and time again now she found herself glancing back, a chill running down her spine. But there was nothing so see; the park was deserted and there was no sign of anything beneath the bridge's classical columns and pedimented porticoes.

Rex halted in the shadow of the bridge as he saw her look back yet again. Had she seen him? No, no she couldn't have, for she was hurrying on again. He smiled a little as he watched her. What a fool she was, leaving civilization further and further behind her as she entered this wild, isolated place where there were only the ghosts of the past to watch over her.

He waited as she reached the foot of the steps and began to climb up to the terrace, and then he left the shelter of the bridge to move silently and swiftly in her wake. She was almost his, his beautiful Lady Domino. . . .

She stood at last on the terrace. The excitement quivered breathlessly through her, fluttering wildly in her breast. What if she was wrong? What if there was nothing there? "Oh, please," she whispered. "*Please* let something come of this." The lights of Bath twinkled far below and she heard the low hooting of an owl somewhere in the woods, but she saw nothing of the stealthy figure on the drive.

Her steps sounded loud on the flagstones as she approached the shadowy space at the entrance of the cellars. The walls shut out the moonlight and the air became instantly cooler as she descended. The boards that had been nailed over it shortly after the fire had long since been broken away by thieves. The door creaked loudly in the silence as she pushed it open, shivering as the dank, icy air from within swept out over her, bringing with it the mustiness of damp stone and mortar, the tang of rotting wood and rope, and above all the stench of decay. The black opening yawned before her.

Hesitantly she went forward, knowing that the steps led down beside the wall, but as she passed inside the wayward breeze seemed to deliberately catch the door, swinging it to behind her. The noise echoed over and over until she wanted to put her hands to her ears. The sounds died away at last and there was only the velvet silence once more, an impenetrable, almost palpable shroud. Forcing such fearsome thoughts to the back of her mind, she fumbled for a lucifer. The moments seemed to pass on leaden feet before it flared into life, a vibrant flame that sent the shadows reeling into the distant corners and illuminated her face with a fiery, almost demonic glow. The candle was reluctant to light, but at last the weak flame grew stronger and the soft halo lit up the steps stretching down before her.

Slowly she looked around, gasping aloud as she saw a rat crouching on the cellar floor, its red eyes bright and sharp for a moment before it moved silently away into the murky shadows. She could see broken barrels and lengths of ancient rope, all that remained now of the contents of a once-great house. The hiding place behind the stone lay some way away to the right. Putting her hand to the damp wall, she began to descend slowly, the flame gyrating wildly and the shadows spinning monstrously all around.

As Rex reached the terrace he heard the slam of the door and he turned immediately in the direction of the sound. Softly he hurried toward it, and as he neared the shadows he saw the door. His eyes glittered unpleasantly as he smiled again. Had she been cooperating in his design, she could not have done more to serve his purpose. He descended to the door, pushing very gently upon it, but no amount of stealth could silence the eerie groaning of the hinges. Briefly he saw the glow of candlelight from within, but then instantly it was extinguished and there was only the inky darkness. Moments later the thin drifting wisps of smoke from candle reached him, pricking his nostrils with its recent warmth. She was somewhere very close.

Terrified, Adele was standing at the foot of the cellar steps looking up at the man's silhouette, picked out so very clearly against the starry sky. It was Rex, she knew it instantly. That moment of recognition lent her more fear and dread than anything else in her life, and she was trembling as she stretched out a hand toward the wall. Her questing fingertips touched the cold stone and she began to edge away from the steps. Her mind was a blank, terror robbing her of memory so that she could not think which way the cellars went, whether she was edging herself into a corner or whether she was moving away where there was more room, more chance of escape.

A whimper caught in her throat as she stared up at him, backing slowly away, but then she stumbled against a barrel. It rolled away on the uneven floor, clattering and rumbling like the roar of a hundred cannon. The whimper escaped her lips then and she turned blindly into the enveloping blackness, knocking aside another barrel as she did so and catching her foot in one of the coils of rope that seemed to lie everywhere. She fell heavily to the floor, winding herself and lay where she had fallen, the thundering of her heart so loud that she was sure he must be able to hear it.

A lucifer glowed suddenly at the top of the steps and at last she could see him clearly, so very handsome and elegant in his evening clothes, a diamond pin gleaming in the folds of his cravat. She also suddenly saw where she was lying. There were barrels all around her and several ransacked tea chests. One of these was pushed almost into a small corner where there was just enough room left for her to crawl behind it. Stifling the terrified sobs that rose in her throat, she crawled toward that little space, the only protection she could see.

The lucifer flickered and died, and there was darkness once more. The moments passed before the next one flared and she pressed back into the shadows as if she would become part of the wall. The shuddering light raised shadows and demons all around her and she hid her face in her hands. There was no escape from him this time; it was only a matter of time before he found her. He would have his revenge.

She heard him descend the steps, and through a small crack between the tea chest and the wall she saw him glancing carefully all around. He looked down then and bent out of sight, and when he straightened she saw that he had found the candle she had dropped. A moment later the steady flame had been lit and he held the candle aloft.

He searched methodically, leaving nothing to chance. More than once the moving light almost threw its telltale glow over her, but each time fell just short of her pale face and wide, frightened eyes. The minutes passed and he became irritated, kicking a barrel aside. The sound echoed from wall to wall.

It was then that he saw the tea chest in the corner. A slow, triumphant smile spread over his fine lips as he saw the fringe of her shawl peeping from beneath it. Setting the candle down on another chest, he approached her hiding place, reaching down suddenly to push the chest aside and grab her arm. She screamed as his fingers closed painfully over her and he dragged her toward him.

"So," he said softly, ignoring her pathetic struggles, "at last there is nothing to come between us."

"Please, my lord!"

"I am deaf to your pleas, my lovely, for I have been denied that which I am due for long enough."

"Please let me go, I *beg* of you!"

"You might as well beg for the moon, sweetheart."

"You don't think I have come here without expecting someone to join me!" she cried then, desperate to halt his purpose.

"If you expected someone, why then did you extinguish the light when you heard me?" He laughed a little. "You will have to do better than that, Miss Russell, much better."

"Please let me go," she whispered, ceasing to struggle, "Please—"

"You are mine, my fine *lady*, and before many minutes more you will know that fact only too well." He pushed her back against the wall, holding her chin roughly with one hand as he looked down into her panic-stricken face. "You are so very beautiful," he murmured. "I have dreamed of this sweet moment since first I saw you. You wore a domino but I could sense how beautiful you were." He bent his head forward to kiss her on the lips and she could taste the maraschino on his breath.

The cry was muffled and choked in her throat as he pulled her into his arms then, kissing her all the while. She felt his hand move to touch her breast and in absolute dread she began to struggle feebly, trying to fight his superior strength. She felt him laugh; there was none of Sir Mask's gentleness about him now. He was savage and urgent, forcing her to the floor as his passion lent him more and more strength. She was completely at his mercy, helpless and unable to even begin to fend off his brutish attack.

"Unhand her, Talbourne, if you value your miserable life! Unhand her, I say!"

With a disbelieving cry, Rex whirled about in the direction of that voice. "Blaisdon!"

David Latimer stood at the top of the cellar steps, a dim, barely discernible figure beyond the rim of candlelight. Slowly he began to descend, his gaze holding Rex transfixed. Adele scrambled away, fighting back the sobs and tearing her skirt on a piece of stone.

Rex got to his feet, his face growing paler. "This has nothing to do with you, Blaisdon. I advise you therefore to stay out of it."

"Do you indeed? And since when have I needed to pay heed to your advice?" David halted, his glance moving then to Adele. "You are all right?"

She had no time to answer, for Rex seized his opportunity to draw a pistol from inside his coat and level it at David. Adele screamed a warning, her fingers closing instinctively over a piece of stone which she threw with all her might at Rex. It struck his shoulder and the pistol discharged harmlessly into the ceiling, the blast cracking like thunder in the enclosed space. The echoes died away very slowly and Rex lowered the pistol, his face ashen now. He was himself now as helpless as Adele had been but a minute before. His tongue passed nervously over his dry lips and his face seemed to take on an even more ghastly pallor.

David had not moved a muscle from the moment Adele had screamed. His eyes were as hard as flint, and the utter contempt and loathing he felt for Rex was plain to see on his cold face. "So, my little dukeling," he breathed softly. "Yet again you would shoot a defenseless man. I should have put an end to you in India, for you are not fit to breathe this earth's sweet air!"

Adele stared at them both. India? David Latimer had been in India? What was all this about?

Rex gave a short, nervous laugh. "Everyone knew that Ramchund deserved to die, Blaisdon; he tried to cheat me over that diamond."

"The diamond had nothing to do with it; you shot him because he tried to stop you assaulting his daughter."

"Ramchund's daughter was a whore; the whole of Madras knew that!"

"The whole of Madras knew nothing of the sort."

"She became your mistress within days of your arrival!"

"And how that one fact pinched your miserable little soul, Talbourne. It pinched you until you tried to take by force that which she had every right to deny you, and it drove you to commit murder. Ramchund may have been a diamond merchant and he may have sailed close to the wind, but he was no rogue and he did not deserve to die for protecting what he held most dear in all the world."

Rex's eyes were bright and beads of perspiration gleamed on his waxen forehead. "You are free with your accusation, Blaisdon, but you have done nothing about it!"

"Not because I dare not, I promise you that, my little

193

dukeling. You have been safe from me simply because I gave Ramchund's daughter my word. Her sister was promised to a great lord and that match would have been ruined had any scandal touched the family name. Everyone believed Ramchund had been murdered by an unknown thief, but I learned the truth because she told me. You should have learned a salutary lesson from all that, Talbourne, but you learned nothing at all. You left India and came back here as filled with your own arrogant importance and as puffed up with pride and a sense of your own superiority as ever. I still stand by my word to Ramchund's daughter, but that word does not bind me now, for you have again attempted to take by brute force that which has been refused you.''

''And what of Miss Russell's reputation?'' cried Rex desperately. ''Have you no thought of that?''

Without warning, David suddenly lunged forward and Rex did not even have time to cry out. Adele stared, mesmerized for a moment, but then she struggled to her feet and ran to seize the earl's arm.

''Stop, please stop! He's not worth it, David. He's just not worth risking the gallows for!'' Desperately she tugged at his sleeve, and at last he drew back, contenting himself at the last with flinging Rex against the wall, just as he had once flung him against the shelves in the haberdashery. The wall was hard and the blow knocked Rex unconscious. He slumped to the floor and with a gasp Adele knelt beside him, fearing that he was dead, but then she felt his pulse. She closed her eyes with relief.

David bent to take her by the shoulders, drawing her to her feet and holding her close for a moment. ''It's all right now,'' he murmured. ''You're safe.''

She clung to him, burying her face in his coat. She felt his fingers move gently against her warm hair and she could feel his heart beating close to hers.

Slowly he pulled away, looking into her pale face. ''You are sure you're all right? He didn't—''

She shook her head weakly. ''You came in time. But how did you know I was here?''

''Miss Rogers came to me.''

''Cat? But—''

''She saw Talbourne's phaeton and realized that you were in danger. Why in God's own name you could not have

194

waited until daylight and then taken someone with you I'll never know!''

"I didn't think."

"No, and in that I believe you run true to form." He bent to tie Rex's arms and legs with some of the old rope that lay about on the floor. Then he turned to her again. "There is nothing for it but to let him go in a while; to do anything other than that would indeed bring your name into something which would ruin your reputation.''

She stared down at Rex's motionless body. "Did he really kill that man in India?''

"Yes. He has much to answer for."

"Was she very beautiful, your mistress?''

"Very."

She said nothing more and he looked at her for a moment before speaking again. "I have once again done my impersonation of St. George. The dragon lies vanquished and the fair maiden has been rescued. Shall we now look for the long-hidden treasure so that one of us may live happily ever after?''

"One of us?''

"I speak of you, Miss Russell.''

She could not help but notice that he had returned to a more formal mode of address. A short while before he had called her by her first name. "Yes," she said. "Yes, let us look for the treasure, my lord.''

She picked up the candle and glanced around, taking her bearings. Going to one wall, she began to count the stones. "Thirteen, fourteen, fifteen. It's this one, the sixteenth from the end.'' Pushing the candle into his hand again, she felt around the stone, seeking the well-remembered places. Dust scattered to the floor as she dragged the stone out with a slow, grating sound that made her glance nervously around.

The stone fell with a resounding clatter and the flame trembled as he held the candle closer to the dark space in the wall. Spiders scurried back into the shadows and Adele shuddered as she reached inside, her hand brushing against the heavy gray lace of old cobwebs. She felt around for anything remotely like a ledger or notebook, and then with a cry drew out a small leather-bound volume. Wiping the dust away from its cover, she stared at it, afraid at the last moment of opening it for fear of bitter disappointment.

Returning the candle to her, he took the book and opened it. Page after page of Denzil Russell's neat handwriting and precise figures was revealed and Adele closed her eyes with joy. It was all there, every detail her father had found out about the fraud for which he himself was to be blamed. Nothing had been omitted, from Frederick Repton's first false entry to the huge sums finally transferred so cleverly to the Duke of Bellingham's accounts.

David closed the book at last. "It may have taken five years," he said softly, "but in the end your father is vindicated."

"Yes," she whispered.

"Then we had better take this precious item to a safe place."

Tears shone on her cheeks. "It *will* convict my father's murderers, won't it? I mean, there isn't any room for doubt?"

"It will convict them, and it will make you a very rich woman again, or had that not occurred to you?"

She stared at him. "No, it had not," she said. "I was thinking only of clearing my father's name. Beyond that—" She shrugged, for it was true, she *hadn't* really considered anything more.

"No, I begin to see that that is so. Well, I suggest that you begin to give the matter some consideration, Miss Russell, for the moment I take this book to the relevant authorities, wheels will be set in motion which will eventually return to you all that was taken five years ago."

"But if you had not come up here tonight—"

"For that fact you must thank Miss Rogers."

"But you came."

"I trust you are not going to again ask me why."

"No."

"Good, for once a gentleman has given his word about protecting a lady, then it ill becomes that lady to question his actions."

She looked away from him. He had given his word to her five years before, but it had suited him to break it then. But now, when she owed him her very life, it would indeed ill become her to question his motives. Her glance fell on Rex, still lying motionless where he had fallen. "What shall you do about Lord Talbourne?"

"I shall untie him and leave him to come around in his own good time. The turtle feast of scandal which is about to break over his family's head will make further punishment a little unnecessary. You should be smiling, Miss Russell, for after five years of suffering taunts at Euphemia's hands, the tables are about to be sweetly reversed.''

She stared at him. ''But you are to marry her, how can you speak of her like that?''

''Whatever my intentions are toward her, Miss Russell, I am not blind to her faults. I never have been and I never will be.''

He untied Rex again and then took Adele's arm, leading her to the steps and up into the cool, fresh night air. After the dank cellar, the perfume from the balsam trees down in the woods seemed headier than before, and she took a long, deep breath, shaking her hair.

He lifted her onto his horse and then mounted behind her, his arm strong and steady around her waist as he urged the horse away down the slope. She looked back at the silhouette of Beech Park against the starry sky. Was the nightmare of the past five years really over at last? Was it possible that her life was about to undergo yet another drastic change, only this time for the better? Was it?

Chapter 24

It was still dark but the Bellingham landau was drawn up outside the house in the Circus. The house was ablaze with lights. The noise and confusion besetting the household had aroused several neighboring families, and there were a number of people gathered outside on the pavement. Trunk after trunk was carried out to the waiting carriage by footmen who had obviously dressed hastily and who looked pale and nervous.

The watch stood looking with interest, leaning on their staves, their patrol forgotten as they discussed what might have happened to reduce the icy, imperious Duchess of Bellingham to such hysteria that her cries could be clearly heard as she ordered maids here and there. There could be little trace now of the intimidatingly composed paragon before whom Bath trembled, not if all the noise was anything to go by.

Realizing that they had dallied too long already, the watch at last began to move on, but then one of them caught his companions by the sleeves, pointing across the Circus at the solitary, hurrying figure of Rex, Lord Talbourne, making his way toward his home. They all stared, for he looked, as the saying goes, as if he had been dragged through a hedge backward. His hair was a mess and his clothes in such a state that his London tailor would no doubt collapse of the vapors if he had seen. They watched him push his way through the small crowd, shaking off all those who tried to ask him what was happening, and then he vanished into the house.

The leader of the watch took out his immense fob watch and, taking a deep breath, called out. "Four o'clock in the morning, and all's well!" His companions broke into helpless laughter. All's well? Not for some it wasn't!

Alarmed at the chaos reigning in the house and horrified at the sound of his mother's hysteria, Rex went to find his sister. She was sitting alone in the candlelit drawing room, looking very composed and in every way the complete opposite of her frantic mother. She was pale and drawn, and had her brother looked closer he would have seen that she had been crying, although the tears were over now.

She looked up as he entered. "Ah, so the prodigal returns again," she murmured. "And does so too late to witness the fireworks."

"What's happened?"

"I might ask the same of you, my handsome but untidy gamecock."

"Footpads."

"Really?" Her eyes flickered disdainfully. "Well, I suppose that a fine lord walking alone should expect to fall foul of such villains—although I must also wonder if you met with more than a defenseless woman when you set off in the direction of Beech Park."

He flushed angrily. "That damned clacking tiger!"

"Told me all he knew when I demanded it of him!"

"Does it matter what's happened to me? I am more concerned now to find out what's going on here? Where's Father?"

"He's been arrested."

He stared, his face draining of what little color it had left. "Sweet God above!"

"I believe that Sir Frederick Repton has been arrested too, which might give you some idea of what lies behind all this."

"Denzil Russell?"

She inclined her head once. "Right the first time, brother mine."

He reached for the decanter. "Is there proof?"

"Of course there is!" she snapped irritably, "You don't imagine they arrest a nobleman of Father's importance without proof, do you?"

"But how? I mean, where did they—"

"Your precious Adele and the—the Earl of Blaisdon . . ." Her voice broke off, the slight trembling of her lips the only sign of the huge emotion lurking just beneath the surface of her strange calm. The moment passed and she continued. "They found evidence which Denzil Russell had apparently hidden in the cellars at Beech Park before the fire. The earl acted on her behalf and went to the authorities. Papa and Sir Frederick were arrested about an hour ago."

Rex gave a short, disbelieving laugh. "The cellars," he murmured, swirling the cognac, "the damned cellars!"

"You followed her, didn't you? What happened? Did you exact your revenge."

"No. Blaisdon, would you believe, arrived yet again."

"And bettered you again, by the look of you." She sneered, looking at him with something akin to loathing. "Dear God, how pathetic you are, Rex. I swear that I'm twice the man you'll ever be!"

"Are you? One thing I know you are, sis, and that is only half the woman you'd like to be, for Blaisdon will never be yours."

She looked away from him.

He smiled. "We are quits, sis. We share the same fate, both doomed to be humiliated by Blaisdon and his haberdasher's assistant."

"Stop it!"

"What's this, a crack in your formidable armor?" He went closer to her, studying her tear-stained face. "Twice the man, are you? I think not."

She watched him drain the glass and turned to pour himself another. "What are you going to do now? Drown your sorrows?"

"I've ordered my phaeton to be made ready immediately—I was going to leave Bath even before what you've told me about Father's arrest. Now I'm twice as determined to be gone before daylight."

"Mother's leaving too; she's returning to her family's estate in Westmorland. The Bellingham rats are leaving the sinking ship with all possible haste."

"I see no reason to allow Bath a glimpse of our disarray, do you?" he replied.

"I shall not leave until well after daylight. I ordered my carriage for after breakfast and shall not alter that order."

"What's this? The supreme gesture?"

"Yes, but not for the reason you think. Like you, I had ordered my carriage before I knew what was going to happen."

His eyes were shrewd. "Blaisdon ended your hopes once and for all, did he?"

"Yes."

"Poor sis, you really love him, don't you?"

She didn't answer.

"So, you are going to make your exit with your chin in the air. I salute your nerve." He raised his glass to her. "How the tables have turned upon us, eh? The great and noble

House of Bellingham now suffers the same fate as Denzil Russell and his daughter, although to be sure we are far from impoverished.''

Slowly Euphemia got up. ''No, we are not impoverished, but the ruin is there for all that. It will be a long, long time before the name of Bellingham is revered again. You know, I despise Adele Russell, God knows that I do, but I admire her too. In the face of all that happened to her, she still kept her pride, she didn't give in. And if she could do it, then so can I. I may have lost, but the world will never see that in my face. I've done my crying; there'll be no more tears, and when I go out to my carriage I shall not show by so much as a flicker how I really feel.''

''If that's your pleasure, you carry on, but I've no wish to prove anything to anyone and am quite set upon leaving this cursed hole before the world claps eyes on me. I didn't do anything five years ago. I was far away in India, and the slight scrape I've got myself into with Blaisdon will smooth over. I shall rise above it all and I don't give a damn about anything or anyone else.''

''No, I didn't imagine for one moment that you would.''

''You are in no position to be superior, sis,'' he said softly. ''You are as callously selfish as I am. You and I are true scions of the House of Bellingham; we think only of ourselves. Father may have come the proverbial cropper, but that cannot be helped. *C'est la vie, n'est-ce pas?* Mama may have the hysterics, but it is not because she is worried about him. It's because she's worried about how much will leave a mark upon her, that's why she's scurrying away to Westmorland. I swear that if there was an estate near John o'Groats, she'd go there instead! We're all Bellinghams, sis, rotten to the core.''

''You may be a Bellingham, Rex, but there isn't an ounce of that blood in my veins.''

''Ah, yes,'' he said, grinning. ''You're Wenworth's brat, aren't you? The outcome of the first of Mama's brief amours. Well, that's an accident of birth; it doesn't make the slightest difference to the real you, for you've been brought up a Bellingham and a damned Bellingham is what you'll always be. You'll always scheme and plot, always allow your spite free rein, always take your revenge for the slightest iinsult, imagined or otherwise. You'll always present a smiling, charming face to the world, but inside you'll always be as poisonous as a nest of vipers. You're one of us, sis, there's no getting away from it. Only a Bellingham would have gone to all that trouble to find out the nasty little secrets in Dr. Enleigh's cupboard, only a Bellingham would have stooped to hiring a dilapidated chaise in order to meet a sly fellow whose only business in life is to pry into the affairs of others. It was a masterful effort, sis, a true Bellingham effort, but all in vain as it turns out, for your luck ran out.''

''All in vain?'' she said lightly, ''I think not.''

''There is little point in getting your scheming hands on those deeds now, for it will make no difference whatsoever to Adele Russell. If Father has been arrested, then it is only a matter of time before she is restored to all her wealth. She'll be able to give her precious nurse a hundred haberdasheries after that, in the heart of London probably.''

''I must admit defeat where Adele Russell is concerned, but that fat, holier-than-thou clergyman will not escape.''

''You'll expose Enleigh anyway?''

''Yes, he had the temerity to refuse what I asked of him.''

''You see?'' He smiled, raising his glass. ''You're a Bellingham to your fingertips.''

Chapter 25

Someone was drawing back the heavy velvet drapes at the windows and the gentle sound made Adele stir in the canopied bed. The sunlight streamed in and she instinctively turned her face away from it, curling up again between the soft, lavender scented sheets. She felt warm and drowsy, too deliciously comfortable to open her eyes, but at last she did so.

The room in which she lay was very elegant indeed, its walls hung with Chinese silk on which a beautiful design of pastel-hued flowers had been painted. The furniture was all of polished mahogany and there was an exquisite Wilton carpet on the floor. Through an adjoining door she could see a dressing room, as daintily furnished as any lady could wish with its primrose brocade dressing table on which stood a small looking-glass and many little bottles, jewelboxes, combs and brushes, and all the paraphernalia of a lady's toilet. A jug of water, a bowl, and a towel stood on another table and there was a large cheval glass before the sun-lit window. Her puzzled gaze moved to the fireplace where an immense bowl of summer flowers stood in the hearth next to the rushlight, which had burned overnight and which someone had recently extinguished.

A shadow passed between Adele and the window and Cat asked her how she was feeling.

"Cat?" Adele blinked. "Where—?" Memory flooded back then and she sat up with a start.

Cat smiled, sitting on the edge of the bed. "You are in the Earl of Blaisdon's house on Royal Crescent."

"I know, I remember." She glanced toward the window as she heard a sound outside. "What's that?"

"The crowd."

"What crowd?"

"The one which gathered there directly news of what had happened spread through Bath."

"But how do they know so quickly? I don't remember anything at all after drinking that mulled wine the countess insisted I take."

"You fell asleep. I think you were totally exhausted, both in your mind and in your body. I suggested that it might be better to take you home to the haberdashery, but neither the earl nor the countess would hear of it. They said that that would not be at all wise for once the furor began, the shop would be the focus of a great deal of unwelcome attention. And I think they are right, for if a crowd that size can gather outside a grand house on Royal Crescent, then the Lord alone knows what's happening in Milsom Street."

"How did they all find out?"

"The moment the earl was satisfied you would be remaining here, he went directly to the authorities with the evidence. The duke and Sir Frederick were arrested within the hour. I gather that the Duchess of Bellingham herself was the reason the tale spread so swiftly, for she made such a dreadful fuss, ordering her carriage and having the vapors, that the whole of the Circus was soon aware what had happened."

Adele hardly dared believe what she was being told. They had been arrested—after all this time they were to pay for their dreadful crimes. She looked at Cat again. "What of Euphemia? And Lord Talbourne?"

"Well, I don't know about Lady Euphemia; as far as I am aware she is still in the Circus. Lord Talbourne left before first light in his phaeton, driving like a madman along the London road, so I'm told. The duchess, as I've already said, ordered her carriage immediately and left at about the same time as her son. I believe she's going to Westmorland or some such place."

At that moment the door opened and the countess entered, her black bombazine skirts rustling and her cane tapping. "Please leave us, Miss Rogers," she asked, nodding at Cat who hastened to obey.

The countess came to the foot of the bed. "I trust you are feeling a little recovered after your ordeal, Miss Russell."

"I am, thank you."

The countess's bright eyes rested thoughtfully on the young woman in the bed. "We have only met once before, Miss Russell, and on that occasion—the occasion of your betrothal to my son—you were attired in the finest silk; you had jewels in your hair and at your throat. You looked quite the most enchanting creature I had ever set eyes on, and now, in your borrowed night robe, your hair uncombed and unadorned, you are still captivatingly beautiful and I can understand only too well how my son became so enamoured of you.''

"On that other occasion, my lady,'' said Adele, holding the other woman's gaze, "I was in no doubt that you did not approve of me, that you would much have preferred to be welcoming Lady Euphemia as your future daughter-in-law.''

"I *was* in favor of the match with the duke's daughter, but not, I hasten to say, because I disapproved of you personally.'' The countess came around the bed, sitting down stiffly on the edge of the elegant coverlet and resting her cane carefully. Clasping her bony, lace-covered hands in her lap, she spoke again. "Maybe I should be very honest with you, Miss Russell.''

"You were honest then, although you said nothing outright.''

The countess smiled. "You interest me greatly, for I do not believe I have ever met anyone quite like you before. You are certainly capable of some quite alarming escapades, and yet I do not think for one moment that you are at all as forward and impudent as some of your recent behavior might suggest.''

Adele listened to this judgment without replying.

"I said that my opposition—such as it was—to the betrothal was not caused by my disapproval of you, and that is the truth. I opposed the match simply because it had not been calmly and objectively arranged, because it was a love match, Miss Russell, and I view love matches with a great deal of suspicion, and rightly so.''

"Why?''

"Because they are entered into with such high hopes and nearly always seem to end in disillusionment. On so many occasions, it seems, I witnessed the marriages of friends and relations turn sour because reality could not possibly match up to the soaring dreams love promised, and I did not want that for my son. To me, the arranged marriage is the perfect beast, Miss Russell, and that is why I opposed the match with you—for no other reason, and certainly not because Lady Euphemia was the daughter of a duke whereas you were the daughter of a banker.''

"Was your own marriage arranged?''

"Yes. Oh, at the time I was very young and I rebelled a little, wanting to marry the man I loved instead of the man my parents chose for me, but in the end I did as I was told, and I believe I made the right choice."

"Were you happy?"

"Happy? I suppose I was, but then one does not look inside one's marriage for happiness, one looks outside for that. I did my duty to my husband, I produced David, and then considered myself free to take a lover if I chose. I took as my lover the man I had loved in the first place, and by him I had my other son, Jamie." The countess gave a short laugh then, flushing a little as she looked at Adele. "Do you know, I have not ever volunteered that information in my life."

Adele felt very uncomfortable. "There is no need—" she began.

"There is, if only to make you see that I was against the marriage between you and my son for perfectly valid reasons."

"Valid to you."

"Yes, valid to me."

Adele glanced away, wishing she could change the subject, for she was finding this conversation very unsettling. "H-how is Jamie?" she asked at last, "I remember meeting him once. I think it was the same evening I met David—I mean, the earl."

"Jamie is dead, Miss Russell."

Adele looked up with swift dismay. "Forgive me, I did not know."

"Why should you know? He died in India, about five years ago now. He left for that cursed land the day after you met him, and had barely arrived there when an ague took him."

"I'm so very sorry."

The old woman nodded sadly. "Thank you, Miss Russell. I have nothing left now to remind me of the man I loved; his son is dead and he himself was killed when thrown from a brute of a thoroughbred which no man in his right senses would have attempted to ride. Jamie had his father's headstrong ways, a chip off the old block in so many, many ways."

Adele hesitated before asking the next question, but she was curious, and besides, if the countess was giving her views on marriage as being the cause of past opposition, then the question had some relevance. "My lady, did you only ever love Jamie's father?"

"I have not had a string of lovers like the Duchess of Bellingham, if that is what you mean," came the tart reply.

"That is not what I was thinking."

The countess glanced at her. "Very well, I will tell you. I only ever loved Jamie's father; there was never anyone else in my heart."

"Then your arranged match, the right choice in your own words, in fact offered you less than a love match would have done. If you had followed your heart and married the man you loved instead of the man your parents chose for you, then you would have known a great deal more happiness, wouldn't you? Forgive me for being blunt, my lady, but that is what I think."

After a moment, during which Adele thought she had gone far too far, the countess suddenly smiled. "You are too sharp for your own good, missy."

"I merely don't agree with your views on marriage."

"So it seems."

"But your son does, doesn't he?"

"What do you mean?"

"I may have foolishly entered into the betrothal because I loved him, but he certainly did not approach the matter in the same way, did he?"

The countess seemed taken aback. "Why do you say that?"

"Because he sought to end the betrothal the moment scandal touched upon my name, and I became not only notorious but also penniless. The note he sent to me could not have been more cruel or deliberate. Again you must forgive me for speaking plainly, my lady, but that is how I see it. Indeed, it would not surprise me in the slightest to learn now that he has already striven to dissociate himself from his more recent courtship of the Marchioness of Heydon for exactly the same reasons: she is suddenly not at all a suitable bride for the great Earl of Blaisdon!"

For a long moment the countess looked at her, seeming somewhat bemused by the forthright attack upon her son. "You do indeed believe in speaking your mind, don't you?" she said at last.

"I have learned my lessons well over the past five years, my lady. Besides, I believe that the cards were put on the table the moment you entered this room, weren't they?"

"Yes, I suppose they were, for I wished so much to understand you, Miss Russell."

"And do you?"

"I begin to think so. You appear to have a very low opinion of my son."

Adele said nothing.

"He would strongly challenge your description of his recent association with the marchioness as being tantamount to a courtship."

"How else should it be described? I'll warrant even you believed he was about to ask for her hand."

The countess nodded. "I did. I now know better."

"So I'm right, he has terminated all connection with her."

"Not all connection, just any notion of marriage."

"I don't think there is anything more to be said, do you?" Adele got out of the bed. "I think it would be better if I left your house now, my lady, for I do not merit your continued kindness after all I've said. Please believe me when I say that I am very grateful for your kindness and for the immeasurable help the earl has given me. I owe him more than I can begin to say. But the past is too close; things were said and done which make it impossible for me to remain under your roof. Please say that you understand."

"Oh, I understand, Miss Russell. Indeed, I've never understood so clearly before." The old woman stood, her hands neatly on the handle of her cane. "I trust, however, that you will remain to take breakfast with us. My son has gone to the authorities again to clear up several small matters, but he will return soon."

"I would rather go immediately."

"That would offend me."

Adele looked at her in surprise. "Offend you?"

"Please stay for breakfast."

"I will stay to thank the earl."

"But not to break bread with him?" The countess smiled. "Very well, that will do to be going on with. Until a little later then, Miss Russell."

The door closed behind her. A little later a maid came to attend Adele. Very neat and tidy in her plain blue gown with its white ruff at the throat, she bobbed a curtsy and then proceeded excellently about her work. In no time at all Adele had acquired a coiffure that would have done justice to a London drawing room and was once again wearing the dimity gown, expertly repaired and cleaned after the ravages of the Beech Park cellar floor.

Before bracing herself to go down to the breakfast room, she asked the maid where Cat was.

"In the kitchens, ma'am."

"Would you tell her that we shall be returning to Milsom Street in a short while and to be ready to leave?"

"Yes, ma'am."

The breakfast room, like all the best such rooms, was sunny and welcoming, its walls richly paneled and its ceiling beautifully decorated with gilded plasterwork. Normally the tall windows would have been open to the summer morning, but the presence of the crowd prevented that. The Earl of Blaisdon and his mother were already seated at the white-clothed table, and Adele noticed immediately that the countess looked a little stormy, her lips pressed tightly together, although she managed a smile as Adele entered.

The earl stood. "Good morning, Miss Russell."

"Good morning, my lord."

"Please sit down."

"I would prefer—"

"I'm sure even you have time to spare for breakfast," he replied, waiting deliberately.

Reluctantly she went to the chair the butler had drawn out for her. As she sat down she noticed the muffins and breakfast rolls keeping warm on a trivet before the small fire and the polished brass kettle with its china handle simmering gently on the glowing coals.

The countess glanced at her son and then at Adele. "I have informed my son that you intend to return to Milsom Street, Miss Russell, and he insists that you reconsider."

His eyebrow twitched a little. "I believe I am capable of speaking for myself, Mother," he said. "Miss Russell, I do indeed think it would be better if you remained here for the time being, for when I passed down Milsom Street this morning the crush outside the haberdashery was quite unbelievable. You and Miss Rogers would be much more comfortable if you stayed here."

"I would prefer to leave, sir."

His blue eyes met hers for a moment and then he nodded. "Very well, I will see that a carriage is made ready for you."

"There is no need."

"How else do you imagine you will get there?"

"Is it so bad?"

"It is. Word that Repton and the duke had been arrested

spread like wildfire and the whole of Bath is agog to set eyes on you. You are the darling of the day, Miss Russell; your hometown adores you again and wishes to shower attention upon you whether you wish it or not. Why, I believe they have had you betrothed to at least two dukes, several mere lords, and even an exiled French *comte*—and all that before breakfast."

His mother looked very put out, her glance somehow a little defiant. "David, I wish you would not—"

He threw her a swift, angry look. "That is enough, Mother."

"But—"

"Enough!"

She lowered her gaze to her plate and fell silent, but her lips were pressed together again, and it looked as if she were struggling considerably against her better judgment.

He turned once more to Adele. "Are you still set on leaving this house?"

"Yes."

"Very well, that is the end of the matter." He beckoned to the butler. "See that the landau is brought to the front immediately."

"Very well, my lord."

Adele toyed with her coffee cup. "My lord—"

"Yes?"

"I wish to thank you again for all that you have done for me."

"I have done very little."

His mother seemed unable to contain herself any longer. "David!" she cried, her whole body trembling. "This has surely gone far enough! How can you sit there like that?"

"I thought I conveyed my thoughts precisely to you a little earlier, Mother, and that you had given your word. I am holding you to that."

A thousand expressions passed across the countess's face as she fought to control her tongue. "Very well," she said at last, "I will say nothing more for the time being, but I make no promise whatsoever that I will not return to the subject later."

"My attitude will not change, no matter how often you return," he said shortly, glancing at his fob watch. "And now, is it not time for you to go to the Pump Room again?"

She got to her feet and for a long moment mother and son looked at each other before she turned on her heel and left.

Adele sat uncomfortably where she was, wishing that she had not been present at such a sharp exchange.

"You look as if you wish to say something, Miss Russell."

"I do?"

"You are pensive, to say the least."

"I—I was thinking that my affairs have interfered somewhat with your plans."

"My plans?"

"To marry the Marchioness of Heydon."

He sat back, his face very cold. *"Miss* Russell, I have never in my life entertained notions of marrying Euphemia. I did not intend such a course five years ago and I certainly have not intended it recently. I trust that you will now desist from all mention of such matters."

She stared at him. "But how can you say that when you have escorted her everywhere? *Everyone* knew what your intentions were!"

"Everyone knew nothing of the sort. I repeat, I have never thought of asking Euphemia to marry me."

"Then you should not have behaved as if you did." The words slipped out before she could stop them.

His eyes flashed with bitter anger then. "Don't you, of *all* people, presume to tell me how to conduct myself! What right have you to criticize me when your own actions in the past have been so questionable?"

Slowly she stood. "What actions?"

"I think you know well enough."

"No, I don't." She looked into his angry eyes—oh, so very angry. "I think I had better go," she whispered.

"Yes, I agree. Good day to you, Miss Russell, I trust we will never meet again!"

Fighting back the tears, she hurried to the doors, flinging them open before the butler could reach them. Gathering her skirts, she ran down the stairs, so upset that all she could think of was leaving this dreadful house.

Cat was waiting in the hallway and she looked around when she heard the light, swift steps on the stairs. Her face became anxious when she saw how distraught her former charge was. "Adele? What is it?"

Trying to control the tears, Adele put a hand on the anxious's woman's arm, but turned to the footman waiting by the door. "Is the landau there yet?"

"It's just arriving, madam."

"Then please open the door."

Even though she had been warned, she was still not prepared for the stir her appearance would cause among the crowd. They pressed excitedly forward, eager to see the woman who seemed set to be the center of yet another cause célèbre, and the coachman had the greatest difficulty controlling the team, which danced nervously around, eyes rolling and heads tossing.

Cat put a shielding arm around Adele's shoulders, and the footman did his best to conduct them safely to the carriage. At last the door slammed behind them and Adele sat weakly back, staring out at the sea of inquisitive faces that peered in at her. Cat held her hand as the landau began to move forward, the coachman shouting angrily for the way to be cleared. The parish constables seemed virtually powerless, and it wasn't until the coachman cracked his whip that the crowd parted hastily to allow the carriage through. The team came swiftly up to a smart pace, leaving the crowd behind as it entered Brock Street and the approach to the Circus.

In the hallway of the Bellingham residence, Euphemia took a final glance at herself in the hand mirror the maid held up before her. The judicious application of French rouge and Chinese papers had repaired the damage left by the tears she had shed earlier. There was no trace now of the tiredness around her eyes or the anxiety and disappointment lining her lips. Her hair looked as perfect as she wished, and she had chosen very carefully what she would wear when she emerged from the house to the curious gaze of the crowd still gathered on the pavement.

She wore a buttercup-yellow pelisse, which was very jaunty and bright and which she felt was quite the most lighthearted garment she possessed. It had cheeky frills and ruffs and was very eye-catching, which was how she wished to be. On her head was a little hat set at an angle so that the large, bouncy plumes adorning it could curl down the side of her head. Did she look as carefree and unperturbed as she intended? Yes, yes she did. Taking a deep breath, she nodded at the waiting footman, who flung open the doors.

She followed him out and the crowd immediately began to whisper. She smiled, her head held high, but her smile faltered just a little as she saw the Latimer carriage enter the Circus. Adele looked out and for a long moment the two

212

women looked at each other, then the landau passed from sight down Gay Street. Euphemia recovered, her smile returning as the footman handed her into her own carriage, and a moment later she was being conveyed away from the prying eyes of the crowd.

In Milsom Street the crush was immense, and the parish constables had long since given up all attempts to clear it. Cat leaned out. "You'd best brace yourself," she warned Adele, "for it's worse by far than what we've left behind. I only hope that foolish Joanie has wit enough to be on the lookout for us returning."

The landau swayed to a standstill a little way up the street from the shop, the team being far too agitated now to go any closer. The footman jumped down to open the door, and as he did so his livery was recognized. A great cry went up and the crowds surged hopefully toward the carriage.

"There she is," cried someone as Adele emerged.

Cat caught her hand and they began to run to the shop, where Joanie's anxious, frightened face was peering out of the bow window. In a blur Adele saw the sea of faces all around as the crowd pushed, and by the time Joanie had at last opened the door to admit them, Adele's coiffure had been ruined again and the sleeve of her gown torn.

Together Cat and Joanie forced the door closed, locking and bolting it to make sure no one would get in, and then the three women left the shop to go through to the relative peace of the kitchen.

Joanie was shaking from head to toe. "What's been happening, Miss Rogers?" she asked, her voice catching as if she was about to cry.

Cat looked sadly at Adele's bowed head and shaking shoulders. "Well you might ask, Joanie Smith," she said softly, "Well you might ask."

Chapter 26

The Earl of Blaisdon lounged silently on the sofa, a faraway look in his eyes. Beyond the windows the crowd still gathered, but at last the parish constables were beginning to have some success.

The countess was seated in her favorite chair, a tray of coffee on the little table beside her. She removed the lid of the pot and sniffed the aroma, wrinkling her nose disapprovingly. "The coffee in this accursed town is not as excellent as that which Berry's supply."

He didn't reply, indeed he didn't even hear her.

"You don't have much to say for yourself," she said, pouring herself a cup.

"I beg your pardon?"

"After having far too much to say for yourself at the breakfast table, you are now apparently struck dumb."

"I'm sorry for my earlier behavior; it was inexcusable."

"It was indeed, but I forgive you. However, you certainly left me in no doubt that I was to hold my tongue."

"That was the intention."

"You are wrong about this, David, very wrong."

"No."

"I spoke with Miss Russell this morning, as you know, and she was very adamant that *you* ended the engagement."

"If it pleases her for some reason to lay the blame on me, then let her proceed."

"She appeared to me to firmly believe she was speaking the truth."

"You and I both know that she was not. She was the one who ended the betrothal."

"Well, one of you must be fibbing, for you cannot possibly both be right, can you?" she said, eyeing him carefully. "And yet somehow I have the strangest feeling that you both are."

He looked at her in some exasperation. "I am not in the mood for damned riddles!"

"Don't swear, David."

"I apologize."

"Apologies uttered in that tone are hardly gracious; however, I accept."

His eyebrows flickered, but he refrained from replying.

She stirred her coffee, even though it contained no cream or sugar. "Now then, let me tell you how this whole sorry affair begins to appear to me."

"You will do that whether I wish you to or not."

"Yes, for when only you and I are present I have no need to pay any heed at all to your pompous male blusterings."

"Well, I suppose I can at least take solace from the knowledge that the rest of the world is under the impression that I'm master in my own home," he said dryly.

She smiled at him. "Don't be facetious. To the matter in hand: I have met Miss Russell twice now and I confess to believing her to be a forthright, honest and high-principled young lady. Oh, maybe she fell a little from grace when she was unwise enough to attend that masquerade, and she certainly did when she consented to meet that dreadful Talbourne, but apart from those slips, she is everything a young lady should be."

"Including rich enough to be a suitable wife," he said dryly.

"That *is* an added asset, I do not deny it."

"I find your mercenary and cold-blooded approach to the state of holy matrimony somewhat alarming."

"You are not the first person today to say something of the kind. Your Miss Russell did too."

"She isn't *my* Miss Russell!"

"No, but you wish she were."

He stood, going to the window to look out over Crescent Fields. The day was very bright and sunny, the buildings of Bath looked golden, and the trees were particularly handsome, their leaves moving just a little in the soft breeze. "Whatever I may wish," he said at last, "*her* wishes are quite plain. She loathes the very sight of me. And as to your riddles, everything is quite clear to me; she deliberately chose to misinterpret the letter I wrote to her before I went to India. There was no mistaking the contents of her reply, which reached me so promptly on the day I was to depart."

"The timing of it all was really quite remarkable," said his mother thoughtfully, beginning to stir the untouched coffee once more.

"The timing was coincidental."

"No, I don't believe it was. David, why do you believe she accepted your proposal in the first place?"

"Because I was a catch, even for Denzil Russell's daughter."

"Why then do you think she changed her mind."

"I don't even begin to know!" he said sarcastically. "I only know that I believed her when she told me she loved me. Oh, she was a consummate actress."

"But *why* go through such an act? Well?"

He shrugged. "I said that I did not know."

"No, because you cannot put a reason to such an apparent contradiction. You say she accepted you because you were a catch—you have never ceased to be a catch—and yet you say she ended the engagement. I don't believe she was a consummate actress, David, I believe she accepted your proposal because she loved you."

"I think not."

"Oh, you really are a stubborn creature—and so is Miss Russell. But then they do say that it takes one to find another one!" She put down her cup and subjected him to her most stern gaze. "Admit to me, David Latimer, that you still love Miss Russell."

"And what good would such an admission do?"

"It would at least serve to tell me that I am on firm ground!"

"Very well, I still love her."

"And she loves you, I'm sure of it."

He laughed. "Come now, you will say you are sure there are fairies next."

"Can you prove to me that there *aren't* fairies?"

"No, but then neither can I prove that there are."

"So, anything is possible."

He smiled fondly. "Yes," he said softly, "anything is possible."

"Even that Miss Russell loves you."

"Even that."

"I have already said that I have formed a very high opinion of her. I believe her above all else to be an honest woman. She would never, *never* have accepted your proposal in the

216

first place if she had not loved you. She does not believe in arranged marriages; she believes very much in love matches. She left me in no doubt as to her opinion of *my* opinion on that score. So I began this morning to seriously reconsider the events of five years ago, and I believe that I have formed a very clear picture. To begin with, I don't believe that she received the actual letter you wrote. And I don't believe she ever wrote to you in return.''

''But she did—I received the damned thing!''

''Think,'' she said gently. ''Think to whom you entrusted your letter; think who conveyed it to Beech Park, and then think who it was who brought her so-called reply to you. In view of all we have learned since arriving in this dreadful town, I believe that a great deal of intrigue was going on behind your back, intrigue which served to ruin both your happiness and Miss Russell's.''

He turned slowly to look at her, his face very still. ''Go on.''

''For the five years since the ending of the betrothal, Miss Russell's existence has hardly been delightful. She has been forced to wait upon those who once regarded her as their equal, she has endured the shame of both that and the ruining of her father's name, and above all, she has had to contend with the apparently cruel and callous betrayal she suffered at your hands. No, hear me out, David, for this must be said. I can well imagine the contents of the letter which was purported to come from you—for I have seen the letter which in turn was purported to come from her. You think she loathes you, and probably she feels that she should do just that, but I don't believe she does. She behaves as she does toward you now because she has to salvage her pride. And when I look at the way *you* have conducted yourself toward her since you rediscovered her, I see exactly the same conflict of emotions taking place. You love her, but your own pride has been badly bruised; you wish to stay away from her but you have found your path crossing hers time and time again. And you have been unable to prevent yourself from doing all you can to put things right for her. You would protect her with your very life, because you love her, but you would never tell her that—you would spout of honor, or some other such foolish male uttering.''

He smiled, for that was exactly what he had done—to the very letter.

His mother nodded. "I know you so very well, my laddo," she said, "Well enough to have always known in my heart that you would never marry because there was only ever one woman for you: Adele Russell. So, you now know that she is very much alive. She is within your grasp."

"I wish I could honestly think that."

"Think again about who you were so utterly addle pated enough to entrust that precious letter to, think who handed her letter to you, and think who subsequently told you that Miss Russell had perished with her father in the fire. Does it not all come down to one man, the man who had beavered so hard to get you to the altar with his daughter? I speak of the Duke of Bellingham, who we now know to have been behind so very much else which happened to Adele five years ago."

The countess paused. "I would not have suspected anything, but for Adele making me think so much. The fact that the duke had told you she was dead was so glaring, so deliberate, and yet until this morning I had forgotten it. There simply *has* to be more to his role in this. Now then, David Latimer, are you still going to prate to me about your express wish being unalterable? Or do you perhaps begin to see that someone has to make a move if things are to be resolved. It's up to you, and I shall not rest until I prod you into doing something, for if there is one thing I cannot bear, it is a miserable man about the house."

He smiled, but shook his head a little. "Even if I agree with you, there is still one fact which prevents me from ever approaching her now."

"What fact?"

"That she is now restored to her fortune. How do you imagine it would look if after an interval of five years the noble Earl of Blaisdon took himself along to profess his undying love all over again? It would not look at all well, Mother, and she would be bound to put the very worst light upon my actions."

His mother took a long, weary breath. "Possibly."

"Highly probably."

She stirred the almost cold coffee once more. "Some time ago, last year I believe it was, I attended a ball held by Mr. and Mrs. Daniels of Farnham in Hampshire," she said suddenly.

He was amazed at the apparent ease with which she shrugged

218

off such an important topic as his broken affair with Adele. "Did you?" he said coldly.

"Bear with me, David, for I am not being as contrary as your tone suggests you think. There is a very good point to this."

"I can't even begin to imagine what it is."

She looked crossly at him. "Unfortunately, you appear to be the supreme master of the lowest form of wit! Now then, I was telling you that I attended the ball. I was not going to at first, because I considered it a little presumptuous of them to invite me as we had only met once. However, I was staying not far away, and when the evening came I suddenly found myself at the proverbial loose end. So I decided to go, and I was very glad that I did, for I met Miss Austen. You have heard of Miss Austen?"

He nodded nonplussed. "Which Miss Austen?"

"The authoress."

"Yes, I have heard of her," he replied, a little bemused.

"She resides now at Chawton."

"How splendid for her."

She ignored him. "She was telling me that she intends to one day write a novel about a young lady who is persuaded by those closest to her that it would be better for her to end her betrothal to the young man she loves. She does as they advise and is very unhappy as a consequence, but then, miraculously, she is granted a second chance when the young man reenters her life some time later. After a great many misunderstandings, they eventually realize that they should never have listened to the persuasion of others and at last they are united." The countess glanced thoughtfully at the fireplace. "I do believe Miss Austen was speaking from experience—or at least from lost experience."

"It is a very pretty story, Mother, the very stuff of such novels as Miss Austen's adherents revel in."

"It is also the stuff of your predicament, my lad," his mother replied tartly. "I have a very high opinion of Miss Austen's books. They are very entertaining and so very sharp and observant. Maybe they do not deal with high society, but people are really the same from whatever level of life they hail. You have been granted a second chance with Miss Russell, and my advice to you is that you take that chance and risk your insufferable pride receiving a blow on the snout. And I offer you this advice as one who did not receive a second chance but had to abide by the dreadful mistake, made at the persuasion of others, that she made at the tender age of sixteen. I should never have married your father. I should have defied them all and married Jamie's father. But I did not. I was never happy with your father, nor he with me. Over the years I have spouted a great deal about the advisability of arranged marriages, when all along I knew full well that they are not admirable institutions. I am being utterly honest with you, painfully so perhaps, but I would do anything in my power now to bring you together with the woman you love."

He saw the tears shining in her eyes and crossed the room to her immediately, crouching beside her to take her hands. "I am very honored to have such a fine lady as my mother," he said softly.

"Go to her, David, before it is too late and you lose her forever. No one ever gets a third chance."

"And if I receive a bloody nose for my pains?"

She smiled. "You won't, I'm sure of that."

Adele was sitting on a bench in the garden behind the haberdashery. There was still a crowd at the front of the shop, although the parish constables' threat of bringing in the military had had quite an effect. The shop had not opened its doors and many an elegant carriage had drawn up hopefully at the curb, only to have to drive on. It was peaceful in the garden, the atmosphere was soothing, but her embroidery lay untouched on her lap and she felt anything but calm and relaxed. The roses smelled so good and the air was warm and sunny, but the beauty of the summer's day received no answer in her heavy heart. His parting words to her seemed to echo over and over in her head. *Good day to you, Miss Russell. I trust we will never meet again.* How cold those words had been, and how final—so very final. . . .

The breeze whispered through the sweet-smelling herbs edging the ash path, ruffling the hem of her gown, and playing with her hair, which was brushed free, unribboned and unpinned. Some of the colorful silks spilled over to the ground, but she did not even notice. She felt quite desolate, bereft of any of the joy with which she should have been contemplating her future. She had everything to smile for, but she would always be a prisoner of unhappy love.

She did not hear Cat emerge from the back door. "Adele? You have a visitor."

Adele looked up in surprise, her eyes widening as she saw David. "My lord?"

He removed his top hat, bowing. "Miss Russell."

Cat cleared her throat nervously, smoothing her apron and making some vague excuse about having something to attend to.

He looked at Adele, seeing the marks of weeping on her pale face. Slowly he removed his gloves, dropped them into the hat which he then placed on the bench beside her. Resting one shining boot next to it, he looked down into her eyes. "Miss Russell, I did not come here merely to be polite, I came to discuss events of five years ago. I realize full well how this must appear to you, for it cannot seem anything but suspicious now that you are about to be a rich woman again, but nevertheless I am—persuaded—that we should talk about our former betrothal."

She stared at him. "What is there to say? You ended the matter and I had to accept that fact."

"No, Miss Russell—*you* ended the matter."

She flushed then. "Sir, if this is some unkind jest—"

"No jest. I swear that I am telling you the truth. Please look at me again, for I am not finding this at all easy and if you look away so haughtily then I fear that I will not be able to say that which I know must be said."

"If you do not jest with me, sir, what is this really about?" Her eyes met his once more.

"Five years ago, Adele, I was the happiest of men. I had just become betrothed to the only woman who had ever truly turned my head. I loved her completely and believed she loved me, and I imagined that I was destined to achieve the one thing I had always sworn I would achieve—a marriage which was a love match. Then something happened which forced me to have to postpone the wedding."

"*Postpone* it?" she cried immediately. "You wished to cancel it completely!"

"No, Adele, I said postpone and that was precisely what I meant. Word had reached me from Madras that my brother Jamie was seriously ill. My mother was distraught and I promised her that I would go to India as swiftly as humanly possible. I therefore wrote to you explaining my predicament and begging you to postpone the arrangements so that we

221

could wed the moment I returned. Your reply reached me on the very day I was to set sail—you severed the engagement completely, offering no explanation and going so far as to say you did not wish ever to have dealings with me again.''

She stared at him, totally bewildered. "None of this is true, my lord, none of it. I didn't write a letter to you—what letter was there to write after receiving your cruelly curt note?''

He resisted the temptation to reach out to her. "I know that you are speaking the truth—or what is apparently the truth—just as I am. You see, when I wrote to you about the postponement, I happened to be in London at my club. The Duke of Bellingham was a member of the same club and he was about to leave for Bath, indeed his carriage was waiting at the door. I asked him to deliver the letter to you—an action which I am assured by my mother was the action of a fool to end all fools. And indeed it was, for I was perfectly aware that he had tried very hard to get me to the altar with his daughter. I forgot all that in my haste to see that my letter to you was delivered as swiftly as possible—would to God now that I had sent a courier, or even used the royal mail!''

"The duke delivered your letter," she said, looking away. "It arrived one week to the day after the fire and was brought by one of his footmen.''

"I was on my way to India when Beech Park burned down, Adele; your home was still standing and your father still alive when I wrote to you. The duke timed everything to suit his own aims, delivering a false letter to me from you on the very day I was to depart, and delivering my so-called letter to you after the fire and the scandal, thus making my actions appear all the more odious.''

"You are saying that your letter was forged?''

"I am. Thanks to His Grace of Bellingham, you believed me to be the most callous and unfeeling of creatures, and I departed for India the most unhappy man on earth.''

"But you consoled yourself," she said, glancing at him.

"Why should I not? I make no excuse for taking Ramchund's daughter as my mistress. Indeed to excuse my actions would be to belittle her, which is something I would never do.''

"Did you love her?''

He smiled. "No, Adele, I didn't love her. I have only ever loved one woman and I am looking at her now, although as God is my witness I did not believe I would ever look into

222

your eyes again. You see, when I returned from India, I repaired to my club prior to traveling on to my estate, and there—wonder of wonders—I once again encountered the Duke of Bellingham. When I had last seen him he had been a nervous, worried, somewhat impoverished lord, but how changed he was on my return! Now he was plump and grand, clad in the finest togs and living so well that he was a martyr to gout! But then the reason for the transformation in the House of Bellingham is only too well known now, isn't it?"

She nodded, looking down at the profusion of colored silks in her lap.

"Adele, I must tell you that the duke told me that you had perished with your father in the fire," he said quietly. "Until I saw you that day in Sydney Gardens, I believed you were dead."

She felt quite weak suddenly; this was all too much. "Wh-why have you come to me now?" she asked at last.

"Would you believe me if I told you that I came because of Miss Jane Austen?"

She looked up swiftly. "Not really."

"Nonetheless, it is true, at least in part. Adele, did you love me when you accepted my proposal?" His blue eyes were very piercing in that moment.

She looked away, her cheeks hot. "I did; I loved you with all my heart."

At last he touched her cheek, drawing his fingertips very softly over her skin. "As I loved you," he murmured. "A love which lingered on even though I believed you had gone from me forever, a love which made me notice a dominoed lady at the masquerade. There was something about that lady in sprigged muslin, something which touched a deep memory, something in the way she moved, even in the tilt of her head when she laughed. And then, when for a brief, brief moment she pulled back her hood to pin her hair, that golden hair which reminded me so very poignantly of all that I had lost . . . That is why I asked you to dance with me that night; I was pursuing a ghost—a beloved ghost."

Trembling, and hardly able to believe her own ears, she got up. "I wish that I had known," she whispered.

"And now that you do?"

Her eyes were very large and soft as they met his. "Now I can tell you that I have never ceased loving you, in spite of all my efforts to escape from that love, and then when I saw you again—"

He reached out to take her hand, drawing her toward him. "Oh, Adele, my dearest Adele," he said softly, pulling her into his arms. His lips were warm, and the air around her seemed to sing with joy.

A Commercial
Enterprise

Chapter 1

It was a lonely part of Dartmoor where the winding track from Selford Village passed over the stream by way of a narrow stone bridge. Floodwater from the melting snow on the high tors foamed in a torrent down through the rocky, tree-lined combe, the sound echoing around the naked branches. Cold, windswept, and desolate, it was a favorite place for highwaymen. All travelers, even the swiftest of horsemen, had to go slowly in order to negotiate the bridge, and highwaymen could wait with ease in the shelter of the concealing trees.

An old post chaise approached the bridge on its way down from Selford to join the main Exeter highway in the valley far below, but the roar of the swollen stream drowned the sound of the little hired carriage. It was a poor vehicle now, although once it had been the proud possession of a marquis. Its panels were a scratched and faded blue, and the heraldic emblems which once graced the doors had been completely obliterated. Perched on the more robust of the two horses, the yellow-jacketed postboy looked anything but cheerful as he glanced nervously around the combe for any stealthy movement which might give warning of someone lying in wait. Called a boy, Charlie Hargreaves was in fact forty-five years old, and he loathed having to turn out in such inclement weather simply to convey a young woman, whom he regarded as stubborn and willful, to the White Boar Inn on the first stage of an unnecessary journey to London. It was ten miles to the inn, miles which were hazardous and which offered too many hiding places for the so-called gentlemen of the road, and he could only view with apprehension the prospect of the next hour or so. On bitterly cold February days like this, only fools and the idle rich ventured forth into such risks; glancing nervously through the tangle of trees again, he urged the team across the bridge, pondering how his passenger, Miss Caroline Lexham of Selford Manor, apparently did not fall into either category.

A solitary horseman waited in the lee of a holly tree, his face hidden by the brim of his tall hat, his damp cloak billowing in the icy wind. He was not a man of fashion, his riding boots were well made rather than modish, and his leather gloves were substantial but hardly elegant. His attention was on the chaise, and in particular upon the mud-spattered window, where he could see the paleness of a woman's face. As the carriage reached the holly tree, he urged his horse directly into its path.

Charlie's face became instantly ashen as he brought the chaise to an abrupt halt. "Let us pass!" he cried fearfully. "We've nothing of value for you!"

The horseman dismounted, his face at last revealed as he looked up at the terrified postboy. "You've never had reason to fear me, Charlie Hargreaves, and you've no reason to do so now. I merely wish to speak with Miss Lexham." The wind almost snatched his voice away and his cloak flapped wildly as he made fast his horse's reins.

"Squire Marchand?" Charlie was taken aback, looking down in amazement at the young master of Selford Manor. "Will you be long, sir? Only Miss Lexham said I was to be as quick as possible as she had to meet the Exeter mail and—"

"I will take as long as is necessary to persuade her to abandon this foolish journey."

Charlie fell silent, watching as Richard Marchand turned toward the door of the chaise, hesitating a moment in obvious doubt. At twenty-eight, he was tall and well built, with tousled blond hair and clear blue eyes, and by any measure he was considered to be a catch in these parts. As master of Selford he could have had his pick of the daughters of nearby landowners, but everyone knew his heart was set upon his cousin Caroline, who at twenty was eight years his junior. Since the death of her mother she had lived alone in a house in the village, with a cook-housekeeper to look after her, and her handsome cousin had long been determined to put an end to that lonely existence. Everyone in Selford knew that he wanted to marry her, and an announcement had been expected for some time; the fact that there had so far been no such announcement was regarded by many as a blessing, for although Miss Lexham was very well liked and respected, she was nevertheless thought to be unattractively overeducated for a female. This fault in her upbringing had led to her being possessed of a singularly independent nature, and no sensible fellow would wish to endure such willful spirit in his wife. It was at the feet of Miss Caroline's late mother that most of the blame lay for this lamentable state of affairs, for she had sought to instill in her daughter all the qualities of a lady of rank, and being unable to afford a proper governess, she had engaged the services of Parson Young. The parson had by some dreadful coincidence also believed that a female should be as well educated as a male, and he had done his best to fill his pretty pupil's head with all manner of facts and figures, from a knowledge of astronomy to a thorough grounding in algebra and geometry. Of what possible use were such things to a woman destined to be mistress of a manor high on Dartmoor? It was not a female's place to be learned and knowledgeable, it was her function in life to find herself a husband, make him happy, and be a mother to his children. Of one thing Squire Marchand could be thankful, however, and that was that the good parson's command of the French language had been appalling and he had therefore not been in a position to instruct his charge in this fashionable tongue. Richard Marchand would therefore be spared constant lessons in history, geography, and arithmetic, which could then be repeated in in the language of England's hereditary enemy!

Charlie huddled himself against the elements, thinking to himself that never had Miss Caroline Lexham's mulish, overeducated, unfeminine traits been more in evidence than at present, for here she was, setting off on an unnecessary journey all the way to London on her own. And for what reason? She intended to be present at the reading of her uncle's will—an uncle she had never even met and who certainly had not entertained fond thoughts of his niece.

Richard still hesitated at the door of the chaise. He knew that what he was about to say would not be well received, for he and Caroline had had many heated arguments ever since her ridiculous and stubborn decision to go to London. Her insistence had angered him, and he took refuge in blaming her upbringing, but in his heart he knew that his anger was born mostly of the recent unease which had sprung up between them. She had begun more and more to want the freedom to conduct her life as she saw fit, not as someone else dictated, and he took this as an implied criticism, an unwarranted criticism of his manhood which he resented deeply. He had said hurtful things to her, he had tried to impose his will upon her, but she had stoutly held her ground. Now, at this eleventh hour, he had to try one last time to make her change her mind. Taking a deep breath, he flung open the door and looked inside.

The interior was gloomy. The drab upholstery was worn and there was straw upon the floor. Caroline sat in the corner, toying nervously with the strings of her velvet reticule. She was very beautiful, although she had never seemed conscious of the fact; perhaps that was part of her charm. Her eyes were large and gray, and the curls peeping from beneath her high-crowned brown bonnet were the color of warm honey. She looked almost lost in her voluminous traveling mantle, the ribbons of which were tied only loosely so that he could just make out the heavy chased silver of her grandmother's necklace, the only item of any value she possessed. Like Richard himself, she could not have been called fashionable, but where he was unmistakably a country squire, Caroline Lexham had the fragile, delicate features associated with ladies of quality. There was something very arresting about her, from the gracefulness of her slender figure and the tilt of her head to the candid expression of her wide eyes. Those eyes met his now, and they were a little reproachful. "Richard?"

"I think you know why I've stopped you, Caroline."

"It will serve no purpose; my mind is made up."

"I must persuade you to turn back to Selford, for apart

from anything else, journeying two hundred miles in these conditions is madness!''

"I am going to London, Richard," she said quietly. "And I do not see why you try so hard to prevent me. I'm only going for a short while."

"Are you?" The words slipped out before he could stop them. He searched her pale face. He was afraid to let her go, afraid that he would lose her forever once the sophisticated gentlemen of the *beau monde* saw her beauty. He was afraid too that after the excitement of the capital she had long yearned to see, the dullness of remote Selford would bore her. "Please stay, Caroline," he begged, his voice barely audible above the roar of the water thundering over the rocks nearby.

She found it hard to withstand this entreaty, but she knew that she must, for both their sakes. "I will not be gone for long," she repeated.

"Damn you!" he cried, his helplessness making him harsh again. "I demand that you stay here!"

Her eyes flashed in angry response. "You are my cousin, Richard, not my keeper!"

"I want to be more, I want to be your husband!"

She couldn't reply, and she lowered her eyes to the reticule lying on her lap.

He struggled to be gentle again, reaching over to put his gloved hand over hers. "Caroline, we grew up together, we've *always* been together, and since your mother died it's been assumed that in time we would—"

"Perhaps that's the trouble, Richard," she interposed quickly. "We've been together too much and now when I look at you I see my brother, not the man I wish to have as my husband."

"I don't believe you mean that, for I know that when I see you I see the woman with whom I wish to spend the rest of my life. My feelings for you are anything but brotherly, I promise you that."

She could only look at him. *Why* wouldn't he listen? Why did he refuse to hear when she tried to tell him the truth?

His fingers tightened a little over hers. "Please stay here, Caroline, forget this foolishness about London."

"I cannot." Her voice was quiet but firm. She loved him, but not in the right way, and in recent months the pressure to marry him had become almost unendurable. She had to escape from Selford for just a little while.

He snatched his hand away, his quick anger sweeping to the fore again. "You think that because you carry the exalted Lexham name that once you reach London your aristocratic relatives will welcome you with open arms! Well, you will be disappointed, for as far as they are concerned you are nothing but a lowly Marchand! They've ignored you all your life and they are not about to change now. Your father was the late earl's only brother, but he scandalized and infuriated them all when he took my aunt as his wife. Catherine Marchand may have been very sweet and beautiful, but by Lexham standards she was virtually a pauper!"

"It was a love match," she said defensively.

"For Philip Lexham it was a grave misalliance. Only if he had married a servant, a divorced woman, or a Cyprian could he have sinned more in their eyes. They never forgave him and he died disinherited, spurned by his own flesh and blood. They will never forgive you for being a living reminder of an episode they would prefer to sweep under the ancestral carpet. Don't go to the reading of that will, Caroline, for it will avail you of nothing and may even prove painful to you. Please listen to me."

She toyed once more with the strings of her reticule. He was right about her relatives, and she knew it, but how could she tell him that she was determined to go to London as much to be free of Selford and free of him for a while as to hear the last will and testament of a man she had never known? She needed time to herself, time to put things into perspective. More and more of late she had come to realize that she chafed at the close-knit rural existence which was all she had ever known. Now she yearned to see something more of the world. She was tired of conversation which turned solely on farming and prices, on cattle and sheep, on the vagaries of Dartmoor weather, on hunting and foxhounds and all the other interminable sporting activities followed with such obsession by country squires like Richard. It was a world for men and there was no place for women of Caroline's spirit. Such an existence forever more would stifle and frustrate her as the years passed and would make any marriage between her and Richard Marchand a very serious mistake. She didn't want to hurt him; she just wanted him to understand and accept the truth, but he didn't want to know what she felt or why she felt it. He was supremely confident that if she married him, then she would be content to forget her stubborn restlessness, which he regarded as mystifying female nonsense anyway. In his blind, unthinking way he was as arrogant as he accused the Lexhams of being, but he would have been appalled had he known she thought such things of him. He simply did not understand her, and she doubted very much if he ever would. She, on the other hand, understood him only too well, and knew that the barrier was insurmountable. As cousins they could be close and loving; as lovers they were as unlike as chalk and cheese, too opposite for there to be any hope of a successful and happy marriage.

Her long silence disturbed him. "Caroline?"

"I intend to go to London, Richard, and nothing you say will make any difference."

He was almost savage then, wanting to cause her pain for all the hurt she was dealing him. "They'll laugh in your face! They'll scorn your country ways and your country clothes!"

"Please, don't."

He looked helplessly into the soft gray eyes and saw defeat at last. Why couldn't she see that he would only love and cherish her? Why couldn't she see that it was marriage that she needed, not foolish escapades like this? Other women were content enough with their lot, happy to contemplate futures with loving husbands and with children, why couldn't she be as they were? Why did she always seem to be seeking something, he knew not what? Was it because she was half Lexham? Was that why? He wanted to say so much to her, but the words would not come. She was and would always be a mystery to him, and his own nature was such that he would never reach through the puzzle to find the answer. Slowly he stepped back, closing the door and nodding at Charlie, who immediately roused himself and urged the team on down the track.

Richard watched the old vehicle lumber away. Instinct told him that she would never return to Selford to live, not because that was already her secret avowed intention, but because events would overtake her. For a down-to-earth country squire, Richard Marchand had a surprising belief in the power of dreams, and recently he had dreamed that she would stay in London. Now, as the chaise disappeared from sight, that belief was stronger than ever. Somewhere in the capital there was a gentleman who was going to see past her country clothes and inexperience of society ways, who was going to fall in love with her charm and beauty, her vivaciousness, her sense of humor, and her compassion; that gentleman, like Richard Marchand before him, was going to want to keep her forever, but where the squire of Selford had failed, the London gentleman was going to succeed.

Sadly Richard remounted. The wind gusted icily through the combe, bending the trees and momentarily making the sound of the water even louder as it foamed and splashed over the rocks. There was a promise of more snow in the air as Richard turned his horse back up the track to ride home. This new year of 1818 was to have been the year he made Caroline Lexham his bride; instead it was to be the year of losing her.

Chapter 2

As the carriage drew away, Caroline resisted the temptation to look back, for to have done that might have made her falter in her resolve. She did not know what she would do on her return to Selford, merely that somehow she would have to make him understand that she would never marry him. She felt that after escaping to London and having separated herself from the influence of Dartmoor and Selford, she would find it easier to face him with the incontrovertible facts. Maybe then he would at last accept that she would never be his wife. She looked out of the ill-fitting window, watching the gray winter scene slip slowly by. Dartmoor in the spring and summer was very beautiful, but in the middle of winter it was desolate, brooding, and unkind.

The chaise jolted at last from the moorland track onto the main highway between Plymouth in the west and Exeter toward the east, but although she expected to see many more vehicles, it seemed that most travelers had decided to shun the raw cold and the risk of flooding. After half an hour, the only others she saw were a carrier and his wagon, drawn by eight oxen, and a smart yellow curricle driven at breakneck speed by a dashing young blood with golden Apollo curls and a tight-waisted crimson coat. She heard his mocking laughter as he shaved dangerously close to the chaise, earning a blasphemous response from the furious Charlie.

Looking out of the opposite window, away to the south across the valley, she could see a great white house set in a magnificent park. This was Petwell, the estate belonging to the young widow of old Admiral Lord Chaddington. Caroline had never met her, but she had heard a great deal about her. Lady Chaddington was rumored to have married the old man in order to inherit his considerable fortune. Now she was an important and influential society hostess in London, and invitations to Petwell and her house in Berkeley Square were much sought after by the *haut monde*. Said to be a very beautiful woman, she was nevertheless not liked in this part of Devon, for she was harsh and unfeeling with her tenants. On balance, Caroline was glad that she had not moved in the same circles as Lady Chaddington, and she hoped that she would not encounter anyone like her in London.

Thinking about London inevitably made her wonder about her Lexham relatives. She knew little of them, beyond the fact that they were very wealthy, that she had numerous uncles, aunts, and cousins, that the country seat of the senior branch of the family was Watermoor Chase in County Durham, and their London address was the famous Lexham House in Mayfair Street. This town house was said to be one of the most luxurious in London, having recently been completely refurbished. It was said to be so modern and exquisite a mansion that even the Prince Regent envied it. She wondered what it would be like to live in such a house, and then she smiled a little wryly, for it was hardly likely that her proud kinsmen would ever afford her the opportunity of finding out, her cousin Dominic least of all. He was the new Earl of Lexham, the thirteenth of the line, and he seemed to her to be the most arrogant and prideful of the whole family. He it was who had returned her thoughtful letter of condolence on the death of his mother, the twelfth countess, three years earlier. With it he had enclosed a curt note, instructing her never to communicate with the rest of the family again. She would willingly have abided by this had it not been for the letter from her late uncle's lawyer, Mr. Jordan of Maitland Court. It wasn't that she expected a bequest, far from it, it was more that she felt it right that she should attend, right for Philip Lexham's only daughter to be there when his brother's will was read. Absentmindedly she toyed with her grandmother's necklace—her grandmother, the eleventh Countess of Lexham.

The chaise drove on, seeming to take an age to travel the ten miles to the White Boar. The clouds had taken on that yellow-gray hue that heralds snow, and even as she noticed, the first flakes began to dance and spin through the freezing air. Charlie urged the tired team along the deserted highway, glancing in dismay at the worsening weather. The old chaise bumped and swayed alarmingly over the ruts and hidden stones, and as Caroline instinctively reached for something with which to steady herself, there was an ominous splintering sound from somewhere beneath the vehicle. Charlie drew the horses to a standstill and dismounted wearily, cursing to himself, for he recognized the sound and knew that the axle had been damaged. That would mean it would be even longer now before he toasted himself in front of a warm fire!

As he bent to inspect the damage, Caroline leaned out. "What's happened?"

"The axle's almost gone."

"Oh, no!"

"We'll be able to go on," he said, straightening and looking slyly at her, hoping that this would deter her from thought of continuing to the White Boar. "But we'll have to go very slowly indeed."

"How slowly?"

"No more than a snail's pace."

"But I have to meet the mail!"

"I daren't take risks, Miss Lexham, for we could get stranded altogether, and what with the weather closing in and the danger of highwaymen . . ." He allowed his voice to fade meaningfully away, intending to frighten her as much as possible with such dreadful thoughts.

But she knew Charlie Hargreaves and his love of his creature comforts. "Continue as best you can," she said. "For if it is possible to reach the inn in time, then I wish to do so."

He scowled. "Yes, ma'am." Muttering beneath his breath, he remounted and urged the chaise on its way again, but very definitely at the promised snail's pace. The axle made alarming grinding sounds at each jolt, but it did not give completely.

The White Boar was a busy hostelry, used by the mails and stages which regularly plied this route between London and the west country. It was also busy with the considerable trade produced by the posting side of the business, although today it seemed inordinately quiet. It was built in a sheltered combe, protected from the worst of the winter weather by the surrounding heights of Dartmoor and by a copse of large trees. The breeze tore wisps of smoke from the chimneys, and there were lights in the windows in spite of the early hour. The weather had closed in still more and the snow was beginning to fall heavily. Caroline could no longer see the high tors, which were shrouded in mist and cloud.

The chaise passed slowly beneath an arch into a galleried courtyard, where the smell of roast beef hung appetizingly in the air. Ivy twined up toward the roof, the shiny, dark green leaves shivering a little as the wind caught them. The only other vehicles were the yellow curricle that had passed the chaise on the highway, and the Plymouth mail, which was preparing to leave. The guard made a final check, the mailbags were loaded, and the lids slammed. With a loud blast of the post horn, the coach drew away, emerging from the shelter of the inn and turning west into the snowstorm.

Caroline alighted. Few snowflakes found their way down to the cobbles, where wisps of straw lay everywhere, and she stepped hastily out of the way as grooms and ostlers hurried about their tasks. The landlord emerged from the taproom, having perceived the chaise's arrival. His practiced eye took in the shabby vehicle and its only passenger's plain, unremarkable clothes. He trimmed his manner to suit her apparent station, being civil but not too courteous. "Can I be of service?"

"I am hoping to travel on the Exeter mail, am I too late?"

He shrugged. "Hard to say, for the Exeter mail hasn't come through yet, but that's probably because it can't manage the floods between here and Plymouth."

"But the Plymouth mail has just left!"

"There's grave doubts that it will reach its destination. I expect it back here within an hour or so. They're getting through from the east, but as soon as they reach the floods . . . It's been like this since yesterday, that's why there's so little on the roads. You might be lucky and get a stage come through, the Red Glory for instance."

"The stagecoach? When?"

"It should have been through over an hour ago and hasn't

arrived yet. It has two fords to come over, mind, so I reckon
it's had to go around the long way to the north. If so, then it
won't call here at all.''

"But it might?"

He nodded. "It might."

"I'll wait then."

"As you wish. Will you take some refreshment? We've
some very fine roast beef."

"Yes, I think I will."

He nodded at a nearby maidservant and then walked away,
considering that he had given enough attention to a traveler
who did not look likely to leave a handsome tip.

Leaving Charlie Hargreaves to attend to the repair of the
damaged chaise, Caroline followed the maid into the hallway
of the inn, where bowls of water had been provided, each
with a clean towel. The maid added hot water from a steaming kettle and Caroline took off her gloves. She didn't realize
how very cold her fingers were until she sank them into the
water and painful feeling began to return. When she had
washed and tidied herself a little, she was conducted into the
dining room, which was very crowded indeed, many travelers
having been stranded by the failure of the mails and stages.
There were very few places left at the tables, except at one,
which was occupied by one dandified gentleman. As she was
led to one of the crowded tables, she recognized him immediately as the man driving the yellow curricle. She made herself
as comfortable as possible in the confined space her chair
occupied between a fat farmer and an equally enormous man
of the cloth, and as she did so she surreptitiously glanced
again at the dandy.

His crimson coat looked very gaudy and bright in the
flickering light from the fireplace, next to which his table
stood. The upturned collar collar of his shirt extended to his
ears and his starched muslin cravat was very elaborate indeed.
A large bunch of seals was suspended from his fob, and the
lower part of his anatomy was attired in a voluminous pair of
cossacks, those full trousers made popular by the Czar of
Russia and which were pleated at the waist and gathered in
with ribbons at the ankles. They were a ridiculous fashion,
not made any more attractive by the fact that his upper
portion was squeezed into a corset that tightened his already
narrow waist and puffed out his chest like that of an angry

hen. His cheeks were rouged and his golden hair teased into unnatural Apollo curls, thus completing the destruction of his good looks. With a blanched hand he raised a quizzing glass, inspecting her in that rude, deliberate way so often affected by dandies. His manner offended her and she felt her cheeks coloring with annoyance and embarrassment.

As the maid brought Caroline's plate of roast beef, he rose languidly to his feet, his tasseled ebony cane swinging in his pale fingers as he crossed to her table. Hastily the maid put down the hot plate and then hurried away. Conversation died as everyone looked at Caroline and her unwanted admirer, who began to speak in a lisping drawl that closely resembled a bray.

"I thay, would you care to join me? I vow it would pleathe me immenthely to share my table with you."

"I am quite content where I am, sir," she replied in a tone calculated to spurn him.

"I'm sure you'd pwefer it clother to the fire," he persisted, being importunate enough to place his hand familiarly upon her shoulder.

Icily she moved away. "Thank you, sir, but no."

"Oh, come now," he insisted. "Why ith a pwetty little thing like you twaveling all alone, mm? I'm sure you'd find it much more congenial if you—"

"Would you please leave me alone, sir?" she interrupted angrily. "I have attempted to be polite to you, but you make that impossible. It is hardly gentlemanly to continue to pester a lady who has made her wishes very plain!" Gasps greeted this hot censure, for everyone knew that it was unwise to cross a gentleman of his obvious character and rank.

At last he snatched his hand away, his eyes suddenly sharp. "Obviouthly I wath mithtaken ath to your bweeding, madam," he snapped, "for you are thertainly not fit to join me!" For a moment he remained where he was, thus giving her a last opportunity to see the folly of her ways, but she calmly began to eat, and so he furiously strode away across the red-tiled floor, slamming the door behind him.

The other diners exchanged glances, but it wasn't long before conversation broke out again and Caroline was able to finish her meal in peace. Indeed, when later she emerged from the dining room, her fingers crossed for favorable news

of the Red Glory, she had put the odious dandy from her
mind.

But the landlord shook his head when she inquired, and he
avoided meeting her eyes. "Er—no, there's no sign of it yet,
but it could be through at any time."

With a sigh, she went out into the courtyard, which was
silent now. Through the rear archway she could see Charlie
Hargreaves arguing with the man who was to repair the
damage to the chaise, and she could also see the dashing
yellow curricle belonging to the man who had so rudely
accosted her, but apart from those two vehicles, there was
nothing else at all. Seldom could the White Boar have been
more quiet. Glancing up at the heavy gray sky, she could see
the snowflakes hurrying through the eddying air. They were
beginning to find their way into the yard now and a thin layer
of white had settled on the wooden steps leading up to the
gallery.

Turning back into the passageway, she found herself
face-to-face with the dandy. His eyes were mocking and
scornful and there was a disagreeable smile on his lips. He
didn't say a word to her, but he sketched a derisive bow
before turning on his heel and vanishing into the inn. His
manner should have warned her that he had not let her escape
scot-free, but she thought nothing as she sat down on an
uncomfortable chair, resigning herself to either a long wait or
to the possibility of having to return to Selford after all.

An hour or more passed as she sat there. Outside the snow
still fell and the courtyard was silent. At last she could bear
the chair no more, and to stretch her legs she went out into
the courtyard again, this time going up the snowy wooden
steps to the gallery. Leaning on the rail, she gazed down at
the yard. Suddenly, she heard the unmistakable sound of a
coach approaching, and she straightened hopefully. It had to
the the Red Glory, it simply *had* to be!

Chapter 3

But the elegant carriage which entered the inn yard was not the awaited stagecoach, it was a very costly private drag. In spite of her disappointment, she could not help gazing down at it in admiration, for it was truly the most magnificent traveling carriage she had ever seen. Drawn by a team of perfectly matched bays, it was attended by gold-liveried footmen, and its similarly clad coachman was obviously one of the very best, for he maneuvered the carriage effortlessly in the enclosed yard, gaining maximum response from the team with the minimum of command.

The coach came to a standstill by the open inn door, its panels gleaming brightly and the heraldic device emblazoned upon it quite easy to see from where she stood. It was a four-headed black swan. She looked at it, her brows drawing together in puzzlement, for somehow that badge was familiar to her. But how could that be so? Her attention was drawn to the occupant of the coach then, for one of the footmen went to open the shining door.

A gentleman alighted. He was arrestingly handsome and was dressed more finely than any man she had ever seen before. He was tall and broad-shouldered, but his hips were slender, and she judged that he was about thirty years old.

His clothes could only have come from London's finest tailor, for the coat fitted his manly figure to perfection and the gray cloth from which it was made must, in her opinion, have cost a fortune. A silk cravat burgeoned discreetly at his throat, a diamond pin nestling in its folds, and his dark green waistcoat struck just the right note of contrast. A heavy Polish greatcoat was flung casually around his shoulders, spurs shone on the heels of his top boots, and his long, well-made legs were encased in breeches that hugged very close indeed. His top hat rested rakishly on his dark hair, and as he glanced around the courtyard, she recognized in him a nonpareil of the first order, a man always to be reckoned with. He needed no rouge to enhance his looks and was the sort of man for whom being immaculate would always come effortlessly. And yet he was not haughty or inordinately grand, for there was no mistaking the glint of wry humor in his hazel eyes as the obsequious landlord came scurrying out, bowing and smiling in a way which contrasted rather too greatly with the greeting he had accorded Caroline earlier.

"Sir Henry! Welcome to my humble hostelry! Welcome to the White Boar!"

Sir Henry! Of course, now she understood the familiarity of the four-headed swan. Her cousin Richard's almost obsessive following of all matters concerning the turf allowed her to recognize the badge as the one worn by jockeys riding Sir Henry Seymour's famous racehorses. Sir Henry was known almost universally by his nickname, Hal, and he was revered throughout the land by every lover of horse racing. He was also well known as a leading light of the *beau monde* and as a close friend of the hero of Waterloo, the Duke of Wellington. Caroline had read much about him, but as she looked down now she thought that what she had read had not done him justice, for he was at least twice as handsome as any journalist had hinted.

The landlord's servile smile was almost unbearable. "May I be of any assistance to you, Sir Henry?"

"You can inform me if Lord Fynehurst has arrived."

"He has indeed, Sir Henry, and he awaits you within."

"Excellent." Hal turned back to the carriage, and it was then that Caroline realized that he was not traveling alone, for he held out his hand and a lady emerged, stepping daintily down to the cobbles.

She was very lovely, although her beauty was marred by a certain hardness. She was dressed very much *à la mode*, for her mauve traveling pelisse was adorned with military epaulets and black frogging, and she wore a miniature of the Iron Duke upon her curving bosom. Her auburn hair was twisted up expertly beneath a little hat bedecked with tassels and braid, and she looked very London, a vision from the engravings in *La Belle Assemblée*. Hal smiled at her. "Your brother has arrived," he said.

Marcia, Lady Chaddington—for it was she if Lord Fynehurst was her brother—did not look well pleased with this information; indeed she was positively disappointed. "What a pity," she murmured a little petulantly, "For I was hoping he would be his usual tardy self so that I could be on my own with you for a little longer."

"I promise I will visit Petwell again soon."

"I still do not understand why you must hurry back to Town. What on earth did that messenger tell you?"

"Come now, Marcia, a lady does not ask such things of a gentleman," he replied teasingly.

"This lady does. Oh, Hal, there cannot be anything *that* pressing, especially as you've only recently returned from rushing off to Brussels and the Duke of Wellington! It cannot be anything to do with your racehorses, or you would have said so, and surely it cannot be that wretched banquet you've somehow become involved with for the duke." She searched his face for a moment. "Dear God, it *is* the banquet, isn't it? Now I feel more miffed than ever with you, for it seems that I must play second fiddle to a mere gastronomic exercise!"

"It is hardly to be spoken of so disparagingly," he protested, laughing.

"I could be even more rude about it if I so chose. I don't understand you, Hal Seymour, for why are you, of *all* men, involved with arranging a banquet. Even if it is on account of the Duke of Wellington, I still find it very mysterious."

"Perhaps I am more of an eccentric than you have hitherto guessed."

"My brother prides himself on being an eccentric, Hal, and you are certainly not even slightly in the same mold."

He smiled. "Then put it down to my desire and willingness to come to the aid of a friend. Reggie Bannister was to have arranged the whole diversion, but now he is ill and has asked me to step in for him.''

She was doubtful. ''That is plausible, I suppose, except that I can think of any number of gentlemen Reggie would have approached before you for such a task.''

''Meaning that you suspect me of fibbing?''

''Meaning that you are not telling the whole truth, which is a different thing entirely. There is obviously a great deal more to this banquet than meets the eye. I don't profess to know yet what it is, but I do know that it is not what it appears to be.''

''It is just a banquet, my dear, no more and no less.''

''That, my dear sir, is rubbish,'' she replied impolitely. ''For the mere fact that you are mixed up in it points to it being anything *but* a simple banquet.''

''How devious you make me sound.''

''Devious? Mysterious, perhaps. There have always been two sides to you, Hal, for you have never been just a privileged man of leisure. You are prepared to live dangerously, you are shrewd and capable, and I wonder greatly about the number of invitations you have to Downing Street.''

''You see mysteries where there are none, Marcia.''

''Do I?'' She spoke very softly, her blue eyes thoughtful as they searched his face.

He smiled, turning to the waiting landlord. ''Please conduct Lady Chaddington to Lord Fynehurst.''

The landlord bowed and smiled, and reluctantly Marcia followed him into the inn. Hal watched them, his expression almost guarded, and it seemed to Caroline that his thoughts were anywhere but upon the White Boar or any of its patrons, even the beautiful Lady Chaddington. Suddenly, as if he sensed the close scrutiny to which he was being subjected, he looked up at the gallery, straight into her horrified eyes.

She was transfixed with dismay at having been detected staring down at him. Her cheeks flamed and her gray eyes widened with embarrassment, but at last she found the wit to step back out of sight.

Amused, he continued to look up at the spot where she had been. One glance had told him immediately that she was not a grand or fashionable lady, but that same glance had also told him that she was breathtakingly lovely—and so bewitchingly mortified at having been caught spying! He wondered who she was. Smiling to himself, he left thoughts of the delightful stranger, and went into the inn to seek Marcia and her brother.

Caroline felt dreadful and was careful to remain well back out of sight from the courtyard. What *must* he be thinking of her? How *could* she have stared down so blatantly?

A maid emerged from a nearby doorway. It was the same one who had shown her into the dining room earlier. Smiling, the girl bobbed a curtsy. "Begging your pardon, ma'am, but should you not be thinking of taking a room for the night? There's only one room left now, and as there won't be any mails or stages through today now—"

"But I was hoping that the Red Glory would be able to get through."

"Oh, no, ma'am, it's been taken off. A rider arrived to say so about five minutes after you sat down to your meal."

Caroline stared at her. "Five minutes after? Are you sure?"

"Yes, ma'am, I distinctly heard him telling Mr. Baldwin— that's the landlord."

Perplexed, Caroline could only look at her. The landlord had known that the stage was not going to arrive and yet had not told her so? Belatedly she remembered how uneasily he had avoided her eyes, and the triumphant scorn upon the dandy's face. Suddenly it was only too clear. Determined to punish her for spurning his attentions, the dandy had made it his business to inquire about her. Making her wait in vain for a stage which was not going to arrive was his revenge, and the landlord had placed more value upon pleasing such a gentleman than upon doing the right thing by a more lowly traveler!

She thanked the maid, who was looking curiously at her, and then went slowly down the slippery, snow-covered steps to the courtyard, but she misjudged her footing, and with a scream tumbled forward—straight into Hal Seymour's arms as he emerged once more from the inn.

Catching her with ease, his arms firm and strong, he held her for a moment before releasing her. Then he smiled into her flushed face, framed so prettily by honey-colored curls. "So," he murmured, "angels do still fall from the heavens."

"F-forgive me, sir."

"What is there to forgive? I am sure you did not fling yourself down on purpose." Still smiling, he bowed and introduced himself. "Sir Henry Seymour of Daneborough, at your service."

Hesitantly she accomplished a reasonable curtsy, robbed of true grace by the fact that she was again covered with confusion. "Miss Lexham," she replied.

The name conveyed nothing to him, for he could hardly be expected to guess that she was first cousin to the new Earl of Lexham and her clothes proclaimed her to be anything but grandly connected. "I trust you are not injured in any way, Miss Lexham," he said.

"I am quite all right. Thank you." She lowered her glance shyly, horribly mindful of having been seen peering down so rudely from the gallery. To her relief, she saw the landlord emerging from the inn, and she made him her excuse to escape from an embarrassing situation.

The landlord turned as she called his name, and once again he looked anything but comfortable. "If it's about the stage, then I'm afraid there's no word—"

"That, sir, is an untruth," she said coldly. "As I believe you know only too well!"

His guilt was written plainly on his face, plainly enough to intrigue Hal, who watched the exchange with growing interest. Now he came to her side. "Is something wrong, Miss Lexham? Perhaps I can be of some assistance."

Before she could reply, the landlord spoke up hastily. "It's nothing, Sir Henry, nothing at all!"

"Allow me to be the judge of that," replied Hal, glancing at Caroline's angry gray eyes.

"I swear it's of no importance," insisted the anxious landlord, wishing that he'd remained safely inside instead of coming out to this possible hornets' nest.

Hal's tone was clipped. "I asked what was going on, and I await an answer."

"It was merely a prank, Sir Henry, nothing serious. The lady was stranded waiting for the Exeter mail and so was hoping to take the Red Glory stagecoach instead. The stage isn't coming through after all, but she was not informed of the fact."

Hal's hazel eyes were bright and hard. "Indeed? And may I ask why not?"

"It wasn't my fault, Sir Henry!" protested the landlord, "for how could I go against Lord Fynehurst?"

Caroline stared at him in sudden dismay. The dandy was Lord Fynehurst? She hardly dared to look at Hal, who was on such intimate terms with Lord Fynehurst's beautiful sister.

For a moment Hal was silent, and then he waved the relieved landlord away. "Very well, I know his lordship's ways only too well." He looked at Caroline. "Unfortunately this hostelry is part of the Petwell estate, which goes a little way toward explaining the landlord's actions, although I do not excuse his conduct. Or the conduct of Lord Fynehurst, for that matter. Miss Lexham, am I to understand that you wish to reach Exeter?"

"Yes, for I am on my way to London, where I have an appointment tomorrow morning."

"Then consider your difficulties to be over, for London is my destination and I too have an important appointment there in the morning. I am on the point of leaving now, if you wish to take me up on my offer."

She was taken aback. "You are offering to convey me all the way to London?"

"Yes, Miss Lexham, that is exactly what I am doing."

"Oh, but I couldn't possibly—"

"Why not? There is more than enough room and it would please me to be of some service to you, especially as the good name of the English gentleman must be redeemed."

She was torn, for she wished to accept his offer, not only because it would mean her timely arrival in London, but also because it would mean being in the company of a man she found more than a little attractive. There was something about his warm hazel eyes and almost teasing smile which quite set her at sixes and sevens, although she hoped that he did not realize the fact. Yes, she wanted to accept, but would such a course be proper? She hardly knew him. Then she remembered Lady Chaddington—surely her presence would put things beyond reproach? She smiled a little shyly at him. "Thank you, Sir Henry, I would be pleased to accept."

He conducted her to the waiting carriage and a footman was dispatched to retrieve her solitary valise from Charlie Hargreaves' chaise, her other belongings having been dispatched a day or so earlier on the mail and thus undoubtedly already at the lawyer's premises in London.

The carriage shook a little as the coachman climbed up to his seat, and Caroline glanced expectantly at the door of the inn, thinking that at any moment Lady Chaddington would emerge. But, to her horror, the carriage door was slammed and the whip cracked. A second later the heavy vehicle was pulling out of the inn and turning east toward Exeter and London! Nervously her fingers crept to her grandmother's necklace, something she frequently did when anxious, and now she had good reason to be anxious, for suddenly the situation had ceased to be at all proper. She was traveling alone all the way to London, a distance of some two hundred miles, with a gentleman she had only just met, and whose intentions might be anything but chivalrous or honorable.

Chapter 4

There was nothing of a snail's pace about the speed with which Hal's coachman urged the team along the snowy highway. The horses moved with seeming effortlessness and Caroline could only compare the comfort in which she now traveled to the undoubted *dis*comfort of Charlie's rickety old chaise. In place of the worn upholstery of earlier there was soft green leather, and it was the fine smell of this that permeated the air, not the unpleasant odor of stale straw. The glass in the windows did not rattle and the springs protected the occupants from the worst of the ruts and potholes. She was comfortable and warm, for there was a hot brick wrapped in cloth by her feet and a woolen rug tucked around her knees.

For a while they traveled in silence, for she was preoccupied with the impropriety of the situation into which she had got herself. Hal, on the other hand, was preoccupied with other things, things which were obviously of great importance. At last she felt she must break the silence and say something to make herself feel a little easier about her predicament.

"It really is most kind of you to convey me to London, Sir Henry."

The faraway look vanished from his eyes and he smiled at

her. "It seemed the obvious and sensible thing to do, Miss Lexham. But tell me, do you make a habit of setting out on such long journeys all by yourself?"

She colored a little. "No."

"I'm relieved to hear it. I know your destination is London, but from where have you come?"

"Selford."

"I confess I have never heard of it."

"It is only a small village on the moor."

"And you have always lived there?"

"Yes."

"So, you are most definitely a country mouse, but I rather warrant you'd make a very fetching town mouse."

Was the compliment simple gallantry? Or was it perhaps the opening move of her seduction? She smiled a little nervously.

"Please do not look so painfully anxious, Miss Lexham, for I assure you I am no Fynehurst."

Her color deepened at his perception. "Oh, I did not for one moment—"

"Oh, yes you did, Miss Country Mouse, oh, yes you did. If you had but seen your face when you realized that Lady Chaddington was not to accompany us after all!"

Her embarrassment was so great that she did not know where to look.

He grinned a little wickedly. "Do I embarrass you?"

"A little."

"Forgive me, I did not mean to."

This reply made her suddenly bold. "Oh, yes you did, Sir Henry, oh, yes you did."

He threw his head back and gave a roar of approving laughter. "*Touché* But your swift riposte is confirmation that you are indeed at heart a town mouse."

She smiled too, feeling inexplicably at ease with him, in spite of her earlier uncertainty. He was so much more worldly-wise than she was, so easily able to make her blush, and yet there was nothing disagreeable about his manner—no unpleasant touch of a Lord Fynehurst. Indeed, there was something disarming about his smile and his willingness to laugh at himself. She was drawn to him and found herself wondering what it would be like to be courted by him, what it would be like to be kissed by him. The color which had seemed to flare so frequently on her cheeks since first she had seen him flushed hotly again now, and she looked quickly out of the window.

He did not seem to notice. "Do you often go to Town, Miss Lexham?"

"I have never been before."

"And you choose this appalling weather to do it for the first time? You must indeed have a pressing reason."

"I go for the reading of my uncle's will."

He did not reply, but his glance moved in puzzlement to her clothing, which did not display one token of mourning.

She felt the need to explain. "I did not once meet my uncle, Sir Henry; indeed his dealings with my part of the family were less than cordial. And before you think my reasons for going to hear his will are purely mercenary, let me assure you that they are anything but."

"You do not need to be so defensive with me, Miss Lexham, for I have not condemned your motives unheard. However, since you have brought the subject up, let me admit that I find it curious that a delightful little country mouse should scuttle off to London when there is no tasty bit of cheese at the end of the journey. I shall, therefore, be impudent enough to inquire what your motives really are."

"It is simply that I have seized the opportunity to see London."

His shrewd hazel eyes seemed to see right into her soul. "Oh, you fibber, Miss Lexham, you fibber."

"I'm not a fibber!" she protested.

"Yes, you are, for there is far more to your flight from Selford than a mere desire to see London."

"Just as there is more to your banquet than a mere banquet?"

His glance was quizzical. "Little mice have large ears, it seems."

"I could not help overhearing."

He grinned at that. "No, from the way you were positively hanging over the edge of the gallery, I can quite believe it!"

"I'm sorry about that."

"I'm not, for if you had not been there, then you would not have fallen into my arms and I would now be traveling to London all alone and without your stimulating conversation to keep boredom at bay. However, we digress, for I believe we were discussing your intriguing reasons for fleeing to

London. Let me see now, what does my vast experience of the world tell me has happened in your case?" He studied her face for a moment and then nodded. "I have it. You are fleeing from an importunate suitor."

She lowered her eyes. "Yes, I suppose I must concede that you are right.

"Do you wish to talk about it?"

She looked at him again. "Are you really interested in the goings-on of the Selford mousehole, Sir Henry?"

He smiled. "If you knew me better, Miss Mouse, you would know that if I was not interested, then I would not have asked. Who is this dastardly fellow? Is he a Lord Rat? A Sir Rat? Or just a Mr. Rat."

She smiled. "He is a mister, but he is not a rat at all; he is my cousin Richard and in fact I am very fond of him." To her surprise, she found herself telling him all about herself, although she somehow omitted to mention her grand connection with the House of Lexham.

When she had finished, he nodded in approval. "You are right to escape, even if only for a short while, Miss Lexham, and I applaud your spirit."

"I would like to believe that, Sir Henry, but I wonder if you would say what you just did if I was—say—your sister, or your cousin? Would you not then condemn me for being willful, obstinate, and opinionated?"

He seemed amused. "You appear to know me very well all of a sudden. It so happens that if you were my sister, I would still applaud your actions, as indeed I have already proved with my real sister. The many spinster aunts and maiden cousins with which the Seymour family appears to be endowed had set their communal hearts upon matching my unfortunate sister with the dull and elderly Marquis of Wye. She, on the other hand, had set her sights upon the less wealthy but considerably younger and more congenial Lord Carstairs. She told me her wishes and I upheld her. Does that answer your question?"

"Yes, I suppose it does. Forgive me, Sir Henry."

"Because your cousin is the epitome of unthinking male arrogance, it does not signify that every man has to be colored from the same paintpot."

"I apologize, Sir Henry."

"Apology graciously accepted, Miss Lexham." He bowed his head.

"But it is still a fact, is it not, that gentlemen are much more free to decide their own destiny than are ladies."

"Possibly."

"Definitely, Sir Henry. Do you honestly expect me to believe that when you marry you will have to bow to the wishes of others, or even that others will attempt to impose their will upon you in the matter? No, because you will be free to choose whichever bride you wish."

He smiled. "I do not think it is quite as simple as that for the male of the species, Miss Lexham. However, since that is your belief, I put it to you that you are yourself in the process of deciding for yourself about who you marry. Is that not what this precipitate flight to London is all about?"

She had not thought of it quite like that. "Yes, I suppose it is."

"Thank you, Miss Lexham," he said infuriatingly, "that is another apology I will graciously accept." Glancing at her again, he added softly, "I sympathize with the unfortunate Marchand, for his loss is great indeed."

She didn't hear, but instead was looking out of the window once more. There was less snow in the air now, and she could see the trees swaying in the fierce wind, but the well-fitting glass kept out all sound except the rattle of the wheels. When she next spoke, it was on a completely different subject. "Is it true, Sir Henry, that you have sent one of your very best racehorses to America to challenge all comers? Foxleaze is the horse, I believe."

"You are remarkably well informed, Miss Lexham. Yes, it is true. But how do you know about it?"

"My cousin Richard is very interested in horse racing. I believe he must purchase every racing publication in the country."

"I trust he has not lost a fortune on my nags."

"No," she replied, laughing, "but I know that he would never forgive me if he discovered that I had met you and yet had failed to ask for a reliable tip concerning the coming season."

"Deuce take it, madam, you are impudent!" he said, pretending to be stern. "And you are by far too concerned still with pleasing your disagreeable cousin."

"He isn't disagreeable, truly he isn't."

"I say that he is, Miss Lexham, for any man is disagreeable who thinks only of himself and refuses to see the point of view of others. However, as it is you who asks for a tip, and not Mr. Rat himself, then I shall oblige you. I have a nag named Nero which is believed to have excellent prospects for this year's Derby. I warn you, though, that my rivals have put it about that the beast has woodworm in its peg leg, which is a damnable lie, for the wood is perfectly sound."

"How fortunate for the horse."

He smiled. She interested him greatly, for it was not often that one found a young lady with such an impish and irrepressible sense of humor, or one who had come direct from a secluded, restricted country life and yet was prepared to parry words with a man like himself. Initially he had wondered if he would soon regret the impulse of offering to convey her to London, but already he knew that he would not. He studied her as she looked out of the window again. Put her in fine lace and costly silks, and she could be from one of the highest families in the land. There was something mysterious about her. She was cousin to a lowly squire and she dressed accordingly, but there was nothing of the country squire about the quality of the silver and ruby necklace at her throat which she toyed with so frequently. How did she come to possess such a costly piece of jewelry? His idle curiosity prompted him to wonder what her first name was. Had she been of aristocratic birth, undoubtedly she would have been a Georgiana or a Henrietta, but she was not of aristocratic birth and so was most likely a Susan or an Anne. Almost before he realized it, he found himself putting the question into words.

"Forgive my curiosity, Miss Lexham, but what is your first name?"

"Caroline. Why do you ask?"

"Oh, no particular reason." So, she was a Caro, which was as aristocratic a name as any.

"May I ask you a question, Sir Henry?"

"Not if it is inquire what my other names are, for I promise you that wild horses could not drag that embarrassing information from me."

She smiled. "I was merely going to ask you if you could tell me a little about the Duke of Wellington, for I know that you are his friend."

For a fleeting moment she thought his smile seemed to falter. She even imagined she saw a guardedness creep into his eyes, but then it had gone and his former good humor had returned. "And what is it that you wish to know?"

"Everything, I suppose."

"That is too tall an order."

"Just tell me if he is indeed the paragon the newspapers say he is."

"On the whole I have to say that he is, unbelievable as that may seem. He is first and foremost a soldier, of course, and his manner is therefore that of a soldier, but he is also very witty and entertaining company. He is a staunch and loyal friend, and an infuriatingly stubborn fellow when he so feels, especially where his own personal safety is concerned, for he believes that overattention to such things frequently interferes with the performance of his duty. On the field of battle he shows genius and diabolical cunning, which qualities he also shows in the corridors of Westminster. With one glance he can make a man his friend for life, but he can also with one glance quell an army. So you see, Miss Lexham, he is indeed a great man."

"And you admire him very much indeed."

"I admire no one more."

"Is it true that the Bonapartists attempted to murder him in Brussels last summer?"

Again she thought for a moment that she detected a wariness in his manner. "Yes, Miss Lexham," he said after a slight hesitation. "It is true."

"What happened? The newspapers said so very little."

"There was not a great deal to comment upon. Two French journalists lay in wait for the duke in a Brussels park after he had been to a dinner engagement, but purely by chance he took a different route."

She was horrified. "And but for that chance decision, the duke could have been assassinated?"

"I fear that that indeed could have been the case."

"But how was the plot discovered?"

He looked swiftly at her. "You ask a great many questions, Miss Lexham."

"Oh, forgive me, I did not mean to—" She broke off, suddenly flustered.

His eyes softened. "No, you must forgive me, Miss Lexham,

for I should not have addressed you so sharply. You are quite right to wonder how an unsuccessful plot should have been discovered, and the answer—I should imagine—is that governments employ secret agents, spies to infiltrate enemy organizations.''

"Such men must lead very dangerous lives."

He smiled faintly. "They do indeed, Miss Lexham."

"However, at least the duke is safe now."

"For the moment."

"What do you mean?"

"You surely do not imagine that the Bonapartists will let the matter rest there?"

"Well, I—"

"They will not, Miss Lexham, they will not cease until they have put an end to the Iron Duke, or until the day Bonaparte himself passes away."

Something about the way he spoke made her want to shiver. She fell silent, looking out of the window. He smiled to himself. What, he wondered, would the delightful Miss Caro Lexham say if she knew that within the last week in Paris there had been another attempt to assassinate the duke? This latest attack had come perilously close to success, with a shot being fired at the duke's carriage as he returned to his mansion in the Rue Champs-Elysées. The duke had not been hurt and the whole affair was being kept secret for the time being, but there was immense and deep concern in Downing Street. These Bonapartist plots were becoming more daring and more efficient, for to be able to claim the life of the hated Iron Duke would be the greatest of feathers in their evil cap. They would be encouraged as never before and their cause would be given an impetus which could lead to the restoration of Bonaparte upon the throne of France. That was something which could not be contemplated by the victors of Waterloo.

He took out his fob watch. They were making good speed, and if the roads were clear all the way to London, he would be well in time for his appointment with the prime minister. He smiled a little, for Marcia had been right when she guessed that there was more to his recent activities than met the eye; it was this latest attack on the duke's life which had cut short the pleasant dalliance at Petwell.

He glanced out at the Devon countryside, so bleak and forbidding, and thoughts of Marcia faded away as his concentration returned to the matter in hand. The situation was far more serious than anyone in the government wished to admit, for the Bonapartists had now daringly brought their cause across the Channel and were known to be in London itself. Unless they were foiled, and their most ruthless assassin captured, the Duke of Wellington could be murdered in the heart of England's capital.

Chapter 5

They continued to make excellent speed, the roads proving to be as clear as Hal had hoped. He had arranged in advance for fresh horses to be in readiness at a number of inns along the way, as well as another coachman to replace the weary man who had driven so magnificently through the dangerous Devon terrain.

Hal's air of quiet urgency made Caroline wonder greatly about the nature of the appointment he had in London. What could it be about? Whatever it was, it was important enough for no expense to be spared, for the extra horses and coachman must have been costing a great deal. But he gave no intimation of his purpose, and she could not even begin to guess.

The farther east they went, the milder the weather became. There was no snow now and the teams of fresh horses moved swiftly and easily over the broad highways. Their halts were as brief as possible, but toward the end of the afternoon, with Exeter behind them now, they paused at another inn to eat, Hal insisting that she join him at the table. However, such was his desire to press on that they did not remain long at their repast.

Day gave way to night, and now the lamps pierced the

darkness as the carriage sped onward. Caroline's head lolled against the green leather, her eyes closed. Her bonnet lay on the seat beside her and her tousled hair was coming free of its pins. Hal leaned across to tuck the rug around her once more, and as he did so he paused to look at her face. How very lovely she was, and how charmingly unaware of the fact. She was a beguiling, unaffected creature, a challenge, and if she weren't a lady, he would not have refrained from attempting to seduce her. Also, affairs of the heart had no place in his life at the moment.

Drawing the blinds down over the dark windows, he sat back again. He did not feel at all tired, his mind was too active, too preoccupied with the danger surrounding the Duke of Wellington, the hero of Waterloo, his own personal friend, and the man it had become his duty to protect at all costs.

As dawn approached he was still awake, but Caroline slept on, her head rocking very gently to the motion of the carriage and her honey-colored hair tumbling in profusion over her shoulders. Hal glanced outside and saw the pale gray lightening the eastern sky and he felt more relaxed suddenly, for now there could be no doubt that he would be in time for his appointment in Downing Street. With a snap he raised the blinds, and Caroline's sleepy eyes opened.

"Good morning, Miss Lexham."

For a moment she forgot where she was. A stray curl rested against her cheek and she pushed it aside, sitting up swiftly as memory returned and she realized what an untidy, disheveled sight she must be.

He smiled. "Don't look so concerned, for I promise you that even now you look disconcertingly splendid."

"I don't, I look positively dreadful," she replied, returning the smile. "Where are we?" She glanced out at the unfamiliar, flat countryside.

"I don't know precisely, but I do know that London lies not too far ahead now. We should both be in time for our respective appointments."

She took the few remaining pins from her hair and began to swiftly comb it. It was not a ladylike thing to do, but really she did not feel able to sit there without doing something to rectify her appearance. In a matter of minutes she was neat and reasonably tidy again, and as she straightened her grandmother's necklace, she felt much more presentable.

He glanced at the necklace, his curiosity about it returning. "That is a very handsome bauble, Miss Country Mouse."

"It belonged to my grandmother. She was the eleventh countess, I believe."

Her words startled him. "Your grandmother was a *countess*?"

"Yes, she was the Countess of Lexham. The late twelfth earl was my uncle and it is his will I am going to hear."

He was unable to conceal his surprise. "So, you are one of *the* Lexhams?"

She nodded. "Perhaps a great deal would become more clear to you if I explained that my father was Philip Lexham, the late earl's only brother."

"The black sheep of the family. Yes, that does explain a few things, and it certainly accounts for my never having encountered you in society before."

"It also accounts for my unfashionable, plain appearance."

"I did not say that."

"No, Sir Henry," she said with a smile, "but you could not be blamed for thinking it."

"I admit that I did not for one moment imagine you would belong to the exalted Lexhams, for to begin with you are too sweet and charming. Have you ever met any of them?"

"No."

"Then I cannot in all honesty say that you have missed a great deal."

"You do not mince your words, Sir Henry."

"Where the House of Lexham is concerned, I do not, and that is especially so of the new earl, who, I realize now, is your first cousin."

"Dominic? Yes, he is."

"He is a harbinger of mischief, Miss Lexham, and I warn you to be on your guard where he is concerned. He is, without a doubt, the most disagreeable, odious, untrustworthy, and sly insect it has ever been my misfortune to come across. He does everything to excess, whether it be gambling, indulging his considerable appetite for the ladies, lying, cheating, or anything else. In my opinion there is no depth to which he is incapable of sinking. He would, as they say, sell his own grandmother for sixpence."

She was shocked at this blunt assessment of her cousin and his apparent legion of faults. "He cannot be as black as you paint him, Sir Henry."

"He can be and he is, Miss Lexham. Unfortunately, however, his looks are deceiving, for he has the appearance of an angel." He looked at her again. So, the mystery about her was explained. Of *course* she was closely related to Dominic Lexham, how had he failed to note the incredible likeness before? They shared the same honey-colored hair, the same large gray eyes, and the same fine-boned features; but where the new Earl of Lexham was all that was bad, his lovely country cousin was in truth the angel of the family.

She sensed that he was still thinking about her unexpectedly grand connections. "Well, my cousin's character is hardly likely to be of any concern to me, Sir Henry, for I do not expect to have much to do with him during my brief stay in London. But now that you know I am one of *the* Lexhams, would you be very cross with me if I asked if it would be possible for us to drive along Mayfair Street when we reach Town?"

"To see Lexham House? Of course I am not cross, and certainly we may drive along Mayfair Street." He looked outside at the ever-brightening morning. "Miss Lexham, I believe I am hungry enough to eat the proverbial horse. At what time did you say your appointment was?"

"Eleven o'clock."

"Excellent, for my appointment is a little after that, which means that we have more than enough time to partake of a hearty inn breakfast." He lowered the glass to instruct the coachman to pull in at the next suitable hostelry.

She felt that she had already imposed too much upon his generosity, and could not, therefore, enjoy breakfast at his expense too. "Sir Henry—"

"Think nothing of it, Miss Lexham," he interrupted, knowing exactly what was on her mind, "for I have more than enjoyed your company. Besides, I loathe eating alone; it is uncivilized and disagreeable in the extreme. Tell me, in the far recesses of Dartmoor, do you usually enjoy a gargantuan breakfast?"

She smiled. "My cousin does, Sir Henry, but I certainly do not. He likes nothing better than a spread of cold meat, beefsteak pie, cheese, and beer, to say nothing of the more usual bacon and eggs and fresh bread."

"Dear God," he murmured dryly, "the fellow must be

built like Goliath. However, you will be pleased to note that I am a genteel London weakling, and I breakfast accordingly.''

''I'm relieved to hear it,'' she replied, her tone a clever reproduction of his own.

It was not lost upon him. ''Miss Country Mouse, I perceive that you have already begun to metamorphose into a sharp-tongued town rodent.''

''I am told that I have always been thus, Sir Henry,'' she said, smiling.

''By your overbearing cousin Richard and his clique of hunting, shooting, and fishing friends?''

''Yes.''

''They would naturally say that of you, for such dull fellows have little appreciation of a woman's wit.'' He smiled.

''I know,'' she said with a sigh.

''You would make a dreadful lady of Selford Manor, Caro Lexham, you may take my word for that.''

''Is that a compliment?'' she asked hesitantly.

''Oh, yes, it most certainly is,'' he replied softly, his hazel eyes almost lazy as he looked at her.

She colored just a little, for she could not help but be affected by what he said and the way he said it. From the outset she had been drawn to him, sensing that he was a man apart, so singular and different that she would never be able to forget him. Never before had she experienced an emotion so strong and instantaneous; but she knew that it was an emotion she must put firmly from her mind, for she was no Lady Chaddington, and it was to the Lady Chaddingtons of this world that men like Hal Seymour turned, not the Caroline Lexhams.

He watched her, wondering what she was thinking. How easy it was to bring that charming color to her cheeks and to make her look so delightfully confused and uncertain. It would indeed be pleasant to lay siege to her, for the prospect of her eventual sweet surrender was tantamount to the blackmailing of his senses. He smiled wryly to himself, for had she known his present train of thoughts, her illusions about the gallant and gentlemanly Sir Henry Seymour would have been more than a little shattered. Best to speak of other things. Breakfast, perhaps. ''I trust we do not have to travel much farther before we find an inn,'' he said. ''And I also trust that when we do find it, it provides an acceptable table.''

''Surely all the inns on such an important road to London would be excellent, Sir Henry.''

''Possibly. Whatever they provide, however, it will not be up to Oxenford standards.''

''Oxenford? I don't understand.''

''The Oxenford is a fashionable hotel in Piccadilly. My sister and I lodge there at the moment while my house in Hanover Square is being refurbished.''

''You lodge in a hotel?'' She was surprised.

''Why yes, is that so strange?'' He was amused at her reaction. ''Hotels like the Oxenford are not like inns, Miss Lexham; they are exclusive and expensive and are fast becoming very fashionable indeed, especially since the Czar of Russia and his sister, the Duchess of Oldenburg, stayed at the Pulteney three years or so ago. Kings and princes find the best London hotels very much to their liking, and that in turn means that it is quite proper for gentlemen to take their wives, sisters, and daughters there too. Ladies do not like to stay at inns, but they find the new hotels very acceptable indeed. And of course, the hotels provide the very best of French cuisine, which is exceeding fashionable. In fact, I would say that French cooking is practically *de rigueur* at the moment, as you will no doubt discover for yourself.''

''Oh, I doubt if I shall be lodging at an establishment as grand as the Oxenford, Sir Henry.''

''Has your uncle's lawyer made arrangements for you?''

''I do not know.''

''Who is he?''

''Mr. Jordan of Maitland Court.''

''Ah, I know him. He is an excellent fellow and you may rely upon him to do right by you, for although he acts for the Lexhams, he is in fact a most honest and upright fellow—as lawyers go, of course.'' He grinned mischievously. ''He also looks after the welfare of his stomach, so I think you will most certainly be sampling French cuisine, Miss Lexham, if Jordan is involved.''

''What is French cooking really like, Sir Henry? Richard says that it is nothing but overrich sauce poured over indifferent ingredients and is not to be in any way compared with good, plain English cooking.''

He laughed. "There is John Bull personified! However, in one thing he is right, and that is that French cooking is in no way to be compared with the English variety, but when I say that, of course, I speak from personal preference. No doubt your cousin would loathe the fare at the Oxenford, and that is his privilege."

"Presumably the Oxenford has a French chef?"

His eyes took on a thoughtful expression, an almost far-away look which she did not think was entirely on account of her innocent question. "Yes," he murmured, "it boasts the services of one of the finest French chefs in England, one Gaspard Duvall, late of Chez Grignon in the Rue Vivienne, Paris."

"He sounds very impressive."

"Oh, he is, Miss Lexham. He is. As a master of his art I believe that he excels Escudier, Ude, Jacquier, and possibly even Carême—although I would be strongly challenged on that last name."

The names meant nothing to her. She lowered her eyes, feeling suddenly very Selford indeed.

They drove on for a mile or so before the carriage turned at last into the yard of a busy inn, where they partook of an excellent breakfast, which while it was obviously not the work of a Gaspard Duvall, was very tasty. The eggs were done just as she liked them, the bacon was perfectly crisped, the bread warm and fresh, and the coffee strong and aromatic. Much fortified and refreshed, they drove on toward London, and with each mile now, Caroline's excitement mounted. For as long as she could remember, she had longed to visit the capital, and at last the moment was almost upon her.

In spite of the smoke and mist which hung in a pall over the city, she was not disappointed in it. It was so immense, so noisy and thronged after the quiet of Dartmoor, and as the carriage passed through Tyburn turnpike, she felt she was entering the heart not only of London, but of the world itself.

Mindful of her wish to see Lexham House, Hal instructed the coachman to take that route for Maitland Court, and so instead of driving on down Oxford Street, the carriage turned south into Park Lane and then east once more into Mayfair. Through tree-lined avenues they drove, and around quiet, gracious squares where the houses were very elegant and exclusive. At last she looked up and saw the name "Mayfair

Street'' engraved high on a wall, and the carriage began to go more slowly as it approached a high brick wall with a pedimented gateway, and it was through this gateway that she caught her first glimpse of the house in which her father had been born.

It was a beautiful mansion, not all that large by London standards, but certainly very handsome indeed. Set at the far end of a cobbled courtyard that was flanked by coach houses, stables, and other offices, the house rose splendidly against a background of evergreen trees in the gardens at the rear. Perfectly symmetrical, it was breathtakingly simple with its tall, rectangular windows, the flight of white marble steps to the plain door, and the grand balcony extending the width of the floor immediately above. She gazed at it, oddly overcome by seeing at last the house from which she would always be excluded. There was something sad about the building, something closed and unused. There was no smoke rising from any of the chimneys and the windows were all shuttered.

The carriage drove on and she sat back. ''What a lovely house it is, Sir Henry.''

''The Duchess of Devonshire considers it to be the prettiest house in Town.''

''I'm sure it must be,'' she declared, ''But tell me, Sir Henry, are my relatives not residing there at the moment? It looks closed.''

''The Lexhams are only in Town for the Season, Miss Country Mouse, and therefore will not officially be in residence until April or thereabouts. They have come up from County Durham because of the old earl's death, but I believe they are staying at the Clarendon in New Bond Street. Opening Lexham House for a stay of such short duration would be prohibitively expensive.''

''I don't know anything at all, do I?'' she asked suddenly, painfully aware of the gulf between the life she knew and the world he moved in.

''But you will learn swiftly enough,'' he replied. ''Have no fear of that.''

They were driving along Piccadilly now, and in a while he pointed out the Oxenford Hotel, with its pink walls and the balconies overlooking Green Park opposite. Liveried footmen paraded up and down the pavement outside the entrance, rushing to greet a gleaming barouche which drew up at the curb. He also pointed out the Pulteney Hotel, which was nearby. It was here that the czar and his sister had greeted the huge crowds from their balcony.

Apart from exclusive hotels, Piccadilly seemed to contain a vast number of coach offices, for the street was thronged with mails and stages, and with countless travelers, either just arrived in Town or just about to embark for the country. Private curricles and cabriolets threaded their way in and out of the crush, the ribbons tooled with great dash by young blades, some of whom reminded her only too much of the unpleasant Lord Fynehurst, for they too were almost ridiculously fashionable and foppish.

Had Caroline not been so excited and enthralled by it all, she would have been overwhelmed. Hal watched in amusement as she gazed almost breathlessly out of the window. There was more Lexham in her than there was Marchand, he thought, for she was a town mouse to her fingertips. If she returned to the wilds of outlandish Dartmoor, it would not only be her loss, it would be London's loss too.

Just as the church clock in Maitland Court struck eleven, the travel-stained carriage drew up outside Mr. Jordan's premises and the footmen jumped down to open the door and carry her valise into the building. Hal alighted and then handed her down to the pavement.

"I believe I have delivered you on time, Miss Lexham."

"I hope that you will not be late for your appointment, Sir Henry."

"There is no fear of that."

"Thank you for your kind assistance, I am truly indebted to you."

"No, Miss Lexham, I am indebted to you," he corrected.

"In what way?"

"Your sweet presence was a delight and certainly brightened a long and lonely journey."

She looked up into his eyes, realizing quite suddenly that this was the moment of parting and she would probably never see him again. The realization came as a shock, and was not without a little pain. "Good-bye, Sir Henry," she said, her voice deceptively light.

Without warning, he pulled her close, kissing her fully on the lips. "Good-bye, Caro Lexham," he murmured. "Please do not cherish too saintly an impression of me, for I have been struggling against very base thoughts concerning your person.'' Fleetingly his lips brushed hers again, and then he had climbed back into the carriage, which immediately drove swiftly away in the direction of Westminster.

She stood on the pavement, her senses reeling and her lips still tingling from his kiss. Tears pricked her eyelids as the carriage turned the corner of Maitland Court and passed out of sight, out of her life forever. ''Good-bye, Hal,'' she whispered.

Chapter 6

Before going into the chambers, she glanced along the pavement, where several elegant carriages waited at the curb, and on the panels of one she saw the Lexham coat-of-arms. She knew that this was Dominic's carriage. Looking up at the facade of the building, she was suddenly aware of how close she was to the family of which she was part, but which did not want even to acknowledge her existence. A nervousness overtook her; gone was the excitement of seeing London, the sense of having escaped from Selford for a little while; instead there was the uneasy certainty that no pleasant experience awaited her when she entered the building. With a final glance at the corner where last she had seen Hal's carriage, she went up the shallow, worn steps and into the cold hallway.

A clerk hurried up the stairs to inform the lawyer of her arrival, and a moment later Mr. Jordan came down to greet her. He was a short, stout man, and his round face was pink and flustered, as if he was anticipating a disagreeable hour or so at the hands of the Lexhams. His short-queued wig rested uncertainly on his balding head as he bowed over her hand, and she noticed that his black coat appeared to be several inches too small around his ample waist. She tried to bolster her flagging courage by telling herself that before he had

discovered the delights of French cuisine, his coat had probably fit him excellently.

"Good morning, Miss Lexham, I'm so glad that you have
been able to come all this way."

"Good morning, Mr. Jordan."

"I was concerned that you should be present."

"I gained that impression from your letter, Mr. Jordan, but
truly I cannot imagine why you think I should be here, for it
is hardly likely that I am a beneficiary." Still aware of the
need to screw herself up to a certain pitch in order to face her
family, she went on: "Indeed, my only real reason for making the journey was so that I would at last be able to see
London. There, is that not a dreadfully impious admission?"
She laughed nervously.

"Please don't be anxious, Miss Lexham," he said kindly,
"for in me you have a friend. You are Philip Lexham's
daughter, and for me you need no other recommendation."

She stared at him. "But you are my late uncle's lawyer—"

He smiled. "I am a man of business, Miss Lexham, and
perhaps I have not always allowed my heart to rule my head.
Of late, however, as you will soon discover, I have attempted
to correct that fault in my character. Shall we join everyone
else now?"

Slowly she nodded, accepting the arm he offered, and
together they went up the staircase. She heard the low sound
of refined conversation emanating from beyond the door at
the top of the stairs. In spite of her efforts, she could not
dispel her nervousness, and she knew that the hand resting on
the lawyer's black sleeve was trembling as they approached
the door.

A large group of elegantly clad ladies and gentlemen occupied the room. Dressed uniformly in the deepest mourning,
they presented a daunting sight as they turned as one to look
at her. Their eyes were cold and their faces unsmiling, and
the room fell horribly silent. Their icy disdain was almost
tangible, and not one word was uttered by anyone. Her heart
began to pound, for this ordeal was already far worse than
she had imagined. It seemed that she could hear Richard's
warning echoing in her head. *They will never forgive you for
being a living reminder of an episode they would prefer to
sweep under the ancestral carpet. They'll scorn your country*

ways and your country clothes. They've ignored you all your life and they are not about to change now.

A young man stood apart by the window, and she knew immediately that this was her cousin Dominic, the new earl. His honey-colored hair, so like her own, was disheveled and bright in the pale winter sunlight, and his profile was quite perfect as he gazed out, not even glancing at her, although he must have known she was there. He was tall and slender, and dressed very fashionably, although he was no fop. He made no concession at all to his father's death, and in this he was alone among the Lexhams, with the exception of Caroline herself. His coat was dark green and excellent, his breeches a tight-fitting pale gray, and golden spurs gleamed on the heels of his top boots. His cravat was worn in the unstarched style so popular with young gentlemen of fashion, and a large bunch of seals was suspended from his fob. He was very handsome, there could be no disputing that, but there was a chill about him that made her feel instinctively that what Hal had said of him was the truth.

He turned at last and she saw the hard twist of his sensual mouth. For a moment he surveyed her in silence, and then he deliberately crossed to a vacant chair, flung himself impatiently into it, and then glanced at the lawyer. "Get on with this circus, Jordan, I haven't got all day."

His action in seating himself while she remained standing was a calculated insult which only a fool could have failed to note. She lowered her eyes, wishing that her ordeal was over so that she could escape and forget that she was part of this prideful family.

Mr. Jordan hastily conducted her to a chair and then sat at an immense desk. Unlocking a drawer, he took out a rolled, sealed document, which he opened and then set on the green baize before him. Clearing his throat, he began to read, and as he spoke the familiar opening lines, it was evident that everyone expected the will to be merely a formality, but as he progressed, all eyes were suddenly on him, for it was soon obvious that this was no ordinary last will and testament.

. . . I have always been a proud, strict man, conscious of my duty to my family and aware at all times of my rank and position in life. Unlike my foolish, contemptible brother, Philip, I saw to it that I married suitably, into a titled and respected family, thus forming a union which was acceptable

in the eyes of the society of which I was part. My brother's actions brought shame and scorn upon the name of Lexham, but through me it has been restored to the respect and dignity it should always command. Philip was unworthy to bear such a noble and ancient name, and I see it as my duty to make certain that my successor proves to be in my image and not in the image of my brother. I have viewed with some alarm the profligate conduct of my son Dominic, and I have no intention at all of allowing him to fritter away the family fortune which he so fondly imagines is now his to do with as he pleases. In order to curb his many excesses, I have imposed certain strict conditions if he wishes to inherit that which I have chosen to leave him. . . .

For some time an increasing stir had been passing through the gathering, but now an incredulous murmuring broke out. Caroline kept her eyes lowered as she quelled the anger her dead uncle had aroused with his disparaging remarks about her father. Dominic remained motionless and silent, his handsome face very still indeed.

Mr. Jordan glanced uneasily around and then cleared his throat once again. Silence returned, and he continued to read.

For a period of six calendar months from the day upon which this document is read, my son will not receive one penny from my estate. At the end of that period he will receive almost everything, provided he has limited his conduct and proved himself to be reformed. He must be entirely free of debt, both gaming and otherwise, he must no longer keep company with rogues and women of no character, he must have taken a suitable wife, a woman of name and property, and his own name must be free of any ignominy. If he does not do these things, then another period of six calendar months will ensue, and then another, and so on until he bows to my wishes and becomes a man worthy of the title of the thirteenth Earl of Lexham. . . .

At this there was immediate uproar, for no one could believe what they were hearing. Dominic had been listening in stunned silence, but now he leaped to his feet, his eyes diamond bright and his lips thin with fury. "Is this some jest of yours, Jordan? If it is, then I'll have your miserable hide!"

"It is no jest, Lord Lexham," replied the lawyer, raising his voice to be heard above the clamor.

"I'll contest it!" cried Dominic. "I'll take it to every court in the land if need be!"

"You cannot contest it with any hope of success, my lord, for your father was most definitely of sound mind when he made the will. And perhaps I should warn you that he deliberately chose as one of the witnesses a gentleman of such rank and eminence that I do not believe you would wish to offend him by challenging a document to which he had appended his name. I speak of the Prince Regent himself."

Dominic stared at him, and the prince's name was not lost upon the others, who heard it in spite of their disorderly protests. Abruptly the room was quiet again, and everyone looked at Dominic. His face was very pale, and his demeanor chilling as he held the lawyer's nervous gaze. "Correct me if I am wrong, Jordan," he said softly, "but did you not read out that I would inherit *almost* everything?"

"That is indeed what I read out, Lord Lexham." The lawyer was uneasy.

"From which I understand that this damned charade is not yet over."

"I fear not, my lord."

"Then proceed, lawyer." Dominic's voice was almost silky.

"If you w-would please be seated once again, m-my lord," stammered the unfortunate Mr. Jordan, beads of perspiration clearly visible on his glistening forehead.

"I will remain standing."

Mr. Jordan's hand shook as he picked up the will again, and he was obviously very uneasy indeed, just as Dominic intended he should be.

As I believe that my son will think me not to be in earnest about these conditions, I am going to demonstrate my firmness of purpose in a most signal way. I do, therefore, omit from his inheritance a very important part of my estate. That part is Lexham House itself. . . .

The lawyer paused, expecting another angry outburst, but the room was absolutely silent. From where she sat Caroline could see Dominic's face very clearly, and although he did not move a muscle, she could tell that he was immeasurably shocked. But when he spoke, his voice was very calm. "To whom does the house go?"

"It is not quite as simple as that, Lord Lexham; indeed it is very complicated."

"Goddammit, man, will you get to the point!" cried Dominic, his control snapping.

Mr. Jordan flinched as if he had been struck. "Y-yes, my lord, I will c-continue immediately." He took a deep, steadying breath.

That part is Lexham House itself, together with its contents, which are enumerated in the inventory appended to this document. The inventory is necessary in order to prevent anyone from removing any item from the house until such time as my conditions are met. The person I am about to name will be subject to restrictions similar to those pertaining to Dominic's portion of my estate. The house must be lived in for a period of six calendar months, commencing not later than one week after the reading of this will. During those six months the property must be opened up completely, no rooms may remain closed, and no debt must be incurred in order to do this, nor may there be any gift or loan taken out. If the person should wish to marry during this period, then nothing may be received from the new spouse in order to finance the running of the house. The occupancy of the house must be completely respectable, with no hint of scandalous or licentious activity. If at the end of six months these conditions have been complied with in every detail, and provided that the inventory is complete down to the last spoon, then the house will become the full and undisputed property of the person to whom I now leave it. However, if the conditions are not met with, then the house will revert to the rest of the inheritance and will become subject to the conditions I have placed upon my son. I have taken this drastic action in order to convince my son that I mean what I say. He prides himself upon being a gambling man, and so I trust that he appreciates that in these particular stakes, he is still the odds-on favorite, the new owner of the house having in truth little more than an outside chance of success. Indeed, I have entered the new heir simply and solely to goad the favorite, to spur him into doing exactly as I wish. But an outside chance is still a chance, and I fully intend that my son should realize

*this and do all in his power to meet my terms and thus make
sure that the delay before he receives his patrimony should
only involve the first six months. All this having been said, I
now tell you that the person to whom I leave Lexham House
and its contents, is my niece, Caroline Mary Lavinia
Lexham. . . .''*

Chapter 7

It seemed that as one the gathering gave a gasp of horrified disbelief, and Caroline could only look up in swift amazement at hearing her name. One of the gentlemen leaped furiously to his feet, shouting that the whole affair was an outrage and an insult, while the ladies looked at one another in dismay, obviously already concerned with the ridicule the family would be subjected to once the story began to circulate in the drawing rooms of London.

For a moment Dominic seemed stunned, but then he whirled about to face Caroline, his body as taut as a bowstring and his hands clenched so tightly that his knuckles were white. An immediate hush fell over the room and Caroline could hear her own heartbeats as her cousin slowly approached her. Incongruously she found herself remembering Hal Seymour's description of him. *His looks are deceiving, he has the appearance of an angel, but he is a harbinger of mischief and I warn you to be on your guard where he is concerned.* But in spite of his golden, masculine beauty, there was little of the angel about the Earl of Lexham in that moment, for he was in the grip of ugly rage, his gray eyes as hard and unyielding as flint.

Before he could speak, she rose to her feet. "My lord, I promise you that I knew nothing of this!"

"No? I think you lie, madam, and I shall make you pay dearly for this incredible impudence. You wish to play the lady, do you? Well, it seems that for six months you may attempt to do just that, but you will never be a lady, coz, for you are nothing, an upstart who thinks she may claw herself up at my expense! You are wrong, so very wrong, for before I am finished with you, my dear, you will wish that you had remained in the safety and obscurity of Devon."

She was trembling. "I swear that I knew nothing," she repeated.

His eyes flickered. "The whole thing is purely academic anyway, is it not? You do indeed have only an outside chance of keeping the house, for in order to live in it as the will instructs, you will need money, which if I am any judge, is the one thing you most certainly do not possess." He allowed his disparaging, contemptuous glance to move slowly over her plain bonnet, the voluminous, concealing mantle, and the laced ankle boots peeping from beneath its hem.

"Please, sir—"

"Save your breath, madam, for you will surely have need of it! But I warn you here and now, that notwithstanding the Prince Regent's involvement, I shall do all in my power to prove the will to be invalid, and I shall also see to it that you find it utterly impossible to meet the conditions. The kid gloves are off, dear coz, and you would do well to glance frequently over your shoulder from this day forth."

Turning, he went to the table where he had left his top hat and gloves, and then he looked for a last time at Mr. Jordan. "You have crossed me, lawyer, and that was very foolish of you."

"My lord, I merely carried out the late earl's wishes."

Dominic smiled just a little, but there was no warmth or humor in him. "You have crossed me," he repeated, and then he had gone. They heard his light, swift steps on the staircase.

For a moment no one else moved, and then the rest of the Lexham family followed in his wake. The gentlemen avoided meeting Caroline's eyes, and the ladies flicked their costly black skirts aside from her as if they feared she might in some way contaminate them.

At last they had all departed, and Mr. Jordan did not disguise his sigh of relief as he sank into his chair, wiping his shining forehead with a large handkerchief. "Forgive me, Miss Lexham, but I fear I have long been dreading this morning, for I knew only too well how that will would be received. I fully expected to lose the Lexham family as my clients, of that you may be sure. However, at least now you understand why I wrote to you asking you to attend if it was at all possible."

She nodded. "It was in fact that phrase, 'if at all possible,' which made me feel that I should make the journey. But in spite of the will, Mr. Jordan, I feel that I can only agree with my cousin, the earl."

"Agree with him?" The lawyer looked taken aback.

"Oh, not with his conduct, merely with his statement that my tenure at Lexham House can only last for the initial six months, for he is quite right, I don't possess sufficient funds."

"That is a grave obstacle," he admitted. "But at the same time I feel I must advise you to think most carefully about the whole matter. Have you any idea of the value of the house and its contents?"

"No."

"Well, the building itself is worth a great deal, for it is a first-class property occupying a prime Mayfair site. The contents comprise many art treasures, paintings by great artists, an irreplaceable collection of jade and Chinese porcelain, magnificent silver and gold plate, furniture from Versailles itself . . . At the end of six months all that would be yours, if you could meet the terms of the will." He held her gaze. "Miss Lexham, you would be a considerable heiress."

She was silent for a moment. "That's as may be, Mr. Jordan, but it will be quite impossible for me to achieve, because my uncle laid his plans with great care. He calls me an outsider, but what he really means is that I have no chance at all. He had no intention at all of allowing me to slip through, for he has effectively tied my hands by imposing conditions which present an insoluble problem. I am cast in the role of goad, no more, and no less, and to judge by my cousin Dominic's reaction, I would say that my uncle chose his goad with admirable skill."

"And so you mean to give up without a fight?"

"I do not have any choice. Besides, if I am honest, I do

not think that I have any right to the property, for in spite of my cousin's odiousness, he is the new earl, the new head of the family, and Lexham House should go to him.''

Mr. Jordan was appalled at this sentiment. ''My dear Miss Lexham,'' he exclaimed, ''you have *every* right to the house, for it has been left to you. It does not matter what ulterior motive your uncle may have had, it is an indisputable legal fact that for the next six months at least, Lexham House belongs to you and only to you. And I tell you here and now, that nothing would give me greater pleasure than to see Philip Lexham's daughter as mistress of the house in which he was born and from which he was so cruelly excluded by his own flesh and blood. Of all the Lexhams, he alone was worthy, he alone could really lay claim to the title of gentleman. I know that at the moment it seems impossible that you can win, and indeed I have been putting my legal mind to the problem ever since I knew your uncle's intention and I have been unable to see a way through—but there is still one week left in which to solve matters, and in law I promise you that a week can be a very long time. Your uncle used you heartlessly and deliberately, with no thought of your feelings, but he forgot one cardinal rule in racing, Miss Lexham, and that is that sometimes outsiders romp home by a distance. My advice to you is that you thumb your pretty nose at your disagreeable family, and at the new earl in particular, that you take your deceased uncle on and play him at his own game. Fight for your inheritance if you can, my dear! You owe nothing to any of the Lexhams, except perhaps to yourself and to your father's memory, which has been so cruelly disparaged here today. Don't give up just yet, Miss Lexham, I beg of you.''

''And if I do,'' she said quietly, ''the result will still be the same—the week's grace will pass and still I will not have thought of a solution.''

He rose to his feet, coming around the desk to take her hands. ''But you will at least think about it, won't you? You have so very much to gain by trying to meet the conditions, and so very much to lose by throwing in the towel.'' He smiled. ''But you will be in Town for a while, won't you? You wish to see the city, and that will allow me time to show you over your inheritance in Mayfair Street.''

''Not if that means any risk of encountering my relatives, sir.''

"The house is closed, I promise you, for they lodge at present at the Clarendon in New Bond Street. The house is in the care of the housekeeper, a Mrs. Hollingsworth. Look at it this way, Miss Lexham, you have an opportunity now of seeing over the house in which your father was born, the house which bears your name. Does that not mean anything?"

She smiled. "It means a very great deal, Mr. Jordan, and so I thank you and will indeed be pleased to see it whenever it is convenient. But my first priority must be to find somewhere to stay."

"You do not need to worry about that, my dear, for it has already been attended to."

She was a little alarmed, fearing that his choice might be expensive and beyond her poor purse. "Mr. Jordan, I do not have a great deal of money. . . ."

He smiled in a way that could only be described as both sleek and satisfied. "Your stay in London will not cost you one penny, Miss Lexham, for it will be paid for by your late uncle's estate."

She stared. "But how can that be?"

"I made it my business to point out to your uncle that if he wished to use you to spur his son, then it would be achieved to greater effect if you were present—which would entail your coming to London and so on. He thought this a capital notion and instructed that a clause be entered. He intended me to install you in the meanest accommodation available, but there was nothing in the wording of the clause to indicate any such thing; I saw to that. I have reserved for you a suite of rooms in one of London's finest hotels, Miss Lexham, the Oxenford in Piccadilly."

She heard the name with something like a jolt. The Oxenford! Her first thought was that she would be seeing Hal Seymour again after all, but such notions were immediately replaced by more sobering considerations. "Mr. Jordan, I thank you for your kindness, but there is no way at all that I may stay at the Oxenford; it is far too exclusive and I am not at all the sort of person they wish to have as their guest. I am traveling without a maid—because I do not possess one—and I am obviously far from fashionable. No, the Oxenford is quite out of the question."

"My dear, you are the first cousin of the Earl of Lexham, whether or not that gentleman appreciates the fact, and you are also the new owner of Lexham House; of *course* you are worthy of the Oxenford. Besides, the apartment has already been paid for and all arrangements made. I am sure you will not regret staying there, for it is acknowledged to be one of the foremost hotels in Town."

"I know."

"You do?"

"Yes, although until this morning I had never even heard of it."

He was puzzled. "But how did you learn of the Oxenford, Miss Lexham?"

"Sir Henry Seymour told me all about it."

Now he was startled. "You are acquainted with Sir Henry?"

"He was kind enough to convey me to London in his carriage; indeed, but for his kindness, I would probably still be stranded in Devon."

Mr. Jordan looked at her. "Am I to understand that you traveled all the way to London with Sir Henry Seymour?"

"Yes."

"There was another lady present, of course."

She colored a little. "No, I'm rather afraid there wasn't."

He was appalled. "Oh dear, I do not think that that was at all wise or proper."

Her color heightened. "It came about quite by accident, sir, for I truly believed Lady Chaddington was to travel with us. By the time I realized my mistake it was too late and we were leaving the inn. But Sir Henry was a perfect gentleman in every way, Mr. Jordan." She had to look away, however, for she remembered Hal's last words to her only too clearly, and she could almost feel again the warmth and excitement of his lips over hers.

The lawyer shifted a little uneasily. "Miss Lexham, I know it is none of my concern and you would be perfectly justified if you told me to mind my own business, but I feel a little responsible for you, because you are not only Philip Lexham's child, you are also here simply because of my invitation. Forgive me for saying so, but it was not at all proper for you to have been alone with a gentleman like Sir Henry, especially as you can have had little experience of the ways of such men. Those like Sir Henry can be so very charming, attentive, and amusing; they are rich, intent upon the pleasures of life, and they are only too skilled in the pursuit and flattery of the fair sex. You are a young lady of great loveliness, my dear, and that fact will not have been lost upon Sir Henry, for he is no laggard when it comes to such things, that much I promise you.''

Her cheeks were aflame now. ''Maybe so, but he was a gentleman toward me, Mr. Jordan.''

''Well, perhaps I wrong Sir Henry by implying that he could be otherwise, but you were still very much at risk, for you did not know him at all, did you?''

''No.''

''You were alone with a stranger in his carriage, you traveled overnight with him a distance of some two hundred miles, and had he chosen to behave like a blackguard and a libertine, there would have been very little you could have done to defend your honor. Please do not think ill of me for speaking so bluntly, my dear, but I would not feel I had myself behaved with any honor if I had not said something.''
He smiled then, determined to set such a disagreeable topic aside. ''Come now, I do not wish to sound as if I enjoy lecturing, especially as I hope to have the pleasure of dining with you tonight at the Oxenford.''

She returned the smile, the uncomfortable flush dying away from her cheeks. ''I do not think you are lecturing me, Mr. Jordan, for I know that you are truly concerned about my welfare, and of course I would be delighted to dine with you tonight.''

''And you do not still object to the Oxenford?''

''No.''

''Excellent.''

She briefly lowered her eyes. ''Mr. Jordan?''

''Yes?''

''Is Sir Henry to marry Lady Chaddington?''

He looked surprised at the question. ''Why, I believe such a betrothal is soon expected, and rumor has it that her ladyship has been endeavoring for some time to win him.''

She looked up at him. ''What do you know of the banquet he is arranging for the Duke of Wellington?''

He seemed amused. ''Why do you ask?''

''Well, I overheard Lady Chaddington express extreme surprise at his involvement in such an affair, and I must confess that I too am most surprised, for he does not seem at all the sort of man to bother with banquets.''

He nodded. "It is indeed a strange affair, especially as until recently there was a very curious, although utterly discreet, rumor that Sir Henry was involved in things of grave national importance—grave things."

"What do you mean?"

"I will tell you, but you must remember that it is a rumor and probably has no foundation whatsoever; indeed, I do not see that it can have, in view of Sir Henry's subsequent activities. It was being said that he was working on behalf of the government, involved secretly with matters on the Continent, in Brussels and Paris. There was even one suggestion that he was assigned to guard the Duke of Wellington!" The lawyer chuckled, shaking his head. "Well, if he is guarding the Iron Duke, then he has a very strange way of doing it, for he returned to England, promptly decided that his already excellent town house must be completely refurbished from cellar to attic, and then he and his delightful sister, Miss Seymour, took up residence at the Oxenford, where he took over the arranging of the banquet from poor Reggie Bannister, who is so sadly indisposed with the gout at the moment. Now then, Miss Lexham, does that sound to you like the movements of a man who is involved in life-and-death affairs of state?"

She smiled. "No."

"I agree. Now, however, I will take you to the Oxenford, for you must be tired, and then this evening we will dine together there, and you can sample the exquisite cooking of Mr. Duvall—which, I trust, will prove an unforgettable experience and which is to blame for the immense amount of weight I have put on in recent months."

She smiled again, but then a thought struck her. "Oh, Mr. Jordan, I trust that my baggage has arrived. I took the liberty of sending it ahead to this address, I do hope that that was not too much of a liberty. . . ?" Her voice died away at the look of surprise on his face.

"Baggage? Why no, Miss Lexham, nothing has been delivered here."

"Oh, no!"

"Perhaps it is still at the coach office. I will send a man there immediately. Please do not look so concerned, my dear, for I am sure that all is well."

But his words lacked conviction and they both knew that

her baggage was gone forever. Dismayed, she allowed him to usher her to the door. Things were now even worse, for she was not only going to stay at one of London's most exclusive hotels, she was going to do so with a wardrobe of only two dresses, the one she was wearing and the one in her little valise! Why, oh why had she been so foolish as to dispatch her other things ahead? She had only done so in order to make her determination to go all the more plain to Richard—now she was, as the saying went, hoist with her own petard!

Chapter 8

Caroline's heart thumped nervously as she and Mr. Jordan entered the Oxenford a little later, having crossed London in the lawyer's chariot. Her worst fears about the exclusive nature of the hotel were fast being realized, for even as she alighted from the chariot she had witnessed the exchanged glances of the two liveried footmen parading so importantly up and down on the pavement outside the building. Passing through the discreet doorway into the black-and-white-tiled hall, she was conscious of a rather intimidating hush pervading everything, as if no one dared to speak above a whisper.

Little or no daylight pierced the hall, which was consequently lighted by an immense crystal chandelier suspended from the elegant domed ceiling high above. There were footmen everywhere, and long-aproned waiters hurrying to and from the nearby dining room, where it seemed that the guests were enjoying light luncheons. She felt very provincial indeed in her old mantle and sensible ankle boots, and she was horribly aware of her lack of a maid or lady companion; she was aware too of how glaring were the scratches on her old valise, which the porter had placed so prominently on the floor directly beneath the glowing chandelier. As the porter hurried away in search of Mr. Bassett, who was, so Mr.

Jordan whispered to her, the *maître d'hôtel* or majordomo, she knew already that she would not enjoy staying in this place.

Mr. Algernon Bassett proved to be a very superior being indeed. Wearing a discreet and tasteful coat of the darkest blue cloth, and pantaloons which she thought would be more suitable for evening wear, he approached the two new arrivals, his lofty glance taking barely a second to discern that the Miss Lexham who was to occupy the elegant apartment on the second floor was not at all the sort of person he had been expecting. Like Mr. Baldwin of the White Boar, he too trimmed his courtesy to suit her apparent social standing. His smile of welcome, while not exactly withering, was not warm either, and his pale blue eyes seemed to flicker coldly.

He said very little as he snapped his fingers, calling a black boy dressed as a rajah and instructing him to conduct madam to her apartment. She felt her cheeks flush with embarrassment as the little boy picked up the valise, after first glancing around curiously for the rest of her luggage. After arranging to dine with Mr. Jordan that evening, she followed the little black boy up a very grand staircase, along a carpeted passage, and through an ornate doorway into the magnificent apartment she was to occupy for the next few days.

Never before had she been in such elegance, indeed the rooms were almost palatial. There was a small drawing room, a bedroom with a magnificent four-poster bed, and a little dressing room. All were hung with gray brocade, all had beautiful Axminster carpets on the floor, and all overlooked Piccadilly and Green Park, and the magnificence of nearby Devonshire House. Gold-framed mirrors hung on the walls, candles were placed in girandoles on either side of the white-and-pink marble fireplaces, and the mahogany furniture had been polished until it gleamed.

When the little boy had gone, she walked slowly around the apartment, gazing at everything, touching the lacy curtains, running her fingers over the elegant upholstery of a sofa, and testing the softness of the bed. The noise of Piccadilly was muffled and the lace curtains muted the sunlight. The atmosphere of the hotel seemed to fold inexorably over her. She felt very, very alone.

She slept for most of the afternoon, more tired than she had realized after the long journey and the harrowing experience of her first meeting with her father's family. Outside it was dark now and across Green Park she could see the lights of Buckingham House, while nearby Devonshire House was brilliant, every room illuminated. A maid came to draw the curtains and light the candelabra, and it was time for Caroline to dress for her first London dinner.

With a sigh she opened her valise and took out her only other gown, the turquoise lawn. She held it up a little doubtfully, for there was no mistaking the fact that it was a morning gown, not an evening gown, but then she had packed it in the valise merely as a standby in case her gray wool became travel-stained. Now it was to serve for a fashionable dinner in London! Wryly she smiled a little, for there was no doubt that even had her baggage been delivered as promised, the gowns she wore for evenings in Selford would still have looked dreadfully ordinary here in the Oxenford. Still, there was no way out of her predicament and she must do the best she could with the few clothes she had—and at least she had her grandmother's necklace, which was surely grand enough for any occasion.

She washed in the porcelain bowl provided in the dressing room, shivering a little from the cold water, and then she lightly applied rouge to her cheeks and lips. Her hair proved a little difficult, for she so wanted to look as modish as possible, which was not easy when one was not used to such things. It was one thing to peruse past issues of fashionable publications, it was quite another to achieve an acceptable imitation of their engravings.

At last she had finished combing and pinning and she surveyed the result in the cheval glass. She had twisted the honey-colored tresses into a creditable knot on the top of her head, and one long curl hung prettily down over her left shoulder. At Selford she had always called upon the capable services of her cook-housekeeper, Mrs. Thompson, who could dress her hair up with considerable skill, if not in accordance with each successive whim of fashion, and Caroline had found it unbelievably difficult to do the job herself, bending and turning to try to see in the mirror. She patted the length of matching turquoise ribbon which she had managed to twine through the knot of hair, and she was pleased with the way it fluttered a little when she moved.

Next she stepped into the turquoise lawn, puffing out the

little sleeves and arranging the soft folds to fall evenly from
the high waistline. She had wondered how well her grandmother's rubies would look with the turquoise, but she was
pleased to see that they went very well indeed, for the rubies
were dark and the turquoise was a muted, almost dusty shade.
Picking up her plain white shawl and draping it over her bare
arms, she surveyed herself in the mirror again. She sighed,
for there was no mistaking the fact that she was provincial, a
country mouse newly come to Town. Well, there was nothing
for it but to brave the dining room, which would in all
probability be thronged with the most fashionable, most critical of the *haut monde*!

For a moment her courage almost failed her, until she told
herself that Hal Seymour had complimented her upon looking
good even when she had just awoken; if such a gentleman
could say such a thing and mean it, then she must hold her
head high and believe her appearance tonight to be adequate.
As she left her apartment she wondered if Hal would be
dining at the hotel tonight.

Her shaky courage wavered anew, however, as she descended the magnificent grand staircase and a group of ladies
and gentlemen in the hallway all turned as one to survey her.
Her hand shook upon the gleaming rail and her cheeks became very pink as the gentlemen raised their quizzing glasses
and the ladies whispered together behind their fans.

To her relief, Mr. Jordan had already arrived, and he came
forward immediately to greet her, bowing gallantly over her
hand and saying that she looked very fetching indeed. She
was very conscious of how exquisite were the gowns of the
nearby ladies, so obviously the work of the finest London
couturières, whereas the turquoise lawn was as obviously the
handiwork of Eliza White of Selford. She was so preoccupied
with this thought that she hardly heard Mr. Jordan telling her
that unfortunately there was no sign at all of her missing
luggage; it had indeed gone completely astray somewhere
between Selford and London and had probably been stolen.

The dining room of the Oxenford was a very severe chamber,
decorated in dull colors and illuminated by so many chandeliers that the light was harsh and glaring. The lower portion
of the walls was paneled in dark-gray, while the upper portion was hung with silk the color of the sea, which last
seemed somehow to drain the warmth from the faces of the

seated guests. The white-clothed tables were not large and were partitioned from their neighbors to give a little privacy to the small parties of diners. Candelabra stood upon each table and the gleaming cutlery had been set out with such precision that Caroline felt it would be a crime to actually pick up a knife and use it. Waiters hurried to and from the immense sideboards lining the far wall, their long starched aprons crackling, and the drone of polite conversation and the clatter of knives and forks filled the air.

Caroline glanced swiftly at the other guests, but to her disappointment she saw no sign of Hal Seymour. She and Mr. Jordan descended the shallow flight of steps to the floor of the room and another of the little black boys greeted them, his splendid Indian clothes made of the very finest cloth-of-gold. He beamed at the lawyer, recognizing him immediately. "Good evening, Mr. Jordan, sir."

"Good evening, Hercules."

"Follow me, sir. Madam." Hercules bowed very grandly and conducted them to an empty table, where he drew out Caroline's chair for her and then presented her with the *carte*.

She glanced at it in dismay, for it was entirely in French, for which language Parson Young's careful tuition had not prepared her. She was suddenly very aware of the shortcomings of an education which the folk of Selford had regarded as unfemininely thorough but which here in London seemed very inadequate indeed. A little self-consciously she smiled at the lawyer. "Please order for me, sir, as I am sure your choice will be excellent."

He smiled. "I would be delighted, my dear." After regarding the card for a moment, he gave instructions to Hercules, who nodded several times and then scurried away.

The lawyer sat back, looking pleased with himself. "If I said that I had ordered mere chicken broth, then beefsteak and then apricot tart, no doubt you would be singularly unimpressed, but I promise you that those dishes, when prepared by a chef of such genius as Gaspard Duvall, are in a class of their own."

She smiled, but although she tried to appear at ease, it was almost impossible. Under the glare of the chandeliers she felt more conspicuous than ever and quite out of her depth. On reflection, she did not know if she was sorry or relieved that Hal Seymour was not present, for surely the shortcomings of her background and appearance would be only too evident to him in these surroundings—perhaps he would not even wish to acknowledge her.

In spite of these private thoughts, she still found the dining room very interesting. She watched as the waiters spirited heavy silver dishes to and fro with such dexterity that she did not once see a risk of accident. She saw the superior Mr. Bassett wending his regal way between the tables, smiling sleekly at the influential guests, and qualifying his manner even with them. She pondered that in all probability he had a chart upon the wall of his private room: a prince of the blood would receive a deep, scraping bow and a sickly, servile smile, a duke would merit a slightly less scraping bow and an equally servile smile, and so on. Yes, the more she watched him, the more convinced she became of the existence of such a chart. A waiter called the majordomo to carve at a table occupied by bejeweled dowagers, and he stepped up with great verve, picking up the implements with a flourish and proceeding to give the entire room a display of swordsmanship. Caroline hid a smile, for had he challenged the motionless joint of roast beef with a dashing "On guard!" he could not more have resembled a fencing master. How different such carving was at Selford, where Richard hacked with gusto rather than grace, and where the carving knife and fork were discarded afterward with a loud clatter, not with refined daintiness.

Mr. Jordan drew her attention away from the majordomo. "Tell me, Miss Lexham, are you comfortable in your apartment?"

"Oh yes, indeed, the rooms are most elegant."

"Mr. Bassett assured me that the Earl of Lexham's cousin would be most pleased with that particular apartment. I understand it has a fine prospect over Green Park."

"Yes, it has."

"And what do you think of the Oxenford? Are you not glad now that I took rooms here for you?"

He seemed so anxious that she should be pleased that she had not the heart to be honest and say that she found the Oxenford too intimidating and that she would much have preferred a comfortable room at a good inn. Instead she murmured complimentary things and smiled.

He seemed satisfied with her response, for he sat back once

more, glancing around and nodding. "Yes, indeed, when I think back to the days of my youth, there were no such establishments—certainly nowhere quite as eminently suitable for ladies. Now persons of great rank are content to lodge in these hotels. Why, the Prince Regent has a private suite at Mivart's, so that he may enjoy the cooking of its French chef whenever he pleases, and the King of France recently stayed at Grillion's on his way back to Paris to claim his throne. Jacquier, who keeps the Clarendon, was until recently chef to that same King of France, which makes one wonder if perhaps there was some disagreement, for his majesty must have declined the Clarendon in favor of Grillion's. Yes, the fashion has changed a great deal in recent years, and now one is as likely to find members of the aristocracy taking suites in hotels as purchasing town houses. The most recent development, however, is that a very important society wedding is to take place in a hotel—right here at the Oxenford in fact. I speak of the marriage of Lord Carstairs and Miss Seymour."

Caroline was immediately more interested. "Sir Henry's sister?"

"Yes. A most charming and delightful young lady. She wishes, so I understand, to set a new pace, and that is why she insists upon marrying here instead of at the Seymour country seat at Daneborough in Wiltshire, or indeed at fashionable St. George's in Hanover Square." He smiled. "I believe she will succeed in starting a new mode, for ladies of rank and fashion are very receptive to new ideas. Don't you agree, Miss Lexham?"

"I do indeed, sir."

At that moment a waiter brought the chicken broth the lawyer had ordered and Caroline's attention left the interesting topic of Hal's enterprising sister and turned instead to the matter of French cuisine. She had only taken a spoonful when she knew that this meal was an entirely new experience. The chicken broth was magical and deserved its grand title of *consommé princesse;* the beefsteak was called *tournedos à la béarnaise* and was a succulent dream; and the apricot tart was composed of exquisitely sharp fruit upon a feather-light pastry, and it fully deserved to be known by the more interesting name of *tarte aux abricots.*

Mr. Jordan waited until the meal was at an end before at last inquiring what she thought. She smiled. "It seems small wonder to me, sir, that the French were defeated at Waterloo, for if their army had dined upon such wonderful delicacies, no doubt they were feeling too good to put up too much of a struggle."

He laughed. "So, you approve of this rage for French cooking?"

"I think I must, sir."

"Then maybe you will shortly be able to congratulate the chef in person, for I believe he is about to appear among us." He glanced behind her and she turned with interest. There was a slight stir among the other guests and then the incredible figure of Monsieur Gaspard Duvall descended the steps to the floor of the room.

She looked at him in utter amazement, for he did not present at all the traditional figure of a cook: there was no white hat and no apron. He must have been about forty years old, although he moved with the sprightliness of a much younger man. He was small and dark, and with his bright brown eyes and animated expression, was very French indeed. His hair was beginning to go gray at the temples, and had he been of greater stature, he would have been pronounced a very handsome fellow. However, it was his choice of attire which was the most startling thing about him, for it was not at all conventional. His hat was a floppy blue beret, worn at a rakish angle over one ear, his waistcoat was a vivid peacock blue, and his trousers were as close fitting as some gentlemen wore their breeches. His tight-waisted, full-skirted coat was aquamarine in color, and altogether his appearance was such that he could not have passed unnoticed in a crowd. Whatever his taste in clothes, however, his smile was infectious, and it was immediately obvious to Caroline that the little Frenchman was liked as much for his good humor as for his eccentricity.

Fascinated, she watched him progress from table to table, exchanging greetings with the gentlemen and bowing gallantly over the hands of all the ladies. At last he approached her table, and Mr. Jordan rose immediately to his feet.

"Ah, Monsieur Jordan!" exclaimed the chef, recognizing the lawyer, "How pleasant it is to see you here once more."

"The frequency of my visits are proof of my delight with your brilliant cuisine, monsieur. May I present to you Miss Lexham, a lady who has tonight tasted French cooking for the first time."

The chef looked quickly at her. "Miss Lexham? Miss Caroline Lexham?"

She was surprised. "Why yes, monsieur. But how—" She broke off, glancing around as she realized that those at nearby tables had heard the chef say her name, and that that name was not unknown to them. She received many curious glances and people leaned together to whisper.

The chef smiled. "You see, you are already famous, mademoiselle. I think everyone in London knows of the amazing Lexham will."

"Oh." She colored, lowering her eyes.

Mr. Jordan was comforting. "Don't look so uneasy, my dear, for the story was bound to get out, and will have circulated through every drawing room in Town by now."

"I didn't think anyone would hear of it."

The lawyer chuckled. "My dear Miss Lexham, I doubt if a single person present at the reading of that will would have been able to keep his or her tongue still about what happened. Discretion was never a Lexham trait, you know."

She smiled at that. "No, I begin to realize that.

Gaspard Duvall still stood at the table. "So, mademoiselle, you have today become an heiress, and you have also sampled French cooking for the first time. This must surely be a momentous day for you."

"It is indeed, monsieur. I cannot with honesty say how I feel about my inheritance, but I can say that I found the cooking to be quite superlative."

"To hear such praise from the lips of one so very beautiful is sweet indeed, mademoiselle," replied the chef, obviously as pleased as he said he was. "And I am all the more delighted since I have been forced to labor in the bowels of the earth."

"I beg your pardon?"

"The kitchens, they are in the cellars. They are, therefore, *odieuse et abominable*." He spoke with considerable feeling as he lapsed into his native tongue. "Such kitchens are not worthy of Duvall," he went on, tossing an almost venomous glance at the unknowing Mr. Bassett, who stood nodding and smiling just out of earshot. "For they are small and dark, their ovens are old-fashioned, and there is no range at all! In Paris I had magnificent kitchens, large enough to serve *twenty* dining rooms, equipped to produce *thirty-four* soups and *one hundred and twelve* fish dishes on one *carte* alone! Here, everything is *abominable*!" With this, the little chef took his leave of them, moving on to the next table, where he was once again all smiles and charm.

For a little longer Caroline and Mr. Jordan remained at their table, but she was aware of still being the object of much curiosity now that her identity was known, and so at last she asked Mr. Jordan if they could leave. Without hesitation, he agreed, and a minute later they were being shown from the room by little Hercules, into whose upturned turban Mr. Jordan dropped a coin. In the entrance hall, the lawyer took his leave of her, arranging to call upon her at eleven the following morning, when they would drive to Lexham House so that she could see her inheritance.

No sooner had the lawyer departed, however, than the porter was opening the doors again to admit two returning guests, a young lady in delicate lilac muslin, and a tall, distinguished gentleman whom Caroline recognized immediately: Hal Seymour. Her heart almost stopped as she paused at the foot of the grand staircase, and again, as if he sensed her gaze upon him, he turned swiftly in her direction. Their eyes met, and for a moment he seemed surprised, but then he smiled at her. "Why, Miss Lexham," he said, coming toward her. "What an unexpected pleasure this is." He took her hand and raised it to his lips.

Chapter 9

"Good evening, Sir Henry," she replied, wishing that she looked cool and collected, but knowing that a telltale color was flaming on her cheeks.

The young lady he was with now joined them. She was very attractive, with her fluffy dark hair and large, dancing green eyes, and she wore jewelry which was so costly that the precious stones winked and flashed at the slightest movement.

Hal turned to her. "Jennifer, allow me to introduce you to Miss Lexham."

"*The* Miss Lexham?"

"Yes, indeed. Miss Lexham, my sister, Miss Seymour."

Jennifer Seymour smiled, holding out a white-gloved hand. "I am so pleased to meet you, Miss Lexham, for as you will have gathered, I have heard all about you, both from my brother and from the rumors which have today been racing around Town."

Caroline's cheeks continued to burn. "I trust you have heard only good of me, Miss Seymour."

"But of course, for how could there be anything bad about the damsel my brother rescued upon the king's highway, and who has subsequently become Dominic Lexham's *bête noire*!"

"Jennifer!" reproved her brother sternly. "It is not at all

the thing to make one's personal feelings about someone quite so obvious.''

"Well, I am being honest, Hal," she replied firmly. "I do not like Dominic Lexham, and I haven't ever since he locked me in that cupboard and left me there for five hours. He was a beastly little boy, and now he's a beastly big boy. I'm glad Miss Lexham is to have that house, and I have no intention of pretending otherwise.''

Hal rolled his eyes at the ceiling, smiling. "You see, Miss Lexham? My sister has had a privileged upbringing, an expensive education at one of the very best academies for young ladies, and still she does not know how to conduct herself in public.''

"Don't be a disagreeable bear, Hal," went on his irrepressible sister, "for you know that I am only saying what you've said yourself on many an occasion. Dominic Lexham is in sore need of a salutary lesson and I trust that this one will be very salutary indeed. In fact, I hope with all my heart that Miss Lexham will be able to meet all those wretched conditions so that in six months' time she will be the full and undisputed owner of Lexham House." She turned to Caroline then. "Since you will be in Town for some time, I do hope that we may become better acquainted, Miss Lexham, for from what Hal has said of you, I am sure that you and I could become firm friends.''

Caroline glanced quizzically at Hal, wondering what it was that he had said, but she had to shake her head at his sister. "I am afraid that I will not be staying in London more than another day or so.''

Jennifer looked shocked. "But that cannot be so! You will be living in Lexham House!''

Caroline lowered her eyes. "I do not think that that will be possible.''

"But—"

"Jennifer," interposed her brother swiftly. "Do not presume to comment upon something of which you know little or nothing. I think you embarrass Miss Lexham with your rattle.''

Jennifer was immediately contrite. "Oh, forgive me, Miss Lexham, for I know that I speak too often and too thoughtlessly.''

Caroline smiled, liking her very much. "There is nothing

to forgive, Miss Seymour, for no doubt if I had been in your place I would have said exactly the same thing.''

"I am very sorry that you will not be in Town for long, because I was indeed looking forward to furthering our acquaintance.'' Her green eyes brightened suddenly. ''But I have an idea! Miss Lexham, will you join us in our box at the Italian Opera House tonight? We are to see von Winter's *Il Ratto di Proserpina* and the opera *The Haunted Tower*. It will be excellent fun, and you will be able to meet Lord Carstairs, who is to be my husband. Do say that you will join us.''

Caroline would dearly have liked to accept this kind invitation, but her turquoise gown had barely done service for the Oxenford's dining room, it would not do at all for a venue as glittering as the Italian Opera House. ''I would like to accept, Miss Seymour, but—''

"No buts,'' cried Jennifer delightedly. ''You *shall* join us!''

Hal instinctively knew Caroline's dilemma, however, and for the second time he intervened discreetly on her behalf. ''Jennifer, I think that Miss Lexham has a prior engagement.''

Jennifer's face fell. ''Oh, I did not think.''

Caroline was touched at such genuine disappointment, and she liked Hal's lively sister too much to allow her to remain ignorant of the truth. ''Miss Seymour, Sir Henry is being very kind and considerate toward me, for he has perceived the true state of things. I cannot join you tonight because I have nothing even remotely suitable to wear, not because I have an engagement elsewhere. My baggage has unfortunately disappeared *en route* to London, and I confess that even had it arrived, my wardrobe would still not have contained a gown elegant enough for the Italian Opera House. Were it not for that, I would most warmly have accepted your generous invitation.''

Jennifer, initially crestfallen, now brightened again. ''Oh, Miss Lexham, again you must forgive my lack of tact, for I am truly most thoughtless at times. But since you have been so very honest and forthright with me, perhaps I may be the same toward you. There is a very simple solution to the problem, a solution which I would be only too pleased to be of assistance with if you would let me. I believe that you and I are the same size, and up in my apartment there is an immense wardrobe of togs from which you could choose.''

Caroline did not quite know what to say. ''Oh, but I couldn't possibly,'' was all she could think of.

''Why not?'' inquired Jennifer, obviously seeing this as an admirable answer to the problem and dearly hoping to persuade Caroline to take it up.

Hal smiled, looking at Caroline. ''For once, Miss Lexham, I believe that my sister has had an excellent idea, and I assure you that I would be delighted to have your company tonight, for you will save me from the ignominious role of gooseberry.''

Jennifer was indignant at this. ''You, Hal Seymour, are being a bear again!''

He grinned, but then returned his attention to Caroline. ''Please consider my sister's plan, Miss Lexham, for I know that you will enjoy the opera house, and I would be pleased to be your escort.''

To be with him for the whole evening? To be escorted by him? Her pulse was racing as she looked helplessly from one to the other, but at last she capitulated. ''I would love to join you. Thank you so much for your kindness.''

Jennifer was triumphant. ''Oh, I'm *so* pleased! Come, we will repair to my rooms immediately and see what you would like to wear; it will have to be something very splendid indeed if it is to show off that beautiful necklace, of which I am already green with envy!''

In something of a daze, Caroline allowed the other to spirit her away up the staircase. The unbelievable had happened. She was going to the Italian Opera House, she was going to wear a costly and fashionable gown, and she was to be on the arm of one of England's most handsome and fascinating men!

Jennifer's apartment was very fine indeed, the rooms lofty and elegant, the furniture more classical than that in Caroline's apartment. Fires crackled brightly in the hearths as Jennifer's maid, Simpson, was brought hurrying up to assist her mistress. In the dressing room, the maid flung open the wardrobe doors to reveal a bewildering array of beautiful, extremely expensive, and fashionable garments.

Jennifer was almost apologetic. ''I'm afraid that when my brother suddenly announced that we were coming here because our house was to be completely refurbished, I simply could not decide which togs to bring—so I brought absolutely everything.''

"That I can well believe," murmured Caroline, running her fingertips in awe over the shimmering fabrics.

"I shall be wearing this apple-green silk," said Jennifer, taking down a gown which was so soft and light that it seemed to slither over her hands.

"Oh, it's so beautiful," breathed Caroline. "And you will look quite perfect in it; it will go so well with your eyes."

Jennifer was pleased. "That is what I am hoping, for tonight I mean to positively devastate my beloved Charles."

"Charles?"

"Lord Carstairs." Jennifer removed the glove from her left hand, revealing a betrothal ring of the most dazzling diamonds Caroline had ever seen. "I love him so much," she murmured dreamily, gazing at the ring.

"When is the wedding to be?"

"On the evening of Friday, the twentieth of March, by special license here at the Oxenford, but it is simply *ages* away!''

"It's only a month!"

"Which is a lifetime. It would have been earlier in March but for my brother's odious and incomprehensible decision to move here. The house in Hanover Square is perfectly all right; it doesn't *need* refurbishing. Still, I suppose that coming here does have its advantages, for by having my wedding in a hotel I will surely be starting a new vogue."

"Soon all brides will wish to marry *à la Seymour*," laughed Caroline.

"*À la Carstairs*, you mean! Oh, I shall positively float down that grand staircase in my silver tissue, a wreath of diamonds in my hair, followed by twelve bridesmaids, six in primrose and six in lilac. I shall *glow* with happiness. I know it is not considered the thing to adore one's intended husband, but I love my dearest Charles with all my heart and believe myself to be the most fortunate of creatures for having won him." Slowly her smile died away and her green eyes became less happy. "I only wish that a similar happiness lay ahead for my brother."

Caroline received the distinct impression that Jennifer Seymour did not hold out much hope for the granting of this wish, and that this was because she did not like Marcia, Lady

Chaddington, with whom her brother's name was so firmly linked.

Jennifer smiled a little self-consciously. "I know I am foolish to worry so about him, for as he says, he is big enough and ugly enough to do as he sees fit."

"I'm sure he is right."

"I know. I can't help it, though, for he seems set to choose the wrong bride, and what with that and all the danger he seems to involve himself in . . ." She broke off, biting her lip, and it was obvious that she had been at the point of saying something she should not. She smiled again then. "Come, we must hurry and decide upon your togs for the opera house, for if we don't hurry, we will be late."

An hour later, with the final minutes ticking away to the moment they were to depart, they were both ready. Jennifer was attired in the apple-green silk, her hair got up in the style known as *à la Rome*. A golden fillet rested across her pale forehead and a trailing gauze scarf was pinned to the back of her hair, the ends draped elegantly over her bare arms. Emeralds shone at her throat, in her ears, and on the bracelet worn over her long white gloves. Her cashmere shawl put Caroline's plain white one to shame, for it positively glowed with colorful embroidery, and its long silken fringe shivered as Simpson arranged it with great care over her mistress's arms.

After much deliberation and consultation, Caroline had chosen a high-waisted gown of the palest rose muslin, sprigged with tiny silver leaves, and as she looked at herself in the tall cheval glass, she had never dreamed that she would one day wear a gown so modish and beautiful. Its low, revealing neckline displayed her flawless skin and set off her grandmother's silver and ruby necklace to perfection. Its hem was heavy with little pink satin bows, and similar bows adorned the long, diaphanous sleeves which were gathered in at the wrists, the resultant frills spilling over to hide most of her hands. Her toes, peeping from beneath the gown, were clad in white silk stockings and pink bottines tied on with ribbons. She gazed in wonderment at her reflection. Gone was the countrified cousin of the squire of Selford, and in her place was a fashionable lady, the Earl of Lexham's cousin.

Jennifer smiled. "I vow that that necklace enhances the gown more than any I have. Goodness, is that the time? We will have to go down now. Oh, don't forget the fan I gave you, for the opera house is always suffocatingly hot, even in the middle of February!'' Tweaking her shawl to make it hang more satisfactorily, she hurried to the door, which Simpson hastened to open. Jennifer laughed as she and Caroline walked along the passageway toward the staircase. ''I do hope that tonight's performance goes as well as last night's was reported to have done.''

''What do you mean?''

''I have been informed that the rowdier elements in the gods so disliked the performance of *The Haunted Tower* that a positive hail of missiles was rained down upon the stage!''

''At the *opera house*?'' gasped Caroline, startled.

''Oh yes, it is quite usual,'' replied Jennifer as they reached the head of the staircase. There she paused, gazing down. ''Oh, I can just imagine sweeping elegantly down here in my wedding gown! Never will a bride have made a more impressive entrance!''

Hal was waiting in the entrance hall, looking very distinguished in his black velvet evening coat. The coat was very fitted and had ruffles at the cuffs, and he wore a complicated white cravat which looked very startling against the coat's somber velvet. His white waistcoat was unbuttoned to reveal the frill of the shirt beneath, and his knee breeches sported handsome golden buckles. A sword swung at his side and a tricorn hat was tucked under his arm, two formal items of apparel which were *de rigueur* for gentlemen attending the opera house. He was donning white kid gloves as the two women approached, and he turned to greet them.

Jennifer put an apologetic hand upon his arm. ''Are we very late, Hal?''

''Surprisingly enough,'' he replied dryly, ''you are not late at all, which for you, my dear sister, is little short of a miracle.''

''Don't be facetious,'' she retorted. ''Besides, if I *had* been late, I would have had excellent excuse, for there was Miss Lexham's apparel to decide upon.''

''So there was,'' he remarked, allowing his glance to move slowly over Caroline, taking in every last detail of her appearance. His eyes met hers then and she saw in them that lazy warmth which almost bordered on the cynical, but did not quite. Had he said again those last words of their parting outside Mr. Jordan's premises, they could not have hovered more audibly in the air in that moment. She was aware of a heightening color on her cheeks and a trembling in her breast which had no place at all in the makeup of a proper young lady and everything to do with the senses of a woman in the presence of a man to whom she was irresistibly attracted.

He smiled. "You look exquisite, Miss Lexham, but then I would expect that of you."

"Thank you, Sir Henry." Oh, please don't let him guess how much he was affecting her!

"You should always be clad in such elegant togs, for as I said before, you were fashioned for London, not for the provinces. Such beauty as yours should be displayed to the discerning eyes of gentlemen such as myself, and not to the cloddish glances of inconsequential country squirelings." There was a continued amusement in his eyes and she did not know if he only teased her or if he meant what he said.

The porter announced that the landau was waiting at the door, and they left the Oxenford, emerging from the warmth of the hotel into the ice-cold February night. She sat back on the cool gray velvet seat, glancing out of the small window in the hood. Her borrowed gown felt gossamer light, too flimsy for a winter occasion, but the silver sprigging shone and the satin bows looked frivolous and lighthearted. Renewed excitement swept through her as the carriage drew away from the curb.

Chapter 10

The Italian Opera House, which was also known as the King's Theater, stood on the corner of the Haymarket and Pall Mall. It was a large, classical building, its base surrounded by an arcade illuminated by beautiful wrought-iron lamps and by the windows of the little shops which formed part of the ground floor. Caroline noticed immediately that this arcade appeared to be the haunt of ladies of dubious character, who openly approached any unattached gentleman alighting from the throng of elegant carriages drawing up outside the opera house.

As Hal's landau halted at last, Caroline thought fleetingly of her distant home and of Richard Marchand. Selford Village would be so dark and quiet now, the only sound being the moaning of the wind sweeping down over the moor. What would Richard be doing? Would he be seated at his estate ledgers? Or would he be seated comfortably before the fire reading Captain Flint's informative treatise on the breeding, training, and management of horses? She smiled as she gazed out at the glittering scene before her, for no doubt Richard would be poring over Captain Flint again, a pastime he found much more congenial and satisfying than the humdrum of estate ledgers. But then all thought of Richard Marchand fled from her mind as the carriage door was opened and Hal Seymour's fingers closed over hers as he handed her down into a night that was loud with the sound of hooves and carriage wheels, of laughter and conversation.

Her first glimpse of the immense auditorium took her breath away, for it was a splendid vista of red and gold. The horseshoe-shaped pit was encircled by tiers of red-curtained boxes, and there was a very large and spectacular chandelier above the gallery, its brilliant light making that part of the opera house very bright indeed. Everywhere there was the sparkle of jewels and the tremble of ostrich feathers, the subtle shades of dark velvet coats and the flash of military orders upon crimson uniforms. It was a scene never to be forgotten, and as she paused for a moment before taking her seat in the box, she committed every detail to memory, so that for the rest of her life she would be able to recall the breathless excitement of this incredible night. Looking up toward that area of the auditorium known as the gods, she saw a sea of faces peering down, and she wondered if there would indeed be a disturbance such as there had been the night before. The orchestra was tuning up, the sound almost drowned by the babble of voices, and she leaned forward a little to watch the musicians. Behind them the drop curtain shielding the stage moved a little as someone brushed against it, and she was conscious of a surge of anticipation, for it would not be long now before that curtain rose and the performance began.

Down in the pit, the fashionable young men were on display in their elegant clothes. They lounged gracefully on their seats, affecting to be in the grip of an ennui which was only to be dispelled when an interesting new arrival in one of the boxes required a closer inspection with the aid of their quizzing glasses.

At last Caroline sat down, suddenly realizing that until she did so Hal must remain politely standing. A swift blush warmed her cheeks as she smiled apologetically at him, her borrowed fan wafting busily to and fro before her hot face.

Jennifer, who had obviously attended the opera house on countless previous occasions, was quite uninterested in the magnificence of her surroundings; she was occupied with wondering what had happened to Lord Carstairs, who had yet to join them. Then, barely a minute before the curtain was due to rise, he arrived, explaining that he had been forced to walk due to the crush of carriages. He smiled, bowing lovingly over his bride-to-be's hand.

Charles, Lord Carstairs, was of medium height and rather slender. His hair was dark, his complexion pale, and his eyes were soft and brown. He dressed fashionably and yet without that effortless elegance which was Hal's stamp. There was something very appealing and romantic about him and Caroline could well understand how he had won the heart of his vivacious future wife.

He exchanged a friendly greeting with Hal, who then introduced him to Caroline. He smiled warmly as he bowed over her hand and she realized that he knew all about the notorious Lexham will and that he agreed with Jennifer that it was a long overdue lesson for Dominic. As he took his seat next to Jennifer, there was some cheering from the gods, and Caroline turned her full attention upon the brightly lit stage.

Il Ratto di Proserpina was obviously an established favorite, for the audience sang its opening melody, but as the opera progressed, the noise gradually ceased. Caroline enjoyed every moment, for the company gave a creditable performance, and when the final notes were played, there was lengthy and appreciative applause.

It was during the intermission that she first became aware that she was attracting many glances, and that the cause of the interest lay in the presence in the pit of a group of gentlemen who had dined earlier at the Oxenford and who had heard Gaspard Duvall mention her name. These gentlemen pointed out the intriguing Miss Lexham to their friends, who then spread the interesting information to others, and so on, until the whole auditorium seemed to be aware of her identity. This was bad enough, but then things were made suddenly much worse by the arrival in an opposite box of the new Earl of Lexham himself. He too soon perceived that he was the object of much unwelcome whispering, and when he realized why, his handsome face became cold and angry, his eyes flashing when he looked across at Caroline.

She lowered her eyes, toying with the tassels of her fan, and Hal leaned a little closer to her. "You do not seem to appreciate your newfound glory, Miss Lexham."

"It is hardly glory, sir, especially when in spite of my

cousin's unpleasant nature, I find myself in sympathy with him.''

Hal looked at her. "I do believe you mean what you say, and that is very much to your credit, but your sympathy is sadly misplaced.''

"He has every right to resent me, for after all, who am I to interfere in his life?''

"You are the new owner of Lexham House, that is who you are, and you must not forget that.''

She smiled a little. "But I am afraid that I will have to forget it, Sir Henry, and soon.''

The second half of the concert began, the curtain rising for *The Haunted Tower*, which against Caroline's expectation, proved to be a comedy. She forgot about Dominic for a while as she laughed at the performance, but she was suddenly very rudely reminded of her aristocratic cousin when one of the players, a Mr. Braham, stepped forward to sing a ballad entitled "Come tell me where the maid is found." Immediately there was an exceedingly loud and raucous shout from the gods. "She's in the box opposite my lord of Lexham! The one togged in pink!''

This was greeted with a burst of laughter from the audience, and she saw Dominic rise furiously to his feet.

The voice was merciless. "Can't you see her, my lord earl?''

Caroline felt quite dreadful, the flush returning to her cheeks as she kept her glance lowered. Hal leaned close again, putting his hand reassuringly over hers, but it did little to make her feel better, for the audience was quite set upon bringing the performance to a halt now.

On the stage, the unfortunate Mr. Braham endeavored to continue, but even his splendid voice was drowned by the mirth that followed Dominic's precipitate departure from his box. The atmosphere of the evening was ruined for the company of singers, but undeterred, Mr. Braham drew himself up for another song, having decided to move on, but his choice proved even more unhappy. "Slow broke the light," he began, but he got no further, for at that moment another member of the company knocked over a tall candelabrum, which fell with a clatter. The humor of this coincidence was too much for the audience, which dissolved into delighted laughter. This uproarious mirth was the signal for the unruly elements in the gods to begin pelting the stage with a barrage of orange peel, apple cores, and nutshells. The performance came to an abrupt halt, the curtain beginning to fall, only to become stuck with barely a yard to go, so that only the performers' feet could be seen.

Caroline had been staring openmouthed at all the mayhem, but the sight of those feet scuttling around behind the curtain was so funny that she too began to laugh, her earlier mortification disappearing completely. Tears streamed down her cheeks as the curtain gave a shudder and then collapsed completely, trapping the hapless Mr. Braham, who struggled valiantly beneath it, arms waving feebly under the considerable weight.

Jennifer and Lord Carstairs were helpless with laughter, Jennifer holding her aching sides. Hal rose to his feet, trying to hide his own mirth. *"Eh bien, mes enfants,"* he said. "I think it time we removed ourselves from his unseemly melee."

Still laughing, they emerged at last from the opera house, and were soon being conveyed back to the Oxenford. There, Jennifer and Lord Carstairs elected to enjoy one of the suppers for which Gaspard Duvall was becoming famous, but Caroline was too excited to even begin to think of eating. She smiled a little apologetically. "I fear I would not be able to do justice to a supper, Miss Seymour, and so will retire to my bed instead."

"Oh, what a shame," replied Jennifer disappointedly. "But maybe there will be another time."

"I do hope so. Thank you all so much for this evening. I truly enjoyed it."

Jennifer smiled. "As we enjoyed your company, Miss Lexham. Perhaps you and I could spend tomorrow morning together?"

"Tomorrow morning I am to go to Lexham House with Mr. Jordan."

"Perhaps the afternoon instead?"

Caroline smiled. "That would be most agreeable and I shall look forward to it. Good night, Miss Seymour. Lord Carstairs." She was about to say her farewell to Hal too when he smiled at her and offered her his arm once more.

"I will escort you to your apartment, Miss Lexham."

"There is no need, Sir Henry," she began, but he would not hear of anything else.

Jennifer was anxious to go into the dining room. "Shall we order for you, Hal?"

"No, not tonight, Jennifer, for I shall not be able to join you."

A swift anxiety came into his sister's eyes. "Why?"

He hesitated. "I have to see someone."

There was no mistaking Jennifer's alarm. "Hal?"

He drew her hand gently to his lips. "There is no need for you to worry, my dearest, I promise you."

Her fingers closed over his. "You do promise it, don't you?"

He smiled. "Yes."

Caroline watched this little exchange in surprise, remembering Jennifer's reference earlier to the danger in which Hal involved himself and remembering too the rumors of which Mr. Jordan had spoken. The realization that Hal was not joining them because he had an appointment to see someone had caused Jennifer too much anxiety, and Caroline could only wonder if perhaps there was some truth in Mr. Jordan's rumors after all; perhaps Hal Seymour *was* involved in matters of the gravest national importance.

She and Hal left Jennifer and Lord Carstairs then, and Hal walked with her to the door of her apartment, but he did not leave her immediately.

"Miss Lexham, you spoke earlier of having to soon forget your inheritance."

"Yes."

"My advice to you is that you consider very carefully indeed before coming to any decision."

"That is also Mr. Jordan's advice, Sir Henry, but even though I would dearly like to keep the house, I really don't think there is any way in which I may do so. My uncle's conditions are really intended to prevent me from any permanent enjoyment of my inheritance."

"Thwart his intentions and you would be a very wealthy woman."

"I know."

"And so you will instead merely return to Selford, and the dull, frustrating existence you have just escaped from?"

She looked away. "Yes."

He put his hand to her chin and turned her face toward him again. "Will such a life suit you ever again?"

"It will have to, Sir Henry."

He smiled a little wryly. "Selford will *never* satisfy you again, Caro Lexham, for you have tasted London now. I watched you when first you looked out on the streets of this city, and I watched you tonight at the opera house. I told you earlier that you were fashioned for London, and never have I said anything truer. You came home today, which I believe you realize only too well."

She lowered her eyes, very conscious of how close he was and how warm his fingers were against her skin. "And if you are right," she said at last, "what good will it do me to acknowledge my happiness here? I may be fashioned for London, but fate intends me to live my days in Selford."

"Does it?" he murmured, searching her gray eyes.

"Yes, Sir Henry, it does."

For a moment longer he continued to look at her, then he lowered his hand. She sensed a subtle change in him, a withdrawal which was as tangible as it was inexplicable. "Perhaps you are right," he said then, taking out his fob watch and flicking it open. "I fear I must leave you now, Miss Lexham, but no doubt we will encounter each other again before you depart. Good night." He inclined his head in a way that could only be described as cool, and then he left her.

Her eyes filled with tears. "Good night, Sir Henry," she whispered after him. Why had he changed? Had she said something wrong? If she had, she did not know in what way she was guilty, which made his abrupt withdrawal all the more hurtful. And yet what did she expect of him? He was kind and courteous toward her when the occasion demanded it; he had treated her most cordially and with consideration. He conducted himself in a perfectly gentlemanly way toward a woman who meant nothing to him, but who had been thrust into his company. She watched him walk away, and a tear wended its slow way down her cheek. She meant nothing to him, but he meant everything to her, for tonight she knew that she had fallen in love with him.

Sleep proved elusive that night, for she had too much on her mind and there seemed to be so many different sounds to disturb the silence of her bedchamber. Outside there was a constant rattle of carriages passing along Piccadilly, while inside there were the noises of the hotel itself, from the distant clatter of plates in the basement kitchens to the soft, hurrying footsteps of a pageboy conveying a late order to a nearby apartment. She heard a group of noisy, rather tipsy gentlemen returning from a successful night at a gaming club, and she heard a woman's low, teasing laugh as she spurned the hopeful advances of the gallant who had escorted her to her door.

Caroline lay there, gazing up at the shadowy patterns on the canopy of the bed, and it seemed that sleep would never come, but come it did, for she was awoken at dawn by the low humming of the bootblack as he collected the footwear left outside the door of a gentleman who was temporarily without the services of his valet. For a moment she forgot where she was, but then she remembered everything and sat up, shivering a little as she slipped from the bed and her bare feet touched the cold floor. Her breath stood out in a silvery cloud as she went to the window, flinging back the heavy curtains and unfastening the shutters.

Outside everything was frozen. The eastern sky was a pale primrose and a low mist clung beneath the trees of Green Park. There were lamps burning in the windows of a nearby house, and wisps of smoke rose from its chimneys. She knew that the Oxenford possessed gardens at the rear, and on impulse she decided to walk in them while everything was deserted and quiet.

She donned her gray woolen gown and mantle, pulling a face as she looked at her reflection in the cheval glass this morning. She was herself again; gone was the fine London lady of the previous evening. She had done her best with her travel-worn clothes when putting them away, but somehow they still looked in dire need of laundering. She had not dared to call upon the services of the Oxenford, first because she did not possess an abundance of money with which to reward such labors, and second because she shrank from sending such lowly garments to servants accustomed to handling the clothes of the wealthy. She could well imagine the disdain with which her poor mantle would have been received, and so she had endeavored to do what she could herself, but it had been to little effect. With a resigned smile, she twisted her hair up into a tidy knot, put on her bonnet, and tied the ribbons firmly beneath her chin.

She encountered no one as she slipped down through the hotel, and she soon found her way out into the gardens, where the bitter cold caught her breath. The mist had frozen the trees, which loomed frosty and white in the dawn light. As she strolled along a path, she noticed the snowdrops on the lawn, and beneath a hedge the waxy blooms of the last of the Christmas roses. Beyond the confines of the garden, London was beginning to stir. She heard a milkmaid calling in the mews lane, and a boy selling freshly made toffee began to shout his wares at the top of his lungs. In the distance a church bell began to ring, followed by another and then another until the air seemed to vibrate with the noise. Never before had she heard so many, for she was used to the gentler tones of Selford church's solitary toll.

As the bells stopped, she heard voices close at hand, and saw some shadowy figures coming from the direction of the

mews. There were two men, followed by three small boys
pushing barrows, which appeared to be laden with meat, fish,
fruit, and vegetables. One of the two men was Gaspard
Duvall, and she realized that the little procession had been to
all the various markets to choose the choicest items for the
tables at the Oxenford. There was no sign this morning of the
chef's sprightly joviality, for he was engaged in a low, urgent
conversation with the other man, who appeared to be another
Frenchman. Something was obviously wrong, for even allowing for a certain Gallic tendency to gesticulate excitedly,
the chef's manner could only be described as exceedingly
agitated. He argued heatedly with his more taciturn country-
man, whose attitude was one of muted but determined disagreement. It was this dark-haired, thickset second man who
suddenly saw Caroline standing in their path. With a sharp
word of warning, he nudged the chef, who immediately fell
into a confused silence, seeming to find it difficult to collect
himself sufficiently to manage one of his usual smiles of
greeting.

"Wh-why, Mademoiselle Lexham, how early you are out,"
he said at last.

"Good morning, monsieur," she replied, glancing curiously at the other man, who now retreated to join the kitchen
boys waiting obediently with their heavily laden barrows.

The chef followed her glance and seemed to think he
should explain who his companion was. "That is Boisville,
mademoiselle, he is my *entremettier*."

"My French is very poor, monsieur, and I am afraid you
will have to explain."

He appeared relieved that she had not understood anything
earlier, and he beamed. "Ah, forgive me, mademoiselle, and of
course I will explain. An *entremettier* has charge of preparing
the soups, the vegetables, and the desserts, whereas I am the
chef de cuisine, and I am in charge of everything. I am call
the *gros bonnet*, which in English means the 'big hat,' because chefs wear tall white hats. Do you understand?"

"Yes." She was surprised, however, to learn that Boisville
was Duvall's subordinate, for his manner before he had realized she observed them had been anything but subordinate;
indeed, it had been the very opposite!

Boisville bowed then, smiling, although it was not a smile

she particularly liked, and murmuring in excellent English that he would, with the chef's permission, proceed to the kitchens with the boys. Duvall nodded his agreement and the little group moved on toward the hotel, vanishing into the swathes of mist.

She smiled at the chef. "Please don't let me detain you, monsieur, for I know you must have a great deal to do."

"But it is a pleasure to be detained by so lovely a lady," he replied, his bright eyes dancing with his usual gaiety. "Besides which, I welcome any diversion which keeps me from those *odieuse* kitchens!"

"Are they really as bad as you say?"

"They are worse!" he cried with feeling. "And today I shall inform Monsieur Bassett as much. I shall complain and I shall demand improvements."

She wondered what the superior majordomo would make of such animated and impassioned criticisms, for the chef was evidently determined to carry out his threat.

He gestured angrily toward the hotel. "I must make do with old-fashioned ovens and open fires, when in Paris I had closed ranges. But here they expect me to create the most *recherché* of banquets, the most exquisite of wedding feasts! I am the *gros bonnet*, I have the best *brigade de cuisine*—that is the kitchen team," he added almost as an aside. "And yet I must work in the most *odieuse* of kitchens! It will not do, and today I will say so."

"I wish you well, monsieur."

He smiled, drawing her hand to his lips. "I thank you, mademoiselle. But now, I fear, I have to go and see that the *brigade* carries out its tasks correctly. They may be the finest team in the world, but they do not always do things the way I like. *Au revoir, mademoiselle.*"

"Good-bye, monsieur."

With light, swift steps, he hurried away into the mist, and as she watched him she thought again of Boisville's curious attitude. The *entremettier* had not conducted himself as if Duvall had been his superior, and there was no mistaking the fact.

She walked alone for a little while longer, thinking of other things, and then she decided to return to the hotel to write a letter to Richard before taking breakfast. Inside she inquired of the porter where she might find writing implements, and she was directed to the library, where she found an escritoire. A housemaid was attending to the fire, but she hurried out immediately when Caroline entered. Sitting at the escritoire, she took a sheet of the Oxenford's superior parchment and settled down to write.

Oxenford Hotel, Piccadilly. Before breakfast. She smiled, for it was so very grand. Dipping the quill in the ink again, she continued writing. She knew that Richard would be very anxious about her, in spite of his anger at her insistence upon going, and so she wrote in great detail about everything that had happened, even describing the evening gown she had borrowed from Jennifer Seymour. She worded the letter with great care, for she wished it to strike just the right note of affection, neither seeming to encourage him to hope she had changed her mind about marriage or seeming to rebuff him too much, for that would have been hurtful. She wanted him to know that she thought of him, that she loved him still, but that he must not hope she would return to become his bride. She was glad now that she had thought of asking Hal Seymour for a racing tip, for that gave her the perfect ending for her letter. *I was exceeding impudent on your behalf,* she wrote, *for when I traveled with Sir Henry I shamelessly pumped him for some inside information about the turf. He was good enough to tell me that he sets great store by a horse named Nero for this year's Derby—that is surely as good as from the horse's mouth and will make you a very knowing one with your cronies. I will end now, but I promise to write again before I return to Selford. Your affectionate cousin, Caroline.*

After sanding the letter, she folded it, melted some sealing wax against the flames of the crackling, smoking fire, and a moment later the letter was ready to be posted. But as she went toward the door to take it down to the porter, the door was thrust open and she halted in shocked dismay as she saw Lord Fynehurst standing there.

The pale morning light from the window fell coldly on his Apollo curls, making them seem more contrived than ever. He was dressed from head to toe in pale blue, and he held a lace-edged handkerchief lightly between the thumb and first finger of his left hand. His eyes flickered unpleasantly, and he stepped aside, and Caroline realized that he was accompanied by his sister, Marcia, Lady Chaddington.

She advanced slowly into the room, and Caroline instinctively backed away from her. Marcia was clad in chestnut velvet, the same color as her lovely hair, and there was deep fur trimming at her throat, cuffs, and hem. She wore a beaver hat at a rakish angle, and her hands were plunged into the largest fur muff Caroline had ever seen. She was a vision of modish style, but there was something malevolent about her as she halted before Caroline. Lord Fynehurst slowly closed the library door, leaning back against it to prevent anyone from entering unexpectedly.

"Well," murmured Marcia quietly. "You have looks enough, I suppose, but in other ways you are rather drab, are you not?"

Caroline said nothing, swiftly gathering her skirts to hurry to the door, but Lord Fynehurst wagged a reproachful finger at her. "Not yet, dearetht, not yet."

"I wish to leave, sir, please allow me to pass!"

Marcia turned. "I have not done with you yet, miss."

"What do you wish of me?"

"I have come to issue a warning."

"A warning? About what?"

"About interfering with that which does not concern you."

"I'm afraid that I don't understand," replied Caroline, but she sensed that it was because of Hal Seymour. It could be nothing else.

A cool, contemptuous smile played about Marcia's lips. "You don't understand? Come now, don't let us pretend, for you are a scheming, conniving jade and you know full well why I have felt it necessary to come here like this."

"No, my lady, I do *not* know."

"I note that you appear to know who I am."

"Yes."

"Then you must also know in what way you have transgressed."

"No."

"What a vulgar, little creature you are, to be sure, for your conduct has been that of a *demimondaine* of the meanest order."

"A *demimondaine*?" gasped Caroline, her gray eyes widening with shock and anger.

Marcia's rich hem swung as she walked slowly along the tall shelves of books, an elegant gloved finger dragging along the embossed spines. "What else are you but a common Cyprian? Only such a creature would stoop to the level you stooped to in order to gain a place in Sir Henry's carriage. You flaunted yourself quite outrageously, or so he tells me."

Caroline felt as if she had been struck. Hal had said that of her? Her trembling fingers crept to her grandmother's necklace, moving nervously over the chased silver.

Marcia turned to face her, her eyes cold and filled with loathing. "You are an adventuress, Miss Lexham, and your purpose is quite plain to one and all. Why, you even went to the length of taking rooms in this very hotel!"

"I didn't reserve the apartment here; Mr. Jordan, the lawyer, did."

"At your instruction, no doubt."

"No!"

"It doesn't matter, for you will not succeed. You will not succeed in this and you will not succeed in retaining your hold upon Lexham House. I mean to be rid of you, my dear, and quickly."

"I do not wish to hear any more of this, Lady Chaddington. Please allow me to leave."

"In a moment. First I warn you that I mean what I say. I intend to be rid of you, and soon you will have proof of how determined I am and how powerful is my influence. Take my advice, Miss Lexham, forget your notions of grandeur and forget Sir Henry Seymour, whose derision you have already earned. Take yourself back to the remotenesses of Devon, where you belong. Now, I will bid you good day, and I trust good-bye as well. Be sensible and remove yourself from Town as swiftly as possible. Be tardy or obstinate, and it will be the worst for you. I am an implacable enemy, I promise you that."

Her rich skirts rustling, Marcia swept out, followed by her mean-hearted brother. Caroline leaned weakly against the escritoire. She was shaking, her emotions swinging between anger at being so unjustly threatened and abused and a dreadful humiliation that Hal should have expressed such an opinion of her. To her face he had been charming and courteous; behind her back he was false and contemptuous. Furiously she blinked back the hot tears, forcing them away as she strove to retain her poise. Then, her head held high, she emerged from the library into the deserted passageway.

Chapter 12

Such was her mortification at finding out what Hal had said of her that the thought of perhaps seeing him at breakfast was quite dreadful. To her immeasurable relief, however, neither he nor his sister appeared in the dining room. She did not enjoy her first fashionable breakfast, for she was too distressed after her confrontation with Lady Chaddington. She sat almost alone in the elegant dining room, for most of the guests had yet to rise. Although it was now bright and sunny outside, the room was gloomy and depressing, for its windows did not catch the morning sun, and she was glad enough to escape into the lighter hallway to await Mr. Jordan's arrival.

The hall was very busy now, the porter was always rising from his chair to open the door, and a constant stream of waiters, their long aprons crackling, hurried up and down the grand staircase with trays, or in and out of the dining room, which was beginning to attract more guests now. Mr. Basset occupied a prominent position on the tiled floor, smiling obsequiously at the more exalted guests, and outside she could see the liveried footmen parading importantly up and down, exchanging disdainful glances with their opposite numbers outside the nearby Pulteney.

Sitting on one of the elegant sofas, Caroline watched everything, and she was surprised that she found something with which she could most certainly find fault. A door opposite stood open, and she could see that the room beyond was the coffee room. It was sun-filled and bright, with many white-clothed tables, and it was a much more welcoming proposition for breakfast than the dark dining room. Had she been in the majordomo's place, she would have seen to it that breakfast was served in the sunny coffee room, of that she had no doubt.

As she dwelt upon this, a carriage was pulling up at the curb, and its arrival was greeted with immediate service by the footmen, who hurried to open the door, which was adorned with an aristocratic coat-of-arms. A young gentleman with honey-colored hair alighted and entered the hotel, his expression dark, and he had advanced to where she was sitting before she sensed his presence and looked up sharply into those gray eyes which so mirrored her own.

"My lord earl!"

Dominic's lips were thin and cruel. "I would have words with you, madam. In private."

"I am sure that whatever you have to say can be said here," she began, a little apprehensively.

"In private," he repeated, the tip of his ebony cane indicating the open door of the deserted coffee room.

Seeing that they were attracting the interest of both the porter and Mr. Bassett, she decided against her better judgment to do as he wished, and in the coffee room she turned nervously to face him.

The sunlight streamed over his elegant figure, burnishing the brown of his coat and flashing upon the jeweled pin in his cravat. He did not deign to remove his top hat. His whole being exuded utter contempt and disdain for her. He did not pretend to be polite, for he regarded her as an inferior creature without any right to civility. "I think, madam," he said in a chilling tone, "that I have been foolish to allow this charade to progress this far. I speak of your unwelcome presence in Town and your impudent pretensions to my property."

"The impudence was not mine, sirrah," she replied coldly, her anger aroused. "It was your father's for bringing me into his will."

"Don't think to be clever with me, missy!"

"I'm not being clever, I merely repay you in kind for your arrogant rudeness."

His gray eyes flashed furiously. "Be careful, I warn you. Besides, it is immaterial what you think or say, it is what you do which concerns me—and I intend that you shall leave London immediately and that you will renounce any spurious claim you may have to Lexham House." He gave a brief, mirthless laugh. "You fancy yourself to be a fine lady all of a sudden, don't you? You languish in one of the best hotels in Town, flaunt yourself in an opera box in borrowed fripperies, and believe yourself to be very much the Lexham! But you are only a vulgar little Marchand, and your posturings are laughable."

"Really? I did not notice you laughing last night, my lord."

His control snapped at this sarcastic defiance, this unwanted reminder of the humiliation he had suffered because of her presence at the opera house. With an oath, he seized her roughly by the arms, shaking her with a savagery that frightened her. She began to struggle, wanting to shout for help but somehow unable to do so. Her efforts were in vain against his furious strength, but then she was saved by the sudden opening of the door as a maid came in with a pile of freshly laundered napkins.

Dominic released her immediately, turning away with an air of apparent nonchalance, and needing no prompting, Caroline gathered her skirts and hurried out past the startled maid.

To her immense relief, she saw Mr. Jordan waiting for her in the hall, and she slowed to a sedate walk, composing herself as she approached him. She would not say anything of what had just taken place, for there was no point, and it was probably better left untold. She smiled. "Good morning, Mr. Jordan."

"Good morning, Miss Lexham." His shrewd eyes took in her flustered appearance and noted the emergence of the new Earl of Lexham from the doorway behind her. Dominic walked past without a word, and Caroline lowered her eyes as the lawyer looked at her again. "Another unpleasant confrontation with your kinsman, my dear?"

"Yes."

He waited, but she did not elaborate, and so he offered her his arm. "Shall we go?"

"By all means, Mr. Jordan."

Dominic's carriage had gone when at last Mr. Jordan's chariot drew away from the curb and proceeded west along Piccadilly before turning north into Mayfair. The lawyer glanced at her, wondering what had passed between the two cousins, for whatever it was she was greatly upset by it, he could see that by the way her hands trembled. To break the silence, he spoke of the housekeeper at Lexham House, Mrs. Hollingsworth.

"She is expecting us and will conduct you over the house, which I fear is very cold, having been closed since last autumn. She has been under some difficulty since the late earl's demise, for she has hardly any staff, barely sufficient even for an unoccupied house."

"Why is that?"

He cleared his throat. "I—er—believe they were reluctant to fall under the jurisdiction of the new earl."

"I can sympathize with their dilemma," she replied shortly.

They drove on toward Mayfair Street in silence, and he began to wonder if her quiet mood was caused solely by her disagreeable interview with her cousin. The more he considered it, the more the lawyer sensed that there was something else of concern to her, and he hoped for her sake that it had nothing to do with the handsome, charming Sir Henry Seymour, in whose company she had apparently spent a great part of the previous evening.

The chariot turned into Mayfair Street, and Caroline sat forward, putting aside her problems and thinking instead of the house which was so briefly to be hers. She was aware of holding her breath as the carriage rattled beneath the pedimented gateway and entered the wide, cobbled court before the house. She saw again the flanking wings of stables, coach houses, and kitchens, but it was at Lexham House itself that she gazed as the sound of the carriage's approach echoed all around.

It was a handsome, red-brick building, symmetrical and harmonious. The ground-floor windows were arched, while those on the two floors above were rectangular, and the raised double front doors were approached by a magnificent flight of seven white marble steps. Above this regal entrance was a

long balcony stretching across the front of the house, offering
a commanding view of the court, over the wall, and into
Mayfair Street itself.

They alighted at the steps, and Caroline looked up at the
house where her father had been born and where, but for fate,
she too might have been born. It was a strange feeling to be
looking at this building which carried her family name, and
she was suddenly glad that for six months at least it would
belong to her.

Mr. Jordan glanced approvingly around. "It is indeed a
handsome place. It was designed by Sir William Chambers—
Mr. Chambers as he then was—in 1771 and was built on the
site of an older house, which had been purchased by your
grandfather, the eleventh earl, for the princely sum of sixteen
thousand five hundred pounds." He gave a wry laugh. "It is
worth considerably more than that now, I promsie you."

She did not reply, for at that moment the double front
doors of the house were opened and a woman appeared at the
top of the steps. She was about fifteen years Caroline's senior
and was handsome in an austere, almost forbidding way. Her
dark hair was swept up severely beneath a crisp white mobcap,
and she wore a plain brown wool gown and a starched apron.
A large bunch of keys was suspended on a chain from her
waist, and those keys immediately proclaimed her to be the
housekeeper, Mrs. Hollingsworth. With a silent curtsy, the
woman stood aside to admit them, and slowly Caroline and
the lawyer mounted the wide, white steps.

Inside the echoing vestibule it was ice cold, the chill
emphasized by the pale blue walls and black-and-white-
checkered marble flags on the floor. Some sofas were hidden
beneath dust sheets, and the chandeliers above were wrapped
in ugly brown holland bags. To one side there were rolled
carpets, lying limp and colorless against the wall. Caroline
gazed around, her glance carried from the vestibule and into
the heart of the house by a vista of arches opening on to the
inner hall where rose a truly magnificent black marble staircase,
more impressive even than that at the Oxenford.

Her first impression was one of vastness, but that was
because her eye was deceived, as the architect had intended.
As London mansions went, this house was not very large at
all; there were many others which were more than twice its
size. Her second impression was that the house, like its

housekeeper, was austere and forbidding, and this feeling was reinforced by the dull, echoing thud with which the house-keeper closed the outer doors. The sound reverberated through the empty rooms and corridors, and Caroline felt the urge to shiver.

Chapter 13

Mrs. Hollingsworth's keys chink-chinked as she came to where they stood. "Shall I conduct you on a circuit of the house, madam? Sir?"

Mr. Jordan hastily declined, declaring that he had taken circuits enough when compiling the inventory, and turning back the dustcover on the nearest sofa, he prepared to sit down the moment the two ladies had left him.

Caroline turned a little apprehensively toward the housekeeper. "I would like to see the house, Mrs. Hollingsworth."

"If you will come this way, madam." The keys chinked together again as the woman crossed the vestibule to an impressive doorway above which was fixed a coat-of-arms emblazoned in the bright green, white and gold of the Earls of Lexham.

The door opened onto the private apartments, formerly occupied by the late earl and countess. The rooms were in darkness, for the curtains were drawn and the shutters closed, but in a moment Mrs. Hollingsworth had opened everything up to allow the sunlight to stream in. The light revealed still more ghostly dustcovers, more brown holland over the chandeliers, and more rolled-up carpets. The paintings on the walls were covered with brown paper, and the only item of furniture which did not appear to have been protected in some way was the immense canopied bed with its carvings and heraldic devices.

From the private apartments they proceeded into the library, which was once again in darkness, its furniture covered. The opening of the tall bay windows revealed a prospect over the extensive gardens to the rear of the house; it also revealed a magnificent painted ceiling which was dazzlingly colorful and depicted mythical scenes. Caroline gazed up at it in admiration.

Mrs. Hollingsworth spoke with some pride. "It was painted by Cipriani, madam, the Florentine master."

"It's very beautiful."

"Everything in the house is beautiful," replied the housekeeper, her voice catching unexpectedly. To hide this display of emotion, the woman hurried across the library to the great pedimented doors opening onto the red saloon beyond.

The same cold, desolate atmosphere pervaded this handsome chamber. The opened shutters revealed dull crimson brocade walls and elegant French furniture stacked to one side. Their steps echoed in the carpetless floor as they proceeded quickly through to the next room, which was the dining room and which occupied the opposite corner to the library.

Immense Sheraton sideboards were ranged down one wall, but they were bare now of the gleaming plate which would set them off to such advantage. Indeed, as Caroline glanced at them, she realized that she had seen no porcelain, silver, or gold, none of the treasures Mr. Jordan had mentioned, except the paintings, all of which were so carefully covered by brown paper. The dining room was dominated by the long mahogany table which stretched almost from the window bay to the low Ionic colonnade screening the entrance to the butler's pantry, the kitchens, and other offices forming the one flanking wing of the courtyard.

Mrs. Hollingsworth did not conduct Caroline to these lowly places; instead she led her out of the dining room to the inner hall and then up the grand black marble staircase to the next floor. Here the rooms were smaller in size but more in number, and like their counterparts below they were all shuttered and in darkness, their paintings concealed and their furniture covered. There was something so very sad about these unused chambers with their cold, yawning fireplaces and musty, closed atmosphere, for this was a house which cried out to be occupied again and needed to be warm and lively.

Before ascending yet another flight of stairs to the next floor, they emerged briefly onto the balcony overlooking the courtyard. It was a magnificent vantage point and afforded a view as far as Piccadilly, the chimneys of Devonshire House, and the trees of Green Park. Down below, Mr. Jordan's chariot waited, the stamping and snorting of the impatient horses echoing around the empty stables and coach houses and the long dormitories above them where the male servants normally slept.

The circuit of the next floor was completed more swiftly, and they spent little time in the attics, which comprised storerooms and small bedchambers for the lower female servants. Descending the grand staircase to the ground floor once more, Mrs. Hollingsworth inquired if Caroline would like to see the cellars, where all the valuables were stored, as well as a considerable stock of wines and other such beverages.

Lighting a candle and shielding the weak flame with her hand, the housekeeper unlocked the door and led the way down into the icy darkness, where the raw cold was such that it took Caroline's breath away.

Mrs. Hollingsworth heard her gasp and turned with a smile that quite transformed her stern face and told Caroline that the housekeeper was not as unamiable as she had at first appeared. "I'm afraid that these cellars are said to be the coldest in London, madam."

"That I can well believe!"

"But such cold does have a singular advantage for a fashionable household."

"It does?"

"Such low temperatures ensure that ice placed here in the winter endures almost through the hottest summer." The housekeeper indicated a deep hole in the floor, where by the candlelight Caroline could just make out the straw that would be packed around the ice to insulate it. "The late earl regularly purchased large quantities of ice from the Icelandic suppliers; indeed I recall one memorable summer when Messieurs Gunter, the confectioners of Berkeley Square, had to come to him for ice when their own supply was exhausted. He charged them handsomely for the privilege."

They walked a little farther into the cellars, past casks and barrels, racks of wine, and boxes of expensive candles. There were numerous crates packed carefully with the porcelain, plate, and Chinese jade Mr. Jordan had spoken of, and finally they reached the coal cellar, which was filled almost to capacity with enough fuel to warm the house for several months. It was here that Caroline halted, for she detected a strange gurgling sound.

"Whatever is that?"

"The Tyburn, madam."

Caroline stared. "Do you mean the river?"

"Yes, madam, it flows directly beneath the house."

"What an unpleasant thought," replied Caroline, moving away with a shiver.

The housekeeper smiled. "It passes beneath several May-fair houses, and I know for certain that it flows beneath the Pulteney Hotel in Piccadilly before disappearing somewhere in Green Park. They do say that it is because of the invisible waters of the Tyburn that that part of Piccadilly is so often enveloped in mist."

Caroline was not sorry to emerge again from the sepulchral cellars. Mrs. Hollingsworth carefully extinguished the candle and then locked the cellar door again. The sound of her keys echoed through the house. The housekeeper turned to Caroline again then. "Apart from the grounds and the kitchens, madam, you have now seen the entire house."

"I would like to see the kitchens, if you please."

The woman could not conceal her astonishment. "You would?"

Caroline had to smile a little. "It will not have escaped your notice that there can be little hope of my becoming the permanent mistress of this house, Mrs. Hollingsworth, which naturally means that soon I must return to my home in Devon. That home contains a stout country cook by the name of Mrs. Thompson, and she would never speak to me again if I failed to examine the kitchens of a great London mansion. She will hear of my visit here and she will fully expect to be regaled with every last detail, especially the kitchens."

Mrs. Hollingsworth smiled, and again it was a genuinely warm smile which revealed a kinder nature than one would have expected. "I see that you are truly Master Philip's daughter, madam, for it was your father I heard in your voice then. Of all the Lexhams, he alone was kind and concerned about the servants, just as you are about your Mrs. Thompson.''

"You knew my father?"

"I was a very young parlor maid then, and like all the other servants, I thought the world of him because he was so natural with us. He did not give himself airs and graces, he laughed with us and he sympathized with us. He was sorely missed when he left." The woman looked away for a moment, as if afraid to say fully what was on her mind, but then she looked at Caroline once more, taking a deep breath. "It is this house's great misfortune that Master Dominic does not more resemble his uncle Philip, madam, for all those who had places here have looked elsewhere for employment rather than exist under the new earl's tyranny. Apart from myself and three others, everyone has gone, finding the hazard of seeking positions elsewhere preferable to the thought of your cousin as master. Forgive me for speaking out of turn, madam, but I thought you would understand."

"I do, Mrs. Hollingsworth, for I too have made my cousin's acquaintance now. But tell me, why do you remain here?"

"Because I was paid for one year only last August, just before the old earl closed the house and went back to County Durham for the winter. I am an honest woman, madam, and when I undertook to serve in this house for one year from that date, I considered myself bound by honor so to do, even if Master Dominic had succeeded to the title." The housekeeper smiled a little. "When first Mr. Jordan told me that you were the new owner of Lexham House, I confess that I was overjoyed, for I knew in my heart that the daughter of Master Philip could only be a good and kind woman, but my joy was short-lived, for Mr. Jordan pointed out that it was unlikely that you would be able to keep the house. But I tell you this, madam, if you were to retain this house, I would regard it as an honor to serve you."

"I wish too that I could keep the house, Mrs. Hollingsworth, but as Mr. Jordan told you, I am afraid it will be impossible. Come, shall we look at the kitchens now?"

Mrs. Hollingsworth nodded, leading Caroline back into the dining room, beneath the Ionic colonnade and into the butler's pantry, with its special repository for the most valuable plate. Before conducting her to the kitchens proper, the housekeeper showed Caroline her own little rooms, comprising a parlor, bedroom, and tiny storeroom. There were other such rooms for the upper servants, such privacy being regarded as a necessary acknowledgment of their superior position.

The kitchens were bright, warm, and welcoming after the main house, for the fires were lit, the windows unshuttered, and there was a delicious smell from the joint of mutton turning slowly on a spit. The walls were a gleaming white, their lower portion tiled in the same color, and against them stood enormous dressers laden with crockery for everyday use. On their tops were the largest of the numerous saucepans, while smaller utensils occupied rows of shelves next to one of the immense fireplaces. Copper shone around the hearths and the flames reflected warmly in the burnished metal. At the windows were sheets of fine metal gauze to exclude insects when the casements were open, and the walls that were free of dressers or shelves were hung with countless implements, the uses of which Caroline could only begin to guess.

There were ovens and larders, cupboards and washrooms, pantries and laundry rooms, and in the main kitchen there was even a miraculous supply of hot water from a tap protruding above a stone sink, supplied, Caroline was told, by a heated boiler in the adjacent airing room. In this same large chamber the rafters were laden with cages, baskets, and hooks from which were suspended bunches of herbs, muslin-wrapped hams, and dried mushrooms. Meat and bread occupied their respective cradles, and there was one of the largest sugarloaf cages Caroline had ever seen. She gazed around in wonderment, for never before had she seen such modern, well-equipped kitchens, and she was sure she would not be able to remember even half of it to tell Mrs. Thompson.

There was one marvel she had yet to see, however, and now Mrs. Hollingsworth proudly led her to a curious, low, red-brick construction about the height of a table, occupying the center of the flagstoned floor. This was, announced the housekeeper, the famous set of closed ranges designed scientifically by Baron Rumford, Fellow of the Royal Society and creator of the much lauded kitchens of the Royal Institute in Albemarle Street. These ranges were a very modern invention, a brilliant advance in cleanliness and convenience for the cook. Special long-handled pans nestled in the holes provided for them in the flat top, and Mrs. Hollingsworth pointed out that it was a simple and swift exercise either to damp down the heat or to bring it up to full strength. There were few houses in London which possessed such magnificent closed ranges, and none which possessed finer examples, and Mrs. Hollingsworth took immense pride in telling Caroline all she knew about them.

Caroline could only wonder what Mrs. Thompson would make of such an innovation—or indeed what Gaspard Duvall would say of these kitchens, which were everything he desired and everything the Oxenford's *odieuse* offices were not!

When she had seen all there was to see, she was conducted briefly into the servants' hall where waited the only three remaining members of the staff: the woman cook, an underbutler, and a kitchen boy. Then Mrs. Hollingsworth prepared to conduct Caroline around the grounds, but Caroline thanked her and said that she would prefer to walk alone. The housekeeper quite understood and showed her to the little door opening onto the kitchen garden.

She emerged into the surprisingly warm February sunshine, went through a wicket gate and onto lawns studded with fruit trees that would soon be in blossom. She sat on a wrought-iron seat by an ornamental pool, gazing across the lawns at the house, its red bricks bright in the sun. She no longer felt that the house was austere or forbidding, for now that she had been all over it, she felt a strange affinity with it. Her gaze moved from window to window, from the library with its Cipriani ceiling to the crimson-walled saloon, from the dining room with its Sheraton sideboards to the low roof of the kitchen wing, just visible from where she sat. What would those elegant, sumptuous rooms be like if they were opened up again and filled with all those treasures hidden away in the safety of the cellars? She could imagine the gleaming chandeliers, free of their ugly holland bags, the paintings without brown paper to hide them, the carpets rolled out once more to cover the floors with beautiful designs and colors. And then there was the staircase. Oh, *what* a staircase! It was far more regal and beautiful than that boasted by the Oxenford, and she smiled a little, thinking to what advantage Jennifer Seymour would appear in her silver tissue and wreath of diamonds descending the Lexham House staircase; and also thinking what a wedding feast Gaspard Duvall would be able to prepare in the magnificent kitchens, which were everything the Oxenford's were not.

Suddenly, and quite without any warning at all, an impossible thought entered her head. It was a ridiculous thought, but it would not go away, it insisted upon being considered. Her eyes became pensive as she stared at the house, and then slowly she stood. The thought was improbable, nonsensical even, but with a sudden excited gasp, she gathered her skirts and hurried back to the house, calling Mr. Jordan's name.

The lawyer came running into the kitchens as a startled Mrs. Hollingsworth inquired if something was wrong. Caroline's eyes shone and she shook her head. "No, Mrs. Hollingsworth, indeed I believe the very opposite may be the case." She looked at Mr. Jordan's alarmed face. "I think I have thought of a solution, a way to defeat my uncle's conditions."

The housekeeper gasped hopefully and Mr. Jordan stared at her. "You have?" he asked in amazement.

She smiled. "What would you say if I told you I intended turning Lexham House into an exclusive hotel?"

Her words fell onto a stunned silence.

Chapter 14

Mrs. Hollingsworth's lips parted in astonishment, and the other servants looked askance at one another and then at Caroline. Mr. Jordan was rendered speechless for a moment, but then he recovered. "You cannot possibly be serious, Miss Jordan! You mean to turn this great house into a—a *hotel*?"

"I am perfectly serious, sir."

"It's quite out of the question."

"Why? Does it contravene the terms of the will?"

"Not as far as I can say on the spur of the moment, but it is by far too risky a venture!"

"But I have nothing to lose, Mr. Jordan, as you yourself have pointed out. You told me to play my uncle at his own game, and that is exactly what I am doing. Until this morning I still had sympathy with my cousin Dominic's dilemma, but after his conduct at the Oxenford I no longer have any sympathy for him whatsoever. I believe I have thought of an admirable solution to my predicament, and if I possibly can, I will go ahead with it."

"But to turn this princely residence into a hotel . . ." he began.

"A hotel such as I envisage is very respectable, sir, for who can find fault with establishments considered suitable for the Czar of Russia and his sister, for occasions like the Duke of Wellington's banquet, and for the solemnization of important society marriages, like that of Miss Seymour and Lord Carstairs? The terms of the will demand that I live here for six months, that I open up the entire house, and that I do all this without incurring any debt whatsoever. As a hotel, I must hope that the house will pay for its own upkeep—and there is nothing in the will to say that I may not do that."

Mr. Jordan clearly thought she had taken leave of her senses. "But you are a lady, and ladies do not involve themselves in commercial enterprises of *any* kind!"

"Except when the devil drives, sir, and as far as I am concerned, he most certainly holds the reins at the moment."

"And I do not believe," he continued as if she had not spoken, "that society would accept such a wild venture! Not in Mayfair!"

"Because this has been until now the town residence of the Earls of Lexham?"

"Yes."

"But what was the Oxenford originally if not a private residence? And the Clarendon, the Pulteney, Mivart's, or Grillion's? Were not they also private and exclusive houses?"

"Maybe they were, but now they are in male hands, Miss Lexham, owned or managed by men who were formerly great chefs, experienced and knowledgeable house stewards or butlers. You know nothing of such things, you are a young lady, fresh from the country, and green as to the ways of high society."

"Do you tell me, sir, that these men know more about the running of a great house than a woman like Mrs. Hollingsworth? I cannot agree that there is some mystery about running a hotel, a mystery known only to the male of the species and which a more than competent housekeeper cannot hope to solve. Running a private residence with many titled and wealthy houseguests must be the same as running a hotel, with similar guests—what do you say, Mrs. Hollingsworth?"

The housekeeper was startled at being asked to express an opinion. "I—er—agree with you, madam, there cannot be a great deal to choose between the two situations."

Mr. Jordan was appalled that the sensible and practical housekeeper was apparently allying herself with the lunatic plan. "Mrs. Hollingsworth," he exlaimed, "I am surprised at you!"

"But I must agree with Miss Lexham," explained the housekeeper, "for her idea is *not* as wild and impossible as it at first appears."

Caroline was triumphant. "There!"

Mr. Jordan took a cross breath. "I still say the whole thing is harebrained, for you have not considered anything in detail. In order to throw open the doors of this house to guests you will have to employ a full complement of staff; staff must be paid, Miss Lexham. You will also need to heat the whole house, for it is a long time until the warmth of late spring and summer, and you will need to illuminate it, which will require a great deal of fuel and candles. And then we come to the not insignificant matter of food and drink. Guests of consequence expect fine French cooking and excellent wines; they also expect their own servants to be fed and accommodated. No, Miss Lexham, your idea is out of the question, it simply cannot be done."

Caroline was not defeated yet, for she had found an ally in the housekeeper, and she detected a crack or two in the lawyer's argument. "Sir, it seems to me that you are guilty of a faulty memory."

"Faulty? In what way?"

"You declined earlier to accompany me on a circuit of the house because you had done several circuits when compiling the inventory. During those circuits you are bound to have seen the stocks of wines, candles, and coal in the cellars, stocks which I do not believe are entered in the inventory. Am I right?"

He colored just a little. "You are right, Miss Lexham."

"So, we will take your other arguments. Staff can soon be hired, and even I know that they are not paid for the first three months of their employment, nor are the tradesmen who supply food and so on. I'll warrant that reluctance to immediately pay bills applies more in London than it does in Selford! As to any other consideration, well, the house contains everything in the way of accommodation for both guests and servants, it has immense supplies of crockery, cutlery, bedding, and other such things, because it has *always* had to provide for large parties of guests and their servants. There will be no difference whatsoever, Mr. Jordan, except that from now on those guests will pay for the privilege of lodging here.''

"And the small matter of providing French cuisine? No hotel worth its salt would dare to open its doors to the *haut ton* without being able to boast the services of a French chef.''

"Chefs are surely not impossible to find.''

"My dear Miss Lexham, you dismiss this culinary matter too lightly. Last night at the Oxenford you saw how important Duvall is. Society *expects* the finest cuisine, they *expect* to pay four guineas for such meals, for that is what the Oxenford charges, and they *expect* to enjoy for their money the work of a Duvall, a Carême, an Escudier, or an Ude. Such men do not come two a penny. Have you any idea how much they may command?''

"No,'' she confessed.

"I happen to know that the Earl of Sefton pays Ude three hundred pounds a year, that sum being supplemented by the promise of two hundred guineas for life when Ude retires. The sum offered to Carême by the Prince Regent was astronomical and far in excess of that. You cannot possibly contemplate opening this house as a hotel unless you have such a chef, Miss Lexham, and in order to lure one here you will need money—which I need not remind you is the one thing you do not have.''

She was silent for a long moment. All eyes were upon her, but she was still resolute. Her plan was possible, it gave her a chance to meet the terms of her uncle's will, and she would never be able to forgive herself if she turned her back on it. Slowly she reached up and unfastened her grandmother's necklace, laying it gently on the surface of the table before her. The sunlight pouring in through the windows flashed blood red on the rubies and made the chased silver gleam with an almost blue light.

Mr. Jordan stared at it and then slowly raised his eyes to her serious face. "I beg you reconsider,'' he said gently. "For it is my belief that you are about to cast this precious, beloved item away, and to no purpose.''

"I am set upon my course, Mr. Jordan, and as I will need money, the necklace must be sold.''

"It will not finance you for six months.''

"No, but it will give me the finance to begin. I trust that the hotel would soon begin to support itself."

He looked helplessly at her, seeing the determination in her eyes and feeling in his heart that the idea was doomed from the outset. "Miss Lexham, you speak as if you regard success as a matter of fact!"

"I don't, sir, I promise you that."

Still he could not give up. "And what of your cousin the earl? He is hardly likely to stand by and let this happen to his house—"

"*My* town house," she interrupted calmly. "For the next six months, anyway."

A glimmer of humor touched his eyes at this, for he recognized his own words. "Very well, *your* town house. It matters not, for in the end it comes to the same: the Earl of Lexham will not let you proceed."

"Can he stop me?"

"Not legally, but I doubt very much if he is a man to let such niceties stand in his way."

"Then his interference is something to be coped with if and when it occurs. Oh, Mr. Jordan, don't you see that I *have* to do this now I've thought of it? Now that I've been in this house, it means far more to me than I would have dreamed possible, and if I give up without a struggle, I will regret it for the rest of my life. And there is more; Sir Henry Seymour said to me last night that when I came to London, I came home, and that is very true. I don't want to go back to Selford; I loathe it there. I want to stay here; this is where I feel I belong. I must do everything I can to keep this house; it may be the only chance I ever have of changing the course of my life. Please, at least say you understand."

He saw there there was no point in further argument, for she did indeed mean to go ahead with her plan, her commercial enterprise. "And is there nothing at all I can say to instill wisdom into your pretty head?"

She smiled. "Nothing whatsoever."

He nodded heavily. "Very well, I capitulate. I have grave doubts and reservations, but I will do all I can to help you."

"You will? Oh, *dear* Mr. Jordan!" she cried in delight, forgetting both herself and his dignity by flinging her arms around his neck.

The servants' eyes widened at this uninhibited display, but

Mrs. Hollingsworth saw it as still more evidence that Philip Lexham's warm, open, and genuine nature had been passed on to his daughter.

Caroline turned to the housekeeper then. "You will help me too, won't you?"

"Oh yes, Miss Lexham, have no fear about that."

Caroline smiled, biting her lip a little ruefully. "Mr. Jordan was right about one thing; I certainly do not know the first thing about the running of hotels or great houses."

"I believe I know all that is necessary. We will begin by engaging staff. Advertisements must be placed in the correct publications and the various tradesmen informed. Tradesmen are very useful for such purposes, for they put word about in the hope of benefiting in the form of orders."

Mr. Jordan cleared his throat. "Miss Lexham, nothing can be done until the necklace is sold, for until then you will have no money at all."

She picked it up and pressed it into his hands. "Will you sell it for me?" She smiled a little wickedly then. "I am sure a lady should not participate in anything so mercenary and vulgar!"

He laughed. "You are incorrigible, Miss Lexham, quite incorrigible."

A short while later, Caroline was being conveyed back to the Oxenford in the lawyer's chariot. She was still in a state bordering on elation; it seemed that her plan could not fail, for it had only to succeed for six months! She had arranged with Mrs. Hollingsworth that she would return to Lexham House that very day, cutting short the duration of her stay at the Oxenford, and she did this in part to avoid any further meetings with Hal Seymour. She tried to push all thought of him from her mind, but that was impossible, for in a very short time he had stolen her heart completely, which made the pain of knowing what he had said of her all the more distressing.

Mr. Jordan had placed his chariot at her disposal for the rest of the day, and so she instructed the coachman to wait for her outside the Oxenford as she did not intend to be long. As she entered the quiet vestibule, however, the porter informed her that Mr. Bassett wished to see her immediately. There was something in the porter's manner which told her that her meeting with the majordomo was not going to be pleasant, and she went apprehensively to the dining room, where she was told she would find him.

The dining room was deserted, and so she heard the sound of raised voices before she entered and recognized them as belonging to Mr. Bassett and Gaspard Duvall.

The little chef was obviously very angry. "The kitchens are *not* satisfactory, monsieur!"

"And I say that they must suffice!" replied the equally cross majordomo.

"I am a master, a *genius*, not a slave! A banquet of the size and importance as that for the Duc de Wellington requires finer facilities than those you provide here!"

Mr. Bassett endeavored to take a little of the heat out of the argument. "I agree with you, monsieur," he said in almost conciliatory tones. "And I understand your predicament, but in order to meet your demands it would be necessary to close the hotel completely while the kitchens are rebuilt. That is simply not possible, for how can we close our doors when we have accepted many functions such as the banquet and Miss Seymour's wedding. Be reasonable, monsieur—"

"Reasonable? *Reasonable?*" cried the infuriated chef, obviously quivering from the tip of his floppy beret to the toes of his elegant shoes.

"Please, monsieur," pleaded the anxious majordomo, who was beginning to fear that the chef would resign, which would be a devastating blow to the Oxenford.

Caroline peeped into the room and saw the little Frenchman hesitating. She too believed he must resign, but incredibly he did not; he turned on his heel and walked swiftly toward the door, muttering darkly to himself as he pushed past without seeming to see her. He was so unlike the man she had last spoken to in the garden that she could only stare after him in surprise. After a moment she looked into the room again and, seeing Mr. Bassett wiping his brow with a handkerchief, judged that it would be all right for her to approach him to discover what it was he wished to say to her.

He turned as he heard her approach, and he stiffened visibly. "Ah, Miss Lexham."

"You wished to speak to me?" She could not help noticing that he did not offer her the courtesy of a seat.

"It will not take long, madam, for I merely wish to inform you that your presence is no longer required at the Oxenford."

She was completely taken aback. "I beg your pardon?"

"You will be expected to leave immediately," he went on coldly. "And the sum paid for your stay will be reimbursed to the proper party. That is all."

Her indignation flashed into light. "It most certainly is *not* all!" she said icily. "I expect to be told why this disgraceful request is being made."

"I am not compelled to give you any details, madam, but will say that we have received complaints about your presence."

"From whom?" But even as she asked, she dreaded that she would hear him say Hal's name.

"The identity of anyone concerned is not your business, madam," he replied, his tone very superior as he looked down his pointed nose at her.

"On the contrary, sir, it is very much my business."

He saw the light of angry, determined defiance in her gray eyes and decided that telling her would remove such misplaced impudence and would almost certainly hasten her departure from the premises. "Very well, Miss Lexham, I will tell you. I have this morning received strong complaints from three persons of rank and consequence: Lady Chaddington, Lord Fynehurst, and the Earl of Lexham, your kinsman. All three objected to your presence in this respectable establishment as you are not a person of either quality or good character, and they informed me that unless you were ejected forthwith, they would see to it that they and their friends and acquaintances did not patronize the Oxenford again."

Not a person of either quality or good character? Her eyes darkened with anger at such an appalling insult, but she was glad that at least Hal and his sister had not joined in this exhibition of petty and unnecessary spite. Hal may not have been as open and genuine as he had made out, but she was sure that Jennifer had meant every kind word and action the night before.

The majordomo drew himself up importantly. "I trust that the situation is now perfectly clear, madam. Such persons as I have mentioned cannot be ignored, and I therefore have no choice but to—"

"On the contrary, sir, you have every choice, but you have decided that although their complaints are unwarranted and untrue, and although I am innocent and very much the injured party, I am not of sufficient consequence to warrant consideration. You, sirrah, are as despicable as they!''

Giving him a glance of proud disgust, she turned and walked away, her head held high, but as she hurried up the grand staircase, her eyes brimmed with hot tears and her cheeks flamed with the humiliation and injustice of being treated in such an unkind and disgraceful way.

At the top of the staircase, she halted to look back down at the elegant vestibule with its gracious furniture and attentive page boys and footmen. Defiance stirred her then. She would not allow them to treat her as if she did not matter! She would show them! She would show the Marcia Chaddingtons, Dominic Lexhams, and Oxenfords of this world that she was a person to be reckoned with after all! She would not scuttle out of London because they wanted her to; she would stay and she would make a success of what Mr. Jordan called her ''commercial enterprise'' and soon all London would be talking of the new Lexham Hotel and its unusual owner!

Chapter 15

But her moment of bravado began to shrink to a more timorous apprehension as she packed her few belongings into her valise. Glancing around at her magnificent apartment, the enormity of what she was contemplating began to truly dawn upon her; indeed, the sheer audacity of it made her wonder if perhaps Mr. Jordan was right after all and she *had* taken leave of her senses. Why, only a day or so before she had had qualms about setting off for London at all, and now here she was, determining to embark upon turning a great London mansion into an exclusive hotel.

She had almost completed packing when there was a knock at the door, and before she could say anything it opened and Miss Seymour entered in a rustle of red-and-white-checkered silk, the fresh ribbons in her little day bonnet bouncing prettily beneath her chin. For a moment Caroline froze warily, able to think only of what Hal had said to Marcia Chaddington. What if Jennifer shared her brother's views after all? But the warmth of her smile and her obvious dismay when she saw Caroline's packed valise soon dispelled such fears.

"Oh, Miss Lexham, surely you are not leaving already?"

"I fear that I must."

"But I was so looking forward to your company, and you

119

promised that we would see each other today. Has something happened that you must return to Devon so soon?''

"I-I'm not going back to Devon."

"But where are you going then?"

"I am going to Lexham House."

Jennifer stared at her, and then her eyes brightened. "You are going to fight the will after all? Oh, how wonderful! How excellent! And how gladdening, for this means that I will be able to see you often." She paused for a moment. "Do you really have to leave the Oxenford so quickly? I mean, Hal and I were hoping that you would join us for dinner tonight. . . ."

Caroline secretly doubted very much that Hal joined his sister in any such hope, but at least Jennifer's enthusiasm and warmth proved that he had not shared with her his true opinion of the upstart and disreputable Miss Lexham.

"You will join us, won't you?" inquired Jennifer, thus placing Caroline in the unenviable position of having to admit that she was now *persona non grata* at the Oxenford.

"I would have loved to have joined you, Miss Seymour, but I am afraid that it will not be possible, for I have been requested by Mr. Bassett to leave the hotel immediately."

Jennifer was incredulous. "Surely there is some mistake!"

"There is no mistake; he was most definite."

"But why?"

"Because he has received complaints about my presence here." Caroline spoke carefully, hoping that she would not be asked to name any names.

"But who would complain about you?" demanded Jennifer, her eyes flashing with anger that such a thing could have happened. "I suppose it was that odious cousin of yours. I saw him leaving earlier this morning!"

"Yes, it was my cousin," admitted Caroline, determined to say nothing about Marcia Chaddington or Lord Fynehurst, for it would have placed Jennifer in an invidious position to mention Hal's future bride and brother-in-law in such a context.

Jennifer was indignant on Caroline's behalf. "How infamous and despicable your cousin is! And how monstrous it is that this hotel could do this to you! I think them all odious and disagreeable in the extreme. And I feel insulted."

"*You* feel insulted?" asked Caroline, a little taken aback.

"Naturally, for you are my friend, as you are Hal's, and

you were our guest last night at the opera house. To treat you
in this demeaning and cavalier fashion is tantamount to an
insult to us too!''

"Oh, please do not feel like that . . ." began Caroline
anxiously.

"I will not remain in this dreadful place a moment longer,"
declared the other suddenly. "And when I tell Hal, I am sure
that he wil feel exactly the same way."

"Please don't do anything because of me!" begged Caroline,
not wanting to stir things up to such an extent and wishing
with all her heart that she had somehow managed to avoid all
mention of being asked to leave the Oxenford.

Jennifer took her hands. "I like you immensely, Miss
Lexham, for in you I feel I have found a true and constant
friend, and it simply is not possible for me to allow you to be
treated so abominably without showing in some way how
much I abhor what has been done. Nothing on this earth
would prevail upon me to remain here after this! Come, we
will go immediately to tell Hal."

"Oh, no!" cried Caroline, but to no avail, for Jennifer was
carried along by her indignation on her new friend's behalf,
and Caroline found herself being hurried through the hotel to
Hal's apartment.

He had not long returned from riding. His top hat, gloves,
and riding crop lay on a table and his green riding coat was
unbuttoned. He stood by the immense fireplace of the drawing room, which like Caroline's, overlooked Piccadilly and
the green expanse of the park opposite. His valet was just
pouring him a small glass of cognac as his sister entered,
followed very reluctantly by Caroline, who had no wish to
face him, and certainly no wish to see him being informed of
events he almost certainly already knew about.

The discreet and efficient valet conveyed the cognac into
his master's hand and then spirited the top hat, gloves, and
riding crop from the room, closing the door softly behind
him.

Jennifer hurried immediately to her brother, her whole
body quivering with indignation. "Hal, I have something most
dreadful to tell you!"

Caroline could not bring herself to even look at him. She
kept her eyes firmly on the Kidderminster carpet, and Marcia
Chaddington's scornful, taunting voice seemed to ring in her

ears. *You flaunted yourself quite outrageously, or so he tells me. Forget your notions of grandeur, and forget Sir Henry Seymour, whose derision you have already earned.*

Hal glanced momentarily at Caroline's quiet, bowed head, and then took his agitated sister by the hand. "It must indeed be dreadful to bring you bursting in so unceremoniously. What has happened?"

"Miss Lexham has been told she must leave this hotel, and all because her wretched and contemptible cousin complained about her! Is that not awful, Hal? I am so upset about it, so insulted and angry, that nothing will do but that we leave this horrid place too!"

Hal seemed quite nonplussed for a moment, and to Caroline his initial silence was proof enough that he knew precisely what had happened and whose influence lay behind it. Her cheeks flushed miserably and she didn't raise her eyes to look at him. At last he spoke, "Jennifer, I can quite understand how you feel, and indeed I share your indignation, which is more than justified, but I think that to talk of quitting the Oxenford is to go a little too far."

Caroline looked up then, for although he spoke of sharing his sister's feelings, it was obvious that in truth he did no such thing. He had no intention of making any grand gesture on behalf of a woman he held in contempt. Jennifer, however, was visibly shocked and dismayed by his apparently lackluster reaction to something she regarded as of the utmost importance. "Hal! You cannot understand what has been done. This hotel has gravely insulted our friend, it has dealt appallingly with someone we have openly acknowledged to be agreeable and acceptable to us. By doing that, it has insulted us too."

He swirled his cognac for a moment, saying nothing, and Caroline wondered what was passing through his head. "I repeat," he said then, "that although I can understand your considerable displeasure at what has been done, I do *not* share your belief that we should quit this hotel." He glanced at Caroline. "Forgive me, Miss Lexham, for I do not wish to sound as if I in any way condone what has happened."

She held his gaze and said nothing in reply, but inside she felt an immeasurable hurt.

Jennifer was totally astounded. "Hal! You surely do not mean to remain here."

"Yes, that is exactly what I mean to do."

"I cannot believe that I hear you correctly," she replied, withdrawing her hand from his. "Indeed, I think you behave as odiously as the Oxenford and the Earl of Lexham."

Caroline spoke up quickly. "Please, Miss Seymour, don't say any more, for I do not wish to be the cause of any disagreement between Sir Henry and yourself."

But Jennifer did not seem to hear, for she still stared up disbelievingly into her brother's hazel eyes. "You may not think this thing to be of any importance, Hal, but I most certainly do! I will not remain another night under this discredited roof!"

"Jennifer—" he began.

"My mind is made up," she interrupted. "To remain here would be to ignore what has been done, and it would also mean allowing the arrangements for my marriage to go ahead. Nothing would make me celebrate my marriage here now, *nothing*!"

"Jennifer!" he said sharply, his eyes bright with something, Caroline could not gauge exactly what. "I wish you to stop right now and reconsider!"

"No!" His sister's chin was raised stubbornly.

"I have excellent reason to ask you to remain here."

"I know, and that reason is your own convenience. No, Hal Seymour, I will not stay here, I will leave immediately, and nothing you say can stop me."

"I do not think it would be wise to test the veracity of that statement, Jennifer," he replied quietly. "As head of the family, I think you will find that my powers extend considerably further than you appear to think."

"So, you will force me to do as you wish!" she cried, trembling with anger and frustration.

"I have never *forced* you to do anything in your life, and it ill becomes you to suggest that I am capable of such conduct. I merely said that my powers are extensive enough for me to stop you leaving. I did *not* say that I was about to employ those powers. If you insist upon going elsewhere, then you may do so, provided you choose an address which is acceptable. Where do you intend going? Mivart's? Grillion's?"

"I don't know yet," she replied.

"Perhaps you intend to be the new Lexham Hotel's first guest," he said quietly, glancing at Caroline's astonished face. "Oh, yes, Miss Lexham, news does indeed travel with bewildering speed in this capital of ours."

Jennifer stared at him in puzzlement and then turned toward Caroline. "What does he mean?"

Hal spoke again. "When I was returning from my ride in Hyde Park, I encountered Mr. Jordan, the lawyer, and he informed me that Miss Lexham has a notion to turn Lexham House into a hotel, thus defeating the terms of the will."

"Is this true?" asked Jennifer in astonishment.

"Yes," answered Caroline.

For a moment Jennifer seemed at a loss, but then her green eyes began to dance with delight. "What a splendid thing! What a brave and wonderful plan! Oh, I wish I had half the spirit." She turned triumphantly to her brother once more. "Yes, Hal Seymour, I *do* intend to be the new Lexham Hotel's first guest. I shall take great delight in telling that horrible Mr. Bassett what I think of him, and if I see Dominic Lexham I shall tell him too. I shall make a great deal of noise about leaving this place, and about canceling my wedding here and holding it at the new hotel instead."

Caroline gave a start, her breath catching. "Miss Seymour! You cannot possibly!"

"Why not?" inquired the other, smiling almost archly. "I think it is a capital notion, for it does everything I wish it to do: it strikes back at the Oxenford and at Dominic Lexham, and it goes a considerable way toward setting your admirable enterprise up. It also makes my brother's reprehensible inaction look all the more obvious, which is no more or less than he deserves!"

Hal said nothing to this and his face was expressionless.

"But Miss Seymour," said Caroline, "Lexham House is closed, the rooms are not aired and—"

"But you are about to go there, aren't you?"

"Yes, but—"

"If it is good enough for you, then it is good enough for me—unless—perhaps you do not wish me to go there?" There was a sudden hurt in the green eyes.

"Oh, no," replied Caroline swiftly. "Please do not think that, for it is not so. Of course I would love to have you join me; it's just that I don't want you to do anything you may regret. All your wedding arrangements are made, you have told me how delighted you are at the prospect of having

Monsieur Duvall prepare the feast, and how advantageous will be your appearance on the grand staircase!''

Jennifer had to smile. "As I recall, the staircase at Lexham House is *far* more grand, which must mean I will appear to even greater advantage there. As to the feast, well before Hal decided we must uproot and come to this horrid place, I was quite content for Messieurs Gunter to do the feast. The feast is not important, Miss Seymour, but my gesture in leaving the Oxenford and going to the new Lexham most certainly is. My mind is made up and I shall have Simpson begin packing immediately.'' With a final defiant glance at her silent brother and a flick of her red-and-white skirts, she turned on her heel and hurried from the room, calling for the maid in the adjoining apartment.

Caroline hesitated, not knowing quite what to say to Hal, for there was no trace now of the ease she had once felt in his company. She could not shrug off the sense of hurt and betrayal she felt at what he had said about her and she knew a deep pain at his silent complicity in what had been done to her. In spite of this, however, as she looked into his unfathomable hazel eyes, she knew that she still loved him.

"I don't think there is anything more to be said, Miss Lexham,'' he said then. "So do not let me detain you any longer.''

Without a word, she left the apartment.

Chapter 16

That first evening at Lexham House was very strange indeed, for Caroline and Jennifer shared Mrs. Hollingsworth's little rooms, that lady declaring that on no account could she permit ladies of such delicate constitution to sleep in the damp, cold house. For Jennifer, the housekeeper's rooms were a novel experience, but Caroline found them very similar to some of the rooms at Selford and would, therefore, have felt quite at home in them had it not been for her awareness all the time of the echoing vastness of the main house close by.

Caroline had half expected Jennifer's rush of loyal enthusiasm to fade quickly away once she realized how very uncomfortable Lexham House was going to be for a while, but she was soon proved wrong, for Jennifer entered with great relish into the spirit of things. One thing was soon apparent, and that was that Hal Seymour's vivacious and unpredictable sister was nothing if not adventurous, and she certainly had scant regard for what she regarded as foolish and overfastidious rules of etiquette, which she took considerable delight in flouting at the first opportunity. Naturally, she never went too far in this, which was part of her charm, and which was also probably why she seemed to get away with what others would deem to be horrendous sins.

It was quickly decided that Jennifer would have Mrs. Hollingsworth's bed, the housekeeper refusing to hear of anything else and preparing for herself a bed of sorts on the floor of the storeroom where she kept her jars of pickles and preserves. Caroline was provided with a spare mattress in a corner of the parlor, and when everything had been made ready, the unlikely trio sat before the fire to discuss what must be done next to put Caroline's momentous plans into action. There was something very unreal about the situation, and Caroline almost expected to wake up soon and find herself back in her bed at Selford, but when she pinched herself she knew she was very much awake and that this was all really happening.

She glanced approvingly around the parlor, which was an inviting room with a red-tiled floor and whitewashed walls. There were colorful chintz curtains at the window and matching cushions on the dark wooden chairs, and against one wall stood a dresser displaying the housekeeper's prized crockery and the silver-gilt candlestick presented to her by Caroline's grandmother, that same countess who had once owned the necklace which was to finance the first weeks of the great commercial enterprise.

Occasionally they heard bursts of laughter from the servants' hall, where Jennifer's maid, Simpson, was very much the center of interest. Outside, the wind had risen and rattled the panes of glass from time to time. Each gust drew a draft down the chimney, making the fire glow very red, which in turn burnished the fur of the large, gray cat curled up before the hearth. Mrs. Hollingsworth sat on a low stool in front of the fire, toasting bread on a long-handled fork, and the smell was very appetizing indeed, prompting Jennifer to remark that not even Monsieur Duvall could create such a delicacy. This made them all smile, and Caroline found herself thinking what a very strange, ill-assorted trio they were: a lady of wealth and fashion, a housekeeper, and an unlikely heiress, all seated around a fire sharing toast together! Indeed, it was all so improbable that she wanted to laugh, but after all, it *was* said that the truth was often much more strange than fiction. But as she sat there, thinking about the situation in which she now found herself, she was aware more and more that she was flying in the face of adversity, defying influential enemies, and risking all on a venture which many would have been generous to call madcap.

Mrs. Hollingsworth saw her pensive expression, and judged it correctly. "It will be all right, madam, I know that it will."

"I wish I could be so certain, but somehow the whole idea suddenly seems impossible, conceived when the moon was full."

"I recall my mother saying that notions taken at such times were frequently the best notions of all, and far from being moonstruck. We'll set to work here in the morning, we'll open up the house and light the fires, and you'll soon begin to feel better then. I will see to it that suitable staff are found, and I promise you that in a week or so you'll see a complete transformation. Once you see Lexham House as it was meant to be, you will know that your idea of defeating your uncle's will by this plan is a stroke of genius and not to be spoken of as mere moon madness. The Lexham Hotel will become one of London's finest and most exclusive establishments, you mark my words, and Miss Seymour's wedding will be spoken of for seasons to come."

Caroline wanted so much to take comfort from the housekeeper's words, but she couldn't. It seemed that with the coming of darkness, her buoyant optimism had all but completely gone, leaving her feeling very vulnerable and unsure.

Jennifer leaned over to put a reassuring hand on her arm. "Mrs. Hollingsworth is right, you simply cannot fail, for there will be enough talk and interest to carry you through those all-important six months."

"Maybe. Or maybe the whole thing will prove to be a nine days' wonder. We all know that a hotel is nothing at the moment unless it offers the finest in French cuisine; the Lexham cannot do that."

"Yet," replied Jennifer firmly.

"I will need to find another Gaspard Duvall. And not only for the everyday cooking—what of your wedding? At the moment, it seems inevitable that we will have to approach Gunter's, and that will mean providing exactly the same feast as countless other fashionable weddings. There will not be anything memorable about that, will there? So, when the nine days of wonder are over, the Lexham will be judged on its own merits, and will be found wanting.''

Mrs. Hollingsworth inspected the toast and then held it to the fire again. ''Your hotel will only be found wanting in that one respect, in all the others it will be superlative, of that you may be quite sure. It will offer the most elegant accommodation, the most exclusive address, and the finest service—I will personally see to the latter. As to using Gunter's, well I agree that it is not ideal, but they are caterers of the highest quality and can be as French as need be—which should certainly be the case as they charge five guineas for the services of one of their man cooks and one guinea each for his eight attendants. I know these figures because the late earl employed them from time to time.'' The housekeeper paused for a moment, her expression suddenly very thoughtful, and then she lowered the toasting fork, looking directly at Caroline. ''This Mr. Duvall is the finest French chef in London, is he not?''

''So I believe.''

''And he is dissatisfied at the Oxenford on account of the kitchens?''

''Yes.''

''Lure him here then.''

Caroline stared.

Mrs. Hollingsworth smiled. ''I'll warrant this house boasts the very best kitchens in England—excepting the Pavilion in Brighton, perhaps. Steal him from the Oxenford, Miss Lexham, for you owe that establishment nothing.''

Caroline was nonplussed. ''Are you serious?''

''Never more so in my life.''

''I would dearly like to think I *could* lure him here, but I cannot. He may be dissatisfied at the Oxenford, but he is at least very well paid there. I can't offer him anything but an uncertain future and the finest kitchens in Town. Indeed,'' she added almost as an aside, ''I can't afford to do anything at all unless Mr. Jordan manages to sell my necklace.''

Mrs. Hollingsworth was not to be defeated. ''Perhaps it will not be necessary to offer him grand sums of money, Miss Lexham. If your enterprise is a success, at the end of six months this house and its contents will be yours. You could offer Mr. Duvall a valuable item from the house in lieu of payment; and if he has an eye for a good bargain, he'll see the benefit of such an arrangement. In my experience, madam, those who get to such eminent positions as he has reached do not do so without being shrewd men of business as well as masters of their chosen field.''

Jennifer had been listening with great interest, and now she smiled approvingly. ''Mrs. Hollingsworth is right, and you must at least try. And just *think* what a sweet revenge it would be upon that horrid Mr. Bassett!''

Caroline looked from one to the other, and then slowly she smiled. ''Very well, I will approach Monsieur Duvall.''

At that moment they heard a loud knocking echoing through from the front doors of the main house, and all three fell silent with surprise. Mrs. Hollingsworth got up and went to the window, peering out into the darkness, and then she smiled. ''It's Mr. Jordan, I recognize his chariot!'' She hurried out and a moment later ushered the lawyer into the little parlor.

He bowed immediately to both Caroline and Jennifer. ''Good evening, Miss Lexham. Miss Seymour.''

Jennifer smiled. ''You do not seem surprised to see me here, sir.''

''That is because I already knew what had happened, Miss Seymour. Word of your actions has begun to spread already, and there is quite an upset at the Oxenford, as you can well imagine, for your—er—defection is not good for its reputation.''

''Excellent.''

He smiled a little. ''My sentiments precisely. However, I will not beat about the bush and will come directly to the point of my visit. Miss Lexham, I have sold your necklace.''

Caroline stared. ''Already?''

''It was most fortunate. This afternoon a gentleman from Scotland had an appointment with me, and he happened to see the necklace. On learning that its owner wished to sell it, he immediately offered me a most handsome price, saying that it was just the thing to present to his future wife. The transaction was completed there and then.'' He placed some documents in her hands. ''I took the liberty of depositing the money in a very reputable bank, that of Messieurs Coutts, and now you may conduct your business through them, using their checks—a much safer proposition than keeping too much money in the house. There are so many rogues and thieves about, Miss Lexham, and it would not do at all for you to lose anything at this delicate stage."

She gazed in wonder at the very handsome price her necklace had fetched. "Did he really pay this?"

"Certainly."

"But who was he?"

For a moment the lawyer hesitated. "Oh, no one you know, my dear, and perhaps it would be best to leave him as a stranger, for the necklace meant a very great deal to you."

"Yes, I suppose you are right. Oh, Mr. Jordan, I can hardly believe all this is really happening."

"No," he said with some feeling. "Nor can I."

She smiled. "You must forgive me for so unsettling you, Mr. Jordan."

"My dear Miss Lexham, you haven't merely unsettled me, I fear you have quite taken my breath away. However, no doubt the novelty of it all will do me good. Now I must leave you, for I have a dinner to attend and shall barely be in time for the final speech. Good night, ladies."

"Good night."

Mrs. Hollingsworth showed him out, and Jennifer turned to Caroline. "There is something I have been meaning to mention to you."

"Yes?"

"When I departed from the Oxenford today, Mr. Bassett went to great lengths to dissuade me, imploring that it was not his fault, that he had been in no position to defy *three* such eminent persons when they were intent upon having you removed."

"Oh."

"You let me believe that the Earl of Lexham was the only person involved, but I now know that Lady Chaddington and her brother were too."

"Yes."

"Why?"

"I believe you know why."

"Because she is to marry Hal?"

"Yes."

Jennifer lowered her eyes. "I have always loathed Marcia Chaddington, and now I loathe her more than ever. She is everything that is wrong for my brother, and yet he does not seem able to see it. She will make him very unhappy, and I cannot bear the thought, for I love him very dearly. I will tell him what she did to you, for he should know the depths to which she is capable of sinking.''

"Please, don't.''

"Why?''

Caroline couldn't answer, for she could hardly say that she thought Hal already knew full well what Marcia had done, and more, that he approved.

Jennifer was firm. "I mean to tell him. It isn't as if I am breaking a confidence, for Mr. Bassett informed me, did he not?''

"I would still rather you said nothing.''

"His happiness is too important to me. I feel I must do all I can to make him see sense about her. Forgive me.''

Caroline smiled. "There is nothing to forgive, Miss Seymour.''

"Please call me Jennifer; after all we can hardly remain so formal when we are about to share slices of toast which resemble doorsteps!''

Caroline laughed then. "Very well, provided you call me Caroline.''

"Naturally.''

Chapter 17

Nearly two weeks passed and February gave way to March. Preparations at Lexham House went on apace, but although Caroline expected some sign of further action on the part of her enemies, nothing happened. She learned that Dominic had been called away suddenly to his County Durham estate, which explained his silence, but Marcia Chaddington and her brother were very much in Town, and yet they appeared to be ignoring her continued presence. She had written a brief note to Gaspard Duvall, asking him to call upon her at his earliest convenience, but as yet she had not received a reply. In the meantime she and Mrs. Hollingsworth had searched in vain for another chef, but as Mr. Jordan had said, such persons were not two a penny. The matter of a chef caused Caroline more and more anxiety as time went on, for the hotel was set to open in one week's time, on the ill-starred Friday, the thirteenth of March. She had thought twice about tempting providence by choosing this particular date, but to wait another week would have clashed a little with Jennifer's wedding, and to bring the date forward would have meant opening before the house was completely ready. So, with her fingers crossed, she had set the date for the thirteenth.

When she had taken up residence in the house, she had

immediately met the first condition of her uncle's will, and
the second condition was met when the army of nearly thirty
servants Mrs. Hollingsworth engaged opened up the rooms
and lit fires in all the hearths.

It was good to be in the house when it was warm and
welcoming. The dust sheets had been removed from the
furniture, the brown paper taken down from the paintings, the
carpets unrolled and put in their allotted places, and the
crystal chandeliers glittered brilliantly on being released from
their dull holland prisons. Plate gleamed on the dining room's
handsome sideboards, and the mahogany table was a highly
polished mirror in which shone perfect reflections of the
silver-gilt candelabra standing upon it. The red saloon was
also magnificent again, its beautiful furniture and paintings
showing up to perfect advantage in the fresh spring sunlight
which daily poured in through the tall windows. Throughout
the house the story was the same, and in the grounds gardeners tended the lawns and flower beds where daffodils were
now in bud. The greenhouses had been put to full use again,
and evergreen shrubs had been purchased, complete with
terra-cotta pots, to place at various points where their foliage
added a welcome contrast of color against the red brick of the
house. They looked especially well upon the grand balcony
overlooking the courtyard, as Caroline noted with approval
each time she returned to the house after an expedition to the
shops of Oxford Street or to the inexpensive dressmaker Mrs.
Hollingsworth had found for her. Caroline knew that she was
in dire need of new clothes, for the mistress of the Lexham
House could hardly appear alternately in gray wool or turquoise lawn. The thought of paying for such apparel, however,
seemed dreadful, for it drained her resources, but so far her
expenses had been minimal.

Jennifer now occupied gracious apartments at the front of
the house, and she declared herself to be very well pleased,
especially as it was so much more peaceful there than it had
been at the Oxenford, where the noise of Piccadilly had
intruded until well into the night.

After much deliberation, Caroline had been persuaded to
take the private apartments on the ground floor. Her first
instinct had been to take some rooms at the top of the house,
but both Mrs. Hollingsworth and Jennifer had been appalled
at such a suggestion, pointing out that already society was

talking about the new venture, and about Caroline in particular—she would be expected to conduct herself as the mistress of the house, and would therefore have to play the part to the full. Eventually she was persuaded, but she felt ill at ease in rooms which had until fairly recently been occupied by her uncle, and she hated climbing at nights into the huge, canopied bed.

As preparations continued in Mayfair Street, society discussed the piquancy of the situation, for the Lexham will had intrigued many people. Dominic's absence from Town caused a little disappointment, but the appearance one morning of an item in *The Times* assured onlookers of his imminent and furious return. The article detailed the goings-on at Lexham House, and was worded in such a way as to fan the flames of the family feud which had glowed steadily since the very day Philip Lexham had run away to marry Catherine Marchand. Caroline had read the newspaper that morning too, and she could well imagine the effect its appearance at the breakfast table would be having upon her prideful, vengeful cousin. That edition of *The Times* would appear on the table at Selford too, which prompted her to sit down and write a lengthy letter of explanation to Richard, who was bound to be most alarmed when he realized what she was doing. She intended her letter to soothe his worries if at all possible, but when she read it through afterward, it seemed to show up the faults and hazards of her plan rather than conceal them. There was nothing for it but to dispatch the letter, however, and trust that it would serve the purpose for which it was intended.

Of Hal Seymour Lexham House saw nothing. He had remained firmly entrenched at the Oxenford, much to the annoyance of his sister, who was determined to show her disapproval by staying away from him. She wanted him to call upon her, but as yet he had not shown any inclination so to do. Unlike his future brother-in-law, Lord Carstairs upheld Jennifer on every count, declaring himself to be appalled at the conduct of the Oxenford, Dominic Lexham *et al,* and to be totally mystified by Hal's refusal to join in the condemnation.

Hal appeared to be supremely unconcerned, continuing as if nothing had happened. He supervised the arrangements for the banquet, dined every night at the Oxenford, inspected the progress on his house in Hanover Square, and was seen absolutely everywhere with Marcia Chaddington on his arm. As far as Caroline was concerned, he could not have expressed himself more clearly had he placed a notice in a newspaper, but she hid her feelings so well that no one could have guessed that Sir Henry Seymour even crossed her mind.

As the day of the opening approached, Caroline wondered what she would have done without the help of Mrs. Hollingsworth. Having decided that Caroline's plan for Lexham House offered it salvation from Dominic, the housekeeper did all in her power to help. She seemed to have an endless capacity for seeing simple solutions to problems that seemed enormous to Caroline. Every hotel should have two footmen to parade up and down outside, but that meant livery. Caroline could hardly array her footmen in Dominic's livery, but to provide them with entirely new clothes would have been exorbitantly expensive. The housekeeper produced some black braiding from a trunk in an attic room and set some housemaids to remove the silver lace and rosettes from the dark red coats and tricorn hats, replacing both with the braiding. The result was a transformation which Dominic would not be able to complain about with any justification. The housekeeper also solved the less important matter of the lack of hair powder for the footmen, advising the use of ordinary household flour instead. Thus, the two handsome fellows were all ready for their first day of duty on the pavement of Mayfair Street.

If Caroline felt indebted to the housekeeper, she was similarly obliged to Jennifer, for there was no doubting the considerable fillip the forthcoming wedding was giving to the new hotel's fortunes. The mere fact that Jennifer and her future husband were staunchly in favor of marrying at the Lexham had already produced several tentative inquiries from people who wished to hold functions there, from a reunion of old soldiers to a fund-raising subscription dinner for the widows of Trafalgar. But in spite of her delight at these signs of society's interest, Caroline was horribly aware of the Lexham Hotel's one great failing: its lack of a French chef.

This problem had still not been solved when one morning Hal Seymour paid his first call upon his sister. Wearing a wine-red coat, his full cravat ruffled by the breeze, he drove smartly up to the door in his cabriolet. As he drew the vehicle to a standstill, the tiger jumped down from his perch behind and took the reins from his master, who alighted and then paused to tip his top hat back on his dark hair for a moment. He gazed around the elegant courtyard, his expression thoughtful, and then he ascended the steps to the door, which was opened immediately by the vigilant porter.

Caroline was in the vestibule, but she was unaware of his arrival, for she was supervising the surprisingly difficult task of arranging the various sofas and tables to best advantage. The men moving the furniture were becoming harassed, and she was confounded by the seeming impossibility of achieving a suitably balanced and elegant arrangement.

Hal handed his hat and gloves to the porter, watched her for a moment more and then approached, smiling a little. "It would seem to me, Miss Lexham, that everything looks quite well as it now is."

She whirled about. "Sir Henry!"

"The same." He bowed.

It was a shock to see him again so unexpectedly, and his smile confused her, for when they had last faced each other he had been anything but smiling and friendly. "You startled me," was all she could think of saying, and it sounded very lame.

"So it seems," he replied. "Which is a dreadful admission from the chatelaine of such an establishment. You are not permitted to be anything but alert and imperturbable from now on, Miss Lexham."

"I will be sure to remember that in future."

He smiled again, but there was something in his glance that told her he was aware of the reserve of her manner. "You would be wise to do just that, for I fear you may soon receive a very unwelcome visit from a certain titled gentleman."

"My cousin?"

"He returned to Town yesterday, brought hot-foot by what he had read in *The Times*. He then spent a considerable time with his new lawyer, a very sly fellow who knows more about the curves of the law than the straight lines, after which he took himself to Watier's where he lost a considerable fortune. So far your cousin has done nothing whatever to meet the terms of his father's will, in fact he has not curbed his extravagance in the slightest. He now begins to see that you, on the other hand, are prepared to do a great deal, and that is something he will find unendurable. I feel I should warn you most earnestly to be on your guard from now on."

"I will be. Thank you for your warning, Sir Henry." She meant what she said, but her voice sounded stilted. She could not help it, for although he sounded so concerned, she could only contrast his present manner with his actions over the past two weeks. She was anxious to escape from him suddenly, and with a weak smile prepared to conduct him to Jennifer's apartment. "I am sure you did not come here to discuss my family problems, sir, so I will take you to Miss Seymour straight away."

For a moment his shrewd gaze seemed to read her thoughts, but he merely nodded, following as she led him beneath the arch and into the inner hall, where they began to ascend the grand staircase.

"I trust my sister is keeping well, Miss Lexham."

"Yes. Although—"

"Yes?" He halted. "Is something wrong?"

"No, I was only going to say that she is feeling a little low today, so perhaps a visit from you will do her good."

"I trust it is nothing—"

"Oh, I think it is probably just the understandable apprehension of a bride almost on the eve of her wedding." Caroline continued on up the staircase, and after a moment he followed her, but as she approached Jennifer's door, she wondered if her explanation for Jennifer's mood had been entirely truthful. Jennifer had breakfasted with her that morning, and she had been in high spirits, laughing at the morning paper's sly jibes at the Prince Regent, but then the next moment she had suddenly folded the paper and put it to one side. Her smile and humor had gone and she had been quiet and withdrawn for the rest of the meal.

Jennifer was seated by the fire in her apartment, reading Mrs. Edgeworth's *Tales from Fashionable Life*, but she set the volume aside immediately when Caroline showed Hal into the room. Hesitantly she rose to her feet, obviously undecided about how to greet him, but when he smiled and held out his hands to her, she forgot her crossness and hurried gladly to him.

He caught her close, hugging her. "And what is this I hear about you being a little low today?"

"Oh, it's nothing."

He put his hand to her chin and raised her face, searching

her eyes for a moment. "That is not so, sweeting. Tell me what is wrong."

Caroline judged that the time had come for her to leave them alone, but as she began to make her excuses, Jennifer immediately begged her to stay. "No, don't go, Caroline, I would like you to sit with us for a while."

"I am sure Sir Henry has much he wishes to say to you without me being there."

He smiled. "Nothing which would not be made more pleasant by your presence, I assure you. I would be glad if you joined us."

She did not want to sit in the same room with him, but she had little choice, and so she allowed him to conduct her to the sofa. The moment they were all seated, however, Jennifer revealed that she had an ulterior motive for desiring the presence of a third party. Sitting on the very edge of her chair, she faced her brother, her whole manner urgent and anxious. "Hal, you wished to know what is wrong—now I will tell you. I read in the newspaper this morning that the Duke of Wellington is about to return to London for a little while. Is this so?"

His eyes had become very wary and he glanced momentarily at Caroline before replying. "Why do you ask?"

"I think you know why, Hal."

"I hardly think this is a suitable time to discuss it, for I am sure we will only bore Miss Lexham."

"Caroline is not bored, and I am sure that this is an excellent time to discuss it," replied Jennifer, her tone little short of defiant. "*Is* the Duke returning from Paris?"

"He is."

"For how long?"

"Possibly about three days."

"Will you be with him throughout?"

"You begin to sound like an interrogator, Jennifer. Yes, I will be with him."

His sister's eyes filled with tears then. "Why has it always to be you? Why can't they find someone else after all this time?"

"Please, Jennifer," he began, again glancing uneasily at Caroline.

"You've only just returned from attending him in Brussels, and I know you were in danger there. I think it heartless and unkind of the duke to expect so much of you!'' Jennifer's hands twisted miserably in her lap and large tears welled up in her eyes.

He went to her, gently taking her shaking hands. ''The duke expects nothing of me, my love, and you wrong him by saying that he does. Come now, these tears are not necessary.''

''They are, Hal! I worry so about you, and with good reason, for you are so often in great danger!''

He bowed his head for a moment. ''Please, Jennifer, I think you've said more than enough already.''

''I want to say much, much more!''

A little self-consciously, Caroline rose to her feet. ''Perhaps it would be better if I left, Sir Henry, for I have no wish to hear anything which is not my business.''

He smiled at that. ''My dear, discreet Miss Lexham, I think that that would indeed be like closing the stable door after the departure of the horse. My sister has achieved her aim, knowing full well that your presence prevents me from being the bear I should be with her.''

Jennifer had the grace to look ashamed. ''He is right, Caroline, I have used you most abominably for my own purposes. Please forgive me.''

''I am sure there is nothing to forgive,'' replied Caroline.

''So please do not go now,'' went on Jennifer. ''For if you do, I will fear that you are cross with me after all. I could not bear to have you cross with me as well as Hal.''

''Oh, I'm sure Sir Henry isn't cross,'' said Caroline quickly.

''He most certainly is,'' he interposed. ''And with justification. Please sit down again, Miss Lexham, for you may as well hear whatever it is my sister has on her mind.''

Caroline obeyed as Jennifer looked anxiously at her brother again. ''I'm truly sorry for being so devious, Hal, but the moment I saw that notice in the newspaper I knew I had to speak to you. If you had not come here today, then I would have sent Simpson to you, asking you to call on me.''

''You have no need to worry about me, Jennifer.''

''Would you swear that on the Bible?''

He did not reply.

''You see? I am right to be anxious for your safety!''

''I could not swear on the Bible that I will return safely to the Oxenford, Jennifer—swearing such things is not sensible.''

''You are playing with words, Hal Seymour. I am talking

about the danger you get into because of your involvement in perilous intrigues concerning the Duke of Wellington. I want to be a happy bride, Hal, with my adored brother to give me away. I don't want to be in mourning for that brother instead.''

He smiled, putting his hand softly to her pale cheeks. "What a very depressing thought. I promise you that you will indeed be a happy bride, for this brief visit of the duke's will not endanger me in any way.''

"I wish that you no longer had anything to do with the duke's safety.''

"I do what I do gladly, Jennifer. Nothing will change that.''

"I know.''

He squeezed her fingers again and then returned to his seat. "I think we should talk of something more pleasant—your wedding, perhaps.''

Jennifer smiled, struggling to push away her gloom. "Oh, things are going on handsomely, Hal.''

He glanced at Caroline. "I've no doubt they are.''

"I still mean to set new standards of brilliance. I mean to make it the thing to be married in a hotel, to go away to Venice, and to receive invitations to the home of Lord and Lady Carstairs.''

"Society is obviously about to be shaken by the scruff of the neck.''

Jennifer's low spirits were evaporating. "I went to Gunter's yesterday to see the cake. Oh, Hal, they're doing it so well. It is surely the most handsome of confections and will look magnificent reposing in the center of the table with its ribbons and flowers. If they do the whole feast as well as they have done the cake—''

"They are to do the whole feast?'' he inquired, looking surprised.

"We hope not,'' replied Jennifer, before Caroline could say anything. "For we hope that soon the Lexham will have a very celebrated chef of it own.''

"Oh? Who have you found?''

Jennifer was almost gleeful. "Monsieur Duvall! Is it not splendid?''

Hal stared at his sister, his smile fixed for a briefest of seconds before he recovered from his obvious shock at this revelation. "Duvall is to do your wedding feast? But he is surely not leaving the Oxenford?"

"I certainly hope that he is," said Jennifer triumphantly. "Which will leave you with dull English fare again, Hal Seymour, and serve you right."

"You only *hope* he is? Does this mean nothing has been settled?"

Caroline spoke up quickly. "I have communicated with Monsieur Duvall, Sir Henry, but as yet I have not received a reply. I am not as sanguine as Miss Seymour that he will leave the Oxenford in favor of the Lexham."

"He will," insisted Jennifer. "I just *know* that he will."

Hal glanced again at Caroline before replying. "I fear that I agree with you, Miss Lexham, and I do not think you should rely at all upon gaining Duvall's services."

Jennifer sat back and sniffed. "We will see. However, we've talked about *my* wedding, perhaps it is time to speak of yours."

"Mine?" He looked surprised. "I have no wedding to discuss."

"I doubt if Marcia Chaddington would agree."

"I cannot speak for her, of course."

"Does that mean that you haven't asked her to marry you yet?"

"It most certainly does."

"Good, and I trust that that situation will continue indefinitely."

"I had no idea you disliked her quite that much," he replied dryly.

"I like her less and less with each passing day, as you would too if you knew the whole truth about her."

Caroline could see what was coming and she was alarmed. "Please, Jennifer! Don't say anything more!"

"I shall say what I please," retorted Jennifer determinedly. "He should be told what a horrid creature she is."

He glanced from one to the other. "And what, precisely, should I be told?"

Jennifer faced him. "That Marcia Chaddington and her brother also complained to Mr. Bassett at the Oxenford about Caroline's presence there. They demanded that she should be told to leave. Marcia is extremely odious, Hal Seymour, and you will be the biggest fool of all time if you take her as your wife!''

Hal looked silently at his sister for a moment. "And why would Marcia do that?" he asked softly. "What possible reason could she have?"

For the third and final time Caroline determined to leave the room. Her cheeks were aflame with embarrassment, and she gathered her skirts to hurry to the door. "I-I have a lot to do," she said. "So I beg that you excuse me."

Chapter 18

On the eve of the opening, Caroline and Mrs. Hollingsworth worked very hard indeed, checking and rechecking that everything was in readiness for the following morning when the doors of the Lexham Hotel would at last be opened and when some of the huge stock of champagne from the late earl's cellar would be served, chilled by ice from the large block purchased from an Icelandic supplier who had advertised in the newspaper earlier in the week. Notices concerning the opening had been placed in various publications, and now it was only a matter of hours before Caroline would see if all the interest stirred by the novelty and audacity of her actions would bring the required result. She went to her bed at midnight, but she was so nervous about a number of minor details that she doubted if she would be able to sleep. Within minutes, however, she sank into a deep, exhausted slumber.

It was very dark when the noise of hammering at the front doors awakened her. With a gasp she sat up, glancing around the shadowy room. Her night-light had gone out, leaving only the vague glow from the dying embers in the hearth to illuminate the chamber. The hammering echoed urgently through the house again, and as she slipped anxiously from the bed, reaching for her shawl, she heard the porter open the door. An authoritative male voice demanded Miss Lexham's immediate presence, and she paused in surprise, for she knew that voice: it belonged to Jennifer's betrothed, Lord Carstairs. But why come at such an hour and when Jennifer wasn't present? In her nightgown and holding her shawl around her shoulders, she hurried out to the vestibule, where she saw that it was indeed Lord Carstairs, but he was accompanied by several officers of the watch, and they looked very much as if they were present in their official capacity.

Lord Carstairs looked a little uncomfortable as she approached, and he removed his tall hat. "Forgive this intrusion, Miss Lexham, but I fear that I am here on a matter which I find unpleasant."

"Unpleasant?" She stared at him.

"I am here not as your personal acquaintance, but as a magistrate."

"But what has happened?"

"We have been informed that certain rooms in this house are being used by—er, ladies of ill repute."

Caroline's lips parted in amazement. "You have been wrongly informed, my lord."

He looked uncomfortable. "I trust that that is indeed so."

"I don't understand, my lord, why you and these gentlemen have come here. Even if this house were being used by every Cyprian in London, I do not see why a magistrate should come in the middle of the night to—"

"I come because I have been requested so to do by the Earl of Lexham. Forgive me, Miss Lexham, for I would infinitely have preferred someone else to have come in my stead, but the earl was most specific that *I* should undertake this search of these premises. He wishes the matter to be officially investigated as he is anxious to see that the terms of his father's will are not being violated. You must understand, Miss Lexham, that if we do indeed find anything untoward during our search, then we will have to report that we have discovered the house being used for purposes which are other than respectable."

She nodded. So, at last Dominic had made a move against her—and how neat to decide upon Lord Carstairs as his instrument. As she accompanied her visitors up the grand staircase, she knew in her heart that they would indeed discover what they had come to search for: Dominic would have seen to that. She was glad of one thing: Jennifer was staying overnight with friends.

The sound of laughter was faint at first, but it grew louder as they reached the first landing. As one they glanced up to the floor above, Lord Carstairs gave a reluctant nod, and the officers of the watch led the way up the next flight of steps. The noise was much louder now; Caroline could discern that the laughter was a mixture of both male and female, and that it was not at all discreet. Her heart began to rush with anger and dismay as they followed the sound to a remote apartment at the rear of the house, an apartment Caroline knew had never been occupied since her arrival at the house.

One of the watch rapped once upon the door with his staff and then opened it. The dazzling light of the chandeliers leaped out onto the shadowy passageway, and with it came the heavy smell of Spanish cigars. Caroline felt numb as she gazed at the scene now revealed before her. There were three young gentlemen and three ladies, if ladies they could be called, for their muslin gowns were of the sheerest stuff imaginable, their bosoms were almost bared, and their faces were painted in a most brazen way.

Silence fell, and knowing, triumphant glances were exchanged as Lord Carstairs turned unhappily to Caroline. "Are these ladies and gentlemen guests here, Miss Lexham?"

"No."

One of the women approached then, her lips pursed provocatively and her whole figure swaying in a way that reminded Caroline of the courtesans flaunting themselves beneath the arcade at the Italian Opera House. "Of course we're guests here," she said. "As you know full well, dearie, for you met us at the door. There's no point trying to deny it, you took a chance and it didn't work. Cut your losses, we all have to at some time or other."

"I have never seen you before in my life and you are not here with my knowledge or permission," replied Caroline, glancing then at Lord Carstairs. "My lord, I swear that I know nothing about this."

The courtesan laughed. "Oh, that's rich! You took our money gladly enough, and now suddenly you're all prim and proper. You opened your front door to us, you showed us up here, and now suddenly you don't know anything about us." The other occupants of the room burst into laughter at this, and Caroline looked helplessly at them. How could she prove that she was telling the truth?

Lord Carstairs gave a heavy sigh. He had not enjoyed his duties this night in the slightest. "I'm sorry, Miss Lexham, but I will have to report what I have witnessed here tonight."

Another voice interrupted at that point. "Then you will have to report that the whole thing is an artifice, Charles, and was dreamed up by Dominic Lexham for his own foul purposes."

With a gasp Caroline whirled about to see Hal approaching along the passage. His cane swung lightly in his white-gloved hand and his top hat was tipped nonchalantly back on his dark hair. The sapphire pin in his cravat sparkled brilliantly as he paused within the arc of light from the chandeliers.

"Hal?" Lord Carstairs looked dumbfounded. "What are you saying?"

"I am saying that these persons did not enter this house with Miss Lexham's knowledge. They certainly did not receive a greeting at the front door from her, nor did she show them up to this apartment; indeed they entered *after* she had retired to her bed."

"And how do you know this?" asked Lord Carstairs.

"Because I made it my business to find out. They entered illegally from the gardens, breaking a window in order to do so. I think it safe to say that Miss Lexham is innocent of any complicity in this plot."

"And Dominic Lexham is behind it, you say?" inquired Lord Carstairs.

"Don't be tiresome, Charles, of *course* he is!" replied Hal, a little irritated. "He has to be implicated if he was the one who reported things in the first place! Now then, you have done your duty, and you can report your findings—which can only be that Miss Lexham has done nothing to contravene the terms of her uncle's will."

Lord Carstairs cleared his throat uncomfortably, his cheeks coloring a little at the hint of sarcasm in Hal's reply. "Yes, well perhaps you are right. As for you, ladies and gentlemen," he went on, turning to face the six culprits, who were no longer as slyly clever as they had been, "I think it would be best if you left immediately, unless Miss Lexham wishes to press charges against you."

Caroline hastily shook her head. "No, I don't, I just want them to leave and never return."

The six needed no urging, and within a minute they had vacated the apartment and were being shown out through the front door by the porter. The gentlemen of the watch descended to the vestibule, where they waited for Lord Carstairs, who stood for a moment to offer his apologies to Caroline. "Again I must ask your forgiveness, Miss Lexham, for I did not gladly undertake this night's work, but in my capacity as magistrate I truly had no choice."

"I quite understand, my lord."

He drew her hand to his lips. "I pray that that is indeed so, for it would grieve me to think that I had alienated myself from your friendship by my actions." He looked a little shamefaced. "The truth of the matter is that I was anxious because of Jennifer. If there had been anything untoward here tonight—which there would have been <u>but for</u> Sir Henry's intervention—her character might in some way have suffered. I do trust that you understand and forgive my anxiety on her behalf."

"Of course I do."

Still a little embarrassed at the whole affair, he glanced at Hal. "My carriage is outside, can I convey you anywhere?"

"Yes, that would be agreeable, Charles. I will join you in a moment, after I have spoken with Miss Lexham."

Charles nodded and left them, and Caroline looked at Hal. "I must thank you, Sir Henry, for if you had not come when you did . . ." She hesitated. "Why *did* you come here tonight?"

"As I said, Miss Lexham, I made it my business to find out what was happening."

"Because of Jennifer?"

He smiled a little. "Certes, Miss Lexham. Because of Jennifer."

Although she knew she should not wish to hear him say more, she was still inestimably hurt by this fresh evidence of his disinterest in her, but she managed to return the smile. "Then I am indeed most fortunate that your brotherly concern has saved me from my cousin's spite."

"Most fortunate. However, my intervention has only saved you on this occasion, Miss Lexham, for I have no doubt that your odious and disagreeable kinsman will try again. He has not been idle; both he and your other relatives have busied themselves since learning of your activities by spreading word among their friends and acquaintances that the entire Lexham family will be displeased if any sign of favor is shown to the Lexham Hotel.''

She lowered her eyes, wondering if Marcia and Lord Fynehurst had also been thus busying themselves against her—and if they had, did Hal know of it? Slowly she raised her eyes to his face once more, inevitably wondering whether he would do anything to aid her if he knew about Marcia and her brother. It was one thing to thwart the plans of the Earl of Lexham; it was quite another to move against the actions and wishes of the woman he would soon make his bride.

He smiled again, his glance sweeping over her, taking in her cloud of honey-colored hair, the little bare toes peeping from beneath the voluminous nightgown, and the way she clutched her plain white shawl about her. ''Sometimes you are still a little country mouse, are you not? Tonight you stood in need of assistance from this wicked town rat in order to be kept safe from the vile plots of other town rats.''

''It seems I am destined to be always in your debt, Sir Henry.''

''Then tomorrow you may thank me properly.''

''Properly?''

''Tomorrow is the occasion of the grand opening, is it not? I understand my sister intends to return here by hook or by crook in order to celebrate with you.''

''Yes, at least that is what she said.''

''If she said it, Miss Lexham, then you may count upon her doing it. You may also count upon me calling upon you, for I shall make time in order so to do. Oh, by the way—''

''Yes?''

''Did you receive a reply from Gaspard Duvall?''

She was a little surprised. ''No, I'm very much afraid I did not.''

His eyes seemed to clear, although until that moment she had not realized that a veil had descended over them. ''So, you are still without your *chef de cuisine*.''

''Unfortunately that is indeed the case, although I still hope that somehow I will find another chef—certainly in time for your sister's wedding.''

"I am sure that she will be quite content with what Gunter's can offer."

"That isn't really the point, is it?"

He searched her face for a moment. "No," he said softly, "I don't suppose that for you it is. However, I am sure that all will be well in the end."

"I hope so, Sir Henry."

"Until tomorrow then, when I trust you will see fit to broach a bottle of old Lexham's finest champagne with me, for I believe I will have something of interest to celebrate."

"Something of interest?" She could only think that he was referring to his betrothal to Marcia.

"All will be revealed, Miss Lexham. Good night to you."

"Good night, Sir Henry."

She remained where she was as he walked away.

Chapter 19

She slept poorly for the rest of the night, rising especially early the next morning in order to attend to the remaining arrangements before the opening at eleven o'clock. After Dominic's attempt to destroy her careful plans, she felt more uneasy than ever about having chosen Friday the thirteenth, but it was too late to change her mind now.

The morning was dull and wet, gusts of wind carrying the low, gray clouds swiftly over the heavens. It was the very worst kind of spring morning, not at all the sort of weather she would have wished for. She stood by the window of her apartment with a cup of black coffee, gazing out over the forlorn courtyard, where the rain lashed the puddles that had already collected in the dips. As she looked out, wondering how many of the *beau monde* would choose to stay at home rather than sally forth to inspect London's newest hotel in such conditions, a very bright and gaudy yellow chaise drew into the courtyard from Mayfair Street. It passed the Lexham's two footmen, who, although well trained and used to the ways of the wealthy, were nevertheless startled enough to gape after it. They stared even more as it halted by the hotel's entrance and two men alighted. One was the strange, eccentric Gaspard Duvall; the other was his dark, discomfiting *entremettier*, Boisville.

Never one to shun bright colors, the chef wore a purple frock coat, beige trousers, a loosely tied black satin cravat, and a floppy green beret which rested jauntily over his left ear. He advanced to the door with swift, light steps, rapping upon it with his gold-tasseled cane. He was followed at a respectful distance by the more soberly clad Boisville, whose gloomy presence Caroline believed would have cast a shadow over the sunniest of days, let alone one as dismal as this. But the mere fact of the chef's arrival at the hotel was gladdening enough for her to set aside any thought of the strange *entremettier*. Putting down her cup and crossing her fingers for luck, she hurried into the vestibule to greet Duvall.

Mrs. Hollingsworth had been supervising the setting out of the glasses in the dining room, and she emerged just as Caroline reached the two Frenchmen. The housekeeper remained discreetly beneath one of the arches which led to the inner hall, watching as Duvall took Caroline's hand and drew it gallantly to his lips.

"Ah, Mademoiselle Lexham, how good it is to see you once more. I trust that we have not called too early, but I knew that later you would be very busy."

"Of course it isn't too early, monsieur, and I'm so glad that you have called."

"Forgive me that I did not come more swiftly, but there has been so much to do." His dark eyes moved briefly to Boisville's stern, unsmiling face. Then he caught sight of Mrs. Hollingsworth, and he looked at her with obvious and immediate interest, admiration shining in his dark brown eyes. Caroline looked at him with some surprise, and then was more surprised to see that Mrs. Hollingsworth's reaction to him was scarcely less obvious. The housekeeper's cheeks flushed with pretty color and she lowered her glance as coyly as any young girl.

He looked at Caroline again. "Who is the lady in brown?" he asked softly.

"She is my housekeeper, Mrs. Hollingsworth. Allow me to introduce you." Caroline conducted him to the arches. "Monsieur Duvall, allow me to present you to Mrs. Hollingsworth. Mrs. Hollingsworth, Monsieur Gaspard Duvall of the Oxenford."

The chef took the housekeeper's hand, drawing it warmly and slowly to his lips. "*Enchanté, madame.* Mr. Hollingsworth is a very fortunate man to have so beautiful a wife."

Mrs. Hollingsworth's cheeks were aflame now and she was covered with confusion as she drew her hand away. "Mr. Hollingsworth is dead, monsieur."

He said no more, but his eyes were very eloquent as he smiled at her.

Caroline was aware of Boisville, who watched everything without uttering a word and without even the slightest smile touching his straight lips. She spoke again to the chef. "Monsieur, I wonder if you could advise me about the kitchens here?"

"The kitchens? Ah, mademoiselle, there is no one in the world who can better advise you than I, Gaspard Duvall." With another smile at Mrs. Hollingsworth, he offered Caroline his arm, and together they went through into the dining room, through the butler's pantry, the safes of which were filled now with valuable plate, and into the kitchens. Mrs. Hollingsworth followed, walking beside Boisville, who glanced at her but still said nothing.

Caroline and Mrs. Hollingsworth stood watching as the chef, accompanied by the *entremettier,* inspected every inch of the Lexham's wonderful kitchens. Nothing slipped Duvall's attention, and his admiration was complete. He could not have been more impressed by Baron Rumford's magnificent closed ranges, and he spent a considerable time upon them before at last returning to where the two women stood.

"Mademoiselle Lexham, you wished for my advice, but I see nothing upon which I may advise you, for everything seems to be in the most perfect of order."

She felt uncomfortable, for Boisville's shrewd eyes rested coldly upon her face, as if he knew full well what she was about to say and as if he knew also exactly what Duvall's reply would be. She didn't want to ask the chef in front of his oppressive companion, but she did not have any choice. "Monsieur, I have not been entirely honest with you; it is not your advice I would like, it is your presence here, at the Lexham Hotel. Monsieur Duvall, I would very much like to offer you the position of *chef de cuisine* here."

Many emotions seemed to pass through his bright eyes. He glanced very briefly at Boisville's cold face and then turned back to Caroline. "Forgive me, mademoiselle," he said quietly, "but I fear I must refuse your so kind invitation. There is nothing I would like more than to leave the kitchens of the Oxenford and take charge of these magnificent offices instead, but I regret that it is impossible."

She stared at him in the utmost dismay, for somehow she had convinced herself that he would accept. She saw an unpleasant gleam in Boisville's eyes, and she could not help wondering if the chef might have accepted had it not be for the presence of this subtly insubordinate subordinate.

Duvall took her hand and raised it to his lips again. "I am most honored that you should have offered this prize to me, and I am truly sorry that it is not in my power to accept." He looked for a moment at Mrs. Hollingsworth. "Believe me, madame, if it was possible for me to come here, I would come."

A short while afterward, Caroline stood on the steps of the house with the housekeeper, watching as the gaudy yellow chaise swayed away across the windswept courtyard. "Why did he refuse, Mrs. Hollingsworth?"

"I don't know, and that's a fact. I was so sure that he would accept; he was so interested in the ranges." She paused for a moment. "I did not care for that Boisville fellow."

"No, in fact I dislike him somewhat, although he has never said or done anything to make me so feel." Caroline turned to walk slowly back into the vestibule. "So, it is to be Gunter's for Miss Seymour's wedding after all."

"They will do it handsomely," reassured the other quickly, sensing Caroline's dampened spirits.

"As they do for everyone else. The feast will not be a novelty, Mrs. Hollingsworth, and I think that Miss Seymour is disappointed, even though she hasn't said so to me." She turned to the housekeeper. "I am afraid that her kindness and loyalty to me is to cost her the sort of wedding she wished for, and I feel very badly about it." Gathering her skirts, she hurried off to her private apartments, and Mrs. Hollingsworth looked sadly after her.

At eleven o'clock precisely, the first carriage rolled across the courtyard, and at the same moment Caroline positioned herself in the vestibule to receive the Lexham Hotel's first guests. She wore her turquoise lawn, the dressmaker not having completed her other gowns, and she wished that she still possessed her grandmother's necklace, not only because she loved it so, but also because it set off the gown's plain but pretty neckline so well. She felt a little drab, but then as Mrs. Hollingsworth pointed out, the visiting ladies would not wish to find themselves being challenged by the mistress of the house.

As the carriage came to a halt at the foot of the hotel steps, the rain stopped and the sun shone through a break in the clouds. The ladies and gentlemen occupying the carriage were laughing and chattering as they alighted, and the porter threw open the doors as they came up the steps. Her heart thundering, Caroline stepped forward to greet them. This was the all important moment, for she was only too conscious that a great deal of the interest in the hotel centered upon her. Did she strike just the right note as far as they were concerned? Did she look acceptably London? Or was she hopelessly provincial still? Smiling, she sank into a curtsy. "Good morning, ladies and gentlemen. Welcome to the Lexham Hotel."

The gentlemen bowed and inclined their heads graciously, while the ladies gave her that minute examination which only ladies can manage in a glance of a second's duration, decided she was tolerably pretty but in no way to be placed on their level, and were therefore pleased to accord her their smiles of approval. The dreaded moment was over, and with a secret sigh of relief, Caroline escorted them into the dining room, where the long mahogany table was laden with numerous ice buckets containing bottles of champagne, with tray after tray of crystal glasses, and with silver-gilt dishes of Gunter's very finest wafers and comfits. In an affable mood, the ladies and gentlemen accepted their first glasses of the late earl's champagne, sipped them, and murmured favorably. They then strolled through the house, admiring the magnificence of the red saloon and recalling various incidents that had happened there during the late earl's lifetime before going on to inspect the countless books in the library. They proceeded through the entire building, taking note of everything with their critical, knowing eyes.

And so it went, as London's *beau monde* sallied forth to Mayfair Street to survey the unexpected enterprise of a young woman whose name had been on every tongue in every drawing room since her arrival in Town such a very short time before. They all made leisurely circuits of the house, pronouncing themselves to be much impressed and to be beginning to understand why that clever Miss Seymour had deserted the Oxenford and wished to marry here instead. The ubiquitous Mrs. Hollingsworth was able to report with great delight that she had heard several parties compare the comforts of the Lexham favorably with those provided by the Oxenford, the Pulteney, and Mivart's.

As she had promised, Jennifer returned some time after midday, and was pleased to be able to tell Caroline that such was the crush of carriages in nearby streets that she had almost forsaken her landau in favor of walking. Glancing around at the crowded room and recognizing many important faces, she told Caroline that the grand opening could only be described as a success—Dominic and the Lexhams had been put to rout.

Glancing around too, Caroline knew that for the moment this was indeed so. But if Dominic had failed, there were others who might still succeed, and they had actually chosen to honor the Lexham's grand opening with their presence. She had known a feeling of great dismay and wariness when Marcia and her brother had alighted from a carriage, together with a number of their friends. Caroline's smile of greeting was very guarded as they approached. Marcia looked very beautiful in lemon-yellow muslin, a particularly dazzling silk shawl trailing along the floor behind her. She leaned elegantly on her brother's arm, and she paid hardly any attention to Caroline. Indeed, as they passed on into the dining room, Caroline distinctly heard Marcia's purring tone as she extolled the countless virtues of the hotel which was so soon to be the scene of "dearest Jennifer's" wedding.

Bearing in mind the unpleasant threats these two had issued to her at the Oxenford, Caroline took this new behavior very much with a pinch of salt. They were up to something—but what was it? Nervously she watched their progress around the house, but everywhere they were sweetness and light, pointing out things which pleased them and always being sure to bring the Seymour name into the conversation if they possibly could. A reluctant Jennifer was inveigled into joining them, and Marcia made a great point of linking arms with her, as if they were sisters by marriage already.

An hour or more of this passed, and still nothing had

happened, and Caroline began to think they were not planning anything after all, for they were all gathered in the vestibule waiting for their carriages. But then it happened, and Caroline was quite unable to prevent disaster from striking.

With a sudden squeal of disgust and horror, Marcia pointed a quivering finger toward the shadowy inner hall. "Look! There's a rat! Oh, Perry, do you see it?" She clutched her brother's arm fearfully.

The other ladies gasped and moved closer together, staring in the direction she pointed, but no one could see anything—except Lord Fynehurst, of course. "By Gad, yeth!" he cried. "Yeth, I do thee it!"

The ladies squeaked a little and everyone else within hearing had suddenly fallen silent. Caroline stared in dismay, for there was no rat, she knew that quite well, but how to convince everyone else that Marcia and her loathsome brother were "mistaken"?

Lord Fynehurst held a perfumed handkerchief to his nose. "I thay, what a bad show," he murmured, all but shuddering. "One don't expect to find vermin in platheth like thith! Jennifer, m'dear, you can't pothibly still be thinking of marryin' here! No, 'pon me thoul, you can't!"

Jennifer was at a loss for words, glancing unhappily in Caroline's direction, but at that moment a smiling Mrs. Hollingsworth emerged from the inner hall, her large gray cat in her arms. "I'm so sorry Tibby startled you, my lady," she said to a stony-faced Marcia. "The naughty creature slipped past me and he knows that he should not! Large and gray he may be, but he's certainly no rat, I assure you." She smiled, stroking the purring cat.

The ladies relaxed quite visibly, some of them laughing a little, and the gentlemen exchanged knowing glances; how typical of a woman, those glances said, taking to the vapors over an imagined rat!

Marcia gave the housekeeper a positively poisonous glance. "Do you expect me to believe I mistook that great animal for a rat?"

"It was only the cat, my lady," replied Mrs. Hollingsworth. "And from a distance he probably does look a little—"

"I saw a rat," repeated Marcia, two specks of high color touching her pale cheeks.

Lord Fynehurst thought the whole thing was better left.

"Come now, Marthia," he murmured uncomfortably. "It wath the wretched cat."

Jennifer smiled brightly then. "Of course it was, Marcia, you don't imagine I could have lived here for some weeks now and failed to notice if the place was infested with rats."

Several chuckles greeted this, and Marcia knew that she had lost the moment. Without another word, she took her brother's arm and swept out of the hotel, but at the door she paused to glance back spitefully at Caroline. The future Lady Seymour had not finished with the Lexham Hotel and its mistress yet.

Only one thing more happened to mar the day, and it had nothing to do with the Lexham Hotel; it concerned the contents of a specially printed late edition of a newspaper. It seemed that in Paris at the beginning of February, almost a month earlier, there had been another attempt on the life of the Duke of Wellington, several shots being fired at his carriage. The government had decided to keep the whole thing suppressed, and would have had an indiscreet individual not shown a private letter from someone in Paris to an interested London newspaper.

Jennifer became very pale and upset at the news, although she strove to conceal the fact from everyone, but Caroline realized only too well how Hal's sister had received the story. Caroline also realized now what lay behind his urgent journey back to London, the journey which had brought him into her life. He had known about the assassination attempt within days. Glancing at Jennifer again, Caroline knew that Jennifer had guessed this to be the case as well, his efforts to soothe his sister's anxieties about the duke's forthcoming visit to London were now in vain. Catching Caroline's eyes, Jennifer smiled wanly, but she could not conceal her fears for her brother's life. Hal had not seen fit to mention this attempt on the duke's life—what else might he not have seen fit to mention?

Chapter 20

The rest of the day passed without incident—and also without the promised visit from Hal, which inevitably led Caroline to wonder if he was engaged upon something connected with the news now revealed.

It was past midnight before the last of the guests had departed, and for the Lexham Hotel at least the day had been an unmitigated triumph. Even to Caroline's cautious heart it seemed that the enterprise must go from strength to strength, for not only could it now boast Jennifer's wedding, it could also boast reservations for several anniversary dinners and a large reunion of officers who had served under Nelson. A number of rooms and two apartments had been reserved, and apart from the sabotage attempt by Marcia and her brother, not a single word of criticism had been uttered against the hotel throughout the day. But then, as Caroline realized only too well, not a great many people were aware yet that the Lexham could not offer French cuisine; that discovery might put a different complexion upon the whole venture. Somehow she must find another chef; she and Mrs. Hollingsworth would redouble their efforts in the morning and keep their fingers crossed.

As the clocks struck half past midnight, Caroline sat at the escritoire in her private apartment, going over the arrangements for the wedding. Gunter's was to provide the cake, the whole of the feast, and was to send a man known as a *glacier* to carve decorations from the solid block of ice reposing in the cellar. Among these decorations would be vases of the flowers and ferns ordered from the flower market at Covent Garden. From the same ice would come the nests for the butter, and the sorbets and cream ices which would be made by Gunter's main cook and his eight attendants. The wedding over, the bride and her new husband would go away in a white, flower-garlanded landau, drawn by four cream horses with rosettes and white satin bows on their harness, driven by a postilion clad entirely in white. This magical departure for distant Venice would be the perfect ending to a fairytale day—but for Caroline at least, it would be spoiled if she could not provide for Jennifer the same sort of magnificent feast Gaspard Duvall would have prepared for her at the Oxenford.

Pushing the papers away, Caroline leaned back in her chair. Jennifer had gone out of her way to try to reassure her that it did not matter that Gunter's was to do the catering, but Caroline still felt that it *did* matter. There was no point in regretting it, though, for the wedding must go ahead. Thinking about Jennifer brought Caroline to ponder the day's news again. She hoped that Hal had managed to charm his way around his worried sister with whom he was dining at Lord Fynehurst's.

Getting wearily to her feet, Caroline decided that she had pored over lists and figures from Messieurs Coutts, the bankers, for long enough. It had been a long and tiring day, and it was now well past time to retire to her bed. Even as the thought entered her head, however, she heard a loud noise from the vestibule. Someone was shouting! Her eyes widened as she heard steps approaching her door, then the porter called out in warning, "Miss Lexham! Miss Lexham! He's coming in, I can't stop him!"

At this the door opened, and Dominic pushed his way in. His face was flushed, he was a little unsteady, and she perceived immediately that he was the worse for drink. "Good evening, *cousin*!" he said, sweeping a scornful bow.

The anxious porter appeared in the doorway behind him. "I tried to prevent him, Miss Lexham—"

"It will be all right, you may go," she said, still looking warily at her cousin.

"Very well, Miss Lexham, but I'll be within hearing if you need me."

"Thank you."

The porter went out, being careful to leave the door open. Dominic gave her a contemptuous glance. "My, my, aren't we the fine lady now?"

"Did you have something of importance to say to me, sir?"

"Oh, yes, sweetheart, a great deal."

"Please say it, and then leave."

"You seem to forget, my dear, that you were the one who was supposed to leave—but you are still here, aren't you?"

"I see no reason to do your bidding, my lord earl, or to bow to your wicked plots against me."

His eyes darkened. "Guard your tongue!"

"Nor do I have to stand here and listen to your abuse, sir. You obviously have nothing of consequence to say, so I ask you to leave."

He gave a cold laugh. "Leave my own house?"

"It isn't your house, sirrah, not yet."

"You've been very clever, haven't you? Somehow you've dreamed up this way of complying with my father's will—but have you done so legally, eh? That is the question."

"What do you mean?"

His smile was chilling. "How have you financed this little enterprise? Has Seymour filled your purse? And if he has, what manner of payment did he receive? Has he enjoyed your favors, my dear coz?"

She was shaking with fury. "Get out of here, sirrah!"

"You haven't answered my question," he said, coming closer.

"Nor do I intend to. Leave this house immediately, my lord, or I will have you thrown out."

"I think not," he murmured softly, his eyes glittering in the candlelight.

A third voice broke into the silence. "On the contrary, Lexham, I think your ejection from these premises is imminent." It was Hal, who not for the first time had arrived at a very opportune moment.

Dominic whirled about with an oath. "Seymour! Am I to

presume that you have *carte blanche* to enter these private apartments?''

Toying with the frill protruding from his cuff, Hal came a little nearer, his hazel eyes very cold. ''Keep a civil tongue in your fool head, Lexham, for I am not in the best of moods and I can be very touchy when slurs are cast upon the characters of ladies.''

Dominic swallowed but held his ground. ''By what right do you play the master in this house, Seymour?''

''I merely act upon the wishes of the mistress of the house.''

''Mistress?'' Dominic gave a laugh which was almost a sneer. ''Perhaps that is the perfect word to describe my fair cousin!''

With a swiftness that left Dominic breathless, Hal seized him by the lapels and then thrust him disdainfully away. ''I will spare you this time, my maraschino lordling, but only because you are in drink. However, be warned that if you cause Miss Lexham one more moment of distress, you will answer to me. Is that quite clear?''

Dominic clutched at a table to steady himself. ''You will regret this, Seymour!''

''I doubt that very much,'' replied Hal coolly. ''Now, get out.''

For a moment Dominic considered defying this command, but then discretion had the better part of valor, and he strode from the room with as much dignity as he could muster, pushing between the porter and the footmen who waited there.

The door closed, and Hal turned to Caroline. ''Are you all right?''

''Yes,'' she replied, but her voice was a little shaky.

''Come and sit down,'' he said quickly, leading her to a chair by the fire.

She smiled. ''It seems to be my lot in life to be continually indebted to you, Sir Henry.''

''Maybe it is my good fortune to be so often able to come to your rescue,'' he replied.

''Why did you come here?''

''I was under the impression that you expected me.''

''At this hour?''

He smiled. "I would have come earlier, but—er, something came up."

"Sir Henry, it came up in Paris at the beginning of last month."

'So it did," he murmured, lounging back on the sofa opposite her. A half smile touched his fine lips as he surveyed her. "Very well, I will be honest with you. I called here at this hour because a little bird whispered to me at Fynehurst's that Lexham was in his cups at Watier's and threatening to call upon you. I deemed it the honorable thing for me to once again become St. George and dash to the rescue of the fair damsel who was undoubtedly about to become distressed."

She smiled a little. "I am truly grateful, Sir Henry, and I am very sorry that my affairs have interfered with your enjoyment of your dinner."

"Say rather that your affairs *saved* me from that dinner, which was far from being up to Duvall's standards."

"Shall you dine at the Oxenford instead then?"

"I begin to think you believe me to be operated entirely by the moods of my stomach, Miss Lexham."

"Oh, I did not mean—"

He smiled again. "I know. However, I must forgo Duvall's genius as well, for he is most unwell tonight—or so I am told."

"I trust it is nothing serious."

His tone was bland. "No, nothing serious. A headache, I believe. I understand that there are times when he is prey to such indispositions."

"I am sorry to hear that, for he is such a charming man."

His eyes were half closed as he looked at her. "Charming, but disconcertingly attached to the Oxenford. Jennifer told me what happened."

She didn't reply, for she was thinking suddenly that Gaspard Duvall was not the only man who was disconcertingly attached to the Oxenford. The thought made her feel suddenly uncomfortable, for it reminded her of what Marcia had said—of what Hal had said to his future wife about the woman he had conveyed so kindly to London in his carriage. Nervously she stood. "I will not detain you any longer, Sir Henry, for I am sure you have much to do—"

He seemed amused. "First Lexham is ejected, and now it is my turn?"

"I did not mean to sound as if I were ejecting you, Sir Henry," she replied quickly.

"I sincerely hope not, especially as I was expecting to share a bottle of champagne with you. Or had you forgotten?"

She stared at him. "N-no, of course I hadn't forgotten."

"Excellent, then you had best send someone to bring it, had you not?"

Not knowing quite what to make of him, she picked up the little bell, and in a moment one of the footmen appeared. She instructed him to bring champagne and two glasses.

Hal leaned back. "Congratulations are in order I believe, Miss Lexham."

"Congratulations?" Her heart sank.

"Why yes. I must congratulate you upon the success of your grand opening, and you must congratulate me upon the success of my horse."

She could only look at him, quite taken aback. "Your horse?"

"Foxleaze. Come now, Miss Lexham, you surely recall Foxleaze! As I remember, you asked me about the wretched nag during our journey from Devon. I heard a whisper yesterday that the beast had won a famous victory in America, and today I had that news officially confirmed in a letter."

"Oh!" She could not help the way her eyes brightened. "Why, of course I congratulate you, Sir Henry."

"What did you think I was going to refer to, Miss Lexham?"

She colored a little. "I don't really know, Sir Henry."

The footman returned with the champagne, and when he had gone Hal poured out two glasses, pushing one into her hand and then raising his own. "To the success of the Lexham Hotel—and to the continuing success of my nag."

"To the success of both."

He nodded appreciatively at the champagne. "One thing old Lexham could be counted on for was his excellent taste in things alcoholic, especially champagne. Jennifer told me that things went decidedly well today, with many a rosy glow imparted by this same beverage."

"I hope things went well because this hotel deserved its praise too, Sir Henry."

"No doubt that was mostly the case," he replied, smiling at her. "All the effort you went to deserved to be rewarded."

"How is Jennifer tonight?"

He lowered his glass. "Why do you ask?"

"I think you know why, Sir Henry."

"Are you on the point of quizzing me, Caro Lexham?"

"Yes, Sir Henry, I do believe I am."

"You can be most disconcerting at times."

"Don't try to avoid the subject."

He smiled. "How tenacious you are. Very well, I do know why you ask, and Jennifer is now quite at ease again. Will that do for an answer?"

"Partly."

"And what does that mean?"

"It means that I am still concerned for Jennifer. She worries a great deal about you, Sir Henry, and I want you to tell me that her fears are unjustified."

His hazel eyes were almost lazy as they studied her. "And if I decline to answer?"

"That will be answer enough in itself, Sir Henry."

He laughed a little. "So it will."

"I don't wish to be disagreeable or difficult, Sir Henry, but I regard your sister as my dearest friend, and if there is anything I can do to help her, to make things easier for her, then I will do it gladly. Forgive me if I speak out of turn, but you are on your own admission involved in the welfare of the Duke of Wellington, and I believe that you were in full possession of the facts concerning this latest attempt on his life almost as soon as it happened. She realizes that as well as I do, and it is only natural now that she should be concerned about what might happen when the duke visits London soon. Is she right to be so concerned?"

"I will say this. There is no reason to suppose that this forthcoming visit will offer any danger to me. Will that suffice?"

"It is no more or less than you said before, Sir Henry. You, sir, should be a politician, for you are certainly master of the art of appearing to say something important when in actual fact you have said nothing at all."

"What a waspish tongue you have at times, Miss Lexham."

"It is no more than your answer deserves."

He smiled. "Very well, I will try again. What makes you

think there will be any danger? This is London, not Brussels or Paris, and it is on the other side of the Channel that the wicked Bonapartists lie.''

"I am sure they are as capable of crossing the Channel as you are, Sir Henry.''

"But why would they bother?''

"We can fence like this forever, Sir Henry, but in the end it will come to the same. You *will* be in danger because of the Bonapartists' avowed intent of killing the Duke of Wellington, and that killing could quite easily take place here in London, couldn't it?''

He smiled a little, resting his hand against her cheek for a moment. "You are too clever by half, Caro Lexham. But one thing I ask of you.''

"What is it?''

"That you do not let my sister realize anything.''

"You wrong me to think that I ever would, Sir Henry.''

He nodded. "Yes, perhaps I do, and for that you must forgive me.''

"When does the duke come to London?''

He smiled a little ruefully then. "He sails for Dover before dawn today.''

Her eyes widened. "Sir Henry? You will take care . . .'' How lame the words sounded, but they were all she could think of. He had not discounted what she had said about the Bonapartists crossing the Channel, which to her meant that it was indeed what he expected to happen. He would be in danger, and that danger was imminent. She was afraid for him, more afraid than she could ever begin to tell without conveying the truth of how much she loved him.

He took her hand. "My dearest Caro, I think you may count upon me doing my very best to preserve my elegant hide. I must leave you now, but I thank you from the bottom of my heart for your concern about my sister. It gladdens me to know that I may count upon you to do all you can to set her mind at ease. She is very dear to me and I do not wish to cause her any unhappiness, especially at this time.''

She knew suddenly that he did not want her ever to mention the matter again. "I promise to do what I can, Sir Henry.'' *Because I love you.* The sentence was completed only in her thoughts.

Slowly he turned her palm to his lips. "I am glad that this

Friday the thirteenth was not an unlucky day for you, Caro Lexham. Good night.''

"Good night, Sir Henry."

When he had gone, she sat down, gazing into the glowing heart of the fire. Her gray eyes were luminous in the half-light. Tonight he had trusted her; he had admitted more to her than he had to Jennifer, or even to Marcia. A ghost of a smile played upon her lips. He may once have thought badly of her, but he did not do so now, she knew that beyond a doubt.

Chapter 21

At breakfast the next morning, Caroline had her first opportunity to carry out her word to Hal about soothing Jennifer's worries. The few guests who had already taken rooms at the hotel had not stirred when Jennifer came down to take breakfast alone with Caroline in her private apartment. The future Lady Carstairs looked particularly fresh and pretty in a cream muslin morning gown, with lace at her throat and cuffs and a crimson sash at her waist. At first she was determined to set aside the anxieties of the previous day and talk instead about the dinner party at Lord Fynehurst's.

Pouring herself some more coffee, she grinned impishly. "There was one moment last night which I would not have missed for the world."

"And what moment was that?"

"When Hal announced that he was coming back here to see that you were all right. You should have seen Marcia's face! She was absolutely *furious*! I do believe she was jealous."

"I assure you she has no cause," said Caroline hastily, coloring a little.

"What a pity."

"How unkind you are."

"She's horrid and I wish with all my heart that Hal would

see her for what she is. She may soon be my sister-in-law, but I will never like her, and I will never forgive her for what she has done to you, Caroline. First there was that dreadful business at the Oxenford, and then yesterday that imaginary rat! Really, it was too bad of her.''

One of the footmen came in with a tray upon which lay the morning newspaper and a letter for Caroline. The letter was from Richard Marchand, but before Caroline could break the seal she heard Jennifer's gasp of dismay.

"What is it?" she asked quickly, seeing how pale Jennifer's face had gone.

"The newspaper—"

Caroline looked at it where it lay upon the snowy tablecloth, and she saw immediately what had upset Jennifer. The headlines announced further intelligence about the attempt on the life of the Duke of Wellington.

"Will you read it, Caroline? I don't think I could bear to."

Caroline picked the newspaper up and glanced swiftly at the relevant columns. "It says that the Paris police have made several arrests, although they have not caught the actual assassin yet. The man they seek is said to be a man of extraordinary strength and ferocious temper, and they believe they are well on his trail and will soon have him successfully under lock and key."

"He sounds perfectly horrible."

"He does rather." Caroline smiled lightly, setting the newspaper aside.

"I dread to think of Hal being involved with such men."

"This fellow is in France, not England, and Sir Henry told you that he was not in any danger. You must believe him."

Jennifer's eyes were very large. "Do you believe him, Caroline?"

"Yes, of course I do. Now then, drink your coffee before it gets cold, and don't think anything more about the wretched newspaper."

For a moment Jennifer seemed inclined to continue with the subject, but then she smiled. "You are right. I must be more sensible. Who is your letter from?"

"My cousin."

"The earl?" Jennifer was taken aback.

"No, my *Selford* cousin."

"The one who wishes to marry you?"

"Yes." Caroline broke the seal and read the rather brief communication.

"Is it bad news?"

"No, not exactly. He merely says that he intends to visit me soon."

"You do not look very pleased. Is he disagreeable?"

Caroline smiled. "No, he isn't disagreeable; he just doesn't understand, that's all."

"Well, to do him justice, I suppose *any* country squire would find it difficult to understand a woman who on the spur of a moment decided to turn her back on all she had ever known and set up in business in London as mistress of a hotel! The only kind of man who would understand *that* kind of spirit would be a man from London society, someone like Charles, or Hal. They are not narrow in their outlook, they admire a woman who shows she is not merely a cipher, and they accept that she has as much right as they to her opinions and dreams. Hal is right about you, Caroline, you could never be happy in a place like Selford, and you would be wretched and miserable if you made the mistake of marrying Mr. Marchand. London is where you belong, where you should have been all along." Jennifer smiled then. "There, was that not a profound and instructive speech?"

"It was indeed."

"You see? I am not always a scatterbrained creature."

"No, you are the dearest, kindest, and most loyal friend I have ever had, Jennifer Seymour, and I love you as much as I would a sister."

"That is how I feel about you, Caroline Lexham, and it gives me great pleasure to be able to say that, because I have never said it before in my life. Oh, I've had many friends, but no one to whom I have felt so instantly close. It's funny, but I feel as if I've known you all my life, and yet it has been such a very short time. Goodness! Is that the time? I should have been at my *couturière* five minutes ago!"

Caroline couldn't help laughing. "So, the time for profundity is past, and the scatterbrain is to the fore once again!"

"You, Caroline Lexham, are a positive beast!" Jennifer laughed as she got up.

Caroline settled back to enjoy a final cup of coffee before she too would have to attend to her daily tasks; it would be so different today, because this was the hotel's first real day.

The footman returned and she looked up. "Yes? What is it?"

"Lady Chaddington has called, madam, and she wishes to see you."

Caroline's heart sank. "Very well, please show her in here."

Marcia entered, the ostrich plume in her hat trembling and the fur-trimmed hem of her elegant pelisse swinging. She was clad entirely in virginal white and her hands were thrust deep into a muff. She looked as breathtakingly lovely as ever, and as brittle. She halted, surveying Caroline, an expression of disdain on her face. "Oh dear, the turquoise lawn again. How very repetitive."

"You wished to see me, Lady Chaddington?"

"No, I do not *wish* to see you; in fact the very opposite is the case. However, since you have chosen to defy me, I find this disagreeable visit forced upon me. I am not well pleased with you, Miss Lexham, but I am a civilized person, and so I shall endeavor to rid myself of you in a civilized way."

"You surprise me," replied Caroline. "I did not think there was anything civilized about imagined rats."

Marcia flushed angrily, but refused to be drawn. She glanced around the room. "You have indeed begun to do well for yourself, haven't you? Some say this house is the prettiest in London, which would make you very fortunate indeed if you managed to keep your country claws upon it."

"Why did you come here?"

"To make you an offer you would be foolish to refuse."

"I don't think I wish to hear—"

"I am capable of destroying you, Miss Lexham, you may count upon that. But such a course would maybe take a little time, time during which I would be irritated by your continued presence. You may think you are set to succeed here, but it will all come to nought. I will see that it does. I will wreck Jennifer Seymour's wedding, Miss Lexham, and that is no mere threat, it is a promise."

Caroline stared at her. "But she is to be your sister-in-law! How could you think of doing such a thing?"

"It is Hal Seymour I shall be marrying, my dear, not his vapid little sister. Now then, we can all be spared any unpleasantness if you cut your losses now and accept a substantial sum of money from me before leaving Town forever."

Caroline was trembling. "I refuse your offer, Lady Chaddington."

"What a fool you are."

"Please leave, my lady, and take your 'civilized' methods with you."

Marcia's lip curled with anger. "Your days of glory in this house are numbered, just as are the days when you may count upon a courteous word from Hal Seymour and his sister. Soon you will not even receive a nod from them, they will cut you, as will all London society. You and your high-flying plans are about to take a tumble, Miss Lexham, and I shall take supreme delight in being the instrument of your downfall. You've given yourself airs and graces, queening it in this great house, glorying in your important friends. You think you are very grand, don't you? Well, you are nothing at all, as you will shortly discover to your cost. I will not cease until I have trodden you into the ground, and even then I may not relent." With this, she turned and walked from the room, leaving the door open so that Caroline heard her light steps crossing the tiled floor of the vestibule. The outer door closed and a moment later came the sound of a carriage moving away across the cobbled courtyard.

Still trembling, Caroline rose from her chair and went to look out of the window. She saw Marcia's carriage leaving beneath the pedimented gateway into Mayfair Street. She had meant every word of her threat; she would indeed try to destroy Jennifer's wedding. But how? What would she do? And should Jennifer be warned? No, no, that would not do at all, for it would cause her too much distress. This was something Caroline had to face alone.

It was an hour or so later that an anxious Mrs. Hollingsworth came looking for her. Thoughts of Marcia came immediately to the fore. "Is something wrong?"

"I'm afraid there might be. A gentleman from Gunter's has called and says he must speak urgently with you."

"Did he say why he called?"

"He said that there had been a regrettable oversight of which you must be told immediately."

The wedding, it could only be the wedding! Slowly Caroline went into the vestibule, her turquoise skirts rustling and her little shoes making hardly a sound.

The gentleman from Gunter's was perched nervously on

the edge of one of the sofas, turning his hat in his hands. He was plump and balding and did not look happy in his almost formal coat and pantaloons. He leaped to his feet as she approached, and she knew that he was loathing every moment of his unwelcome errand.

"M-miss Lexham?"

"Sir."

"My n-name is Johnson, Archibald Johnson, and I am here on behalf of Messieurs Gunter."

"What may I do for you, Mr. Johnson?"

"I f-fear that I am the bearer of unfortunate t-tidings."

She waited, but she knew already what he was going to say.

"There has b-been a m-most dreadful and regrettable oversight, M-miss Lexham, and I fear that w-we will not after all be able to cater for Miss Seymour's nuptials."

It was what she had feared, but even so it came as a dreadful shock. She paused for a moment, steadying herself. "May I ask why, sir?"

"A p-prior booking." He looked thoroughly wretched.

"Indeed? What booking?"

"I'm afraid th-that I am n-not at liberty to divulge—"

"Whose booking, sir? I demand to know, and I believe I have the right to know."

"Lord and Lady Stapleton."

She looked away. Their daughter, the Honorable Georgiana Stapleton, was soon to be betrothed to Marcia's brother, Lord Fynehurst. "Mr. Johnson," she said at last, "I put it to you that this other booking is fictitious, or at the very least has been made since you were approached concerning Miss Seymour's wedding."

"Oh, no, Miss L-lexham!"

"But yes, Mr. Johnson, and you know it as well as I do, which is why you are so uncomfortable about the whole thing!"

"The other booking was overlooked."

"You, sir, are fibbing."

"Miss Lexham!" he protested, "I swear—"

"You are not telling the truth, sir, but there is little I can do about it, is there?"

He fell silent.

"I find it quite intolerable that a firm of such standing

should lend itself to such petty and disgraceful vindictiveness and be party to something which injures an innocent person. I promise you that this hotel will never again patronize you. Good day, Mr. Johnson.''

''Miss Lexham—''

''Good day, sir!''

Without another word he almost scuttled to the door, escaping gladly from the justified accusation in her gray eyes. But the moment he had gone, Caroline's bravado deserted her and she turned helplessly to Mrs. Hollingsworth. ''What am I to do? What can I say to Miss Seymour?''

The housekeeper put a gentle but firm hand on her arm. ''Don't despair yet, Miss Lexham, for there is another caterer who may be able to help.''

''Who?''

''Messieurs Owen of Bond Street.''

''We will go there immediately, for I must engage someone!'' But even as she spoke, she knew that Mrs. Hollingsworth's suggestion offered little hope. Marcia's hand lay behind Gunter's defection, and she would not have left any obvious loophole; she was too thorough and too clever for that.

Chapter 22

At Messieurs Owen it was immediately obvious to Caroline that Marcia had been at work. The prinked young gentleman who dealt with them had that same rather uncomfortable look worn earlier by the hapless Mr. Johnson, although he brazened things out a little more successfully than had the representative from Messieurs Gunter. The end result was the same, however, and that was that Caroline and the Lexham Hotel were still without a fashionable caterer to do Jennifer's wedding feast, and as she and Mrs. Hollingsworth emerged onto Bond Street, her spirits were very low indeed.

She had reached an impasse that would leave Marcia—and through her, Dominic—the victor, for failure to cater satisfactorily for the wedding would mean the collapse of society's faith in the new venture; she knew this as surely as she knew night followed day. She would lose Lexham House because she would not be able to meet the terms of her uncle's will after all. This she could have borne, for she had come to London with nothing, and she would leave in the same way, but she could not so easily bear having failed Jennifer, whose warm friendship she valued so very much. Tears stung her eyes as she and Mrs. Hollingsworth walked south along Bond Street toward Piccadilly. The housekeeper walked in silent sympathy, knowing the thoughts going through the other's bowed head and sharing the agony of despair at what seemed inevitable disaster.

It was Mrs. Hollingsworth who saw the group of fashionable young gentlemen standing by a handsome landau drawn up at the curb; recognizing one of them, she put a warning hand on Caroline's arm. "Miss Lexham, your cousin the earl is over there."

As she spoke, Dominic turned and saw them. For a dreadful moment the two Lexham cousins looked at each other, and then, unbelievably, a warm smile curved his fine lips. Bowing a little to his surprised companions, he left them and approached the two women. He looked very elegant indeed, clad in a dark gray coat and beige trousers, his honey-colored hair very bright in the March sunlight as he removed his tall hat and sketched a very handsome bow to them.

"Good morning, cousin."

Caroline stiffened, very much on her guard at this unexpected and rather doubtful transformation. "Good morning, my lord."

His gray eyes bore an expression that seemed contrite. "I am glad that I have encountered you, cousin, for now I may attempt to make amends for my odious and unworthy conduct."

She could not trust him. "I don't think we have anything to say to each other, sir."

"Please, can you not take pity upon this poor penitent? Beneath this coat I assure you I wear a hair shirt of the most tortuous nature." He smiled a little.

"Forgive me, sir, if I find the thought of your penitence a little hard to believe."

"I swear that I am truly repentant, cousin, for in the cold, sober light of day I have come to realize that I have behaved atrociously and now the onus is upon me to raise myself in your estimation. We are first cousins, tied by blood, and we should not be at odds." He gave her an almost boyish smile then. "Perhaps I should correct that, for you were never at odds with me, were you? The fault lies entirely with me, and I can only abjectly beg your forgiveness."

Caroline stared at him, for he sounded so genuine, but her every nerve was alive with mistrust. Those eyes, which were so sad and guilty now, had been so cold and full of loathing only the night before; and that mouth, which smiled in hope now, had curled with contempt and venom when last she had spoken with him.

He took her hand then, raising it to his lips. "I know that I do not deserve your kindness, cousin, but I do mean every word I say now. Please, let us take this as our first meeting, and forget all that has passed before."

She withdrew her hand, still unable to credit this new Dominic. "Why should I believe you, sir? Why should I agree to do as you ask? You have indeed behaved odiously toward me, and although you say you are sorry, I see no reason why you should have undergone this miraculous change of heart since last night."

He caught her hand again, as if he feared to release her. "Can you not see that I am ashamed of myself? Dear God, I am not blackhearted, I *know* that what I have done is appalling, but now that I realize in full how much I have sinned against you, I can only come in abject remorse to beg your forgiveness. You are the mistress of Lexham House, but it is entirely my own fault that this situation has arisen. I know that you are not to blame, and yet I have behaved in a way which shames me to my very soul. Forgive me now, cousin, look into my eyes and know that I am speaking the truth."

Still holding her hand, he came a little closer, clasping that hand in both his and looking down into her face. She did not know what to say or do, for his behavior now quite took her breath away. She was aware of his companions watching with great curiosity, and although she still mistrusted him in her heart, she knew that under the circumstances she had little choice but to say she forgave him. A rather tremulous and uneasy smile touched her lips as for a second time she withdrew her hand. "Of course I forgive you, my lord, and I would be glad to take our acquaintance as beginning from this moment."

He smiled then, his handsome face lightening. "Thank you, cousin, you are more kind than I deserve." Before she knew what was happening, he bent his head and in full view of everyone kissed her upon the cheek. Her face immediately flamed with color, but the thing was done now. Smiling and bowing once more, he replaced his tall hat on his bright hair and then took his leave.

She watched him rejoin his companions, and a moment

later they had climbed into the landau, which drew away and disappeared in the throng of traffic on Bond Street.

Mrs. Hollingsworth was skeptical. "Don't trust him, Miss Lexham—he may say that he isn't blackhearted, but he is, through and through."

"I didn't have much choice but to say I forgave him."

"He's up to something."

"You are probably right, but I really do not care what he says or does, for I have too many problems of my own to worry greatly about him. What am I to tell Miss Seymour when next I see her? She will return to the hotel in such high spirits and happiness after having the final fitting of her wedding gown, and I will have to tell her that I have no one to do the catering. Oh, Mrs. Hollingsworth, I feel so wretched about it."

"It isn't your fault," said the housekeeper, putting a comforting hand on her arm. "You have done everything in your power to see that the wedding arrangements are as excellent as she would wish."

"And I have failed."

"Not yet, there is still time."

Caroline wanted to take comfort from this, but she could not. They had time, true enough, but only a matter of days; wedding feasts took weeks of preparation. . . . Slowly she walked on down toward Piccadilly, Dominic's strange new conduct very far from her thoughts.

As they reached the corner of Bond Street and Piccadilly, they became aware of a large gathering outside the premises of Messieurs Hoby, the fashionable bootmakers on an opposite corner, where St. James's Street began. There appeared to be a large traveling carriage drawn up at the curb outside, and it was surrounded by an excited crowd, who were all interested in something going on inside the bootmaker's shop.

"What is happening, do you think?" asked Caroline, stretching up onto tiptoes in the hope of seeing more.

'Well, if it was a print shop, I could understand the excitement," replied the housekeeper. "But what on earth can be of such interest in a *bootmaker's*?"

"Shall we be very vulgar and go and see?"

With a smile, the housekeeper nodded, and they threaded their way across the busy thoroughfare to join the crowd. At first they were afforded no opening, but by chance a way

opened up and in a moment they found themselves right next
to the window. Inside they could see the polished oak counter
and behind it the dark shelves with pairs of boots and shoes
awaiting collection. It was very superior and discreet, and at
first Caroline could see nothing that might cause such a
crowd to collect, but then she made out the shapes of two
gentlemen standing by the counter in the darkest corner of the
shop, inspecting a pair of top boots which had been brought
by a very nervous, wide-eyed assistant. One gentleman Caroline felt looked vaguely familiar, although she could not place
him, but the other she knew only too well. It was Hal
Seymour! With a gasp, she stepped back from the window,
dreading that at any moment he might turn and see her
peering in. Seizing Mrs. Hollingsworth by the arm, she began
to push back through the pressing crowd, anxious to escape at
all costs before he realized she had been there. How dreadful
it would be if he caught a glimpse of her staring in so
vulgarly!

They had hardly emerged from the crowd, however, when
she heard the stir as the door of the bootmaker's shop opened.
Hal called after her. Dismayed, she halted, turning slowly
toward him. She felt too mortified to be aware of the interest
she was receiving from the crowd.

Smiling, he approached her. "I trust you were not about to
depart on anything urgent."

"No. I, er—"

"Excellent, for that means you have time to meet someone
who has expressed a desire to meet you."

"To meet *me*?" She was quite taken aback.

"Please come inside," he said, drawing her hand through
his arm and nodding at the housekeeper to signify that she too
was included in the invitation. Caroline became increasingly
aware of the buzz of envy spreading through the crowd as she
and Mrs. Hollingsworth were led back to the bootmaker's
shop.

The doorbell tinkled pleasantly as they entered the cool,
dark premises, and the smell of leather seemed to close over
them. After the brightness of the day, she was unable to see
much at first, but gradually her eyes became accustomed to
the gloom and she found herself being presented to the other
gentleman by the counter.

He was, she guessed, somewhere in his forties, although

he had the figure of a younger man. His appearance was imposing; he seemed much taller than his five feet nine inches. He was very handsome, with an aquiline nose and a surprisingly youthful and fresh complexion. His brown hair was cropped very short, his eyes were an arresting, far-seeing blue, and although he wore a plain, somber, dark blue coat, he was nevertheless a figure of great presence and authority. To Caroline he still seemed vaguely familiar, although she knew full well that she had never seen him before. He smiled as Hal introduced her.

"Miss Lexham, allow me to present you to His Grace, the Duke of Wellington. Your Grace, this is Miss Lexham, of whom you have heard so much."

She was dumbstruck, her gray eyes huge, and from just behind her she heard Mrs. Hollingsworth's astonished and delighted gasp.

The duke chuckled, pleased at the effect he had upon them both. "Would to God I'd been able to stop Boney in his tracks with such ease—eh, Seymour?"

Hal grinned. "It would have saved a great deal of time and trouble."

The duke looked at Caroline again. "Forgive me, m'dear, but when Seymour glimpsed you passing by, I told him I wished to meet you. I have indeed heard a great deal about you."

Hastily she gathered her scattered wits. "You've heard about me, Your Grace? I cannot believe that that can be the case."

"M'dear, even Paris drawing rooms ring with your name, for you are such a very interesting subject and such a delightful diversion from the more mundane aspects of life. And if I may say so, m'dear, you are also very beautiful indeed, which adds greatly to the piquancy of the situation."

"Y-your Grace is too kind," she murmured, knowing that she should say more but fast finding herself overwhelmed by the great honor not only of being in the presence of such a great man but also of being paid gallant compliments by him. She must say something else—but what? Inspiration came at last. "Your Grace, I congratulate you upon your fortunate escape from the attempt on your life. I trust the villain will soon be apprehended."

"Why, thank you, Miss Lexham. I am reliably informed

by the Paris police that they hope to arrest their man soon." He glanced at Hal, and then smiled at Caroline again. "But enough of me, it is of you that I wish to speak, m'dear."

"Me? But I am not—"

"But you are, Miss Lexham, you are. I confess that when first whispers reached me about you, I could not believe what I heard. No *lady*, thought I, would have the audacity and spirit to do such things; but the whispers persisted and soon I had to believe them. You are indeed a lady of great spirit, m'dear, and I admire that more than anything else."

She colored. "You are being too kind again, Your Grace."

"Nonsense!" He gave an unexpected whoop of laughter. "I am merely an admiring male, m'dear, for even the Iron Duke has human frailty! I wish you well of your enterprise, Miss Lexham, and I trust that your audacity and acumen shakes the very devil out of establishments like the Oxenford, the recent conduct of which I find totally abhorrent."

Uneasily she glanced at Hal, but his face was inscrutable. She smiled then as she thanked the duke for his kind thoughts, but she refrained from adding that she doubted if her audacity and acumen were about to avail her of anything, for Marcia's interference with Gunter's and similar caterers had closed the last door upon the Lexham Hotel's ability to provide the sort of cuisine the *haut ton* of London sought.

The duke detected her reticence, but misread it. "I agree that your rivals should be held in contempt, m'dear; in fact I too wish to show my contempt for them." He shot a meaningful glance at Hal, who immediately stiffened warily. "What say you, Seymour?"

"Your Grace—"

"I have decided," interrupted the duke, almost with an air of relish, "that I do not wish my banquet to be held at the Oxenford."

"But, Your Grace, all the arrangements are made."

"Unmake them."

Hal struggled to conceal the anger this caprice had aroused. "That is more easily said than done," he replied, and Caroline could have sworn she detected a note of warning in his voice.

"Nevertheless, Seymour, my mind is made up. In fact, I will go further and say that the banquet must now be held at the Lexham Hotel instead."

Behind the counter the assistant's eyes were as round as saucers. Caroline started with shock and Mrs. Hollingsworth's sharp intake of breath was clearly audible in the ensuing silence. Then Hal spoke again, his voice tight with anger. "Your Grace, I must protest! You put me in an impossible position!"

"In my experience," replied the duke infuriatingly, "that is when a man is at his best."

"With all due respect, sir, I think you are forgetting certain—"

"I forget nothing!" the duke interposed sharply. "Indeed, I think *you* forget, Seymour! I have no time for all these careful plots and plans, and endure them under sufferance!"

"Ditto!" was the sharp rejoinder, Hal making clear his complete disapproval and, in so doing, showing that he was fully prepared to brave the ducal wrath.

For a moment the duke's blue eyes flashed, but then he grinned, clapping the other on the shoulder. "Point taken, my dear fellow, but I cannot help it if in this particular instance I think you are totally wrong and that you persistently bark up the wrong tree."

"But what if it is the right tree after all?"

"It isn't."

Hal gave a faint smile. "It would not be the first time Bonaparte has humbugged you."

Again the duke's eyes flashed, more angrily this time. "You are probably the only man alive to whom I would allow such liberties, Seymour."

"And you, sir, are the only man for whom I would take such risks."

The duke looked away for a moment. "I still believe you are wrong, and as far as I am concerned that is the end of it. I will not have my reputation and valor celebrated in the Oxenford. The matter is finished." Straightening a little, he turned suddenly to Caroline, taking her hand and raising it to his lips. "Forgive our ill-mannered asides, m'dear, we have been boors to exclude you from our conversation for so long. It is settled; the banquet must be removed to your establishment. My honor will not permit any other course."

"But, Your Grace," she began hastily, seeing how stormy Hal's face was and being anyway only too aware of the

Lexham's inability to cope with such a grand and important function.

"No buts, m'dear, and you shall not rush to Seymour's aid because he is prettier than I am." The duke grinned roguishly at Hal's continued expression of dark anger.

Caroline looked helplessly at the duke. "Your Grace does not understand—"

"I understand perfectly, my dear, and still will not change my mind. Come now, to have a good business head is surely little different from being a good commander on the field of battle. Tactics must be swift and sure if advantage is to be seized. I offer you considerable advantage now, m'dear, and I shall be very disappointed in you if you fail to snatch it up immediately."

"But, Your Grace—" she said again, wanting to tell him of the predicament which prevented her from taking the advantage he so gallantly pressed upon her, but he did not wish to hear her protests.

"I must leave you now, I am afraid, for I have one thousand and one matters to attend to before returning to Paris in a day or so's time. I look forward to our next meeting, m'dear, when I trust you will greet me in person at the door of the Lexham Hotel, on the occasion of the banquet. Seymour here will call upon you to attend to the details— won't you, Seymour?"

Hal nodded stiffly, but he looked anything but pleased, which fact Caroline was finding increasingly hurtful, for it brought with it echoes of other occasions when he had shown himself to be completely uninterested in the success of her plans.

The duke grinned and then drew her hand to his lips once more. "Good-bye, Miss Lexham."

"Good-bye, Your Grace."

He glanced then at the openmouthed assistant, who had been paying great attention throughout. "The boots'll do, fellow, but I promise you that you will hear from me if I experience so much as a single twinge!"

"Y-yes, Your Grace."

With that the duke donned his tall hat and strode from the shop, the crowd immediately breaking into cheers as he pushed his way toward his waiting carriage.

Caroline turned swiftly to Hal, but he was about to leave

too. He smiled a little, his whole manner stiff with reserve. "I will indeed call upon you, Miss Lexham."

"I am so sorry that all your careful arrangements have been disturbed, Sir Henry."

"There is little I can do about that, for the duke's wish is very much my command."

"But there is something you should know—"

"I cannot delay now; he is waiting for me." Inclining his head, he withdrew, leaving her to watch as he joined the duke in the carriage. The crowd pressed around, and it was some time before the carriage could move away. When it did, the crowd surged in its wake, and the whole concourse passed noisily along Piccadilly.

Caroline stood in the silent shop. She should have been dancing on air, but instead she was in the depths of despair. The duke had talked of tactics and advantage, but on her field of battle the opposing commander had closed all avenues. Marcia was still the victor, in spite of the Duke of Wellington's good intentions on behalf of the Lexham Hotel.

Slowly Caroline walked from the bootmaker's, and her heart was heavy as she and Mrs. Hollingsworth proceeded along the pavement to Mayfair Street. Jennifer would probably be waiting there by now, and she would be devastated by what had happened with Gunter's.

Mrs. Hollingsworth put a gentle hand on her arm. "We'll think of something," she said soothingly.

"Will we?" Caroline's eyes stung with salt tears as she walked on, for on top of all her anxiety about the hotel, she knew the certain anguish of having once more seen evidence of Hal Seymour's indifference.

Chapter 23

The dreadful moment of having to confess failure to Jennifer was to be postponed, however, for when they returned to the hotel they found her maid, Simpson, waiting for them with a message that her mistress had encountered some distant cousins and would be spending the rest of the day with them. Thus Jennifer remained unaware of the catastrophe that had befallen the wedding arrangements.

Mrs. Hollingsworth did all in her power to find a solution, resolutely sending out the footmen to other, lesser caterers. That all was at such short notice did little to help, but even so the results of the inquiries were abysmally discouraging. One caterer could provide some of the desserts, another a small selection of cold fish dishes, while a third was eager to positively deluge the guests with countless meat pies. No one seemed able to undertake the complete feast, and Caroline was justifiably wary of engaging the services of so many cooks, for the broth would undoubtedly have been spoiled beyond redemption. Tentatively they discussed the possibility of preparing the entire feast in the hotel's own kitchens, although of course this would necessarily mean very plain fare indeed; but the merest hint of such a thing had immediately reduced the cook to hysteria, and the idea had been hastily abandoned. The day wore on, and Caroline knew she must accept that all was lost.

Meanwhile the duke's decision about the banquet had been fanned around London like a forest fire, the story being carried initially by the excited assistant at Hoby's, and then by the guests in the dining room at the Oxenford when Hal had imparted the tidings to the horrified Mr. Bassett. Within hours of the duke's announcement to Caroline, it seemed that the whole of London knew about it. It was at this point, with the short March afternoon drawing to a close, that Mr. Jordan called upon Caroline, delighted at having heard about the banquet's removal to the Lexham. He had been conversing with an associate at his club when he had overheard some others talking about what had happened at Hoby's and subsequently at the Oxenford. It seemed that when Hal had informed the unfortunate Mr. Bassett of the news, Gaspard Duvall himself had been nearby and had heard every word. The chef had been so staggered by what he had heard that he had halted in his tracks, causing the waiter who had been following him to drop the tureen of consommé he had been carrying. For a while there had been pandemonium in the usually superior and discreet dining room, and the chef had once again taken to his bed with a headache!

Mr. Jordan repaired immediately to tell Caroline what he had heard, and he chuckled as he related the tale. His smile faded, however, when he perceived that far from being overjoyed at her triumph, she was pale and wan. "My dear, whatever is wrong? Here I am, because of the most wonderful news imaginable, and you look more miserable than I have ever seen you before!"

"I have reason to be unhappy, Mr. Jordan," she replied, gesturing to him to sit in a comfortable chair close to the fireplace in her drawing room.

"I don't understand. Did the duke or did he not say that he wished the banquet to take place here instead of the Oxenford?"

"Oh, that is true enough."

"Then why are you not dancing a jig?"

"Because I will not be able to hold the banquet here, or hold anything else for that matter."

"You jest, surely."

She explained in detail all that had happened. "So you see, Mr. Jordan," she finished, "the banquet is quite out of the question. Lady Chaddington has seen to that. I tried to tell the duke and Sir Henry, but neither of them would listen. Now I must tell Miss Seymour that she has no wedding feast, and I must face the fact that my high-flying plans for this house will come to nought.''

He listened in growing dismay. "Oh, my dear Miss Lexham, I'm so sorry. But surely something can be done to save things? I am certain that Miss Seymour would be agreeable to a plain feast if she was to be acquainted with the facts—''

"Oh, of course she would, Mr. Jordan, but I would not be. I could not and would not ask her to put up with anything less than perfection for her wedding. She deserves the very best, for she is truly an angel; I can no longer offer her anything approaching the best, and that is the end of it.''

"I did not mean to offend you, my dear," he said gently. She smiled. "I know.''

"It grieves me very much to think that your fine venture will come to nothing after all. Oh, I admit that in the beginning I was less than enthusiastic, but I had truly come to believe that you would make a resounding success of it all. But for the machinations of a jealous, spiteful woman, you would have done it, wouldn't you?''

"You are a very dear friend, Mr. Jordan.''

At that moment they both heard swift, excited steps approaching the door, and Caroline detected the chink-chink of Mrs. Hollingsworth's keys. It was quite out of character for the housekeeper to run anywhere, and even more out of character for her to burst unceremoniously into Caroline's private apartments, but this is what now happened.

"Whatever is it, Mrs. Hollingsworth?" cried Caroline, getting up in alarm.

"Oh, madam, such wonderful news!''

'News?'' Caroline's tentative fingers crept to touch the vanished necklace.

"We have a chef after all!" Mrs. Hollingsworth's eyes danced with delight and her smile made her whole face glow.

"We do? Who is he?''

"*The* chef, madam!'' Pink with pleasure, the housekeeper stood aside, beckoning to someone waiting in the antechamber.

Caroline stared as two men entered; it was Gaspard Duvall and his dour *entremettier,* Boisville!

The chef advanced, his step as light and bouncy as ever,

and he seemed to have fully recovered from his headache. His mustard-colored coat was oddly bright in the dying rays of the afternoon sun, and he removed his beret with a flourish as he bowed over her hand. "Good evening, Mademoiselle Lexham. Forgive me for calling so unexpectedly, but it gives me great pleasure to be able to say that I can now accept your kind offer and I am immediately at your disposal."

She continued to stare, totally taken aback by this latest development. At last she found her voice. "You-you mean you wish to be *chef de cuisine* here after all?"

He smiled, glancing fleetingly at his silent, unsmiling companion. "*Mais oui, mademoiselle*, but then I always wished to come here. Unfortunately it was not immediately possible."

She did not know what had happened to change that state of affairs, she only knew that by some miracle all her problems had been solved. "Oh, Monsieur Duvall, you have no idea how overjoyed I am to hear you say this!" She could almost have run to hug the beaming little chef.

Mr. Jordan was delighted. "Providence has smiled upon you, my dear Miss Lexham, and no one could be more pleased than I!"

Mrs. Hollingsworth was scarcely less enthusiastic. "Now Miss Seymour will have the finest feast imaginable after all, and then there will be the banquet! Oh, madam, I'm so pleased for you!"

Caroline smiled too, but she could not help noticing how surly and silent Boisville remained. Not once did a smile or any other emotion touch his motionless lips, and such lack of expression was somehow chilling.

Gaspard Duvall spread his hands and smiled quizzically at her. "It is settled then, mademoiselle? I am your *chef de cuisine*?"

"Of course you are, monsieur."

"Then I and my entire *brigade de cuisine* will commence first thing tomorrow, and I will immediately put my mind to the *carte* for Miss Seymour's wedding feast. The dishes I had in mind before will not do now, for there is no time to acquire the necessary ingredients, but I promise to produce a feast which will be worthy both of the occasion and of my good name. After that, I will turn my thoughts to the banquet, *oui*?" He cleared his throat a little and then smiled once again.

"Welcome to the Lexham Hotel, Monsieur Duvall," said Caroline, "And you, Monsieur Boisville." She inclined her head at Gaspard's assistant, but she felt uneasy as she did so. There was something about the *entremettier* which she could not like in the slightest.

His response was toneless. *"Merci, mademoiselle."*

It was with some relief that she turned to the chef once more. "I think we have much to discuss, monsieur, so if you would please be seated?" She indicated a vacant chair.

Mr. Jordan immediately made his excuses and departed, after congratulating her once more upon this excellent turn of events, and soon Caroline was seated with the chef, Boisville, and Mrs. Hollingsworth while matters of the size of his *brigade de cuisine* and their accommodation and so on were gone over in a little more detail. Gaspard pronounced himself quite willing to forgo the usual method of payment for his services, and instead to take something of value from the house at the end of six months. He brushed aside any other difficulties that seemed to offer themselves, quite determined to take charge of the Lexham's fine kitchens.

Boisville sat stiffly and did not speak once. His presence was oppressive and Caroline detected Mrs. Hollingsworth glancing uncomfortably in his direction. Caroline was at a loss to understand why a man as lighthearted and cheerful as Gaspard Duvall should want such a gloomy and disagreeable person at his right hand. There was something else she found disturbing, and that was the distinct impression she received that whenever Gaspard was required to make a decision, no matter how small, he first secretly sought Boisville's silent consent. When she first received this impression, she told herself she imagined it, but it persisted until she knew she was not mistaken. She was reminded of the first occasion she had seen the two men together, in the garden at the Oxenford. She had thought then that Boisville seemed more the master than the subordinate; now she thought it even more.

At last the discussion came to an end and the two Frenchmen departed, leaving a very different atmosphere behind them than had existed before their arrival. Mrs. Hollingsworth stood with Caroline at the window, watching the chef's bright yellow carriage roll away across the courtyard, its color visible even though darkness had almost completely fallen now. "I'm so glad things have turned out this way, Miss Lexham."

Caroline smiled. "I'll warrant you are. You positively glowed the entire time he was here."

The housekeeper blushed a little. "I will not pretend that I don't find him the most charming of gentlemen. Nor will I pretend that I don't find his sour companion Boisville decidedly unpleasant."

"He certainly isn't full of the joys of spring," agreed Caroline, closing the shutters and drawing the curtains.

Mrs. Hollingsworth smiled again. "So, Lady Chaddington hasn't won after all. She'll be positively pinched with rage when she hears what has happened now."

Caroline looked swiftly at the housekeeper. "Miss Seymour is not to learn of Lady Chaddington's intriguing."

"I understand, madam, for she is to marry Sir Henry."

"Yes, so it would not do at all for anything to be said. We will just let her know that Monsieur Duvall is to come here after all, and we will say nothing concerning Gunter's."

The housekeeper nodded and prepared to leave to go about her tasks, but at the door she paused. "Miss Lexham? Why do you think the chef changed his mind?"

"I don't really know."

Mrs. Hollingsworth grinned then. "And nor do you care?"

"Something like that, for I'm only too glad that he is to come here after all. His reasons simply do not matter."

Not long afterward Jennifer returned to the hotel, accompanied by her brother. Caroline happened to be in the vestibule at the time, and so was able impart the good news immediately.

"Oh, Jennifer," she cried, hurrying forward in a rustle of turquoise lawn. "I have something very exciting to tell you. We have a chef after all and so you will have your feast à la français as you've always wanted!"

Jennifer had been a little withdrawn, but now her eyes brightened with delight and she clasped Caroline's hands. "Oh, can it truly be so? After what Marcia told me about Gunter's, I was fearing dreadful news would be awaiting me and instead it was all untrue!"

"Untrue?" Caroline still smiled, but she stiffened inside.

"Yes, she was most distraught, she told me that she had heard that Gunter's could not do the feast after all because of a prior booking. She said that she was so upset for me that she personally went to all the reputable caterers to see if one of them could take the feast on, as a special favor to her, but none of them could. There, I *knew* she was fibbing to be spiteful!'' Jennifer cast a knowing, arch look at Hal.

Caroline spoke up quickly. ''Well, perhaps in part it is true, for Gunter's did indeed back out of the arrangement, and I was very worried indeed, but now all is resolved and the problem at an end.''

Jennifer smiled. ''Tell me, who is the chef? Will I have heard of him?''

''Oh, yes, you certainly have heard of him,'' replied Caroline. ''He is none other than Gaspard Duvall himself.''

Jennifer gasped with instant delight, but Hal's reaction was more puzzling. For a moment he seeemed almost stunned, until he realized that his silence was mystifying his sister, at which he smiled and congratulated her upon getting what she wanted once more and Caroline upon this welcome reversal of fate. His words were spoken warmly enough, but there was something behind them, something Caroline did not understand. For an incredible moment she wondered if, as in the past, he was fully aware of everything Marcia had done, but then she immediately discarded such thoughts, for Hal would never, never have been party to anything that would have brought such chaos to his sister's wedding plans. No, on this occasion Marcia had worked alone and had gone to considerable lengths to conceal her tracks, for her plotting struck a little too close to the Seymours for comfort. This being so, whatever it was that lay behind Hal's reaction now, it was not that he had known what Marcia had done. What was it then?

Jennifer hugged him. ''Oh, I'm so happy again! Only one thing spoils it all for me.''

''And what is that?'' he asked, smiling at her.

''That you persist in remaining at the Oxenford. I have asked you to come here and now I ask you again, Hal. You are my only brother, you are to give me away at my wedding—I want you here, close to me, not beleaguered in that odious place!''

''If that is truly what you want,'' he replied suddenly, ''then with Miss Lexham's permission, I will do as you request.''

Caroline could not help staring at him as he said this, for

with a sudden clear insight into his thoughts, she knew that
this decision had nothing to do with his desire to please his
sister. Unlike the trusting, ingenuous Jennifer, Caroline knew
that his actions were brought about by the removal of the
banquet to the Lexham—and from that, she deduced that it
had something to do with Gaspard Duvall. Stunned at this
realization, she did not at first hear him when he addressed
her.

"Miss Lexham?"

"I beg your pardon?" She brought her thoughts back with
a jolt. "Did you say something?"

He seemed faintly amused. "I asked you if you would be able
to tolerate my presence beneath your roof."

"You are always welcome here, Sir Henry."

He sensed something in her manner, but he said nothing
more, turning back to his sister and kissing her farewell. "I
have to go now."

"Go? But I thought you were going to take supper with
me."

"I forgot that I have an appointment, but I am sure Miss
Lexham would be pleased to sit with you and listen to your
interminable rattle."

Jennifer pretended to be cross. "You are a beast, Henry
Seymour, and I hate you."

He smiled and tweaked her cheek. "Good night, kitten."

"Good night."

He looked at Caroline. "Good night, Miss Lexham."

She inclined her head. "Sir Henry."

For a moment his shrewd glance rested thoughtfully upon
her, but then he hurried out to the courtyard where his
carriage had not yet departed.

"Oh, dear," said Jennifer suddenly, "I forgot to ask him."

"Ask him what?"

"If he would apologize to Marcia for me."

"Apologize?"

"When she came to me about Gunter's and the wedding
feast, I wasn't exactly forthcoming; in fact I was decidedly
cool. Now it seems that she was telling the truth, and I have a
conscience. If I misjudged her about this, perhaps I have
misjudged her about other things—oh, not about the way she
has behaved toward you, for that was unforgivable, but I
didn't care for her before you came to Town."

Caroline said nothing to this, for Jennifer's original assessment of Marcia, Lady Chaddington, was the more accurate.

Jennifer linked arms with her. "So, Monsieur Duvall is to come here after all. How splendid! I insist that you join me for supper, Caroline, and we will celebrate with some iced champagne."

Chapter 24

The speed with which all recent events had taken place at the Lexham was the talking point of society, and the following day, the day Gaspard Duvall and his entire *brigade de cuisine* removed themselves from the Oxenford, saw a constant to-ing and fro-ing of elegant carriages as ladies and gentlemen came in the hope of enjoying luncheon, and later dinner, at the new hotel. After the desolation and uncertainty of the day before, for Caroline it was like a dream come true. She felt like the legendary King Midas, for everything she touched did indeed appear to somehow turn to gold—and consequently she had great reservations about such luck, for things had not gone well for King Midas. . . .

Gaspard's arrival in the Lexham's kitchens had an immediate and electrifying effect upon everyone at the hotel. Such was his genius that he was straightaway able to create a dazzling menu from the ingredients already available; such was his immense charm that he drew a warm response from everyone, even the meanest kitchen boy, and everyone did his utmost to please him. He was one of those rare beings, a man of acknowledged brilliance, feted and adored by society and yet totally unspoiled, and therefore swiftly worshiped by all those over whom he held sway. Within an hour of his arrival, he had the kitchens running exactly as he wished, and he was delightedly experimenting with the wondrous Rumford closed ranges. He sang as he worked, which at first astonished the more staid British, but they soon accepted this French eccentricity, and even came to join in occasionally. Watching him, Caroline began to wonder if maybe she had been wrong to believe Hal's decision to come to the Lexham had something to do with the chef, something sinister.

Gaspard's influence was not only felt in the kitchens; he swiftly offered his advice to Caroline where the dining room itself was concerned. Having come from Paris, city of the world's finest cafés, a place where it was second nature to flatter women, he shook his head disapprovingly at the glare created by the glittering chandeliers. Such a harsh light was not kind to the ladies, he said, and instead the room should be illuminated only by candles, which would throw a soft glow in which even the most elderly of matrons could appear to advantage. This, he pointed out, would also be to the Lexham's advantage, for the ladies were all influential. If they were pleased, then so also were the gentlemen—such things did not work in reverse, for what pleased gentlemen very rarely appeared to please their respectable womenfolk.

He also advised Caroline to have places at the table marked as being reserved, for in this way unwanted persons could be denied entry. If one wished to have respectable ladies as guests, one could not risk them being exposed to the presence of Cyprians. It was a simple matter for the notices to be removed from the places if suitable persons wished to dine, and thus all risk of doubtful respectability was eliminated. This ruse worked excellently in Paris, and must therefore work equally well in London, and was especially advisable in an establishment which was in its infancy and therefore had a reputation to create. She took his advice, bearing in mind Dominic's recent scheming, for respectability was all important if she was to meet the terms of her uncle's will.

True to his word, Hal had quitted the Oxenford and taken an apartment at the Lexham. His arrival, however, inevitably meant frequent visits from Marcia, who swept in every morning, issuing orders and generally behaving as if she were the lady of the house. She played her cards with great care, making all she could of Jennifer's guilty conscience. No one could have been sweeter or more patient than Lady Chaddington, no one

could have been more willing to be of assistance to the bride
during the frequent rehearsals which now took place. Each
day the bridesmaids came, and the bridal procession was to
be seen practicing descending the grand staircase, and Marcia
was to be seen at the foot of the steps, advising and instructing as if she had all the time in the world. Caroline found her
conduct contemptible after her attempt to ruin the wedding
arrangements by interfering with Gunter's. But Marcia was a
consummate actress, and no one could have guessed the truth
about her as she smiled at Jennifer or leaned adoringly on
Hal's arm. She was so very credible, superbly beautiful, and
every inch a lady of rank and fashion; to Hal she obviously
appeared to be the perfect bride, and if the way he glanced at
her was anything to go by, that was exactly what he intended
her to be. Toward Caroline her conduct was publicly
impeccable, containing just the correct degree of courtesy one
would have expected considering Jennifer's frequent state-
ments that Caroline was her very dearest friend. Marcia had
to gauge her behavior very precisely, according Caroline neither
too little nor too much in the way of condescension. Caroline's
position was a difficult one to define as far as society
was concerned, for she was well connected, being so closely
related to the Earl of Lexham, and she was acknowledged to
be socially acceptable by both the Seymours and Lord Carstairs,
but at the same time she was mistress of a commercial
enterprise, which was hardly a ladylike pursuit. All in all,
Marcia had to tread very carefully, which feat she achieved
superbly well in public—in private it was quite another matter.
Only once did the two women encounter each other when no
one else was present, and then Marcia made no pretense
whatsoever. Her eyes were incredibly cold and her face dangerously still, and she spoke very softly indeed. "I have not
done with you yet, of that you may be sure."

But guarding against Marcia was only one of Caroline's
worries on the eve of the wedding day. The last guest went
up to his room, holding aloft the candlestick he had been
handed by the footman in the vestibule. The quivering light
threw monstrous shadows over the walls as Mrs. Hollingsworth
said good night to Caroline and then proceeded to her little
parlor, where no doubt the ardent and attentive Gaspard
would be waiting to take supper *à deux* with his unlikely
quarry. Caroline smiled as she watched the housekeeper hurry

away, her keys chinking busily. Unlikely indeed, for who would have thought that the dapper, excitable Frenchman would have been so inexorably drawn to the prim, correct housekeeper? And who would have expected this feeling to be reciprocated? There was no doubt that this was the case, for Mrs. Hollingsworth had rather too swiftly succumbed to his wish to take his meals alone with her, something Caroline had certainly never expected. Now he was nearly always to be found in her parlor when he was not in the kitchens, and it was here that he seemed to be at his happiest.

He was a creature of sudden moods, lapsing into unexpected and dark silences which only the housekeeper appeared able to laugh him out of, and this she could do with ease. Soon he would be smiling and singing again, and glancing adoringly at his beloved Madame H.

Caroline would have been very happy for Mrs. Hollingsworth, of whom she was very fond, had it not been for her own nagging suspicions that Hal's activities were in some way connected with Gaspard—which led inevitably to the possibility that the chef was involved with the Bonapartist plots against the Duke of Wellington. When Gaspard was happy and smiling, these suspicions seemed unbelievable, but when he was quiet and withdrawn, or when he was with the unpleasant Boisville, then those suspicions did not seem quite as wild. She wanted to ask Hal about it, but somehow she knew that she could not, for when she had given him her word that she would do all she could to ease Jennifer's mind, it had somehow been implicit that she would never again mention the subject. She did not know exactly why she felt this, but she did, and she knew that her instinct was correct; it would not be the thing at all to say anything more.

The housekeeper disappeared toward her parlor, and Caroline returned to her own apartments, intent upon going over the arrangements for the wedding one last time before retiring. Wearily she sat at the escritoire by the light of a candle, taking out all the papers on which she had written seemingly endless lists and notes. One by one she ticked off the items. The white coach had been attended to, the flowers ordered from Covent Garden—including the extra ferns and garlands Gaspard had advised for the dining room—and the cake had been delivered from Gunter's, that establishment being anxious not to find itself left with a specially ordered item

decorated with the heraldic emblems of the Seymour and
Carstairs families. Jennifer's silver tissue wedding gown had
been delivered from her *couturière*, together with the primrose and lilac gowns to be worn by her many bridesmaids,
and on the same day Caroline's new gowns had also been
delivered, although they had not arrived in so grand a style,
being brought to the rear of the house. But at least she could
appear in something other than gray wool or turquoise lawn,
and as she sat in the candlelight, her new white muslin gown
was blushed to the palest of pinks.

"How very pleasing you look in white, Caro."

She turned with a gasp to see Hal leaning against the
doorjamb. He had returned from an evening engagement and
was dressed formally in a black velvet coat and silk breeches.
His waistcoat was of white satin and his cravat edged with
lace. His dark hair was a little ruffled, and this added an
attractively casual note to his otherwise distinguished appearance. He smiled, coming further into the room, dropping his
gloves and tricorn hat upon a table.

"Good evening, Sir Henry."

"Good evening, Caro."

She wondered why he had chosen to come to see her, and
at such an hour. "Is there something—"

"I have merely come to wish you well for tomorrow. Since
I have lodged here I have taken the opportunity of observing
you, Caro Lexham, and what I have seen has impressed me
greatly. You have taken to the running of this house as if you
have known no other life. In short, you appear to have been
born to be the mistress of a great London mansion."

"I think that most of the praise should go to Mrs.
Hollingsworth, for without her I could not—"

"Nonsense, you fully deserve the praise. Mrs. Hollingsworth
is no doubt extremely efficient, but she can only respond to
the lady of the house, and in your case that lady is very
significant."

"I think you are too kind, Sir Henry."

He shook his head. "No, Caro, that is one thing I am not.
In fact, I have not been at all kind, a lamentable lapse on my
part."

"I don't know what you mean."

His hazel eyes moved over her face in the candlelight.
"No, I don't suppose you do, and in a way I hope you never

understand, for that would be a welcome solution." He smiled then. "Forgive me, I think I may have enjoyed a rather too convivial evening."

"Perhaps."

"Don't know me too well, Caro, a fellow likes to retain a little mystery."

She smiled.

"I came here tonight not only to wish you well, but also to thank you."

"Thank me?"

He nodded. "For all you have done for Jennifer. I know that you have toiled as much because you love her as because you need to make a success of this venture. Whatever happens tomorrow, you will have done all you possibly can to make my sister's wedding day the most splendid occasion."

She lowered her eyes then, unable to help wondering if he would still be thanking her at this time the next day, for by then there was no doubt that Marcia would have made some move against her. "I—I just hope that all goes well, Sir Henry," she said at last, raising her gaze slowly to his face.

"Oh, I don't think anything will go drastically wrong," he said softly. "Of that you can be sure."

Could she be so sure? She doubted it very much.

Something in her glance drew him a little closer suddenly, and he put his hand to her chin, stroking her skin gently with his thumb. "How very vulnerable you are at times, Caro, which fact I find quite irresistible—and at this very moment I do not feel inclined to restrain my baser instincts." He slipped his arm around her waist, pulling her toward him and kissing her on the lips, his fingers moving in the warm hair at the nape of her neck. A wild, warm desire coursed through her, a desire to which she momentarily yielded, but then she drew firmly away. He did not mean the kiss, it was merely a passing fancy which would be forgotten within a moment.

"Why, Sir Henry," she said lightly, endeavoring to sound merely amused. "You must indeed have enjoyed a convivial evening."

"I did indeed, and for the sweetest of moments I cherished a hope that it was about to continue."

"That would not be at all the thing, sir."

"So it seems. Pray forgive the trespass."

"Forgive it? Why, I have already forgotten it, Sir Henry."

He raised an eyebrow at that, smiling a little. "Have you, be damned? I must be losing my touch."

"Good night, Sir Henry."

A light passed through his eyes and he gave a low laugh. "Good night, Caro."

Chapter 25

It seemed that she had barely fallen asleep before it was time to rise again. Mrs. Hollingsworth brought her a silver pot of freshly made coffee and, as she set it down, announced that the menu cards, which had had to be hastily reordered when Gaspard came to the hotel, had not been delivered as promised. Nor had the flowers arrived from Covent Garden.

With a groan, Caroline slipped quickly from the bed. Mrs. Hollingsworth hurried away to do her own tasks, and Caroline washed and dressed as swiftly as possible, for if those two vital items had not been delivered by the time she left her apartment, she would have to go out to see what had happened to them.

As she stole a moment or two to enjoy the excellent coffee, the lower servants, who had risen at five to commence their work, were just finishing their early tasks. In the main reception room the fires had been raked out and laid anew, and damp sand had been scattered on the carpets to settle the dust before brushing. Everything was attended to in silence, so that not a single guest was disturbed by all the activity.

In the kitchens Gaspard and his *brigade* had commenced the preparation of the wedding feast, which work would go on at the same time as the guests' breakfasts were begun. So, while truffles were being cleaned and ortolans stuffed, so also were being made ready the bacon and eggs, kidneys, omelettes, and kedgeree which would soon grace the tables of the dining room and private apartments. Everyone worked swiftly and efficiently, with only Boisville apparently having little to do for the time being. Mrs. Hollingsworth was curious about this, until Gaspard pointed out that in the absence of a glacier from Gunter's, it would be Boisville's task to do the ice carving, at which art he was very skilled indeed. She accepted this explanation, but she could not help thinking that Boisville was apparently a very dispensable *entremettier!* The housekeeper had come to dislike Boisville intensely, for she had swiftly realized that it was after speaking with him that Gaspard frequently fell into his quiet, withdrawn moods. However, this morning Boisville had not approached Gaspard, who was fully occupied with all the preparations, and who was enjoying the hard work so much that he sang to himself as he inspected the freshly delivered Severn salmon.

Her coffee finished, Caroline soon ascertained that neither the menu cards nor the flowers had arrived in the meantime, and so, as the rest of the staff sat down in the servants' hall to a well-earned breakfast, she set off to Piccadilly to find a hackney carriage. It would not have done at all to be seen traveling in such a lowly vehicle, and so she went about it as discreetly as possible, trusting that no one saw the mistress of the Lexham Hotel engaged in such an exercise!

The menu cards were ready and so she easily accomplished the first part of her errand, then went on to Covent Garden. The market had been busy for many hours already and the noise and bustle was considerable as porters with baskets on their heads jostled and shouted, as prices were argued, and as wagons and carts struggled to pass through narrow ways. The little single-story shops and open-fronted booths were doing a brisk trade and such was the crush that it was impossible for the hackney to proceed further. Bidding the coachman to wait for her, she alighted and went on foot into the flower market. She stepped carefully over the dirty cobbles where rotting fruit and vegetables had been carelessly thrown, and at last she approached the man who had undertaken to provide the flowers, ferns, and garlands for the wedding.

He was a portly fellow with a bulbous nose and a battered top hat which could have done with a good brushing, but he was surrounded by the most beautiful flowers in the whole market. Buckets filled with daffodils, narcissi, and tulips cluttered the cobbles, together with bowls of roses and carnations from the market garden hothouses upriver from the city at Chelsea. To the rear of the booth, the man's assistants were employed making garlands, their bowed figures almost concealed by large wooden pails of ferns and other greenery.

Caroline hardly dared to ask him about the delivery for the Lexham Hotel, for a dreadful thought had occurred to her: had Marcia chosen this way for her next move? But to her overwhelming relief, the man immediately assured her that the flowers had been sent off barely ten minutes before, the delay having been beyond his control as he had not received his own order until late, the market gardeners having had some difficulty owing to awkward tides and so on. Caroline gladly accepted his explanation, for all that mattered to her was that the order was *en route* for Mayfair Street.

She retraced her steps to the hackney, but when she got there she halted in dismay, for there was no sign of it. She glanced swiftly around, thinking that she had mistaken the place, but no, the hackney had simply gone! Desperately she cast around for another, for she must return as quickly as possible. As if to emphasize her predicament, the church bells chose that moment to chime the half hour; it was already half past nine and she was stranded on the opposite side of London!

She did not see the smart red curricle emerge slowly from a side street, its high-stepping team of bright chestnuts driven with great skill by the young gentleman at the ribbons. He was fashionably dressed and wore his top hat tipped back on his honey-colored hair. He seemed to be searching the busy street, and then he saw her. "Cousin Caroline?" It was Dominic.

She turned in surprise, hearing his voice above the noise. What a strange coincidence it was that he should happen to drive along this very street at the time that she was there. She greeted him warily. "Good morning, my lord."

He halted the curricle in the middle of the street, ignoring the angry shouts from the other vehicles which could not now pass by. "So cool still, cousin? I had hoped we were friends now. Why are you alone here at this hour?"

The complaints were becoming angrier as he waited deliberately for her to reply, and she glanced uncomfortably at the other vehicles. "Had you not better clear the way, my lord?"

"When you have answered my question. You should not be in this disreputable neighborhood on your own, Caroline, it is hardly advisable."

"I had to come because the flowers had not been delivered for the wedding."

"Ah, then your error is understood and forgiven. I trust that you did not walk all the way, but the apparent absence of any vehicle suggests that that has to be the case."

She was suspicious suddenly, sensing that he knew about the hackney. "I did not walk, my lord, I hired a carriage."

He smiled a little, still ignoring the shouts and waved fists. "Is that a delicate way of admitting that you committed the heinous sin of traveling in a hackney? Tut, tut, my dear Caroline, that is not at all the *ton*. However, I am pleased to be at your disposal and would be honored to convey you back to Mayfair Street. Will you accept my offer?"

She looked up at him, knowing that this was a charade he had deliberately staged. He must have seen her alight from the hackney and he had dismissed it, fully intending to just happen along. But why?

He held out an elegantly gloved hand. "Come on, this is hardly the time to demur, cousin; you are in need of transport and I can provide it."

He was right and she knew it, and so she accepted his hand. He drew her easily up to the seat beside him, flicking the whip so that the red curricle leaped away at a spanking pace. She clung fearfully to the seat as he negotiated a corner.

He laughed. "I haven't lost a passenger yet, coz! I assure you that I always drive like this; our present speed is not, therefore, part of a dastardly plot to dispose of you."

She did not know whether to smile or not, for had anyone else made the remark it would have been amusing, but it simply wasn't when uttered by Dominic Lexham.

He glanced at her. "Your silence is ominous, cousin. Does it mean that you still harbor a grudge against me?"

"A grudge? No."

"Then please treat me as if you now regard me as a friend, for I assure you that I am." He reached over to put his hand over hers, and the curricle flew along a wide thoroughfare.

Straightening once more, he urged the team faster, cracking the whip so that the vehicle dashed across a junction, ignoring the traffic passing in the other direction, and entered Piccadilly at what seemed to her to be breakneck speed. Almost in a blur she saw the window of Hoby's, she saw Green Park and the Pulteney and Oxenford hotels before the curricle turned at last into the quiet streets and squares of Mayfair.

She knew a great sense of relief when they passed beneath the pedimented gateway and slowly crossed the courtyard to the main entrance of the hotel. She wondered what he was thinking in that moment, but she could read nothing in his handsome, expressionless face.

The flower wagon was just departing and some maids were carrying the last garlands into the vestibule as the curricle came to a standstill by the steps and Dominic alighted to help Caroline down. Holding her hand, he smiled into her eyes. "There, cousin, I have delivered you safe and sound, and more swiftly I am sure than your phantom hackney."

"I am most grateful to you."

"I assure you that the pleasure was all mine." His glance was so warm that she felt suddenly embarrassed, especially as some guests emerged from the hotel at that very moment. She began to withdraw her hand, but his fingers tightened over hers. "Until we meet again, Caroline," he said softly, bending his head and kissing her fully on the lips.

With a horrified gasp, she stepped back from him. Still smiling, he climbed lightly back onto the curricle and with a swift crack of the whip jerked the team into action once more.

She was horribly conscious of the guests' curious glances, and her face was the color of flame as she gathered her skirts to hurry swiftly into the house, politely murmuring her greeting as she passed. The ladies smiled and nodded, but exchanged quizzical glances; the gentlemen doffed their hats, their eyes lowered to catch a glimpse of her pretty ankles.

As the door closed behind her, the departing guests strolled slowly on down the steps and across the courtyard. They glanced back at the entrance, their heads together as they discussed the intriguing little scene they had just witnessed, commenting that the two Lexham cousins appeared to have become very intimate indeed.

*   *   *

Caroline had no time to consider Dominic's strange conduct, for in spite of the fact that the wedding itself was not to take place until early evening, there still seemed to be a mountain of work before all was in readiness. In advance there had seemed to be sufficient time to do everything, but now the day was upon them there did not appear to be sufficient minutes in each hour. The everyday life of the hotel had to proceed, the needs of the guests attended to, and thus while the servants labored to decorate the red saloon, the dining room, and the vestibules, there was a constant throng of guests and visitors to make their task even more arduous.

As the day wore on, however, the rooms set aside for the wedding took on an entirely new and fairy-tale appearance. Swathes of flowers and greenery turned them into sylvan bowers, with garlands twined around columns, through the banisters of the grand staircase, along pelmets and around doorjambs. White satin bows were pinned to furnishings, and great bowls of bright spring flowers stood everywhere, filling the air with their delicate perfume, so fresh and full of promise. In the vestibule stood the pretty baskets of wedding favors, the knots of white ribbon and posies of primroses, which would be handed to each guest on arrival.

But it was in the dining room that the greatest transformation took place, for it was here that the fashionable gathering could congregate after the ceremony in order to sample the magnificent feast Gaspard and his *brigade* had prepared. In this room had been created a leafy bower in which one could almost have expected to find Titania lying asleep. Ferns and blossoms had been arranged in huge bowls, garlands were draped everywhere, especially around the white-clothed table, and immense épergnes full of flowers, moss, and fruit stood at intervals along its great length. There were silver bowls of melons, pineapples, peaches, pears, and grapes, and dozens of shaded candles to give that muted light which was at once so romantic and flattering. The light shone on gleaming cutlery and cut crystal, and the menu cards stood elegantly in little silver-gilt stands. The Sheraton sideboards were a vision of splendor with the dazzling Lexham plate displayed in all its considerable glory, and in one corner of the room splashed a little fountain, the mechanics of which were a mystery to

Caroline but which were fully understood by the experienced Mrs. Hollingsworth.

In the cellar, Boisville worked away at carving the ice, and had already finished swans and eagles, the emblems of the Seymour and Carstairs families, and had now begun the very delicate vases in which would soon sparkle the more feathery ferns.

Darkness fell at last and the guests began to arrive, and in her private apartment, Caroline put the finishing touches to her appearance. To achieve a singularly fashionable and elegant effect when funds were at a premium was no simple matter, and she had consulted for a long time with her diligent dressmaker. This astute lady had in her possession a particularly splendid ruff, made to closely resemble those worn in Tudor times, and so it had been decided to create a gown to suit this item. The result was a vision of sixteenth-century fashion, with elaborate, puckered sleeves stitched with hundreds of tiny pearls, but made very modish indeed by the use of a very fine rose-pink Indian muslin. The hem was high enough to reveal her ankles, and was emphasized by stiff *rouleaux* to make the skirt stand out a little, and the long sleeves ended in cuffs of lace which almost completely concealed her hands. Her hair was dressed high and back from her face, as she had seen in portraits of Elizabethan ladies, and was twined with little strings of pearls. These pearls had been pressed upon her for the occasion by a very insistent Jennifer, who perceived that they would be the very thing.

Standing in front of the cheval glass now, Caroline surveyed herself from head to toe. Would she do? She touched the stiff ruff which sprang out so splendidly around the neckline of the gown, revealing her pale, bare throat. Oh, how excellent her grandmother's necklace would have looked now! But there was no point in yearning for what had been lost forever; the necklace had gone and she would never wear it again.

Only one thing remained now, and that was the tiny velvet cap which was to be pinned at the back of her head, and as she bent to pick it up, Mrs. Hollingworth came in, her discreet dark gray skirts rustling and her keys chinking in a familiar way Caroline found suddenly very comforting. As the housekeeper helped her with the cap, Caroline went over and over the final arrangements. Surely they had not forgotten something of vital importance?

"Has everything been attended to, Mrs. Hollingsworth?"

"Everything, madam. The maids finished the ribbons from the cake over an hour ago. We can do no more."

"How do I look?"

"Very lovely."

"Does it show that I have not been to a *couturière*?"

"No, Miss Lexham, it does not." Smiling reassuringly, the housekeeper took Caroline's shawl and draped it carefully over her ruched sleeves. "There, now you are ready to be this day's most important London hostess."

"Oh, don't say that, for it fills me with terror."

"You will carry it off splendidly, I know that you will."

"Not if Lady Chaddington can help it."

"We will be sure to watch her very closely, madam, of that you may be sure."

"I wish I could guess what she will do, but I cannot. She is so unscrupulous that it could be just about anything!"

"You must not think about it, Miss Lexham; you must just carry on as if all is well—which it probably will be, for I cannot think that she will do anything to the actual wedding of her future sister-in-law."

"No? Well I think she is quite capable of doing that, Mrs. Hollingsworth, because as far as she is concerned tonight I am at my most vulnerable. Destroy tonight's celebration, and she has destroyed me; the fact that she will also have ruined Jennifer's wedding day will not really enter into it at all. However, you are right, it will do no good to worry about it, for until whatever it is actually happens, there doesn't appear to be very much we can do about it." She paused for a moment, suddenly very nervous. "Wish me luck, Mrs. Hollingsworth."

In reply the housekeeper made so bold as to suddenly hug her. "Of course I wish you luck, my dearest Miss Lexham."

Smiling gratefully at this warm display of affection, Caroline took a deep breath and left the apartment to go out into the vestibule to greet the wedding guests.

The crystal chandeliers glittered above bare shoulders and jeweled hair, and tall ostrich plumes trembled richly in the warmth from the glowing fire in the hallway. The gentlemen wore coats of velvet, dark green, dark blue, and black, and brass or silver buttons shone elegantly on the rich, somber material. The air was filled with the sounds of refined conversation and laughter, and outside more and more carriages turned into the courtyard, their lamps casting arcs of light in the gloom and their wheels and the hooves of their teams clattering above the cobbles. The Lexham Hotel was ablaze with lights, not a single shutter or curtain being closed and every room being illuminated for this most important of social occasions. To Caroline, as she moved among the crush of distinguished guests, it seemed that the whole of the *beau monde* was assembled here tonight—the whole of the *beau monde* to witness either her triumph, or her ignominious defeat at the hands of Marcia, Lady Chaddington.

Marcia had arrived early on the arm of her popinjay brother, and she looked very elegant indeed, clad in a low-necked slip of the palest lime-green sarcenet with an overgown of silver patent net. Fabulous emeralds lay at her throat and hung from her ears, and frothy ostrich plumes quivered above her magnificently dressed auburn hair. Beside her, clad in pale-blue from Apollo-curled head to slippered toe, Lord Fynehurst looked almost as splendid, but decidedly unmanly, and his braying tones could be heard at frequent intervals above the noise of conversation.

A small orchestra had been hired for the occasion, and they played in the background in the red saloon. The vicar of fashionable St. George's, Hanover Square, sipped champagne with the other guests as he waited for the commencement of the ceremony. A very nervous Lord Carstairs, his slender figure very handsome in an embroidered velvet coat of the richest wine red, moved among the guests, and several times she saw him bid the groom's man, his long-suffering brother, to check again that the wedding ring was safely in his pocket.

At last the appointed hour came and everyone pushed into the red saloon, where the chairs and sofas had been placed around the walls to allow as many as possible to witness the actual ceremony. An expectant hush fell over the gathering, and all eyes were turned on the open doorway, through which could be seen the fine rise of the grand staircase.

The first guests to see the wedding party appear at the top of the steps gave gasps of admiration and Caroline smiled as she saw Jennifer make the magnificent entrance she had so wanted. And what an entrance it was, for she looked so very

beautiful and glowing with happiness, and she was the center
of attention as she slowly descended on Hal's arm. Her silver
tissue wedding gown was adorned with two broad flounces of
Brussels point lace, edged with shell trimming, and was
fastened at its tiny waist by a beautiful diamond clasp. A
breathtaking wreath of more diamonds flashed and glittered in
her fluffy dark hair, and there was an air of such joy about
her that she outshone every other woman present and was
truly the most beautiful and enchanting of brides. Behind her
came the twelve bridesmaids, six clad in primrose and six in
lilac, and they carried little ribboned posies of sweet-smelling
heartsease, with more of these flowers pinned in their hair.

Hal wore a coat of indigo with silver buttons, and his shirt
frills and cravat were edged with fine lace. He looked very
handsome and dashing, and very proud as he escorted his
lovely sister, his hand resting protectively over hers. His eyes
met Caroline's for a moment as they passed, and he smiled at
her. It was a smile that almost turned her heart over with love
for him, and she lowered her glance to hide the effect it had
had upon her. Then the procession reached the little floral
dais on which the ceremony itself was to take place, and
Jennifer at last saw her beloved Charles, who had watched
her approach with such adoration that there could be no doubt
at all that this was a love match of the first order.

Caroline watched the service with tears in her eyes, for she
was so very happy for her friend, and as the ring was slipped
onto the bride's finger, nothing could have been further
from Caroline's thoughts than the schemes of Lady Chaddington.
At last the ceremony was over and Jennifer turned into her
new husband's arms as he bent to kiss her, and a loud cheer
went up that would have been totally out of place in a church.

Now at last was the time to adjourn to the dining room,
which had been closed to conceal the beautiful decorations
from view until the last moment. The two footmen, wedding
favors pinned to their liveried shoulders, flung open the
connecting doors from the red saloon, and the wedding gathering proceeded into the feast, led by the bride and groom, and
followed immediately by Hal, with Marcia on his arm.

Gasps of delight greeted the first glimpse of the fairy
bower, and more gasps the magnificent table with its épergnes
and garlands, and above all the cake. Gunter's had indeed
surpassed themselves and had created a confection which

dominated the snowy table. Crisp, dainty ribbons extended from the cake to the four corners of the ceiling, and in these corners there were wedding wreaths, adorned with more knots and trailers of satin ribbon. Boisville's splendid ice carvings glistened on silver trays, and cool, soft ferns trembled with each movement of air as the guests proceeded around the table, seeking their allotted places.

The feast commenced, and it was soon evident that society's feting of Gaspard Duvall was well justified, for the dishes that proceeded from the kitchens were delicate, mouth watering, and well worthy of his reputation. The *potages* were declared to be quite magnificent, the *brochettes d' ortolans* to be quite the most delicious dish of those small birds yet tasted, and the salmon *soufflé* to be the lightest and most flavorsome imaginable. Platter after platter was offered to the delighted guests, from dainty slices of chicken breasts on *pâté de foie gras* to a variety of dishes served with expensive and rare truffles.

From a discreet position beneath the Ionic colonnade at the rear of the room, Caroline watched the feast progress. How different an affair it was from a wedding feast in Selford! She smiled to herself, pondering the incredible changes that had taken place in her life in such a short while. Her gaze moved over the dazzling gathering, the cream of London's society, and she was amazed anew that all this should be happening simply because of a sudden, impossible thought that had occurred to her while sitting briefly in the gardens to look at the house where her father had been born.

Seeing Jennifer's happy, smiling face as she raised her glass to share a toast with her new husband, Caroline found herself suddenly looking at Marcia, who had been so oddly quiet thus far. There was a look about her now which suddenly made Caroline very wary. Something was about to happen; Caroline knew it. Every nerve stiffened as she involuntarily stepped forward, one hand reaching out to touch the cool marble of a garland-entwined column. She was deaf to the noise in the room; it was as if she was alone with her enemy. Across the assembly, Marcia's cool, contemptuous glance met hers, and Caroline became aware of the sound of her own heartbeats. Marcia was about to deliver her *coup de grace*, and she would do it alone.

From behind Caroline, a footman appeared, bearing aloft

Gaspard's *pièce de résistance,* a magnificent silver platter bearing an especially created salmon dish, *saumon Jennifer,* named in honor of the bride. Deliciously garnished, and decorated with peacock feathers, the dish's appearance was greeted with admiring claps as the footman bore it deftly to the head of the table, intending to serve the bride and groom first. With bated breath, Caroline watched Marcia, whose whole attitude now was one of confident, gloating anticipation.

From Jennifer and Lord Carstairs, the footman proceeded to Hal, and then to Marcia, but as he flourishingly placed a spoonful of the salmon upon her plate, she gave a sudden scream and rose shakily to her feet. A shocked silence descended instantly over the gathering and all eyes swung toward her in astonishment. Shuddering with disgust, and somehow contriving to look genuinely ill, she pointed a quivering finger at the offending plate. There, reposing horridly in the midst of the delicious salmon, was a very large, very dead cockroach.

Chapter 26

Caroline found herself hurrying forward, and many of the guests gave shudders and hastily put down their cutlery, pushing their plates away as if all the food might contain similar insects. An uneasy and questioning stir passed around the elegant table, and Jennifer's happy smile faltered, her eyes filling with tears at what seemed the complete destruction of her wedding feast. The unfortunate footman didn't quite know what to do, and he looked toward Caroline for instruction, but she could not think of anything to say. There the cockroach lay for all to see, and as far as the guests were concerned, it could only have come from the kitchens. Were those kitchens then crawling with such vermin? Was the whole establishment perhaps similarly afflicted? Had they all made a dreadful mistake in honoring these premises with their patronage. Caroline could sense their thoughts, and she could not blame them; how were they to know that Marcia was the culprit?

The moments of shocked silence passed on leaden feet, and Marcia managed to squeeze remorseful tears which coursed wretchedly down her cheeks as she turned to apologize to Jennifer for having been the unwitting cause of the feast's ruination. But it was this final touch that was to prove her undoing, for as she turned, she dislodged her reticule from the edge of the table and it fell to the floor, the contents spilling everywhere. There, among the trinkets and scent phials, lay several more cockroaches.

The guests who were close enough to see gave shocked gasps, and Marcia's face drained of color as she hastily bent to push the guilty items back into the reticule. She was forestalled, however, for Hal was the more agile, picking everything up and dropping it coldly and pointedly upon the tablecloth before her.

"Your belongings, I believe, madam," he said softly, his eyes filled with disgust.

Marcia couldn't speak; she cast around desperately for a friendly face, but by now everyone was aware of what she had done. A sea of offended, appalled faces looked back at her. Even her brother could not ally himself with her, deliberately keeping his gaze lowered to his plate. At last Marcia's haunted eyes returned to Hal, but she saw that she had lost him forever. With a stifled sob, she gathered her skirts and ran from the room, the sound of her footsteps carrying clearly to them all as she fled to the outer doors.

Immediately a buzz of comment broke out, turning as much upon Hal's conduct as upon Marcia's, for he did not appear to be in any way upset that the woman who was to have been his bride should have stooped to such a detestable trick, and at his beloved sister's wedding! A great many interested glances followed him now as he swept the reticule onto a plate and beckoned to a waiter, who immediately spirited it away. Hal then turned to Caroline, who had been standing close by all the while, and with a smile he raised her hand gallantly to his lips, which gesture met with much approbation from the assembly.

Jennifer and Lord Carstairs were all smiles again and the feast proceeded, the conversation dwelling almost solely on the intriguing subject of Marcia's dreadful behavior and Hal's reaction to it. Lord Fynehurst remained uncomfortably where he was for as long as he could, but in the end he uneasily took his leave, only too conscious that the ignominy touching his sister's name was inevitably touching his own, for the guests knew him well enough to realize that he had probably been fully aware of what she planned to do.

Caroline retreated to her position beneath the colonnade, endeavoring to look calm and unconcerned, but in reality feeling the very opposite. If it had not been for the accidental knocking to the floor of the reticule, Marcia's cunning trick would have worked, the wedding feast would have been disrupted beyond redemption, the reputation of the new Lexham Hotel would have suffered irreparable harm, and the odium would in the end have fallen upon Caroline herself. She trembled a little with delayed shock, hardly realizing that she had not only witnessed the biter being bitten, but also the severing of Marcia's relationship with Hal.

Mrs. Hollingsworth, as soothing and reliable as ever, appeared as if by magic at her side, pressing a glass of champagne into her hand. "It's all over now, my dear, and she didn't succeed in her wickedness. Smile now and drink this, and think only that in spite of her efforts, this wedding celebration has been a wonderful success."

Caroline smiled. "Thank you, Mrs. Hollingsworth, there are times when I truly do not know what I would do without you."

The housekeeper gently patted her arm and then slipped away to the kitchens once more.

Jennifer was much relieved that from imminent disaster, the feast was now proceeding excellently once more, and she now took the opportunity of quizzing her brother as he took his place beside her once more. "Hal, you do not appear to be much put out by what Marcia did."

"That depends upon what you mean by put out. If you mean angry, then I do not appear to be gripped by rage because I am doing all in my power to hide it. If she had been a man, I would call her out for what she did. On the other hand, if by 'put out' you mean heartbroken, then that is because I am not."

"But I thought—"

"You thought incorrectly, my dear sister, as indeed did Marcia herself. I may for a brief while have entertained a notion of marrying her, but my sojourn at Petwell soon relieved me of that foolishness. Marcia may be an excellent bedfellow, but she would make a tyrannical wife!"

"Hal!" cried his shocked sister. "Don't be so improper!"

"I have only provided you with a fact you have been itching to know for some time," he replied infuriatingly.

She flushed. "Well, I admit that I *did* wonder if she was your mistress."

"Now you know."

"You might at least have admitted earlier that you weren't intending to marry her, for I've been worrying so about you," she scolded. "I *knew* she would make you unhappy!"

"If I had told you, Jennifer, you would not have believed me."

"That is your own fault, for you have too frequently in the recent past deliberately told me untruths or simply omitted to tell me things altogether."

"My sins are evidently legion," he remarked dryly, smiling at her.

"They certainly are." Jennifer lowered her eyes for a moment. "Hal, Marcia did that dreadful thing today in order to hurt Caroline, which means that she was jealous of Caroline. Do you agree?"

His smile revealed nothing. "To agree would suggest that I am *au fait* with the workings of the female mind, which I am not. Now then, are you going to be a good little thing and eat up your dinner, or must I spoon-feed you?"

She studied his face for a moment and then accepted that he was not going to be any more forthcoming. "You attempt to spoon-feed me, Henry Seymour, and I'll kick you on the shins, as I remember doing when you were a beastly little boy."

For another hour or more after that the feast continued, but then it was time for the bride and groom to prepare to leave on the first part of their lengthy journey to Venice. They were to stay at some undisclosed address in Kent on their first night, crossing to France from Dover on the next morning's tide. Walking with her husband on one side and her brother on the other, and followed by the twelve bridesmaids, Jennifer left the dining room to go up to her apartment to change.

Hal did not accompany them up the grand staircase, but waited at the foot of the steps until the bridal party had passed from his sight, then he turned to go back to the feast, but instead found himself face-to-face with an old friend from his school days. "Digby! How good it is to see you again! I caught a glimpse of you earlier on and could hardly believe my eyes! How did you contrive to get yourself invited, you old reprobate?"

The other smiled. "By nefarious means, how else?" He was a tall, blond man, dressed in unrelieved black, and his rather aquiline nose had become red as the evening wore on and he enjoyed more and more of the excellent champagne. "I believe I must congratulate you upon this evening's celebrations. I'll warrant this particular wedding will be very much the thing for some time to come."

"My sister sincerely hopes so," replied Hal, grinning. "But I cannot take the credit for any of the arrangements. That must go entirely to Miss Lexham."

"Ah, yes, the intriguing Miss Lexham. What a beauty, eh? By Gad, I can understand Marcia Chaddington's green-eyed jealousy. Quite an armful, eh, Seymour?"

Hal's smile faded just a little. "Don't tread further along that particular path, my friend, for you are entirely wrong."

"You mean, there ain't anything between you and the beauteous *chatelaine*?" The other could not conceal his surprise.

"Nothing whatever."

"Well, damn me, if that don't stagger me! One thing's for sure, though, and that is that Marcia certainly thought there was."

"Possibly."

"You're very reticent about the whole thing, if you don't mind my saying so."

"Perhaps that is because I don't consider it to be any of your business—old friend."

Digby pursed his lips. "Don't get on your high horse, I don't mean any harm. Besides, perhaps it's as well you are not interested in the lady of the house, for from all accounts there's another with a rather surprising involvement."

"Another?"

Digby nodded, glancing across the crowded vestibule to the doorway, where Caroline was saying farewell to several guests who had to depart rather earlier than expected. "Yes," he murmured, "I am told that there was a very pretty scene outside first thing this morning, a fond farewell between Lexham and Lexham."

Hal's face was very still. "I beg your pardon?"

"I confess to being surprised that Marcia Chaddington attempted anything to harm Miss Lexham, for from all accounts until very recently the likely perpetrator of such a trick would have been the Earl of Lexham. Now it seems that

Lexham and his lovely cousin are far from at odds with one another.''

"Digby, if you don't come to the point, I swear I will wring your scrawny neck!''

"All right, dear boy, have patience. It seems that the two were seen embracing, and enjoying a kiss which was far from being a cousinly peck on the cheek. Far from it. That would be a turn-up, would it not? After all the furor caused by the will, Lexham does a complete turnabout and falls in love with the lady!''

Hal did not reply for a moment, but his eyes narrowed a little as he glanced at Caroline's smiling face as she moved among the guests. "Yes," he murmured, "it would indeed be a turnabout.''

"Still," said Digby, smiling a sleek smile, "it is of no concern to you, is it?''

"None whatever.''

"By the way, no doubt you've been too preoccupied today to have heard the latest news from Paris.''

"News?''

"It seems they've caught the assassin—a fellow named Cantillon. They don't know anything more from him, however, for he's keeping a still tongue in his head. They reckon that this means he still has accomplices on the loose.''

"Probably." Hal's expression was thoughtful.

"Ah, I see old Fennimore over there. I must have a word with him. Good-bye, Hal.''

"Good-bye, Digby.''

At that moment Gaspard Duvall made an appearance among the guests, a number of them having sent requests to the kitchens. He was greatly applauded and congratulated upon having prepared the most sumptuous of wedding feasts, and his bright eyes danced with pleasure and pride. Hal watched him, his face still unsmiling and pensive.

Caroline found herself at his side. "Is something wrong, Sir Henry?'' she inquired, seeing his stern expression.

"Wrong, Miss Lexham?'' he replied coldly. "Why, nothing at all.''

"Sir Henry?'' She was shaken by the change in him. He was almost a stranger, and there was no warmth in him at all.

"You must excuse me, madam, if I find it hard to accept that you would not only be so foolish and misguided, but also so brazen and improper as to indulge in fond and intimate embraces with your cousin in public!'' With a stiff nod of his head, he left her.

Stunned, she remained where she was.

She did not see him again to speak to throughout the evening. The bride and groom departed in their white landau, waved off by their happy friends and relatives, and after that the gathering began to thin. The celebrations continued until well into the night, and it was two in the morning before Caroline could at last take herself wearily to her bed.

There she found that before going away, Jennifer had stolen into her apartment and left a little piece of the wedding cake, together with a traditional little verse, written in her own hand.

> *But, madam, as a present take*
> *This little portion of bride-cake;*
> *Fast any Friday in the year,*
> *When Venus mounts the starry sphere,*
> *Thrust this at night beneath pillow clear;*
> *In morning slumber you will seem*
> *To enjoy your lover in a dream.*

Slowly her fingers closed over the paper, crumpling it, and she closed her eyes as the hot tears of misery and renewed heartbreak stung her lids.

She cried herself to sleep, curled up in the vast bed, her face hidden even from the darkness.

Chapter 27

The rough hand closed over her mouth in the faint gray light of dawn. Terrified she struggled, but his strength was too great and he merely tightened his grip, his uncouth fingers digging painfully into her flesh.

"Be still, wench, or it'll be the worse for you!"

His voice was unrefined and his breath smelled of ale. She knew that he meant the threat and she lay still, her eyes huge with fear as she stared up at him. The dawn was but minutes old and the light so muted that he was barely discernible. He was dirty and unshaven, wearing a battered boxcoat and wide-brimmed hat pulled low on his forehead. As she watched, he turned to jerk his head at someone she could not see.

"Got the letter, Ben?"

" 'Course I've got the ruddy letter!" growled the other, his voice as coarse as the first man's. "Where's it to be put?"

"Shove it on the mantel shelf, and be quick about it!"

She was aware of a shadowy figure moving silently across the room, just on the edge of her vision. It stretched up and left something small, oblong, and white against a candlestick.

Her captor returned his attention to her then, shaking her a little to show that he meant business. "Now then, my pretty, if you know what's good for you, you'll come with us nice and quiet. One squeak, and it'll be the last sound you ever make? Got me?''

Still terrified, she nodded her head. Slowly he removed his hand, jerking his head again to indicate that she had to get out of the bed. His eyes rested leeringly on her bare legs, and she sought in vain to conceal them with the folds of her nightgown.

''Don't worry, my lovely,'' he said coarsely. ''It ain't for the likes of Ben and me to gaze upon you. It's for a certain gentleman to do that.''

''Gentleman?''

In reply he reached forward, and even in the half-light, she saw the glint of a metal blade. The knife pressed against her throat. ''I said no sound, sweetheart, and that means no questions either. Here, get this shawl around you and then come quietly; we don't want to wake anyone from their beauty sleep now, do we?'' The blade's tip pressed a little more against her skin and then was removed.

With a trembling hand, she took the proffered shawl, wrapping it tightly around her shoulders. He pushed her roughly toward the door and she stumbled a little, crying out. With an oath he seized her, twisting one arm up sharply behind her back.

''I'll break every bone in your lily-white body if you open your mouth again!'' he breathed, keeping his grip upon her and nodding at Ben, who softly opened the door and slipped out into the dark, deserted vestibule.

The painful twist of her arm brought tears to her eyes as she was propelled across the cold, tiled floor, her bare feet soft and silent. The dark light robbed the wedding flowers and garlands of their color and made the white ribbon knots pinned to the sofas look ghostly. Gone now was the joyous atmosphere of the marriage celebrations, and instead her fear lent a menace to even the most homely of items. The arches leading to the inner vestibule appeared to open onto a mysterious unknown, the statues in the wall niches seemed to move just a little, and the crystal droplets of the chandeliers jingled very softly in the draft of cold air sweeping in from the open front door.

She wanted to scream out for help, but she was too afraid. She did not know who was abducting her or why they were doing it; she did not know who the unknown gentleman was to whom they were evidently taking her. As she was pushed out into the cold March dawn, she looked desperately back at the shadowy vestibule, willing someone to appear and see what was happening, but no one did.

Tendrils of mist rose from the cobbles where an unmarked carriage stood waiting at the foot of the steps. Its blinds were down, its wheels were muffled, and the team's hooves were wrapped in sacking. It had not made a sound as it arrived, and it would not make a sound when it left again. . . .

Her legs felt suddenly weak as she was half dragged down the steps to the carriage, and she struggled as the door swung silently open to admit her. Sensing that she was about to scream in spite of her fear, her assailant swiftly put his dirty hand over her mouth again, heaving her bodily up into the carriage, where other hands caught her. Another man's hand was put over her mouth, a softer hand with several rings upon its fingers. Desperately she squirmed and wriggled, and she was only vaguely aware of her new captor's sudden gasp and the loosening of his grip upon her. Shaken, but alert enough to seize her opportunity, she twisted wildly away from him, scrambling to the doorway and out of the carriage, tumbling helplessly onto the cold, damp cobbles, where she lay for a moment, winded. Almost in tears, she waited for rough hands to seize her once more, but when someone touched her, it was with gentle concern.

"Are you all right, Caro?"

An overwhelming surge of relief swept weakeningly over her as she gazed up into Hal's eyes as he crouched momentarily beside her. She could only nod, watching as he straightened once more, and it was then that she saw he had a pistol in his hand and was leveling it at the occupant of the carriage. There was no sign of the two men who had abducted her, and she was vaguely aware of their footsteps as they fled into the murky dawn.

The barrel of the pistol motioned to whoever was in the carriage to climb down, and she got slowly to her feet, staring as Dominic reluctantly alighted. He did not even glance at her, his attention was fully upon Hal, whose eyes were as cold and hard as flint. "My lord of Lexham," he murmured, "I believe a word or two of explanation is required."

"I have nothing to say to you, Seymour."

"Oh, but you have, you have a great deal to say, my fine lordling, for kidnapping is not a pretty crime. Well?"

"What a bad penny you are, Seymour, continually turning up when you are least expected and least wanted."

"How unfortunate for you, Lexham, but then my activities would not be of any concern to you if you did not have such foul crimes to conceal." The pistol moved threateningly. "Your explanation, there's a good fellow."

Dominic's fearful eyes followed the pistol, but he said nothing.

"Very well, I shall furnish a likely interpretation myself," said Hal, his tone almost conversational. "If I have to guess why the Earl of Lexham would want to abduct his cousin, I would say that it is because he has perceived a rather neat way of circumventing his father's will, the terms of which state that within six months he is not only to prove himself to be a good boy, he is also to have taken for himself a wife, a lady of name and property." A shrewd smile played about Hal's lips as he saw how Dominic's eyes slid guiltily away. "What better name could that wife have than Lexham? And what more desirable property could she possess than Lexham House? You could not afford to wait for those six months to pass, could you? You saw that she was going to make a success of her venture and so you resorted to this extreme length in order to prevent her from keeping the house forever. Oh, you were cunning enough, I suppose, deciding to be all charm and honor toward the unfortunate lady, making certain that whispers sprang up about the apparent intimacy which had begun to flourish between two former enemies. Her abduction would not then arouse the hue and cry it might otherwise have done, especially as it could be made to appear like a romantic elopement, brought about by true love and encouraged by the happiness and atmosphere of my sister's wedding. There, is that not the truth of it, Lexham?"

Caroline had listened in silence, and as Hal's explanation unfolded, she knew that it was the truth. Now she understood Dominic's sudden *volte-face*, she realized now why he had suddenly been so friendly and charming when encountering her with Mrs. Hollingsworth in Bond Street, why he had appeared so miraculously when she was stranded in Covent Garden market. It had all been part of a careful plan to lull her into unguardedness and to convince society that the bitter feud was ended, and in its place was a romantic involvement. How easily it might have come off, for everyone knew how narrow was the border between love and hate, how closely those two intense emotions marched together. No one would have truly believed her when she protested that she was abducted against her will, and Dominic would have been free to dispose of his detested cousin as and when he pleased. . . . She shivered a little, knowing that tonight she probably owed Hal Seymour her very life.

The pistol motioned again. "Is that not the truth of it, Lexham?" repeated Hal.

"How clever you are, Seymour, so sharp that with luck you will one day deal yourself a mortal wound."

"If I do, Lexham, you will not be around to rejoice about it." Hal raised the pistol a little, seeming to take aim.

Caroline's eyes widened with shock and Dominic gave a start of fear, pressing back against the carriage. The coachman stared down from his perch, believing that he was about to witness a cold-blooded murder.

Hal gave a contemptuous laugh then, lowering the pistol. "Not so brave now, eh? It is one thing to play the bully with a helpless woman, but quite another to face another man. It would give me great pleasure to put an end to you, but to indulge myself in such a way would not assist Miss Lexham, who would inevitably become the center of a scandal—which in turn might put her tenure of the house at some risk. Get out of here, Lexham, but I warn you that if you so much as come near this house again, or if you make one move against Miss Lexham, then you will hear from me—and I promise you that when I catch you, there will be no one around to see what fate befalls you."

For a moment Dominic was rooted to the spot with terror, but then he scrambled back into the carriage, shouting to the stunned coachman to drive on, and with as much speed as possible. The whip cracked and the team strained forward, but their efforts were eerily silent, their muffled hooves making no sound. Quietly the dark carriage drew away, its wheels turning secretly. Only the jingle of the harness broke the illusion that some phantom was abroad in London. . . .

The moment the carriage had turned into Mayfair Street, Hal checked that the pistol was not cocked before concealing it in a hidden pocket inside his coat.

In spite of the shock of what had so nearly befallen her, Caroline still sensed his withdrawal, which was so deliberate that it was almost as if he had walked away from her. Her lips trembled a little as she drew her shawl more closely around herself. "S-sir Henry, I am so m-much in your debt, that I don't know how I may thank you," she began.

"I do not require your thanks, Miss Lexham," he replied abruptly. "Let us just leave it that I happened to be in a position to again be of assistance to you."

"I cannot leave it simply at that, Sir Henry, for I do not know what dreadful fate might have befallen me had you not been here tonight."

He smiled coolly. "That fate, my dear Miss Lexham, would in some ways have been little more than your recent behavior has deserved."

Her breath caught and she flinched as if he had struck her. "How can you say that?" she whispered.

"I can say it, madam, because whatever your cousin may have done, he found it extraordinarily easy to win your favors. I gave you my protection tonight, because it was no more or less than any gentleman of honor would have done, but do not imagine that any word or gesture on my part indicates a softening of my contempt for you. You appear to be a woman of little virtue, Miss Lexham, and therefore my advice to you is that you curb your immodest conduct or you will after all forfeit Lexham House."

She felt quite numb, and the hurt was so great that it became a physical pain, sharp and deep. "If that is truly what you think, Sir Henry," she said at last, "I honestly do not know why you bothered to save me. You are entirely wrong about me, but I shall not attempt to defend myself before your unjust condemnation. I thank you again for rescuing me, and I do not think you will be able to find fault in my future conduct, for I will at all times be polite toward you—which in spite of my indebtedness to you, you certainly do not deserve." Pride made her face him in that moment, for nothing would have allowed her to reveal the infinite suffering he caused her. Her head held high, she turned to go back up the steps, not looking back once as she entered the still-silent vestibule.

But as she reached the safety and shelter of her own apartment, she could not stem the tears. Her whole body shook with anguish, but she did not make a sound. Leaning her head back against the closed door, she closed her eyes as she wept.

The sun had risen in a clear sky when Mrs. Hollingsworth brought her her coffee. Caroline was seated in the window, wearing a plain blue gown, her hair dressed neatly beneath her little day bonnet. She had restored a little color to her pale cheeks with rouge, but she could not hide the marks of weeping around her large, dark eyes. The letter her two abductors had so carefully left upon the mantelpiece now lay in ashes in the fireplace. She had read it once, and it confirmed everything Hal had said of Dominic; it purported to be a brief note from her, explaining her absence as an elopement with her "dearest Dominic."

Mrs. Hollingsworth perceived at once that something was wrong, but for the moment she said nothing. Instead she rattled on about how quiet a day it would be after all the excitement of the wedding—and that peace and quiet would be a blessing for poor Gaspard, who had had something of a fright during the night when returning to his room after taking a walk in the fresh air with Boisville to dispel a headache. "An intruder had been searching his room and can only have left a moment before my poor Gaspard entered!"

Caroline was immediately roused from her lethargy, looking up sharply. "At what time was this?"

"Just as dawn was breaking, I believe."

Thoughtfully, Caroline stirred her coffee. An intruder in Gaspard's room? And at that particular time? Could it have been Hal, who had been so fortuitously abroad at precisely that moment and who had taken the unusual precaution of taking a pistol with him?

Mrs. Hollingsworth looked out of the window, noticing nothing in Caroline's reaction. "What a lovely day it is. I believe it is even more fine than yesterday. I wonder if Lord and Lady Carstairs have sailed for France yet?"

"No, I believe they intend leaving Dover later in the day."

The housekeeper smiled. "How wonderful it must be to be going on honeymoon to Venice. I know that it is considered a little vulgar to use that word, but honeymoon is so much more romantic and descriptive than merely going away. Oh, well, I cannot stand here daydreaming about such things. I have work to do. And today I must convince Gaspard that he must be more careful about locking his window properly. I've told him time and time again that there are more thieves in Mayfair than anywhere else, for it's here that they find the houses containing most valuables.'' She went to the door.

''I will not be long,'' Caroline called after her.

The housekeeper looked gently at her. ''Take all the time in the world, my dear, and if you feel like remaining quietly in here, then you do so.''

Caroline smiled. ''Thank you, but it will do me more good to find something to do.''

''I don't know what has upset you, my dear, but if there is anything I can do to—''

''There isn't anything, Mrs. Hollingsworth, but thank you all the same.''

When the housekeeper had gone, Caroline sipped her coffee, thinking again about the mysterious intruder in Gaspard's room. Of course it had been Hal; that was the obvious explanation for him being out and about at the very time when Dominic's henchmen had come to seize her. Hal had been searching for something in Gaspard's room, but what? Evidence of a Bonapartist plot here in London? Evidence of a connection between the chef and the arrested assassin, Cantillon? The thoughts milled urgently around in her head, and at last she got to her feet. She would have to ask Hal about her suspicions; she would have to confront him and risk his displeasure and continued contempt.

Chapter 28

It was to be well into the afternoon before she found an opportunity of speaking to him, for he had come down very late for breakfast and had then gone out. As he had descended the grand staircase, Caroline had been greeting some newly arrived guests. Her eyes had met his, and he had accorded her the coolest of greetings, which coolness her response matched. He could have known nothing of the truth from her expressionless face. Several people noticed the chill exchange and wondered greatly what had happened to give rise to such a remarkable contrast.

He returned to the hotel in the early afternoon, and after writing a number of letters in the library, he went for a stroll in the gardens, where the daffodils were now in full bloom and the blossom trees were bright with pink and white. It was here that at last she confronted him.

"Sir Henry?"

He turned toward her. "I don't think we have anything to say to each other, Miss Lexham."

"You may think not, but I happen to think differently, sir," she replied. "It concerns the intruder in Monsieur Duvall's room last night."

His eyes narrowed and she saw the veiled expression close over his face. "Intruder?"

"I believe you know full well to whom I am referring, Sir Henry."

"Miss Lexham," he said a little testily, "I have no desire to discuss this or anything else with you."

"I am sorry to hear it, sir, for I have every intention of doing just that," she retorted, an edge to her voice. "Although you may think it is none of my concern, I happen to think that it is very much my concern as it is taking place on property which for the moment at least belongs to me!"

An angry brightness flashed in his eyes at her defiance, but he saw that a lady and gentleman strolling nearby were glancing a little curiously at them, and so he suddenly changed his manner, even forcing a smile as he offered her his arm. "Very well, Miss Lexham, what is it you wish to say to me?"

They walked side by side, but although her hand rested on his sleeve, it was as if a chasm gaped between them. They were complete strangers, with none of the easy rapport that had once distinguished their relationship.

"I am waiting, Miss Lexham."

"I believe that you were the intruder, Sir Henry."

"You certainly have come straight to the point, haven't you?"

"I have little reason to do otherwise, sir."

"So it seems. I do not admit to anything, Miss Lexham."

"Does that include the possibility of Bonapartists in this hotel?"

He halted, turning to look at her. "What a very quaint notion, Miss Lexham."

"Is it? Correct me if I am wrong, but I strongly suspect that your brief to guard the Duke of Wellington has led you to Monsieur Duvall, and that that was the reason why you so suddenly decided to have your town house refurbished and why you took up residence at the Oxenford. I further suspect that the forthcoming banquet is expected to flush out any conspiracy, and that that is why you have arranged it and why you are so closely involved in it. The duke's sudden decision to remove the banquet to the Lexham is the reason for Monsieur Duvall's change of heart, and therefore the reason for a similar change in you, Sir Henry. If I am correct, and I

am sure that I am, then I would like you to tell me so, for I
believe that I have the right to know if my hotel is to be the
scene of an attempt to assassinate the duke.''

For a moment he was silent. ''You have evidently given
the matter a great deal of thought, Miss Lexham.''

''In between my various improper activities, sir, I have
obviously had little else to do,'' she replied coldly.

A faint humor gleamed momentarily in his hazel eyes.

''I am waiting, Sir Henry.''

''Very well, I admit that up to a certain point you are
correct, Miss Lexham, that is indeed why I am involved in
the banquet, it is indeed why I left the Oxenford. That is
where it all ends, however, for there has been reliable intelligence from France that if there had been a conspiracy here, it
was no longer to be put into operation.''

''But you are still at the Lexham, Sir Henry.''

''So I am, to be sure. That is because it has been deemed a
wise precaution, no more and no less. In the past there have
been very definite connections between Gaspard Duvall and
certain Bonapartist extremists.''

She stared at him. ''But that simply does not seem possible,
not of Monsieur Duvall!''

''Come now, Miss Lexham, do not be naive. He is a
Frenchman.''

''But—''

''Even a chef is allowed his political views and his patriotism,
madam; surely you will agree with that?''

''Yes.''

''Duvall supported Bonaparte and this political leaning
brought him into contact with some of those we now know to
have conspired to assassinate the duke. My brief, as you
describe it, was to keep an eye upon him, which is precisely
what I have been doing, to the best of my ability. It is now
firmly believed that there is no danger to the duke on this side
of the Channel, but, with your permission, of course, I intend
to remain here at the Lexham at least until after the banquet.''

''As a precaution?''

''Yes, Miss Lexham, as a precaution.''

''And was your intrusion into his room last night also
merely a precaution?''

His eyes were opaque. ''Yes. You need not concern yourself that your premises are to be the scene of a historic

murder, Miss Lexham. The name of your hotel will not go down in the annals of time as the place where the hero of Waterloo met his doom. Have I allayed your fears?"

"I suppose so." But as she spoke she knew that she was not entirely happy.

"Excellent," he said with some asperity. "Now we may terminate this disagreeable discussion. Good day to you, Miss Lexham." He stepped away, inclining his head with an outward appearance of courtesy for the benefit of anyone who might be looking, but in reality the gesture was insulting.

She fought back the tears as she watched him walk away across the flowery lawn.

Meanwhile a new arrival was approaching the doors of the Lexham Hotel, his rather battered and lowly hackney coach being greeted with curious and astonished glances by the two footmen as it turned into the wide courtyard. Weary and aching after his two-hundred-mile journey from Selford, Richard Marchand gazed out at the great house, unable to conceal the amazement he felt on seeing how splendid was his cousin Caroline's inheritance. Dismay followed closely upon the amazement, for if this was the life she now knew, what possible hope could he have of persuading her to return to Selford with him?

He alighted heavily at the steps, nodding at the porter, who tentatively inquired if he could be of any service. "Yes, you may inform Miss Lexham that Mr. Marchand is here."

"Very well, sir. If you will please take a seat?" The porter ushered him into the vestibule and indicated one of the comfortable sofas.

Richard sank wearily onto the sofa nearest the fireplace, glancing around unhappily at the elegant furnishings, the efficient waiters, and the little page boy who was searching for one of the guests, his high-pitched voice ringing out clearly.

Only seconds passed before Richard became suddenly and sharply aware of the conversation of two gentlemen seated nearby.

"And I tell you," said one, "that you would lose your wager. The lady has succumbed. She's Seymour's mistress, right enough. I knew that when I spoke to him about her yesterday at his sister's wedding. He was doing his damnedest to appear disinterested in her activities, but the opposite was obviously the case.''

''So you appear to think. I'm not so certain,'' replied his companion. ''I don't believe Caroline Lexham has succumbed to anyone—except maybe to her cousin, the earl, who incidentally, has suddenly rushed off out of Town again.''

''Forget Lexham,'' insisted the first man. ''It's Seymour whose name will come out of the hat, you mark my words.''

''I've followed your bright guesses before, Digby, and look where it's got me!'' grumbled the second man.

''This is no guess, my dear fellow, it's fact. Why else has he come rushing here? Why else does he pretend their friendship is platonic?''

''I don't follow—''

''The terms of the will, dear fellow! If she does anything slightly doubtful, then she loses this pile of bricks and mortar. *Ergo,* they make it appear that they mean nothing to each other.''

''Ah, I begin to see what you mean—''

''At this very moment they are out walking in the gardens together, and yet they would have us believe that they practically loathe each other. It's quite clear to me, dear fellow, that Caroline Lexham is Hal Seymour's mistress, which is what poor Marcia Chaddington must have known as well, hence her foolish prank at the wedding yesterday. If you still believe the contrary, then I suggest you put your money where your mouth is.''

''Oh, no, Digby, I won't rise to that. I admit defeat. I've come round to your way of thinking: the lady has indeed succumbed.''

At that moment Caroline herself came hurrying into the vestibule, her plain blue skirts rustling. ''Richard?'' Smiling, she came toward him, her hands extended.

Slowly he rose from his seat. ''Caroline?''

Digby and his companion looked uneasily at each other, wondering how much of their indiscreet conversation he had overheard, and therefore how much of it would be relayed to Caroline, who was evidently a very close friend.

She smiled. ''I trust your journey was not too wearisome.''

''It was as one would expect.''

''Is something wrong?''

"I think it is, Caroline, very wrong. I believe we should speak somewhere in private."

She stared up into his stern blue eyes. "Very well, if you will come this way." She led him to her private apartment, where she turned to face him, her hands clasped neatly before her. "Well?"

"It does not please me at all when the first thing I hear discussed on my arrival here is whether or not you are Sir Henry Seymour's mistress."

"I beg your pardon?" she asked faintly, her eyes widening.

"I am sure you heard me well enough, for poor hearing was never one of your afflictions, Caroline. Are you his mistress?"

"No!"

"But he is something to you, isn't he?"

"No." She looked away.

"Don't lie to me, Caroline, for that I find supremely insulting. I love you very much, too much to enjoy having to question you like this, but it simply isn't on to find that your name is being tossed around in wagers concerning chastity!"

"Don't be so pompous, Richard."

"Forgive me, but I fear I am not well versed in how one behaves in such circumstances."

"And don't be sarcastic either, for it does not suit you. I cannot help it if people make such wagers. All I can say is that I am not Sir Henry's mistress; indeed, I believe you will find that he loathes my very name."

"Yes, I understand that that is what the world is supposed to think."

"I am not telling you fibs, Richard," she said quietly, containing her anger because she knew his anxiety was indeed born of his love for her.

"What is Seymour to you?"

"Nothing."

"That is not so, and we both know it. I know you too well in some ways, Caroline, certainly well enough to know when you are attempting to pull the wool over my eyes."

She turned away with a sigh. "It isn't your eyes I attempt to draw the wool over," she said softly. "I believe it is my own. You want the absolute truth? Very well, you shall have it. I love Hal Seymour with all my heart, but he does not like or even respect me. He is not interested in me, Richard, and certainly would not wish to take me as his mistress. I tell you this, though, were he to crook his little finger, then I would run to him. I would be glad to be his mistress, Richard, glad. There, is that enough honesty for you?'' She looked at him again, her gray eyes very dark.

Slowly he nodded. ''Yes, it is enough.''

''I'm sorry, Richard, I don't want to hurt you—''

''I know.''

She went to him, taking his hands. ''I would have made you very unhappy, for I would have been always dissatisfied, always craving something you could not give me.''

His fingers closed around hers. ''Instead, you will make yourself unhappy, craving something you will never have.''

She lowered her eyes. ''At least only I will be responsible for my unhappiness, and not also for yours. You will get over me, Richard, and you will marry someone like Josephine Leyburn.''

''I cannot bear the creature.''

''She is just the sort of wife you need, Richard Marchand. Now then, we've said enough of all this, so let us begin our conversation again. Why, Richard, how good it is to see you again! I trust you had a not too wearisome journey!''

He was forced to laugh. ''You are incorrigible, Caroline Lexham, and I wonder if I will ever get over you, for as they say in the theater, you will be a very difficult act to follow!''

She pretended to look aghast. ''Why, Squire Marchand, what would you be knowing about such wicked places as theaters? What *would* Parson Aylesbury say? And should Goodwife Whittaker so much as learn one word, why the whole of Dartmoor woud soon learn of it!''

Still smiling, he pulled her close, his cheek resting against her little day bonnet. But she did not see how his smile slowly and thoughtfully faded. He loved her too much to be satisfied with accepting what she said; nothing would do but that he spoke with Sir Henry Seymour and learned for himself how things were.

''Sir Henry?''

Hal looked up from writing to see a tall, fair-haired young man dressed in good, but hardly fashionable attire. ''Sir?''

''Richard Marchand, squire of Selford. Your servant, sir.''

"Marchand? Ah, yes, Miss Lexham's cousin." Hal rose politely to his feet.

"I trust you will forgive this intrusion upon your privacy, Sir Henry, but I wished to thank you for having assisted my cousin on her journey to London."

"Think nothing of it, Mr. Marchand, for I did but do what any gentleman would have done." He felt he should say a little more. "Are you in Town for long?"

"A day or so, I merely came to see how she was."

"She appears to be very well, and certainly is making a success of her venture." Hal's hand indicated the surroundings.

"You—you are a guest, Sir Henry?"

Ah, so that was it. "Yes, Mr. Marchand, but through no actual choice, for I have charge of the forthcoming banquet, which the Duke of Wellington has decided must take place here now, instead of at the Oxenford. I shall be quitting the Lexham directly after the banquet, when I trust my house in Hanover Square will be ready."

Richard was perceptibly easier. "I trust the banquet will be a truly memorable occasion, Sir Henry."

Hal smiled just a little. "Not too memorable," he said softly. "That would not do at all."

Richard withdrew then, feeling satisfied that what Caroline had said was true, for whatever her feelings were, Sir Henry Seymour's were equally as plain: he did not care at all for her. Her honor and good name were not at risk.

Hal sat down again, picking up his pen, but after a moment he cast it down again, the force of the action spattering ink over the page. Would to God the banquet was over and done with and he could quit this damned house!

Caroline waited in her apartment. A table had been laid for two, but Richard was very late. Anxiously she stood by the window, looking out into the darkness of the spring night. Mrs. Hollingsworth had said that Richard was closeted in the library with Hal, and now she could only wait in dread to learn what had been said. Would Hal inform Richard of his true opinion of her? Would he relate to him the tale of her dealings with Dominic? Or worse, would Richard reveal to Hal the truth about her love for him? In an agony of suspense, she could only wait. Then she heard his step approaching.

He entered, smiling quickly at her. "Forgive me, Caroline, I know I am late."

Relief swept through her on seeing that smile. "You are forgiven, sir, especially as I have something to confess."

"Confess?"

"You are not to enjoy your favorite roast beef after all."

"Oh, Caroline! I especially asked—"

"Monsieur Duvall, the chef, threw back his hands in horror at the very suggestion that he should prepare such a plain English dish, and instead he has created something especially for tonight."

"Something French and covered in sauce," grumbled Richard.

"Don't be disagreeable and biased," she reproved. "For until you have tried French cooking, how can you possibly express an opinion. Sit down now, and behave yourself, Squire Marchand."

But as Gaspard personally carried in the first course, it was not of the dinner that she thought, it was of her overwhelming gladness that nothing had been said between Hal and Richard that would have any repercussions. Hal remained in ignorance of her love for him, and Richard had not been regaled with the tale of her apparently disreputable conduct. Her eyes were very bright as she raised her glass of wine, smiling across the table at her cousin.

Chapter 29

Richard remained at the Lexham for two more days and then he returned to Selford, and he and Caroline parted very amicably; indeed their friendship now at last appeared to be on the sort of footing she had always wanted, with him accepting once and for all that she would never take him as her husband. She still did not know what had passed between the two men, but she knew that somehow what Hal had said had put Richard's mind at rest. She knew she would never learn the truth from either man, for Richard behaved as if they had barely exchanged two words, and Hal was as remote and disdainful as he had so suddenly become on the night of the wedding.

Richard was not the only person to quit London that day; so also did Marcia, Lady Chaddington. Having attempted to destroy Caroline in front of witnesses, her failure had inevitably been as public, and by the day after the wedding, the story of what had happened was all over Town. She had become the laughingstock of the *beau monde* and her humiliation was made complete by the fact that Hal had rejected her. The dazzling, successful hostess, the beauty who had reigned for several Seasons and who could have expected to reign for several more, was by her own actions the butt of society's scorn, and she could not bear it. With the Season about to get into full swing, Lady Chaddington closed her beautiful Berkeley Square house and left London in an anonymous carriage, while her brother, feeling that a little too much of the ignominy had brushed off upon him, decided that it would be prudent to return to his own estates for a while.

Dominic's defeat was not so public a thing, but nevertheless he too had immediately removed himself from Town for a while, journeying back to County Durham to attend to "urgent" business there. His departure left Caroline free of her enemies for the first time since she had come to London, but she found no joy in the situation. The Lexham Hotel went from strength to strength as the days passed, providing the most luxurious and exclusive accommodation in Town, as well as the finest cuisine. The distinguished guests and visitors found the new enterprise to be everything they could have wished, and the other important hotels found that the rival they had scorned was a very worthy rival indeed. It seemed to Caroline that nothing could now prevent her from meeting the terms of her uncle's will so that when the allotted period of six months had passed, Lexham House would be hers and she would be a very wealthy woman. But it was a hollow glory, for she was more desperately unhappy than she had ever been in her life. Hal Seymour lodged beneath her roof, she saw him every day, and she endured the contempt in his eyes. She did not approach him, nor he her; it was as if they had never before met, never spoken, and certainly never laughed together. There were many nights when her misery was too great and she cried herself to sleep, her face hidden in the softness of her pillow.

One thing provided her with a welcome release from the pain, and that was the immense amount of preparation required for the great banquet. This might have caused her more distress, for by rights she should have dealt directly with Hal, but she chose instead to delegate this considerable responsibility to Mrs. Hollingsworth. The housekeeper had wondered greatly about this, but had begun to realize now that Hal Seymour was the cause of Caroline's unhappiness. And so each day Mrs. Hollingsworth consulted with him about the banquet, and each evening she sat with Caroline to discuss what had been said.

The banquet was set to be a much more dazzling and

important function than Jennifer's wedding had been, and glancing through the guest list, Caroline saw the names of nearly every gentleman of importance in the land, including several dukes. She realized with quite a jolt that the duke's request that she greet him on his arrival at the hotel meant that she would be the only woman present. Glancing through the guest list again, this time with even greater apprehension, she noticed a name she had missed before: Dominic would be present.

Gaspard was, naturally enough, of supreme importance where the banquet was concerned, and he and Caroline spent long hours discussing the complicated and immense menu called for by the importance of the occasion. She found it difficult to treat him exactly as she had before, for she could not forget what she now knew, but somehow it was hard to believe that there was anything sinister about him. He displayed no unease or secretiveness when speaking of the banquet or the Duke of Wellington, and in fact he seemed to be more jovial than usual, not having been indisposed with a headache or even the smallest of black moods for some time now. He enjoyed creating the menu, and his enthusiasm was quite infectious.

The menu was bewildering, and appeared to offer so many different dishes that no one could possibly sample them all without being decidedly ill for a week. There were to be four soups, two thick and two clear, hot *hors d'oeuvres* and cold *hors d'oeuvres*, intermediate fish courses, intermediate meat, poultry and game courses, and a variety of very splendid *entrées*. There were to be hot *rôts* and cold *rôts*, and last but not least, a seemingly endless list of delicious *entremets*, from *bombes*, *mousses*, and *sorbets* to cream flans, fruit tarts, jellies, and molds. And the *pièce de résistance*, Gaspard's *pièce montée* was to be a splendid confection called *gâteau Wellington*, which was to depict the moment of victory at Waterloo. He had prepared a rough drawing of this magnificent creation, which was to have cannon made of cake, chocolate barrels, standards fashioned from spun sugar and rice paper, and a statue of the Iron Duke himself, mounted on his charger Copenhagen, made entirely from sugar. Inside this *gâteau* was to be a filling of cherry ice with grapes and currants, and the whole thing was to be carried shoulder high to the table toward the end of the banquet and set down on a bed of crushed ice before the duke himself. This was to be the crowning glory of the banquet, and Caroline had to agree with the excited, pleased chef that it would indeed provide the whole evening with a fitting conclusion.

It was an unusually humid, close day for late March and the windows of Caroline's apartment were open as she and the chef discussed the details of the banquet menu. Outside not a leaf stirred on the trees, and sounds seemed to carry much further than usual. At last the whole menu had been discussed in depth and she agreed to all the chef's suggestions, including the *gâteau Wellington*, trusting as she did so that her account with Messieurs Coutts would not suffer too cataclysmic a shock.

Gaspard departed from her apartment in high spirits, determined to set about ordering some of the more particular ingredients immediately. The Severn salmon would come live from the supplier in Gloucester, the mullet from Harper's. The other fish would come only from McDonald's, the *foie gras* and truffles from Rimell's, and so on, each specific item coming from the tradesman who specialized in it. The orders had to be placed swiftly, for with the banquet set to take place in two weeks' time, the chef and his *brigade* had to be sure all the agreed-upon dishes could be provided.

Throughout the day everyone commented upon the unusually close weather, applying the word "thundery" even though there had been no rumble from the cloudy skies, no drop of heavy rain. In the evening the windows of the dining room stood open and the ladies busily employed their fans. Caroline was glad for once of the fashion for wearing the flimsiest lawn, silk, or muslin even in the depths of winter, for tonight such light materials were the very thing.

A group of young gentlemen had taken a private room for a dinner party, intent upon celebrating a handsome win by one of their number at the tables of a nearby gaming hell. Boisterous and a little merry, they insisted upon Caroline joining them, which eventually she did, for in spite of their being just a little the worse for drink, they were chivalrous and agreeable, toasting her health and making no unwelcome advances. The noisy little party had broken up at last at two in the morning, and Mrs. Hollingsworth joined Caroline to hand each gentleman a lighted candlestick. Laughing and shushing, the tipsy guests wended their unsteady way up to their rooms, and after a minute or two silence reigned throughout the house.

Caroline smiled at the housekeeper. "And so to our beds too, and I for one will sleep like the proverbial log." She saw the other's slightly withdrawn face. "Is something wrong, Mrs. Hollingsworth?"

"No. At least, not really—"

"Please tell me, for maybe I can help."

"It's nothing like that, it's simply that Gaspard is not himself at all tonight. In fact I think he is quite unwell."

Caroline stared. "Unwell? But when I discussed the banquet menu with him he seemed in excellent spirits."

"So he was, but that was before something very silly upset him."

"What?"

The housekeeper looked a little embarrassed. "It was so foolish, and the girl meant no harm—"

"Please explain, Mrs. Hollingsworth."

"Earlier tonight there was a flower woman in Mayfair Street and one of the footmen, who is stepping out with one of the parlor maids, bought a posy of violets for his sweetheart. She pinned them to her bodice and came into the kitchens. Gaspard took one look and became so upset and angry about it that he reduced the unfortunate girl to tears. Really, Miss Lexham, it was so unlike him that I fear he must be ill, especially as he then promptly retired to his bed with another headache."

"He has been working very hard, and today has been very close and humid. Perhaps that is all there was to it. He will be himself again by the morning, and he will probably be so kind to the poor maid in order to make up that he will reduce her to tears all over again. Now then, don't you worry anymore tonight."

Mrs. Hollingsworth smiled. "Thank you. I feel foolish for worrying now. Well, I suppose we should all retire to our beds now, for it is very late indeed, and I rather fancy that for that party of young gentlemen, there will be headaches of another sort come the morning."

Caroline laughed. "There will indeed, for it was not only the quantity that they celebrated with, it was the mixture. Good night, Mrs. Hollingsworth, and don't worry anymore about Gaspard."

"Good night, Miss Lexham."

Caroline watched the housekeeper hurry away in the direction of the butler's pantry entrance, and her smile faded a little unhappily. She could not help wishing that the housekeeper's heart was not so engaged by Gaspard Duvall. As she walked toward her own apartment, she hoped that her unease about the chef, caused simply and solely by what she had learned from Hal, was not well founded; in fact, she hoped that Hal was totally wrong about his past.

She lay awake in her bed, the draperies still tied back and the window open just a little to allow a small draft of air from outside. Her hair was brushed loose and not enclosed in a night bonnet, and she lay there, gazing up at the bed's immense canopy. She heard a nearby church clock sound half past two, and then three, and she heard the watch patrolling Mayfair Street, calling out that all was well. She was very tired, but sleep was elusive. A low, distant rumble of thunder heralded the approach at last of the promised storm, and a movement of air stirred the trees in the avenues and squares, creeping into her room and moving the curtains just a little.

Her eyes began to close. The sound of breaking glass or china carried clearly to her ears from somewhere in the house, and her eyes flew open again immediately. Alert now, she listened carefully, but there was only silence. She considered trying to sleep again, but something about the noise she had heard made her get out of the bed, pulling her shawl around her shoulders. Someone was moving about in the house, and there should not have been anyone at this hour. Maybe it was a guest, perhaps one of the drunken revelers, in which case she would see if she could be of some assistance; or maybe it was someone who had no right to be there at all, someone like a thief. . . .

She slipped stealthily from her apartment, crossing the deserted, shadowy vestibule like a white ghost in her nightgown. Silently she entered the red saloon, but all was quiet and undisturbed, as was the library and the dining room. Not an ornament was out of place. She was about to go back to her apartment when her glance fell upon the fragments of porcelain on the floor beneath the Ionic colonnade at the rear of the dining room. Swiftly she bent to inspect them, recognizing them as once having been a comfit dish which had been kept upon the Sheraton sideboard next to the entrance to the butler's pantry and the offices beyond.

Puzzled, she straightened once more, glancing nervously around. Someone had knocked the dish to the floor and that was what had disturbed her; but who could it have been? And where was he or she now? She stood motionless, gazing carefully at the inky shadows, but there was no movement, no sign of anything. Then, very softly, came the sound of a door opening somewhere in the kitchens, and she whirled about with a gasp. There was definitely someone in there! Her heart began to beat more swiftly as with one hand she gathered the thick folds of her nightgown and with the other eased open the door of the butler's pantry. Outside the storm was nearer, a clap of thunder breaking loudly overhead and reverberating eerily through the house.

Raindrops spattered against the window as she passed through the silent kitchens, where in the daytime all was bustle and noise, and she gave a stifled gasp as a sudden jagged flash of lightning pierced the darkness. For a moment she thought of calling out to Mrs. Hollingsworth, whose rooms lay nearby, but something kept her silent. The seconds passed and she gradually became aware of voices, French voices raised in anger. Recognizing one as Gaspard's, she slipped through the laundry rooms toward the quiet, rather isolated room the chef had elected to occupy. The nearer she came to his room, the more she realized that the other raised voice belonged to Boisville, the strangely insubordinate subordinate who thought nothing of stating his disagreement with his superior. She reached the small passage where the chef's room lay. Candlelight shone from beneath the door. Abruptly she halted, her breath catching silently in her throat, for by that faint light she could distinctly see the figure of a man pressed against the wall, an eavesdropper whom she recognized very clearly indeed. It was Hal. He was so intent upon listening to what was being said that he was not aware of her. For a moment she could not move; she could only stare at him in dismay. He had not told her the truth that day in the garden, there *was* still some suspicion about the chef.

At that moment the argument seemed to come to an end and there was the sound of a chair scraping against the stone floor. The candlelight swayed as one of the men inside picked up the candlestick, and in that split second she knew that Hal would have to retreat from his place, and when he did so he would see her. Even as she turned to flee, he caught a glimpse of a phantomlike figure in white, its honey-colored hair easy to recognize.

With a smothered curse, he pursued her, moving with such speed that he had quitted the small passageway before the door opened and the chef and Boisville emerged. Caroline had reached the dining room before Hal caught her, and her breath was stopped with a jerk as he seized her by the hand and swung her roughly back into his arms, folding her in an embrace and pressing his lips urgently over hers. He held her body close to his, his fingers coiling in the soft, warm hair at the nape of her neck, and there was nothing she could do to struggle free, nothing she could do to even move, so strong was he. Helplessly she pushed her hands against his chest, but to no avail. She heard the two Frenchmen approach, obviously meaning to clear away the porcelain from the broken comfit dish. The candlelight flickered, became still as they halted in surprise upon seeing what was apparently a lovers' tryst, and then flickered again, becoming more faint as they retreated.

For a long moment Hal continued to hold her in that ardent, but hollow embrace, and then slowly he released her. Furiously she made to strike his face, but he caught her wrist.

"Now is neither the time nor the place, Caro."

"Don't you presume to call me that!" she breathed. "And how *dare* you lay hands upon me in this way!"

"Don't be irritatingly difficult," he snapped, his tone low and urgent. "I could do without any more problems." Glancing in the direction of the butler's pantry, he took her wrist again, drawing her out of the dining room toward her own private apartment, thrusting her inside, and closing the door firmly behind them both.

"Now you may say your piece, madam," he said. "And I trust that it will be brief and to the point."

"Oh, it will!" she replied angrily. "And it will be in the form of a question. Why did you lie to me?"

"Lie?"

"About suspicion falling upon Gaspard."

"For God's sake, will you lower your tone. We may be private here, but not that private."

"Very well," she said more restrainedly. "Why did you fob me off in the garden?"

"I didn't fob you off."

"Then why are you creeping around at night, eavesdropping upon him and then laying rough hands upon me in order to silence me about your activities?"

"You have the answer to the last in your own question," he said coldly. "It was done in order to keep you quiet."

She flushed. "A word would have sufficed to achieve that, sir."

"The action I took seemed more certain of success."

Her body stiffened. "And what might that remark be taken to mean, Sir Henry?"

"Merely that in order to be absolutely sure that you did not utter an unwise word at a very inopportune moment, I chose to prevent all chance by kissing you. That is all." His hazel eyes rested on her. "Which brings me to wonder why you were abroad at such a time."

"I heard the comfit dish break and came to investigate."

He gave a short laugh. "The damned cat did it."

"The cat?"

He nodded. "Marcia's rat. It seems that Duvall is in the habit of letting the wretched creature back in when it has been put out for the night. He gives it a dish of milk and lets it remain in his room. Tonight it slipped through from the kitchens, jumped onto the sideboard, and knocked the dish over. Duvall and Boisville chased after it, saw what had happened, and went to get something to clear up the bits, and it was then that they fell to arguing." Again he gave a short laugh. "Arguing about a damned cake."

"Cake?"

"A *pièce montée* apparently."

"The *gâteau Wellington*?"

"I believe so. They disagreed about when it should be served, who should help to carry it, where exactly it should be placed upon the table and so on. A blasted culinary discussion! If I'd known that, I could have remained in my bed in comfort."

"Which brings me back to my original question, Sir Henry. Why did you lie to me?"

"I did not lie to you, Miss Lexham."

"You did, sir, for you told me that there was no longer any suspicion where my chef was concerned."

"I said that in the past he had had doubtful connections, but that reliable intelligence had been received that there was no longer a conspiracy here. I also said that I intended to remain here until after the banquet, which inevitably means, Miss Lexham, that I will continue to keep a weather eye open. Tonight was merely another wise precaution, one of many I take. I saw the light in Duvall's window at past three in the morning and thought it worthy of investigation. The rest you know."

She fell silent, for his words had the ring of truth about them.

"I trust that you are satisfied now, madam."

"With your explanation? Yes, Sir Henry."

"Do I detect a qualification in your voice?"

"Yes, sir, you do." She faced him, her anger still burning strongly. "How could I be otherwise satisfied with you, Sir Henry, when I know that you hold an opinion of me which is entirely wrong? I am totally innocent of the immodest behavior of which you accuse me, and of which you still silently accuse me with each cold glance and each contemptuous word. I am no more guilty of having encouraged my cousin to embrace me than I was of encouraging you—or will you now say that I welcomed your attentions tonight, indeed that I responded to them? You have tried and condemned me without a hearing, sir, and with the true arrogance of your sex, which believes itself to be above reproach and believes womankind to be weak and untrustworthy. I will be glad when you leave this house, Sir Henry Seymour, more glad than you will ever know, for at the moment I find your presence both unwelcome and insulting. Now, if you please, I wish you to leave this apartment. Good night, sir."

For a moment he looked at her, his expression impenetrable. "Good night, Caro."

"You do not have my permission to ever address me again by that name."

His inclined his head and withdrew, leaving her standing there alone in the center of the unlit room. Through the slightly open window she could hear the rain falling, and in the distance the thunderstorm, following the course of the Thames. She did not cry this time; she felt unable to weep anymore. But her heart wept with love for Hal Seymour, a love that would never die and would never be returned.

Chapter 30

The evening of the banquet approached with almost alarming rapidity, and the last-minute preparations made life at the hotel very hectic indeed. Now it became impossible for Caroline to deal only indirectly with Hal, for there were simply too many details to be finalized, but she carried these painful meetings off by being always strictly correct, observing every tiny rule of etiquette, and seeming to deliberately distance herself from him. But if that was the outward impression her conduct gave, inside the story was still sadly unchanged. Each time she saw him she wanted to reach out to him, she wanted to tell him how much she loved him, she wanted to feel his arms around her and his lips over hers; but all these things were forever denied her and so she hid the truth behind a facade of cool indifference. His manner toward her remained more or less the same as it had been since the night his sister had married. He was polite, but not warm, he afforded her all the necessary courtesies, but he did not smile at her—and never once did he call her Caro.

In this strained atmosphere, they dealt successfully with all the details, their discussions covering every minute of the evening, from the moment the duke's carriage and its escort of light dragoons arrived, to the moment they departed again in the small hours.

The duke's small procession would inevitably be followed into the courtyard by a considerable crowd. There would be servants carrying *flambeaux,* and the flanking buildings would be bedecked with colored lanterns. The house itself would be ablaze with lights, and the grand balcony would be swathed in patriotic red, white, and blue silk and made bright with more lanterns. From this vantage point young girls would scatter rose petals down upon the duke as he alighted at the steps below, ascending to the doorway on a carpet of flowers and leaves to be greeted by Caroline. They would then proceed through the vestibules between an avenue of orange trees, surrounded by walls decorated with military standards and union jacks, and all the while an orchestra would be playing "Rule Britannia."

It had been agreed with the duke that to satisfy the demands of the adoring crowd in the courtyard, he would make an appearance on the grand balcony. After this, he would descend once more to enter the dining room, once again to triumphant music from the orchestra.

The dining room would be a vision of splendor, its walls draped with scarlet and gold velvet, adorned with military standards and laurel wreaths. There would be flowers everywhere, white carnations, scarlet roses, and blue hyacinths, and on the three long tables that replaced the single one of mahogany, there would be snowy-white cloths and countless tall wax tapers in silver-gilt stands. On a dais opposite the Ionic colonnade and the entrance to the butler's pantry would be the table where the guests-of-honor would sit. Their backs would be to the windows, and the great curtains would be tightly closed, forming a perfect background to the magnificent canopy that would be above the duke's seat. This canopy had been retrieved from the cellars, where it had lain almost forgotten for many years, having originally been made for an entertainment for the Prince of Wales given by Caroline's late uncle. Made of gold-fringed crimson velvet, it was to be adorned with the badges of the duke's favorite regiments, and would make a splendid setting for the hero of Waterloo and the Peninsular War.

When all the guests were seated at their laurel-garlanded tables, the banquet would commence, proceeding through the elaborate menu, to end with the triumphant carrying in of the *pièce montée*, the huge *gâteau Wellington* which promised to be the highlight of the whole evening. It would be borne in by four men and placed before the duke, and there it would be revealed that it was no ordinary *gâteau* but a display of miniature illuminations. At the touch of a lighted spill carried by Gaspard himself, various little candles would cast living light over the confectionery cannon and the equestrian statue of the duke, thus creating the effect of those final moments of victory at Waterloo. This moment was bound to bring rapturous and appreciative applause from a gathering which would have enjoyed a most memorable feast and which had drunk toast after toast with the late Earl of Lexham's diminishing supply of champagne, and it would bring to an end an occasion that should earn the efforts of the Lexham Hotel the acclaim its staff richly deserved.

For Caroline, however, there was a constant and unsettling feeling of apprehension, born not only from the importance of the occasion and the eminence of the many guests, but also of her knowledge of Hal's secret duty. She could not entirely shake off the fear that the conspirators had carried off a successful deception, that something dreadful was to take place at the banquet after all. She felt this when she saw Gaspard and knew that his dark mood had not entirely left him, and she felt it when Hal questioned her very closely about the *pièce montée*, having become very interested suddenly on learning that it was to be lighted. He did not say anything, but she knew that his inevitable suspicion was that it contained more than mere candles; it would not have been the first time that an enemy had chosen to annihilate an opponent in an explosion. These things made her nervous, and she knew that she would not be able to breathe easily again until she saw the duke's carriage leaving through the gateway into Mayfair Street. `

This unease was with her on the day of the banquet, when everything was in readiness and she was dressing in her apartment. Outside the lanterns had been lighted and the courtyard was bathed with lights of different colors. It was a fine, clear evening, without any wind and of just the right amount of coolness. Lowering the curtain into place once more, she turned to look at her reflection in the cheval glass. Her gown was made of delicate white muslin, sprigged with a

delicate design of tiny golden stitches. Its waistline was very
high beneath her breasts and was drawn in by a golden string.
The neckline was low but not immodest, and the sleeves were
very full and diaphanous, gathered in tightly at her wrists.
She wore no jewelry, for she had none, and the only adorn-
ment was in her hair, where she had pinned a few red roses,
stolen from the flowers ordered for the banquet. She surveyed
herself in the mirror for a little longer and then picked up the
shawl. She just had time to visit the kitchens and see that all
was well before the guests were due to arrive.

She crossed the vestibule with its walls of standards and
union jacks, the scent of the foliage of the orange trees filling
the air, and made her way toward the kitchens, where the
bustle was immense as final garnishes were placed upon the
cold dishes and where the ingredients were being prepared for
the hot dishes that had to be cooked at the very last moment.
The smell of cooking was quite delicious as Caroline approached along a passage lined with narrow tables upon
which stood domed silver dishes waiting to be borne into the
banquet.

In the kitchens everyone went efficiently about their allotted tasks, and Gaspard, looking pale and tense, gave brief
orders which were instantly and unquestioningly carried out.
Boisville, as the *entremettier*, was overseeing the assistants
who were preparing the soups, and he hardly glanced up as
Caroline entered. She had barely stepped into the room,
however, when there was a knocking at the garden door, and
Mrs. Hollingsworth hurried to see who it was. Caroline could
see her at the door, although she could not see who was
there, and noticing the housekeeper's puzzled expression and
shaking head, she went to discover what was going on.

"What is it, Mrs. Hollingsworth?"

"This fellow is from Covent Garden market; he says he's
delivering our last-minute order."

"But there is no last-minute order," said Caroline, looking
curiously at the redheaded young man who stood there, a
covered basket at his feet, his cap twisting nervously in his
hands. "What order is it supposed to be?"

"Violets, ma'am, twenty-five posies." He removed the
cloth from the basket and she saw the neat little bunches of
purple flowers.

"We did not order them; there has been some mistake."

"No mistake, ma'am, the man said we was to deliver twenty-five posies of violets to the Lexham Hotel before the banquet tonight. This is the Lexham Hotel, ain't it?"

"Yes, but—"

"Then I've done what I was sent to do. Here you are." He picked up the basket and thrust it into Caroline's hands, then before she could say anything more, he turned on his heel and hurried away across the kitchen garden, through the wicket gate, and on toward the mews lane, soon vanishing from sight among the shadows between the lanterns in the trees.

"Well!" declared Mrs. Hollingsworth crossly. "Did you ever see the like of it? We did not place this order and we certainly will not be paying for it; I'll see to that!"

"We'd better take the basket inside," said Caroline, turning back into the busy kitchen, where she placed it upon the floor in a relatively quiet corner. She saw Boisville turn, his glance going swiftly to the contents of the basket and then immediately toward Gaspard. The chef had paused in the middle of chopping some herbs. His face had drained of what little color it had and he was staring at the innocuous violets as if they were venomous snakes.

"Gaspard?" asked Mrs. Hollingsworth quickly, hurrying toward him. "Whatever is the matter? You look quite dreadful."

The chef did not reply. His eyes were haunted as he dragged them away from the basket at last and looked straight at Boisville. His hand trembled as he put the herb chopper slowly down.

The kitchens had become very quiet suddenly as everyone looked at the chef. The only sound was the bubbling of the pans upon the ranges and the sizzling of the various joints upon the slowly turning spits.

Mrs. Hollingsworth became alarmed. "Gaspard? Are you unwell?"

Still the chef did not say anything, but he seemed filled with dread. Boisville stepped forward then. "I fear, madam, that Monsieur Duvall is—how do you say?—superstitious?"

"Superstitious?" asked Caroline. "About what?"

"Violets, mademoiselle."

"But that is nonsense," she replied firmly.

"Nevertheless, mademoiselle, to him they are an omen of great ill."

"They are only flowers," she said, turning to Gaspard. "Monsieur?"

At last he spoke. "F-forgive me, mademoiselle, but I cannot help . . ." Again his hollow eyes moved toward Boisville's cold, unsmiling face.

"I will have the violets removed," she said then, her tone brisk, but as she turned to do just that, Gaspard shook his head.

"They have come into the house, mademoiselle, their task is done."

"Task? What task? What are you talking about?"

He made a great effort to recover, picking up the herb chopper again and managing a small smile. "It is of no matter." But his tone lacked all conviction and both Caroline and Mrs. Hollingsworth knew that it mattered very much indeed. Caroline looked swiftly at Boisville, who silently returned to his own duties, and as Gaspard brought the chopper down upon the herbs, the whole kitchen began to go about its tasks once more.

Caroline and Mrs. Hollingsworth exchanged glances, and Caroline knew that the housekeeper was wondering exactly the same as she was: who had ordered the violets, and why had they done so? For a moment she considered the possibility that this was the work of one of her enemies—perhaps a final effort from Marcia, or maybe it could be Dominic—but somehow she knew that it had nothing to do with them. Whoever had sent the violets had done so for an entirely different motive. But what?

She had no time to think more on the problem, for a footman came looking for her at that moment to tell her that the guests were beginning to arrive. Swiftly she told Mrs. Hollingsworth to remove the basket of violets from Gaspard's sight, and with a final despairing glance at his ashen, agitated face, she left the kitchens to take up her position in the vestibule. The great banquet was about to begin.

Chapter 31

The distinguished guests had all taken their places and awaited the arrival of the duke. The light of hundreds of tall wax tapers glittered on military orders, glowed on the scarlet uniforms of generals and the dark blue of admirals, shone upon the somber garb of bishops, and showed up to perfection the elegant clothes of earls, lords, and dukes. The orchestra played softly in the background and the dining room hummed with the low sound of male conversation.

Quivering with apprehension and toying nervously with her reticule, Caroline waited in the outer vestibule, her heart beating more swiftly as she distinctly heard the sound of distant cheering from the darkness outside. Nodding her head at the porter, she watched as the doors were opened, revealing the brightly lit courtyard and the smoking *flambeaux* of the servants lining the path the duke's carriage and escort would take.

At last she heard the clatter of hooves and the splendidly uniformed light dragoons rode beneath the pedimented gateway, followed by the landau drawn by four black horses, and behind this poured the excited crowd, shouting and cheering their hero. With only Hal at his side, the duke glanced neither

to the right nor the left as the carriage rolled across th
courtyard toward the flower-strewn steps of the hotel.

Caroline turned once, sensing Mrs. Hollingsworth's presence
Her eyes met the housekeeper's a little questioningly, bu
Mrs. Hollingsworth shook her head, thus conveying to Caro
line the unwelcome news that all was not well in the kitchens
Caroline's pulse quickened and she took a deep breath t
steady herself, forcing a smile to her lips as the carriage cam
to a halt and she stepped forward to greet the duke, as he ha
asked.

From the balcony above, the young girls showered th
duke and Hal with rose petals, and the pressing, excite
crowd cheered again. As before, the duke looked taller tha
he was, and tonight he also looked very dignified in navy
blue velvet, with a sapphire-blue sash across his breast and
magnificent silver star pinned over his heart. Beside him, Ha
wore discreet black, the diamond pin in his lace-edged crava
not in any way vying with the duke's decoration.

The two men mounted the flowery steps and Caroline san
into a deep curtsy, one which she had been practicing tim
after time in the cheval glass in her apartment. She avoide
looking at Hal.

"Welcome to the Lexham Hotel, Your Grace."

Smiling, the duke bent to raise her, drawing her hand to hi
lips. "By Gad, Miss Lexham, you look dazzling. What sa
you, Seymour, eh?"

"Quite dazzling," was the cool response.

Momentarily her eyes met his, and then she looked deliber
ately away again, not revealing by so much as a flicker th
easy hurt he inflicted with that bland indifference.

The duke drew her hand through his arm, glancing wit
approval at the embellishments of the vestibule. "You'v
done me proud, m'dear, I thank 'e."

Her whole body quivered invisibly as she proceeded be
tween the avenue of orange trees on the duke's arm, th
strains of "Rule Britannia" echoing all around. They wer
slowly up the grand staircase and out onto the balcony, wher
an immediate delighted roar went up from the huge thron
pressed into the courtyard. Hats were thrown into the ai
arms waved and coats were shaken aloft, and the duke stoo
impassively accepting the adulation. He smiled just a little
inclining his head several times, and he certainly did n

strain himself greatly to win their rapturous applause, but for all that there was something singularly dramatic and inspiring about him. He commanded them all simply by being there, just as he had done on many a field of battle. He won confidence, loyalty, and reverence, and he did so just by being himself.

Caroline stood nervously behind him, thinking how very vulnerable he was and how he might have done better to have taken Hal's advice and forgone this public appearance where he was so easy a target from anywhere in the milling crowd. Glancing at Hal, she saw how alert he was, how his glance moved constantly over the sea of faces below, watchful for anything which might offer that final danger to the duke. She sensed his relief as the duke withdrew at last into the greater safety of the hotel.

"Damn me," remarked the duke lightly. "I thought this banquet was to be private."

Hal smiled. "You are not permitted to be private, Your Grace."

"Not yet," was the dry reply. "But there'll be a time soon enough when the shine wears off me reputation. Everyone loves a soldier when there's war, but they'll kick him in the pants when peace returns." He glanced out through the closed windows once again. "By Gad," he murmured, "I felt decidedly exposed out there, Seymour, and I began to feel your warnings should have been heeded. Still, it went off handsomely, eh?"

"Yes, Your Grace."

"You'll have heard, of course, that that rascal Cantillon refuses to say a word."

"Yes, but then he wouldn't if he had accomplices still free, would he?"

The duke nodded sagely. "That's only too correct, but in spite of that I believe he will soon go free."

Caroline was unable to smother her gasp of astonishment. "Go free?" she asked in amazement. "But how could that possibly be?"

"Because, m'dear, to convict him we need evidence, and although everyone knows he's as guilty as hell itself, no one will come forward. In these virtuous days, the greatest crime a man can commit in France is to denounce another, even though the crime should be a plot to assassinate a third

person. Cantillon will go free.'' He gave one of his unexpected whoops of laughter. ''Why, it wouldn't surprise me i
Bonaparte remembered the scoundrel in his will!'' Still
chuckling, he offered her his arm once more. ''Shall we go
down to the bean feast, m'dear?''

Her gold-spangled muslin skirts dragging softly behind her
she descended the staircase at the duke's side, parting from
him at the entrance of the crowded banqueting room. Chairs
scraped as the gathering rose as one to respectfully applaud as
the duke made his way to the place of honor beneath the
canopy. His progress to the dais was accompanied by the
strains of a triumphant march.

Caroline stood at the doorway for a moment, and then
slipped unnoticed to stand beneath the Ionic colonnade, close
to the entrance to the butler's pantry. The moment the banquet
began, she would go to the kitchens and see how Gaspard
was.

The assembly sat down once more and there was a great
deal of shuffling and clearing of throats, and in that moment
she became aware that someone in the midst of the gathering
was looking at her. It was not a pleasant sensation, and with a
slight shiver she searched the room. At last she met those
staring eyes, so gray, like her own. Dominic's handsome face
was as chill and full of loathing as it had been when first they
had met. He made no pretense now of liking her; his gaze
was steady and did not waver at all; it was Caroline who
looked away first. To her relief, the line of waiters carrying
the first courses made their entrance, and as the last one
passed into the room, a silver dish borne expertly aloft on his
left hand, she gathered her skirts and hurried along the passageway toward the kitchens.

The atmosphere was strained and it soon became apparent
to her that Gaspard was so upset still that he was, unbelievably
close to collapse. Mrs. Hollingsworth was anxiously fussing
around him as he sat in a chair by the fireplace, his face
hidden in his hands and his shoulders bowed. There was an
air of wretchedness about him that affected Caroline greatly
as she crouched beside him and put a gentle hand upon his
jaunty-checkered sleeve.

''Monsieur?''

Slowly he raised his head. ''It is no use, mademoiselle,''

he whispered, his voice almost lost in the bustle of the kitchens as the efficient *brigade* continued without supervision.

"What is wrong?" she asked anxiously. "Surely it isn't the violets."

"But yes," he replied brokenly. "It is the violets." He looked away, his eyes filled with that hollowness she had seen earlier. "Never before have I so hated one of God's creations. A little flower . . ."

Perplexed, Caroline straightened, looking helplessly into the housekeeper's distraught eyes. "Perhaps he would be better lying down, for to be sure it does him no good to sit here like this."

"I will take him to my rooms, they are closer than his own, and I will be able to go and see how he is more easily."

"Very well, do that. Can everything go on without him?" Caroline glanced around the busy kitchen.

"Yes, that Boisville fellow has taken over."

Caroline said nothing more as Mrs. Hollingsworth coaxed Gaspard to his feet, gently persuading him to accompany her to her rooms. Before he left, he turned once more to Caroline. "Forgive me, mademoiselle, please forgive me."

"Of course I forgive you," she replied, seeing how his haunted eyes flew toward Boisville, who had watched and listened all the while, and whose presence was quite obviously lending an extra edge to Gaspard's fear, for fear it was that had brought the chef to this piteous state.

With a heavy heart, Caroline walked back along the passage, taking up an advantageous position in a shadowy corner of the butler's pantry. From here, by looking in a mirror on a nearby wall, she could see all that was happening in the dining room, which for this one night had become a grand banqueting hall. She could watch the proceedings in complete safety, for no one at the magnificent tables could see her.

For a while she almost forgot Gaspard as she watched the banquet. The many tapers flickered in the rising heat and she could clearly see the flash of the silver star on the duke's breast as he turned to speak to Hal, seated some distance away at the end of the dais. She gazed at Hal, able to do so only because she knew he could not see her. How very handsome he was, and how easily that lazy, almost cynical smile of his twisted in her heart like a knife. Why had everything to be the way it was? Why couldn't fate have

decreed that he should look at her with that same love no
reflecting so plainly in her own eyes? Suddenly the remot
ness and tranquillity of Selford seemed a blessed haven, a
it was the first time she had felt like that since leaving
those weeks ago. Weeks? Sometimes it seemed that she ha
dreamed of Dartmoor, that London was the only life she ha
ever known—and that Hal Seymour was the only thing ev
to have been of deep and lasting consequence to her. Gazir
at him now, the utter futility and hopelessness of her lo
washed painfully over her, and she forced herself to lo
away.

The waiters filed past her once more, bearing aloft anoth
impressive array of dishes. Course followed course as sl
stood there, and all the while the orchestra played discreet
in the background, the soft notes almost drowned by the de
drone of male conversation. In spite of the upset with Gaspar
the banquet was going very well indeed, thanks to the eff
ciency and skill of his wonderful *brigade de cuisine*.

The cheese course was served and she realized with son
surprise that the evening had been in progress for nearly tw
and a half hours now. All that remained to be served were t
entremets, consisting of the magnificent array of hot and co
desserts over which Boisville had been in charge, and tl
appearance of poor Gaspard's prized *pièce montée*. Sadly sl
reflected that in his present state, the chef would not be ab
personally to light the candles on the *gâteau*, and wou
therefore forfeit the moment of glory he so richly deserve
for all the work he had put into the banquet.

She heard a discreet cough at her elbow, and turned to s
Boisville standing there. "Yes?" she inquired, unable to qui
conceal the dislike she so instinctively felt for this reptili
Frenchman.

"Forgive the intrusion, mademoiselle, but there is a sma
problem."

"Problem?"

"It concerns the *pièce montée*. I fear that the filling
cherry ice is proving difficult to keep frozen. I think that
would be best if it was served with the *entremets*. By that
mean that it should immediately follow them to the tables ar
not be delayed until they have been virtually finished."

"What does Monsieur Duvall say?"

He did not reply, but expressively shrugged his shoulders

"He is still unwell?" she asked, knowing in her heart that this had to be so.

"Most unwell, mademoiselle, but then he is a very super-stitious man."

"So it would seem," she replied, disliking him intensely. "Very well, you may serve the *pièce montée* directly after the *entremets*."

His smile was almost sleek as he bowed to her and retreated, making as little sound as he had when approaching her. She contained the urge to shudder and returned her attention to the banquet. She watched as toasts were drunk and the gentlemen then relaxed to linger over their cheese. At last the line of efficient waiters spirited away the remnants and the tables were cleared in readiness for the numerous desserts.

"Miss Lexham! Come quickly!" Her attention was drawn sharply away from the banquet by the sound of Mrs. Hollingsworth's low, urgent voice.

"What is it?"

"It's Gaspard, madam, he's in a terrible way now and he's saying things I think you should hear."

Caroline's blood almost froze at the fear contained in those few words. "Things? What things?"

"It's a matter of life and death, Miss Lexham, and you must come right away."

Caroline gazed in growing horror at the trembling, ashen-faced woman, and without another word followed her along the passage in the direction of her rooms.

Unknown to either of them, their brief exchange had been overheard. A stealthy, elegantly clad shadow slipped from the brightness of the banquet into the relative quiet of the butler's pantry. Dominic Lexham's honey-colored hair was unmistakable as he moved silently after the two women. From his place at the table he had witnessed the housekeeper's hurrying, anxious approach along the passage, and his curiosity had been immediately aroused. Now he was intent upon learning what lay behind their intriguing words.

Chapter 32

Gaspard had broken down completely. He rocked to and fro, whispering to himself as if in prayer, and his whole body shook as if he were ice cold. There was no trace now of the buoyant, cheerful little chef whose charm and kindliness had won him so many friends and admirers. Now he was stricken, overwhelmed with some dreadful fear and guilt, and it was too much for him to bear.

Mrs. Hollingsworth went to him, kneeling on the floor before his chair and lovingly taking his hands. "Gaspard, my love?" she said gently. "Gaspard, you must tell Miss Lexham what you told me."

His tormented eyes fled to Caroline's anxious face. "I cannot," he whispered, shaking his head, "I cannot say it—"

"You must, it's too important."

Tears shone in his soft, melting brown eyes and at last he gave a barely perceptible nod. "I cannot go on with the lies, mademoiselle. I have tried to do as they wish, but now I cannot. Until today, I hoped—I *prayed*—that nothing would come of it after all; now when they sent the violets, I knew that I would have to do their bidding."

"The violets? What do the flowers mean?" asked Caroline, although in her heart she was beginning to guess the answer.

"They were a signal, mademoiselle. Bonaparte once said that when the violets were in bloom, he would return to France. Violets have become the emblem of his followers." He sat forward urgently, his face tormented with the fear and guilt that tortured him. "They have my mother and my sisters, mademoiselle, and they said that if I did not do as they wished, my family would be killed. What was I to do? I am a Frenchman, I love my country, but I am no longer a Bonapartist. I have seen how his grand designs have ruined my country and never would I willingly lend my support to his cause. But I love my mother and my sisters. Their lives depend upon me!" Tears shone on his pale cheeks as he gazed imploringly at her. "I do not wish to be the instrument of their death, but nor do I wish to be part of the assassination of the Duke of Wellington. I hoped, dear God how I hoped, that they would not need to call upon me after all, that their plots would be confined to France, but I began to fear the worst when Cantillon was arrested. Today my fears were realized, for the violets meant that the plan would have to be carried out after all. I am upon the rack, Mademoiselle Lexham, and my body, my heart, and my soul are being torn apart by the burden I am forced to bear."

Caroline could only respond sympathetically to the wretchedness in his eyes, and she believed every word he said. "I'm so sorry, monsieur," she said gently. "Believe me I am, but you must realize that I have to ask you what they plan to do, and when they intend doing it."

His lips trembled and he looked faint at the thought of betraying his countrymen, but Mrs. Hollingsworth drew his hands to her lips, kissing both and looking up into his eyes, her great love for him written plainly upon her face, which in that moment was softened to a great beauty. "I love you, Gaspard," she whispered, "and nothing you have said or done will ever change that."

His fingers tightened convulsively around hers and he smiled a little, seeming to find strength in her love. He looked up at Caroline. "It is Boisville, mademoiselle; he is the assassin." He glanced at the clock on the mantelpiece. "You have time enough, for it is to take place when he accompanies *pièce montée* to the duke. Originally he was to have been one of the four men carrying it, but now he will probably take my place and appear to be there only to light the candles upon it. Instead he will draw a pistol and he will shoot the duke. At that range he will be sure to kill him instantly."

Caroline stared at him, a numbness settling coldly over her. "But we have no time at all," she whispered, "for Boisville has changed the plans. The *pièce montée* will already be on its way to the dais!" Gathering her skirt, she fled to the door.

Mrs. Hollingsworth rose swiftly to her feet, her concern only for Gaspard. "But, Miss Lexham, what about Gaspard? We cannot let them know about him."

Caroline paused for the briefest of seconds. "Keep him here, hide him, I'll do what I can." Then she had gone, her heart pounding in her breast. Pray God she would be in time! Pray *God*!

Dominic emerged slowly from the shadows nearby. He had overheard everything and now his mind was racing. Somehow he must turn all this to his own advantage. Somehow there had to be a way of defeating his beautiful but tenacious cousin and of winning back his property. His gray eyes were sharp and shrewd, lightening a little as he made his way back toward the banquet.

She could hear the applause long before she reached the doorway of the butler's pantry. In the brilliantly lit banqueting hall, all eyes were turned toward the dais. In a frozen moment she saw the duke, she saw Hal, she saw the magnificent *pièce montée* resting on its bed of ice, its little illuminations flickering over the lifelike battle scene; and she saw Boisville, his attention solely upon the duke. His hand began to move slowly toward the inside of his coat.

With a scream of warning she hurried into the blinding light, and it was Hal's name that was on her lips. Everyone turned sharply toward her, a stir passing through the assembly. Hal moved like lightning, darting to the startled duke and flinging him bodily from his seat to the floor behind the dais. Boisville's pistol discharged harmlessly into the crimson velvet of the canopy and immediately there was pandemonium. With a lightness that was astounding, Boisville vaulted over the table, scattering the wax tapers in all directions and knocking over a decanter of cognac. Immediately there were flames everywhere, and people began to shout as the assassin vanished behind the drawn curtains. Caroline heard the shattering of the glass in the tall windows as he plunged through into the darkness and anonymity of the gardens. She was vaguely aware of Hal giving pursuit, his figure barely discernible through the smoke which now rose from the blazing table.

The atmosphere swiftly became choking as the smoke filled the room, and men milled everywhere. She heard someone ordering people to form a chain to pass pails of water through from the kitchens. The smoke irritated her eyes and burned in her throat. It seemed that the noise and clamor went on forever as the chain of men formed, and pail after pail of water was tossed over the flames. Anxiously she searched the smoke and vapor for a sign of Hal, but he was nowhere to be seen. The duke was being attended to by several of the army officers present, and although he was a little disheveled, he did not seem any the worse for wear. She was trembling with the shock of everything, and tears stung her smoke-burned eyes as she made her way down through the devastated room toward the curtains, which someone had now drawn back from the flames. She saw the shattered glass in the windows, the fragments shining on the flagstones outside. Cool, refreshing air swept in, passing revivingly over her. How calm and peaceful the gardens looked, the lanterns shining so prettily in the trees, the spring flowers nodding in the night breeze, but Hal was somewhere out there, pursuing a desperate armed man. "Please keep him safe," she whispered. "Don't let him come to harm."

"Miss Lexham?"

She turned to see a scarlet-uniformed gentleman looking inquiringly at her. "Yes?"

"His Grace wishes to thank you for your timely warning. If you would please come this way?" He stood aside, ushering her toward the duke's small party.

Feeling anything but elegant and composed, she followed him. The duke turned to her, a smile on his lips, and he hastily prevented her from sinking into a deep curtsy. "No, no, m'dear, it is I who should be making obeisance to you! Although damn me if I can think how you guessed what that villainous *parlez-vous* was up to!" Still smiling, he drew her hand to his lips. "I thank 'ee from the bottom of me heart, m'dear, for I owe my life to you."

Another voice broke in suddenly. "Your Grace, I believe

you should know that you owe her your life only because at
the last moment she lost her nerve and could not go through
with it. She is one of the conspirators."

With a horrified gasp, she whirled about to see Dominic
standing there, a cool smile upon his lips. "That is a lie!"
she cried. "An infamous lie!"

"Is it, coz?" he replied, coming closer and bowing rever-
ently to the startled duke. "Forgive me, Your Grace, I do not
mean to insult you in any way by my conduct now, but things
have come to my notice which prove that my kinswoman is
anything but the loyal patriot you now believe her to be; she
is an adherent of the revolutionary cause and a Bonapartist of
the first order."

His words carried clearly through the room and an amazed
silence fell over everyone. Caroline's face had drained of
color; her shock was so great that she could not speak. She
stared in stunned silence at her cousin.

The duke's smile had faded. "I trust you can prove your
accusations, my lord, for if you cannot then I swear I will
have your elegant hide for my next pair of boots."

"I can prove them well enough, Your Grace. Perhaps my
cousin would care to tell us if the felon Seymour now pursues
was working alone. Well, coz, was he?"

Her lips parted, but she could not speak. "I—"

"Why do you not reply, cousin?" he inquired reasonably.
"Could it be that you have someone you wish to protect?
Someone who, like yourself, had not the courage to carry out
the murder?"

"No!" she cried. "It isn't like that at all!"

"So, you admit that there is someone else!"

She looked away, tears wet on her cheeks.

Dominic was triumphant. "You see, Your Grace? She
convicts herself by her silence. In her housekeeper's rooms
you will find hidden the chef, Duvall. He, my cousin, and the
wretch who has escaped tonight were together in the conspiracy to assassinate you. I thought my cousin's conduct was a
little odd tonight and I made it my business to keep an eye
upon her. I overheard her speaking with the chef and it was
quite obvious that she was party to the whole thing, but that
the two of them had lost their nerve and had decided the plot
should be abandoned as it was so unlikely to succeed. That
was why she arrived in so timely a way to rescue you, Your

Grace; she did it simply and solely to cover her iniquitous tracks—which she would have done, had I not listened to all that was said.''

"Is this true, Miss Lexham?" asked the duke.

"No!"

Dominic smiled. "The chef is in the housekeeper's parlor and he can be questioned.''

Caroline looked up swiftly. "He is in no condition to answer questions.''

"So," answered the duke heavily, "the chef *is* where Lexham says he is?"

"Yes, Your Grace," she replied. "But—"

The duke turned to several nearby officers. "Bring him here.''

"Your Grace—" persisted Caroline desperately, but he turned a stern, cold eye upon her.

"Please be silent, Miss Lexham.''

She could do nothing but obey, but she did so with dread in her heart, for she knew that what she had said was right. Gaspard was *not* in any state to answer questions, especially questions from the Duke of Wellington!

Silence reigned in the great room, where pools of water lay upon the floor, flames and smoke had ruined the costly furnishings, and panic had overturned chairs and wrenched hangings from the walls. The once proud and glittering assembly of dignitaries waited in silent groups, and everyone looked at Caroline, whose air of agitation made her appear to be very guilty.

At last the officers returned, half carrying and half dragging Gaspard, who was so terrified of the fate which might now await him that he could hardly stand. He did not at first see the duke; he saw only Caroline. Hope leaped into his eyes. "We were in time, mademoiselle?"

That word "we" sealed her fate. A stir passed through the room and she closed her eyes, nodding. "Yes, we were in time, monsieur.''

The duke's face was very still as he folded his arms, the silver star glittering on his breast. "So, monsieur, you admit that you knew of this intended crime.''

With almost a squeak, Gasped turned his head in the direction of the new voice, and recognition dawned instantly upon his pale, terrified face. *"Monsieur le duc!"*

"Do you admit that you were party to a plot to assassinate me?"

"Not willingly, milord, never willingly!" cried the chef.

"Your complicity is nevertheless proved by your reply, monsieur," replied the duke, nodding briefly at the officers. "Remove them to secure rooms for the time being!"

"I am but a chef!" cried Gaspard desperately, seeing the net closing inexorably around him. "I was forced to do as they wished! But I stepped back from the abyss, milord. I stepped back in time to save you!"

"Remove them both," repeated the duke, his face cold.

Gaspard struggled helplessly as they dragged him away, but Caroline held her ground for a moment more. "Your Grace!" she said. "Please do not—"

"I will hear nothing more from you, madam," he replied. "The Frenchman's acts I can understand, but you are English and your crime is therefore all the more heinous!" He glanced at the waiting officers. "Get her out of my sight until she can be taken to the correct place of detention."

It was as if she were in the grip of a nightmare from which she could not escape. She saw Dominic's grinning, victorious face, she saw the condemnation in the eyes of all those gathered in the room, she saw Gaspard being hauled to the doorway, and she saw Mrs. Hollingsworth, so shocked and horrified by what had happened that she could only cling to one of the columns for support, her face quite ghastly.

In a daze, Caroline allowed the officers to take her away. She stumbled a little as they crossed the inner vestibule, halting in dread as she realized that they intended to immure her in the cellar.

"Please! No!"

"It's the most secure place, and it's fitting for traitors," replied one of them, opening the door and thrusting her into the chill, dank darkness beyond. The door closed swiftly behind her, the sound reverberating through the invisible cellar rooms, and the rattle of the key in the lock seemed to carry on forever, echoing over and over again until it became so faint that she could no longer hear it.

Hesitantly, she edged her way down the steps, clinging to the icy rail. The atmosphere was as cold and clammy as an imagined shroud, and she became aware of the eerie gurgle of the unseen Tyburn, flowing endlessly by somewhere beneath the foundations. Slowly she sank to the floor, burying her face in her hands, and the echoes took up the sound of her sobs, tossing them scornfully back at her as if they were in league with Dominic, whose evil triumph was surely now complete.

Chapter 33

How long she remained there, alone and terrified in the darkness, she did not know. She fell into a light, restless sleep, finding little solace in the dreams that haunted those dreadful hours, but at last she was roused by the sound of the key in the lock again.

She struggled to sit up, her eyes turned hopefully toward the light that poured down into the cellar. A woman's figure appeared, and with a cry of gladness she rose to her feet, for it was Mrs. Hollingsworth.

The housekeeper carried a laden tray, her way illuminated by a candle. She set it down and then turned to embrace Caroline. The two women wept in each other's arms, and at last Caroline drew away, wiping her eyes.

"There-there is news of Sir Henry?"

Mrs. Hollingsworth's expression became distinctly cooler. "No, madam."

"I don't know how long I've been here, but it seems like forever. What is to become of us? Have you seen Gaspard?"

Tears filled the housekeeper's eyes. "No," she whispered. "They've taken him away somewhere, I know not where. Oh, Miss Lexham, I'm so afraid for him, he was forced to do what he did, but he could not bring himself to become party to murder! I know that he will pay with his life!'' The tears wended their slow way down Mrs. Hollingsworth's cheeks, and then she looked swiftly and ashamedly at Caroline. ''Oh, my dear, I did not mean to imply that I was not equally concerned for you—''

''I know.'' Caroline glanced at the tray. On it was a jug of milk, some cheese, and bread. ''Is this my banquet?'' she asked a little wryly.

''I would not leave them alone until they allowed me to see you. I am not permitted to stay long—''

''And you saying that nothing has been heard of Sir Henry?''

''No, but it is still dark outside.''

''I pray nothing has befallen him.''

''That is indeed to be hoped.''

''I must see him when he returns,'' went on Caroline. ''He knows that I had nothing to do with the plot.''

''Madam—''

''Yes?''

''I know that now is not the time to tell you this, but I cannot let you hold out hope that Sir Henry will rescue you, for I know that the opposite is the case.''

Caroline stared at her, her eyes huge and dark in the wavering light of the solitary candle flame. ''What do you mean?''

Mrs. Hollingsworth took a long breath. ''I was in the kitchen when word was sent that refreshments were to be taken to the duke, who has temporarily occupied Lady Carstairs' apartment. I decided to wait upon him myself, thinking that if I could speak to him, I could persuade him that you were entirely innocent and that my poor Gaspard should be treated leniently, for he is not a bad man. When I reached the apartment, however, I found that he was not alone; he was seated with a number of gentlemen and they were so deep in conversation that they hardly noticed my presence as I served them. I overheard the duke relating a tale Sir Henry had told him.''

''What tale?''

''Oh, my dear, I would give anything now not to have to say this to you,'' said Mrs. Hollingsworth, reaching out to take Caroline's hand. ''Sir Henry told the duke of the night you caught him eavesdropping upon Gaspard and Boisville, and of how he convinced you to say nothing. The duke roared with laughter, telling the others that it spoke volumes of Sir Henry's skills as a lover that he could persuade a member of the plot to believe him to be pursuing her.''

In the dim, faintly moving light, Caroline's cheeks flamed with humiliation.

"So you see, my dear," went on the housekeeper. "You must not hope for anything from Sir Henry, for he has believed you to be part of it all along, or at least, he has done for some time."

"I cannot believe it," whispered Caroline hollowly. "I cannot believe he thinks that of me—''

"I know that you love him, my dear, but he is not worthy of your love. Forget him; he has brought you nothing but pain and it would have been better for you had you never met him. You will be saved, of that I am sure, but your salvation will not come at his hands."

Numbly, Caroline turned away.

The key turned in the lock again and a soldier looked in. "Your time is up, missus; you're to leave the prisoner alone again now."

Mrs. Hollingsworth squeezed Caroline's cold fingers comfortingly and then left, and almost absently Caroline noticed the absence of the chinking of her keys. Those keys had been confiscated, for fear that she might contemplate helping her mistress to escape.

The darkness and silence folded over Caroline once more, but she was hardly aware of it. She felt and heard nothing, only the distant pounding of her broken heart.

Dawn was beginning to break, and the great crowd still thronged the courtyard. News of what had happened had spread like wildfire and the whole of London had learned of the events at the Lexham Hotel. The capital buzzed with it, and lights had burned in the windows of Mayfair mansions throughout the night. Everyone now knew that the Earl of Lexham's fair cousin, the lady whose enterprise had taken London by storm, was guilty of being a wicked Bonapartist, that she had almost carried off a dastardly plan to assassinate the hero of Waterloo.

A solitary hackney coach made its way slowly through the crush in Mayfair Street, turning with difficulty into the crowded courtyard, the coachman shouting and cracking his whip in an attempt to clear a way.

Inside, Hal sat wearily, his head resting against the ancient upholstery. His cravat hung loose and his shirt was torn. Mud stained the costly velvet of his coat, and a bloody mark scored his right cheek, a reminder of how very close Boisville's dying shot had come to finding its target. Hal had fired first, picking the Frenchman off the parapet of the appropriately named new Waterloo Bridge, and as he began to fall to his death, Boisville had instinctively returned the shot. How close it had scorched, whining through the cold night air, leaving a scar forever.

He was roused from his thoughts by the sudden halting of the hackney as it at last reached the steps of the hotel, where the flowers were now crushed beyond redemption. He flung the door open and climbed down. Immediately he was recognized and a jubilant shout went up for the man whose swift actions had thrust the great duke to the safety of the floor. He hardly glanced around as he hurried up the steps and into the hotel. The door closed behind him and he came face-to-face with Mrs. Hollingsworth.

He managed a weary smile. "Good morning, Mrs. Hollingsworth."

"Sir." She gave him the briefest of nods, her eyes cold and unsmiling.

"Where is Miss Lexham?" he inquired.

"I would have thought that you could have guessed that well enough for yourself, sir," she replied stiffly.

"Mrs. Hollingsworth, I don't know what is the matter with you, and I am certainly not in the mood for parlor games. Where is Miss Lexham?"

"She is under lock and key, Sir Henry, where the ill-founded suspicions of you and your like have placed her!" cried the distraught housekeeper, her anger and bitterness making her forget her place. "She is innocent, the poor lamb, and you will no doubt be congratulating yourself upon your cleverness. You've destroyed her as much as has the Earl of Lexham, Sir Henry Seymour, and I hope you one day pay the price for what you have done!"

Hal stared at her, but then he recovered. "Where is the duke?"

Mrs. Hollingsworth made to walk away from him, but he

caught her angrily by the wrist, twisting her so sharply to face him that her skirts brushed against the nearby orange trees. "Damn you, woman! Answer my question!"

"The duke occupies Lady Carstairs' apartment until later this morning!" she cried, rubbing the wrist which he abruptly released, and watching him as he pushed his way through the avenue of little trees, thrusting aside a hanging banner and then moving swiftly up the grand staircase.

The duke was taking a very Spartan breakfast and he looked up with a smile as Hal was admitted. Wiping his mouth with a napkin, he rose from his table. "Seymour! By Gad, I'm glad to see you! Did you snare the ruffian?"

"His body will be recovered from the Thames, no doubt."

"Excellent. I must thank you for your quick thinking, Seymour, although if I am to be tumbled to the floor I think I would prefer a pretty wench to do the honors next time, eh?" He gave his strange whoop of laughter again, sitting down to pour himself another cup of thick black coffee and gesturing to Hal to sit down with him.

"With your leave, Your Grace, I would prefer to stand."

The duke looked shrewdly at him. "Come on then, out with it. What's on your mind?"

"I'm told that Miss Lexham is under lock and key."

"That is so, for unfortunately she was part of the plot."

"That cannot be so!"

"It *is* so, Seymour, there's no doubt of it, and we've Lexham to thank for exposing her."

"Lexham?" Hal's eyes narrowed.

The duke stirred his coffee busily. "Yes, the fellow decided to pry a little and overheard an interesting and revealing conversation. She and Duvall were Boisville's accomplices, they admitted it."

Hal stared at this information. "She *admitted* it?"

"What is this, a damned inquisition? Yes, Seymour, she admitted it. Now, if you are going to be disagreeable and sulky, you can take yourself elsewhere to do it. If you have any doubts about Miss Lexham's guilt, then you would be best advised to question her cousin about it. You'll find him somewhere around, conducting himself as if the house has returned to him already." The duke looked up, but Hal had gone. With a shrug, and a slight frown at the continuing noise of the crowds outside, the duke continued with his breakfast.

Dominic lounged elegantly on a sofa in the red saloon, a cigar in one hand and an exceedingly early glass of cognac in the other. He held court, glorying in his triumph and fame and repeating the whole story yet again for the benefit of some new arrivals who were eager for every detail. He set a splendid scene, with a cast of wicked, intriguing assassins and with himself as the intrepid hero, risking life and limb to reach the truth and prevented from warning the duke himself only by the wretched cowardice and funk of his treacherous, despicable cousin, the fair Caroline.

From the doorway, Hal listened in disgust to this highly embroidered tale, and gradually the others in the room became aware of his presence. One by one they turned to look at him, something in his cold glance making them silent, and at last only Dominic's drawling voice could be heard.

"Oh, she was a scheming little adventuress, all right; conniving was second nature to her. She made many an advance to me, you know. I suppose she fancied the notion of being Countess of Lexham, eh?" He laughed, but the sound drew no response. Slowly his smug smile faded and he sat up, his eyes going at last to the reason for the silence. His face paled a little as he saw Hal. His tongue passed nervously over his lips and he gave an uneasy laugh. "Well, the paladin returns—and bearing suitable marks of mortal combat. Your health, Seymour." He raised his glass.

With an oath, Hal came forward, striking the glass from his hand and reaching down to drag him from the sofa.

Dominic gave a startled cry. "Take your hands off me, Seymour!"

Hal flung him contemptuously to the floor where he sprawled ignominiously on the carpet, winded. His face was pale but defiant as he gazed up at his attacker.

"Now, my brave fellow," breathed Hal, his soft, menacing voice very clear in the silent room, "you will tell the truth about what happened."

"I've told the truth—" Dominic ceased abruptly as a muddy boot pressed down roughly upon his chest, and then all color drained from his face as Hal slowly drew his pistol and leveled it at him.

"I'm not a patient man, Lexham," he said softly. "Indeed, at this moment patience is a virtue in which I am singularly lacking." He cocked the pistol and a stir passed through the watching gentlemen.

Dominic stared at the pistol and then at the ice-cold determination in his assailant's eyes. "All right," he cried suddenly, his defiance collapsing. "All right, Seymour, I'll tell you."

"I'm waiting."

"Miss Lexham is innocent, she had nothing to do with it." Dominic's tongue passed dryly over his pale lips and he was a picture of craven fear as the pistol barrel moved closer.

"That is not enough, Lexham," said Hal softly.

"I heard everything. Duvall told her about the plot, and she went straightaway to warn the duke. That is the truth, I swear it."

A disgusted murmur greeted this and slowly Hal lowered the pistol. "You are beneath contempt, Lexham, so low that a snake could aspire to the name of gentleman before you. Now then, up you get!" Reaching down, he dragged Dominic to his feet again. "We'll toddle along to the duke and we'll see to it that your innocent cousin is released, her good name and character unharmed by your foul lies. And after that, you would be best advised to get yourself out of the country, for unless you do, I shall be looking for you, dear fellow, and our next meeting will be the last thing you know in this life."

Dominic's gray eyes bulged with dread, his whole body trembled, and he could only nod his head vigorously in agreement. "Anything you say, Seymour, anything at all!"

Unable to look at such abject cowardice, Hal pushed Dominic toward the door, the others parting instinctively to allow them through.

The duke listened in amazement to Dominic's miserable confession and then turned away in disgust. "Great God above," he muttered. "And this creature is an English gentleman! Get him out of my sight before he makes me sick!"

Gladly Dominic escaped toward the door, but Hal's icy voice followed him. "Remember what I said, Lexham, for if you forget, then it will be a fatal mistake."

Dominic fled, stumbling down the grand staircase in such haste that he almost lost his footing upon the petals which still lay scattered there from the previous night. In his scramble to reach the outer door, he knocked over several of the long-suffering orange trees, a number of which had met with disaster during the night's excitement.

The duke looked at Hal. "I think I owe Miss Lexham a considerable apology, Seymour, and I certainly must admit that I•know I owe her my life." He nodded at a waiting soldier. "Have her brought to me immediately."

In the intervening minutes, nothing was said in the room. Hal waited by a window and the duke drummed his fingers upon the table. At last they heard the sound of footsteps approaching. The door was opened and Caroline was shown in. She did not see Hal; she saw only the duke.

Hal watched her, thinking how very lovely she was, even now. Her hair was disheveled, the honey curls tumbling down over her shoulders, and her gown was smoke-stained and a little torn, but still she was quite breathtaking.

She faced the duke, who had immediately risen to his feet. "You sent for me, Your Grace?"

"I did indeed, my dear Miss Lexham," he said, coming around the table toward her. "And I have done so in the great hope that you will forgive me for doubting you."

She stared, hardly daring to believe what she heard.

He took her hands. "You have been gravely wronged, m'dear, and it was my wretched fault for believing the word of that rodent of a cousin of yours. He has admitted his lies and I now know that you are entirely innocent, that you behaved in a most loyal, brave, and patriotic way last night."

Tears of utter relief filled her eyes and she swayed a little. The duke steadied her. "There, there, now, it's all over, m'dear, and you are free to go. But first you must tell me that you forgive me."

She nodded, half blinded by the tears. "Of course you are forgiven, Your Grace."

He raised her hands to his lips, kissing them upon the palms. "Thank you, m'dear, it's more than I deserve."

Her fingers closed over his. "There is one thing—"

"Yes? Name it."

"It's about Monsieur Duvall. Please be lenient with him, Your Grace, for he was made most wretched, he was forced to do their bidding because they threatened to kill his mother and sisters. He is not a wicked man, sir, he is very kind and gentle, and I regard him with great respect. He could not go through with it, he told my housekeeper and then me, and he

told us in time to save you. There would have been much
more time had not Boisville decided to hasten things by
serving the *pièce montée* very much sooner than originally
intended. You must think of these things, Your Grace, and I
beg you to deal as lightly as you can with him, for it would
be tragic if he paid the full price for a crime he could not
contemplate without breaking down."

The duke looked at her for a long moment. "How very
compassionate you are, m'dear, and how very eloquent a
counsel for the defense. Very well, you have my word upon
it that Duvall will be dealt with as leniently as possible."

"Thank you, Your Grace." At that moment she saw Hal
by the window, and the little smile that had warmed her lips
faded immediately.

The duke perceived the change in her and glanced a little
uncertainly at Hal. Then, clearing his throat, he muttered
something about having things to attend to, and he left them
alone.

"Good morning, Caro."

"Sir Henry." Her eyes were cold.

"Your pleasure at seeing I am safe and well quite over-
whelms me."

Briefly her eyes lingered on the mark on his cheek. "Did
you apprehend Boisville?"

"I did."

"Is he—"

"Dead? Yes. Very."

"I congratulate you."

"Do you? Your tone suggests that you wish me in the
Thames with him."

She hid her anguish with the consummate skill of devastated pride. She was more glad than he would ever know that
he was safe and well. She knew great pain on seeing the mark
of Boisville's shot upon his cheek, for it told her how very
close to death he had come. But she could not forget what he
had said of her, what he had thought of her. "You are wrong,
Sir Henry. I do not wish that at all. I rejoice that you are safe
and that you have defeated the assassin, and I trust that for
Jennifer's sake you will now leave such dangerous things to
others."

The coldness in her eyes and the aloofness of her manner
angered him then, his own pride stiffening him against her.

"Thank you, madam," he said shortly. "Again I am over-whelmed by your warmth and concern."

"I do not know how you can expect anything else of me," she said in a shaking voice. Afraid she was about to cry, she gathered her skirts and fled from the room.

He remained where he was for a long moment and then he brought his fist bitterly down upon the table. "God damn you, Caro, God damn you for that!"

Chapter 34

Another day had passed and Caroline stood with Mrs. Hollingsworth in the ruined dining room. The smoke had dulled the chandeliers and stained the magnificent ceiling. The broken window had been roughly boarded up for the time being and the curtains taken down to be restored. One of the Sheraton sideboards had been badly burned and everywhere there was the acrid, pervading stench of the fire. Most of the military banners and union jacks had been taken down and the room cleared of the tables and chairs, but still the echoes of the banquet sounded eerily, as if it was still taking place but could not be seen.

A moment earlier Mrs. Hollingsworth had been smiling, glad of the news that Gaspard would soon be released, the duke carrying out his word to Caroline, but now her face was shocked. "Close the hotel? You cannot mean it!"

"My mind is made up."

"But—"

"To begin with we have no dining room."

"There are other rooms, and the *brigade* is more than anxious to continue! Please, my dear, don't take this dreadful step."

"My heart has gone out of it, I just want to turn my back on it all."

"This isn't like you," said the housekeeper gently.

"Yes, it is," whispered Caroline. "It's very like me to turn my back on things when I cannot endure them anymore. I turned my back on Selford, now I will do the same to London."

"That will give victory to the earl after all, and that can *never* be right!"

A new voice broke into the echoing room. "It certainly cannot!"

Caroline turned swiftly, smiling as she saw Jennifer standing in the doorway, looking very splendid in pale pink, silver tassels trembling from her little hat. She came toward them. "From all accounts it is as well that Charles and I returned from France when we did, for now maybe we will be able to stop you from being silly, Caroline Lexham!"

"France? But were you not—"

"Destined for Venice? Yes, we were, but Charles confessed that he does not travel well and so we lingered on the French coast instead. Then we became restless, thinking all the while of coming back and doing up Carstairs Place, and so we decided to return to England. We arrived last night, and found my brother had high-handedly moved himself into our house."

Caroline looked away. "Yes, I know."

Jennifer looked shrewdly at her. "Are you going to tell me, or do I have to wring it from you by force?"

"There is little to tell."

"Little to tell?" echoed Jennifer incredulously. "My dear creature, London is bristling with tales about the events here. I've heard so many conflicting tales that I am positively dizzy, and you stand there and say airily that there is little to tell. Now then, I shall stamp my pretty foot with pique if you do not come across properly and behave as a best friend should. Besides which," she added more meaningfully, "I wish to know what has passed between you and Hal."

"Nothing whatever," said Caroline quickly.

"I know when I am being humbugged, Caroline," replied Jennifer briskly, "and I know what the present situation calls for."

"What?"

Jennifer smiled. "Why, toast in Mrs. H's lair, of course."

The smell of toast was as appetizing as ever, even arousing Caroline's appetite when she had had no interest in eating since the night of the banquet. Aided and abetted by Mrs. Hollingsworth, she related the whole story, and Jennifer listened enthralled.

"Why," she said when all had been said, "it is better than the latest novel. And to think that I had the bad sense to be away when it was all going on." Her teasing smile faded then. "But you have not told me it all, have you? You have not told me why Hal left here so suddenly and why he avoids mentioning your name as much as you avoid his."

"There is nothing to tell."

"Please, Caroline, you must tell me, for how can I help if no one will admit anything? I *know* that something has happened between you and my brother, something of sufficient seriousness to make him quit these premises and to make you now consider closing the place completely and go back to Devon."

Caroline couldn't tell her, she couldn't tell her how much she loved Hal, how much she would always love him.

Mrs. Hollingsworth glanced at her and then put down the toasting fork. "Lady Carstairs, she will not say anything because she is in love with Sir Henry."

"Mrs. Hollingsworth!" cried Caroline in dismay. "You should not have said that!"

"No, but I think that her ladyship should be told."

Jennifer looked sadly at Caroline. "Oh, my dearest Caroline, I had no idea—"

"No, and that was how I wished it to remain." Caroline got agitatedly to her feet. "You are not to say anything to him, do you hear me? I don't want him to know."

"If that is what you wish, but—"

"No buts, Jennifer, he is not to know because he already despises me."

Jennifer's eyes widened. "Surely you are wrong."

"No, he thinks me a very low creature, Jennifer, capable of anything, even involvement in the assassination attempt on the Duke of Wellington."

"Now I know you have taken leave of your senses!" cried Jennifer. "Hal would never think that of you!"

"But he did for a while, Jennifer, long enough to say as

much to the duke, who then related the tale to others. Mrs. Hollingsworth overheard him.''

"Did you?'' inquired Jennifer.

The housekeeper nodded reluctantly. "I am afraid that I did, your ladyship, though it grieves me to have to say so.''

Jennifer was brisk and disbelieving. "It has to be a misunderstanding. I know in my heart of hearts that my brother would not think that of you, Caroline. No, it's no use telling me all over again, I just know that it isn't true.''

"Please don't say anything to him, Jennifer.''

Jennifer remained silent.

"Please, Jennifer,'' cried Caroline desperately, "you must give me your word.''

Jennifer shook her head. "I cannot, Caroline, for if I did, I would be being an unworthy friend to you and an unworthy sister to him.''

"Please, Jennifer.''

"No. Oh, don't look at me so reproachfully, for I take this stand for the most noble of reasons. I cannot undertake not to say anything, since I believe him to be innocent, and if that is so, he deserves the right to speak in his own defense.''

"He will not care what I think of him, he will laugh about it,'' cried Caroline. "But I will care very much that he knows my secret. I could not bear it, Jennifer.''

Slowly Jennifer rose to her feet, the tassels on her little beaver hat trembling just a little as she bent to gather up her reticule and parasol. "I will not set out to tell him that you love him, Caroline, of course I will not, but I think I should tell him what it is you think he has said and thought of you. I know my brother, he has never been such a monster that he would say untrue things about a lady, and I know that before I left he held you in very high esteem. He still held you in sufficiently high esteem to wring the truth from Dominic, did you know that?''

"It makes no difference, Jennifer, for the fact remains that he *had* thought me guilty, and he thought many other untrue things about me, things which I am ashamed to say to you. Tell him what you wish, it will no doubt amuse him.''

Jennifer lowered her eyes at the bitterness in these words. Glancing sadly at the silent Mrs. Hollingsworth, she took her leave.

*   *   *

Hal was in the billiard room with Charles, and he straight
ened from the green baize table as his sister came in. "How
charming you look, sis, and where have you been that take
you out before we mere males have even risen?"

"I've been to see Caroline."

His smile faded. "I trust she is well."

Charles glanced from one to the other. "What exactly i
going on? I return from my honeymoon in a state of deliriou
happiness to find my brother-in-law as bad-tempered as
bear with a sore head and my bride obviously preoccupie
with things other than my good self."

Jennifer hurried to him, taking his hand and resting it mo
mentarily against her cheek. "Forgive me, my love, but i
seems my disagreeable brother's life needs a little of m
attention." She turned quickly then, snatching up the cue bal
from the table as Hal resolutely made every sign of continu
ing with his play. "Oh, no, brother mine, you shall not carr
on as if nothing has happened."

"Don't be tiresome, Jennifer," he replied.

"I am permitted to be as tiresome as I like in my ow
house, especially with an uninvited guest." She held hi
gaze. "Did you believe Caroline to have been part of the plo
to kill the duke?"

Hal stared at her. "Don't be so damned foolish!" h
snapped.

"Is it foolish?"

"You know that it is. Of *course* I've never thought that."

"She thinks you did, among other sins you seem to hav
perpetrated against her good name since my back has bee
turned."

She related what Mrs. Hollingsworth had overheard, an
then he gave a short, wry laugh. "So, that was why th
omnipresent Mrs. Hollingsworth spoke to me the way sh
did!"

"Is that all you have to say?"

"No, it isn't, for I will tell you that the duke's version i
somewhat incorrect, embroidered upon by the fact that h
related it after Caro had been arrested."

"Caro?" she asked quickly. "That is an unexpectedl
intimate way to refer to her."

He turned away. "A mere slip of the tongue."

"Is it, Hal Seymour? Or could it be that your pride is making you as obstinate now as Caroline's is making her?"

"Don't interfere in something of which you know nothing, Jennifer," he replied shortly.

"I intend to interfere as much as I possibly can," she retorted, "And for once in your life you will stand there and say nothing more until I have finished. Today a great deal has become clear to me and things which puzzled me a little in the past are now presented to me as solved. I remember how you spoke of Caroline when first you traveled to London with her, and I remember how you enjoyed her company at the opera house. You looked at her time and time again, and I thought you did so with more than amused interest, and now I know that it was indeed something more. Your secret duties forced you to remain at the Oxenford, that I also now understand, but you leaped swiftly enough to her defense when Dominic Lexham posed any threat to her. And you never again felt the same about Marcia once you knew what she had done; you had turned from her even more after the wedding and those beastly cockroaches, hadn't you? You showed the world the truth then when you kissed Caroline's hand in front of us all—didn't you?"

He said nothing.

"Didn't you?" she persisted. "Look at me, you wretch, and admit the truth!"

He smiled a little then, gently touching her cheek. "What a terrier you are at times, Lady Carstairs. Very well, I admit it, but after my foolishly public display—which display I thank God only you appeared to understand—I discovered that she had been seen fondly embracing and kissing her cousin Lexham."

"And you were jealous!"

Again he said nothing.

"The truth, Henry Seymour," she pressed, "for I will hear you say it. Admit that you were jealous and you hid the fact by accusing her of improper conduct. Am I right?"

"Yes, dammit, you are right! Now, will you please be satisfied and leave the matter alone?"

"No, I will not leave it alone, for it is too important. Why were you so concerned and jealous that she kissed her cousin?"

Hal glanced momentarily at Charles, who gave him a

sympathetic smile. "You may as well come clean, Hal, for she will not leave you alone until you do."

"What manner of support is that from a brother-in-law?" demanded Hal.

"It is the support of common sense, Hal, for I do believe that Jennifer has discovered you in the wrong."

"I have indeed," declared Jennifer triumphantly, "and you are going to admit it if it is the last thing I do, Hal. I want you to tell me exactly why you were so upset that Caroline should show affection for her kinsman."

"For the life of me I cannot see what difference it makes now. Caro loathes the very sight of me now and I cannot say that I blame her after what I've said and done."

"Don't avoid the issue," she said crossly. "Admit that you love her!"

He gave a heavy sigh and tossed his cue down upon the table. "Very well, I admit it, Jennifer. I was jealous because I loved her."

"Past tense?"

"By *God,* you are persistent! I love her—present tense. Will that suffice?"

Tears shone in her eyes then and she smiled, suddenly flinging her arms around his neck. "Oh *yes,* Hal, that will indeed suffice! You must go to her, you must tell her what you have just admitted here."

"Never." He drew away.

"Because your insufferable pride gets in the way? Oh, Hal, can't you see that that is what is happening to her too? She loves you, she told me that she did, but she thinks you do not care for her. You must go to her, for unless you do you will lose her forever—and I will lose the sweetest of sisters-in-law."

He caught her hand urgently. "She told you she loved me?"

"Yes." She smiled. "She is the only one for you, and you know it. If you do not go to Mayfair Street now, you will regret it for the rest of your stubborn life."

He looked at her for a moment longer and then pulled her close, kissing her warmly on the cheek. "Very well, I will go to her, but first there is something which must be unpacked from my trunk." He reached over to take up the little handbell.

"Something to *unpack*?" she cried incredulously. "What can possibly be of sufficient importance that—"

He smiled. "You will understand when you see it."

A footman entered. "Sir?"

"Tell my valet to unpack the green trunk immediately and bring me the small leather box he will find in it."

Caroline was seated on the bench where first she had had her startling idea to turn Lexham House into a hotel. She wore her old turquoise gown, for somehow it seemed more appropriate now that she had decided to return to Devon. Her hair was dressed loosely, several long curls falling down over one shoulder, and the ends of the ribbons tied in it fluttered a little in the soft spring breeze. The daffodils nodded on the lawns, and the gardeners tended the flower beds, weeding carefully between the sedate rows of tulips. How beautiful the house looked, just as it had done on that other occasion.

She saw Hal approaching, his tall figure very elegant and distinguished beneath the trees. Swiftly she lowered her eyes, her cheeks flushing. How she wished that Jennifer had not learned her secret.

"Caro?"

"Please don't call me that, Sir Henry," she replied a little stiffly.

"Why?"

"And please don't play games with me, sir, for I do not feel able to parry words."

"I will not waste time then. I will tell you straightaway that I did not tell the duke I thought you were one of the conspirators, nor did I tell him that I persuaded you to silence by making love to you. It is my belief that he placed such meaning into what I said because when he related the tale, you had been apprehended. Look at me, Caro, and know that I am telling you the truth."

Unwillingly she raised her eyes. "Very well, Sir Henry," she said at last. "I believe you about that."

"Will you also then believe me when I say that never in my life have I so much regretted a thing as I have regretted saying those hurtful words to you, and saying them not only once but on several occasions."

Agitatedly she looked away. "Why have you come here like this?" she cried, suspecting him of somehow still mocking her. "Do you do it simply to please Jennifer? Or perhaps you enjoy toying with me?"

"I have come here because I wish to forget that we have become estranged, especially as that situation has come about through my own actions. And if I have seemed to toy with you in the past, it has been because I have wanted you so very much. I wish with all my heart that I had never given in to my jealousy, but I did, and I hurt myself as much as I hurt you. I could not bear to think of Dominic Lexham's arms around you, Caro; it made me want to cause you the pain you caused me." He saw the uncertainty in her gray eyes, and the first stirrings of something more. He took the little leather box from his pocket and gave it to her. "Perhaps this will convince you that you have been in my heart for almost as long as I have known you."

With trembling fingers, she opened the box. Inside, flashing and glittering in the sunlight, was her grandmother's necklace. With a gasp, she looked up into his eyes. "Oh, Hal—"

"I did not want you to lose it forever, Caro. I knew how much it meant to you. I persuaded Jordan to go along with the deception, for I did not think the moment was right to tell you, and besides, it could somehow have looked like a contravention of your uncle's damned will! I did it because I loved you, Caro, and I still love you."

The little box tumbled to the grass and the necklace spilled brightly among the daffodils as she reached out to him. Then she was in his arms, held as close and cherished as she had always dreamed. "I love you too, Hal Seymour," she whispered, before his kiss stopped her words.

SIGNET

Regency Romances From
SANDRA HEATH

"Ms. Heath delivers a most pleasing mixture of wit [and] romance... for Regency connoisseurs." —Romantic Times

Now Available:
Lavender Blue
0-451-20858-7

Winter Dreams
0-451-21236-3

Available wherever books are sold or at
www.penguin.com

S319